PRAISE
CHARLIE N. HOLMBERG

THE SPELLBREAKER SERIES

"Romantic and electrifying . . . the fast-paced plot and fully realized world will have readers eager for the next installment. Fans of Victorian-influenced fantasy won't want to put this down."

—*Publishers Weekly*

THE NUMINA SERIES

"[An] enthralling fantasy . . . The story is gripping from the start, with a surprising plot and a lush, beautifully realized setting. Holmberg knows just how to please fantasy fans."

—*Publishers Weekly*

"With scads of action, clear explanations of how supernatural elements function, and appealing characters with smart backstories, this first in a series will draw in fans of Cassandra Clare, Leigh Bardugo, or Brandon Sanderson."

—*Library Journal*

"Holmberg is a genius at world building; she provides just enough information to set the scene without overwhelming the reader. She also creates captivating characters worth rooting for, and puts them in unique situations. Readers will be eager for the second installment in the Numina series."

—*Booklist*

THE PAPER MAGICIAN SERIES

"Charlie is a vibrant writer with an excellent voice and great world building. I thoroughly enjoyed *The Paper Magician*."
—Brandon Sanderson, author of *Mistborn* and *The Way of Kings*

"Harry Potter fans will likely enjoy this story for its glimpses of another structured magical world, and fans of Erin Morgenstern's *The Night Circus* will enjoy the whimsical romance element . . . So if you're looking for a story with some unique magic, romantic gestures, and the inherent darkness that accompanies power all steeped in a yet to be fully explored magical world, then this could be your next read."
—Amanda Lowery, *Thinking Out Loud*

THE WILL AND THE WILDS

"An immersive, dangerous fantasy world. Holmberg draws readers in with a fast-moving plot, rich details, and a surprisingly sweet human-monster romance. This is a lovely, memorable fairy tale."
—*Publishers Weekly*

"Holmberg ably builds her latest fantasy world, and her brisk narrative and the romance at its heart will please fans of her previous magical tales."
—*Booklist*

THE FIFTH DOLL

Winner of the 2017 Whitney Award for Speculative Fiction

Spellmaker

Spellmaker

AUTHOR OF *THE PAPER MAGICIAN*
CHARLIE N. HOLMBERG

Published by 47North, Seattle

www.apub.com

Amazon, the Amazon logo, and 47North are trademarks of Amazon.com, Inc., or its affiliates.

ISBN-13: 9781542022576
ISBN-10: 1542022576

Cover design by Micaela Alcaino

Printed in the United States of America

To Marlene Stringer, my champion.

CHAPTER 1

Brookley, England, June 1895

Elsie Camden sat on the edge of her bed, reading over something she most certainly was not supposed to have. Folded lines crossed it, one down and three across, the creases growing thin from how often she had opened and closed the page. The scrawl was red—the color of rational aspectors—and in the handwriting of whoever had died to create it. She might never know his or her name, and perhaps it was best not to know. By all means, she was translating a piece of the spellmaker's corpse.

The Latin-to-English dictionary she'd borrowed from the vicar was worn and well used. Peeling along the spine. Elsie had confirmed her suspicions several lines ago, but felt the urge to be thorough. To study the spell all the way to its end.

It was a master spell, without a doubt. A master spell of forgetfulness, of memory stealing. Long term. Exactly *how* long, Elsie wasn't certain, even as she went over the last words on the opus page, but one of the words translated to *years*. Years were tricky—the spell might not be as useful as Elsie had previously hoped, especially since Ogden seemed to have, more or less, recovered from his ordeal at the dock and her discovery of his secrets. He'd been under the spiritual control of another aspector for a decade, forced to help perpetrate crimes he would never condone. Elsie had been used, too, but their adversary had twisted her mind instead, tricking her into thinking she was using her spellbreaking ability for a good cause, when in fact she'd been furthering a perverse agenda. At least neither of them had been made to kill directly. Still, the knowledge that they had, however unwittingly, helped in the demise of so many weighed on them both.

Their adversary had arranged for the murder of several aspectors in order to steal their opuses, and this spell was from one of those books. That made it beyond dangerous to keep, and yet Elsie couldn't bring herself to get rid of it. It was too valuable. But she couldn't sell it, couldn't use it . . .

Sighing, she tucked the spell securely back into her bodice, taking a deep breath to dispel residual anxiety.

Elsie still struggled to stomach the knowledge that Master *Lily Merton*, the cheery old spiritual aspector who spoke like a song and befriended everyone, had done such horrid things. Was she working with others? Others who *knew* what they were doing, like Abel Nash? There was no possible way Master Merton would be able to control multiple people at once. Had she already set her eyes on a new pawn now that Ogden had been released? Or would she try to get him back?

A week had passed since Elsie had pulled Merton's controlling spell off her employer's chest, freeing him from spiritual enslavement. And now . . . she kept expecting something to happen. Merton to turn herself in. Police to show up at her door. Bacchus to . . . to what? She swatted *that* thought away like an annoying fly. She had enough worrying thoughts without a big, hearty man infiltrating them.

But nothing had happened. Lily Merton had stayed to herself, and there'd been no more deaths or robberies. Which was good, of course, except it meant the law wouldn't find her on its own. Ogden had left the authorities an anonymous tip five days ago, pointing to Merton. But there was nothing in the papers. The Wright sisters weren't even gossiping about it. Which led Elsie to conclude the tip had been laughed off. Master Merton was a sweet old woman hopping from dinner to dinner to recruit nice young girls to her atheneum. *Obviously* she wasn't secretly a manipulative assassin. Which meant Ogden and Elsie had to handle this themselves.

It was just . . . neither of them knew exactly *how.*

There was no possible way to turn in Master Merton without revealing themselves. Elsie was a spellbreaker, and Ogden a master rational aspector, both unregistered. Elsie might be able to maneuver herself into life in prison or at a labor camp. But Ogden . . . the courts wouldn't be lenient with him.

Standing, Elsie strode to her window and looked out over Brookley, seeing a few passersby. Nothing and no one of import—no lurking henchmen, no bubbly killers, no constables or bobbies. She sucked in another deep breath, forcing herself to calm down, then smoothed her bodice and hair and left her room, heading downstairs toward the smells of luncheon.

Emmeline was just setting a grouse-and-carrot pie on the table in front of Ogden, who leaned hard into a fist, elbow propped on the dining room table, his reading glasses perched low on his nose as he went over a ledger. He looked up as Elsie approached and simply shook his head. Nothing on his end, either, then. Elsie wasn't entirely sure she'd be able to eat, despite all Emmeline's hard work. The maid's pastries had greatly improved over the last year.

Emmeline turned about and lit up. "Oh, Elsie. Telegram came for you."

Elsie's pulse quickened as Emmeline fished around in her apron pockets and retrieved a small envelope. It had a grayish tint to it. Elsie's stomach hit the floor. The Cowls' letters had been the same color. Their orders—Merton's orders, for they'd been from her—had always arrived in nondescript envelopes slipped into her things. Each had included information about how her actions would help the country's poor, only most of it had been lies.

But no . . . she'd never get another of those letters. Ogden had penned all of them, and he was now free from his spell. Surely Master Merton wouldn't attempt to contact her directly. Not that Elsie could use the evidence to indict her. Even if Elsie hadn't destroyed all her letters from the Cowls, they implicated Elsie as a willing participant in criminal activities, and the handwriting could be used against Ogden.

Offering the best smile she could manage, Elsie thanked Emmeline, took the envelope, and sat at the table, opening the letter as Emmeline sliced the pie. She could feel Ogden's eyes on her, but the note had nothing to do with Master Merton. The handwriting was the post-master's, the message from Bacchus Kelsey. She saw his name before anything else, and her chest tightened.

I'd like to see you soon. Can we arrange a meeting?

Licking her lips, Elsie folded the message tightly and stuck it under her leg. She hadn't seen Bacchus—that was, *Master Kelsey*—since he'd appeared in Ogden's hospital room after being freed from a mound of cement conjured by an opus spell. Something the police still didn't understand, but thanks to Ogden's ability to withstand and deflect the mind-twisting of a truthseeker, they didn't suspect him, Elsie, or Master Kelsey of any wrongdoing.

Elsie badly wanted to see Bacchus, talk to him, stroll with him . . . but she feared for him, too. Merton had to suspect—at the very least—that Elsie knew the truth, and Bacchus had been Merton's most recent target. If he were to become involved in the hunt to get the spiritual aspector behind bars, he would likely become her target again. It would be better for the Algarve aspector to remain uninvolved. Better, indeed, if he were to sail back home to Barbados as soon as possible, regardless of how miserable Elsie would be to have an ocean between them.

"Elsie?" Ogden asked, oblivious to the pie being served to him.

Emmeline smiled. "It's not from Mr. Kelsey, is it?"

Elsie felt her ears heat. "It's *Master* Kelsey, Emmeline."

"Oh, right." Of course, her friend seemed not at all put off by the reminder that Bacchus was now echelons above Elsie in status. "But is it?"

A lie formed in the center of Elsie's tongue, but one look at Ogden had her swallowing it. There'd been too many lies between them, intentional and unintentional. He needed to know.

"It is," she answered, and Ogden's shoulders slumped. "He just wants to visit before his departure."

Emmeline looked despondent. "So he's still leaving?"

Straightening and accepting her own slice of steaming pie, Elsie answered, "Of course he's leaving. He was only in England for his advancement to mastership, and that is done. Why else would he stay?"

She kept her eyes fixed on the small pool of gravy oozing onto her plate, but she felt Ogden shake his head at Emmeline. Did he know her so well, or was he reading her thoughts? That was how rational magic worked—it affected the mind. Mind reading, telepathy, the dampening or surging of emotions . . . But she would know if Ogden used magic on her, wouldn't she? One of her abilities as a spellbreaker was to detect magic. Physical spells could be seen, rational spells had a certain feel to them, spiritual spells had a sound, and temporal spells had a smell. She'd been on pins and needles the last week, waiting for the sensation that Ogden was using his magic on her. But it had not yet happened. Either Ogden had refrained from nosing around or he was very adept at hiding his magic, as he'd been for the near decade she'd known him.

Either way, Elsie couldn't help the tar-thick thought that bubbled up the base of her skull. It *was* better for Bacchus to leave, not just because it was safer, but also because he'd held her hand. Because she was calling him by his first name.

Because she'd kissed his cheek and could still feel it upon her lips.

Elsie had let him get too close. Any closer, and he was liable to discover whatever it was that turned people away from her, that marked her as forgettable, unwanted, unlovable. Alfred had found it, as had her mother and her father, her siblings. With his spell gone, Ogden would likely discover it soon enough, too.

"Oh, Elsie," Emmeline said, reaching for her, "I didn't mean anything by it. I was curious, is all."

Snapping to attention, Elsie bucked up and pasted on a smile. "Oh no, Emmeline. I'm not bothered at all. I was just thinking about the last novel reader we had, and how it seemed so hopeless for the baron at the end."

Emmeline nodded. She appeared to believe her, but Elsie wasn't sure. "Only one left in that story. Oh, it should be here any day now!" Emmeline snatched a teacup and filled it, handing it to Ogden, who added far too much sugar and cream, as usual.

In truth, Elsie had completely forgotten about her novel reader schedule. Was it that time again already?

She pressed the tines of her fork to her pie. It *did* smell good, which helped unwind the knots in her stomach. The utensil cut easily through the crust—Emmeline had baked it perfectly. Elsie couldn't remember the last time she'd made a pie herself . . . last summer, perhaps? When Emmeline had rolled her ankle. It had been perfectly edible, but it hadn't looked or smelled nearly this good.

Elsie slid the morsel into her mouth. The meat was almost too hot, but the buttery flavor eased her tension. She chewed, smiled, and said, "Bless you, Emmeline, this is—"

A firm knock sounded at the front door.

Elsie nearly dropped the fork. The telegram beneath her leg burned like an ember. Had Bacchus meant *today*? Perhaps the telegram had come yesterday and Emmeline had forgotten about it? Her body knotted up again, muscles straining, bones near to crunching. She touched her hair. He could join them for lunch. That would give her a moment to get her thoughts together . . .

Emmeline, who'd been about to sit down, said, "I'll answer it," and hurried from the dining room into the workshop, which occupied the front of the house. Elsie couldn't see her, but she paused, listening—and then stiffened.

Like a feather across her skin, she felt the birth of a rational spell. But the rune wasn't directed toward her. No, Ogden had leaned back in his chair, his attention focused on the front of the house. Could he really read a mind from this far away? Or had he cast something else? Elsie was the least experienced with rational spells, so she wouldn't be able to tell without more practice.

"What are they saying?" she whispered, but Ogden was concentrating, so Elsie stood, tossed her napkin on the table, and went to see for herself. Likely just an order for something chiseled; Elsie had delivered all of Ogden's finished pieces yesterday, so it wouldn't be a pickup.

But when Elsie entered the studio, Emmeline glanced back at her with fright in her eyes. Two policemen stood in the doorway, their dark-navy uniforms buttoned up tightly to their chin straps.

"Is that her?" the taller one asked Emmeline, but the maid didn't answer.

Elsie's heart lodged into her throat so tightly she could barely talk around it. "Is that who? Might I ask what has given our maid such a fright?"

"Elsie Camden?" the other officer asked.

A chill coursed up her arms, but Elsie stood erect. "I am she."

The officers glanced at each other before stepping into the house. Only then did Elsie notice there were more beyond the threshold. The taller man lifted a pair of handcuffs. "You're under arrest for the practice of unregistered spellbreaking. Come with us gently if you'd like to avoid a scene."

CHAPTER 2

Bacchus Kelsey lifted his eyes to realize everyone was staring at him.

It wasn't a large party gathered for luncheon, just the family—Isaiah Scott, the Duke of Kent; his wife, Abigail; and his daughters, Ida and Josie. But they all looked at him intently, causing Bacchus to rub his half beard to see if there was food in it.

Fortunately, Duchess Scott clarified their interest before he had to ask. "You're not even halfway through, dear."

He glanced down to his plate, to the half-eaten mutton and vegetables staring back up at him. Everyone else's dishes had already been taken away by the help.

Offering a weak smile, he said, "I suppose I'm lost in thought today."

Josie perked up. "Not about Miss Camden, is it?"

Duchess Scott frowned. "Josie."

Bacchus didn't reply, but she was correct. He *had* been thinking about Elsie. He'd sent a telegram to Brookley that morning. Brief but to the point. He would have contacted her earlier, but he'd thought it best to wait. Alas, there weren't any straightforward rules of decorum for how to comfort a lady after she was nearly murdered by her possessed employer. Cuthbert Ogden had still looked unwell when Bacchus had left the hospital in London, and Elsie had appeared little better. She'd told Bacchus everything, and although he believed her, he still struggled to wrap his head around it.

Cuthbert Ogden, behind all the murders and stolen opuses. Except he wasn't.

So who was?

Bacchus dug his knife into the mutton and finished sawing off the piece he'd been halfheartedly working on for the last couple of minutes. "Just upcoming plans," he finally said.

"You're welcome to stay, of course." The duke leaned his elbows on the table.

"You are very generous, thank you." Bacchus chewed the mutton, swallowed. Thought. "I should be getting everything arranged this week." Barbados called to him—he had responsibilities there, friends, employees who depended on him—but he was too anchored in England to want to leave. Anchored by unanswered questions and an unsure future. He didn't have the same limitations he'd suffered for half his life, for one. That changed things. And then there was the question of how to approach a certain woman—

Baxter, the butler, stepped into the second dining room just then, the sound of the door echoing against the high ceiling. It wasn't as large as the usual dining room, but that one was still under repairs following Abel Nash's attack on Bacchus. The attack Elsie had nearly died to stop. And Bacchus was far more skilled at putting holes in floors than repairing them. Even a master physical aspector—a spellmaker who could affect properties of the physical world—could do only so much.

The butler bowed. "I apologize for interrupting, Your Grace, but there's a visitor in the drawing room for Master Kelsey."

Meal forgotten, Bacchus stood from his chair, trying not to notice the way Josie lit with excitement. His own pulse quickened. "Who?"

"A Mr. Ogden, from Brookley."

Bacchus tried to mask his surprise. "He's alone?"

"Yes, my lord."

Bacchus glanced back to the duke, but it was the duchess who waved at him. "Go on. We'll see you at tea, perhaps?"

Bacchus nodded and followed the butler, nearly mowing him over on their way to the drawing room. When Baxter opened the door, Cuthbert Ogden turned from the window, dressed modestly but with finesse, his hair combed back. He was a stout man, solid, his color fully returned. He was a few inches shorter than Bacchus and had his hands clasped behind his back.

He smiled. "Ah, Master Kelsey. I was hoping to discuss the ornaments you wanted before your return home."

Bacchus's brows drew together. "Orna—"

<Play along, if you would.>

Bacchus nearly choked on his question as Mr. Ogden's voice inserted itself into his mind. Gooseflesh rose on his arms. It was true, then. This man was a rational aspector, a magician of the mind. Something Elsie had uncovered during their chase through the St. Katharine Docks.

"Yes, thank you for seeing me." He nodded to the butler, who gave a cursory glance to their visitor before silently excusing himself. "I was hoping you'd be able to work on a tight schedule."

Mr. Ogden nodded. "Of course." *<Not here.>*

Bacchus gestured past the door. "Would you care to discuss it on the grounds? My legs are in need of exercise."

"Gladly." Another smile, and Mr. Ogden followed Bacchus's direction. Neither of them said another word as they followed the hallway to the first door that led outside. Mr. Ogden waited until they were some distance from the house before speaking again.

"It is my understanding that you're aware of certain things," he said, hands still clasped behind him as they walked.

Bacchus matched his posture and speed. "If you're referring to the events a week prior, then yes, I am."

"Excellent." He stopped suddenly, peering briefly at the house. "Forgive my intrusion, but I'm in need of your aid, Master Kelsey. I've neither the funds nor the standing to help her, and we need all the allies we can get."

"Help her?" Bacchus repeated, stomach tightening. His voice dropped. "Has something happened to Elsie?"

Mr. Ogden's jaw tensed. "She's been arrested."

Dropping his hands, Bacchus stepped back. "On what charges?"

"Illegal spellbreaking, what else?"

Mr. Ogden began walking again, and it took a moment for Bacchus's thoughts to connect to his legs so he could follow. He did, half hissing, "You're awfully calm about this."

"I am calm because I have to be." The words were hard as wrought iron. "Because even I can't get into the minds of every bobby and magistrate and convince them that Elsie is innocent. We'd best be on our way; I'm not certain how to proceed, or how quickly she might be sentenced. You know far more about the workings of the atheneums than I."

Bacchus's heart thudded against his chest, and his spine grew stiff as marble. "I'll call for a carriage right away."

"No need. There's one waiting for us. I convinced one of your servants it was of utmost importance on my way in."

The thought of this man penetrating the staff's minds, *his* mind, should have bothered him, but Bacchus couldn't tear his thoughts from Elsie. "When did they take her?"

"This morning. I'll explain everything I know on the way there."

Sure enough, as they neared the front lane, one of the duke's drivers came around with a carriage. The fastest in the fleet, if Bacchus wasn't mistaken. Good, they couldn't waste any time. Not when Elsie's life was on the line.

To think, only two fortnights ago, Bacchus had been ready to throw her into a cell himself. Now he'd give his right arm to keep her out of one. She'd saved his life twice: first by detecting and removing the siphoning spell that had been draining his strength and energy since adolescence, and second by thwarting Abel Nash's plan to shoot him through with a lightning bolt. But even without the acts of valor, she had startled him with her courage, her tenacity, the soft heart she kept tucked away in a vault of her own making. She made him laugh, made him think, made him *feel*, and envisioning a rope around her neck made Bacchus sick to his very core.

He quickened his pace, Mr. Ogden keeping up well enough. Before they reached the lane, however, Mr. Ogden asked, "You haven't perchance seen Master Lily Merton this past week, have you?"

Bacchus slowed. "No, why?"

Mr. Ogden's eyes stared dead ahead. "Because she's the only one who could have turned Elsie in."

Elsie didn't know what to think. What to do. What to hope. So she just gazed at the crisscrossing bars of the door to her tiny cell, listening to occasional footsteps, blank and scared and cold.

The ride here had been long and hard, for the wagon they'd taken her in had lacked even a simple bench for sitting. She'd thought they'd take her directly to the London Physical Atheneum, but apparently the assembly did not want criminals of her ilk near their precious books. No, she'd been brought to Her Majesty's Prison Oxford, a facility designed by the London atheneums to hold aspectors—men and women who could potentially melt their bars or sway their jailers to let them escape. There were spellbreakers among the patrol as well, she noticed, outfitted with violet badges that stood out from the color-coded badges of the spellmakers—blue for physical, red for rational, yellow for spiritual, and green for temporal.

They'd put her in a cell the size of a closet, protected only by bars and stones. For Elsie, they were all the precautions needed. While she could unwind any spell used to entrap her, she could cast nothing to get herself out. The cell was about five feet tall, five feet long, and three feet across. Not quite large enough for her to lie down without bending her knees, or stand without stooping her head. Perhaps that was the point. The centuries-old stone was mottled gray and white, the plaster chipping at the corners of the ceiling. No mattress, no straw, but she did have a rough blanket and a pot for excrement. No one stood outside the cage-like door, but even so, Elsie couldn't imagine hiking up her dress to use the pot when someone might pass by at any time. She hadn't yet, though her bladder was growing more and more uncomfortable.

Night would fall eventually. Then she would use it. She could wait. They'd already brought her a dingy tray of food for supper. Darkness wouldn't be long now.

She wasn't sure she wanted darkness to come.

Perhaps it would have been better if she weren't alone—if she were instead in one of the larger cells with other prisoners. At least then she'd have someone to talk to. But that company might consist of bandits, murderers, and other ruffians.

The chill finally grew sharp enough that Elsie took the blanket. It didn't smell good, but it was clean, and she wrapped it around her shoulders, leaning onto one side to alleviate some of the pain building in her rump. At least they hadn't put her in the stocks. She'd seen two of them on her way here, one of them in use. The man locked within it had great iron bowls strapped over his hands to dissuade him from using any magic. Praise the Lord, they hadn't taken her hands away. Yet.

Elsie's imagination bristled as the sunlight coming through a window in the hallway—there were none in her cell—faded to orange.

Would they cut off her hands? Send her to the workhouse? Or merely put a rope around her neck and end it quickly?

A sob caught halfway up her throat. Elsie fumbled with her dress until she could loosen her corset and breathe. Then she brought her knees to her chest and rested her forehead on them, hiding her face with the blanket. God help her, she'd never been so scared in her entire life. Even after her family had abandoned her and the Halls had brought her to the workhouse. At least then she hadn't feared *dying*.

Shivering, she pulled the blanket closer. She wished she could just sleep and wake up when this was all over, but her fear-riddled body refused to rest. Elsie was fairly certain she'd never sleep again.

Clenching her jaw, she tried to pull her wits together.

Dear Lord, I know I'm not the most devout, but please help—

"What a drab place this is."

Lightning shot up her limbs at the familiar voice, and she bolted upright, the blanket falling from her shoulders, the crown of her head knocking against the low ceiling. She looked wildly to the door, which remained firmly locked. The woman who had spoken was just inside it, against the left wall.

The cold seeped down to Elsie's bones as she gaped at Master Lily Merton.

The middle-aged woman tucked a short curl behind one of her ears. "But it suits our purposes, doesn't it, dear? We wouldn't want to be interrupted."

Elsie retreated until her back touched the wall behind her. "*You* did this."

Master Merton waved a dismissive hand. "I couldn't talk to you at the stonemasonry shop, now could I? Not with that lug lurking around the corner." She clicked her tongue. "What a sorry loss. I really should be angry with you, Elsie."

Her stomach curled. "Angry? After what you did—"

The words caught on her tongue as she stared at the shorter woman. She could see through her face and shoulders to where the stone behind her shifted from dark to light; the violet dress she wore seemed made of air, the edges blurry.

A projection. Of course. Most master-level spiritual aspectors had the ability to cast one. Yet the projection was solid enough that she had to be close. Perhaps not on the grounds, but in the wood surrounding them?

Elsie swallowed. "Where are you?"

Master Merton chuckled. "I'm not going to tell you that." She looked behind her, but Elsie couldn't tell if she was studying the prison outside the bars or perhaps peering at something in her true location. Maybe she'd heard a noise.

Elsie's breath caught—if she could keep Master Merton talking, perhaps a guard would come by and see her! Then Elsie could tell the authorities everything and have Master Merton arrested. Elsie had nothing to lose, so long as she could keep Ogden out of the confession.

Calculating, she said, "That night, at the duke's house—"

"I'm not here for chitchat, dear," the projection replied, voice just above a whisper. No footsteps sounded overhead or in the halls. Did Master Merton know the guards' schedules, or had she distracted them somehow? "But I will make you an offer. I'll clear your name if you'll come with me."

Elsie gaped. "But why?"

The projection folded her hands together. "You really are valuable, Elsie, especially after what happened with Nash."

Elsie pushed off the wall. "What happened with Nash was *your* doing—"

"And I'd hate to lose you," Master Merton went on. "Really, you're like a daughter to me."

The sentiment pricked her. Once Elsie had considered the Cowls her treasured secret—the anonymous benefactors who had plucked her out of obscurity and given her something important to do . . . and then she'd learned the truth. She shook her head. The opus spell beneath her bodice pressed against her, reminding her of its presence, but it would do her no good here. "You're a murderer and a thief. You used me from the start!"

"Hardly." She looked away, expression downcast. "I didn't involve you, in the beginning. I wanted you to learn your ability and use it to good purpose. The rest . . . it's all happening much later than I had hoped."

Elsie stared at her. *In the beginning.* Was she referring to the childhood tasks she'd assigned to Elsie? Dis-spelling the wall in the middle of farmland and bringing bread baskets to the orphanage? Did she think such small acts could really counterbalance murder?

"What do you mean it's happening later than you'd hoped?" Elsie pressed carefully.

Merton glanced over, meeting her gaze. "I wanted to adopt you, dear child, when I saved you from that workhouse. But I knew if I were to use your talents, the connection would be too obvious. So I set you up in Brookley instead."

"A-Adopt me?" Surely Merton was jesting. Yet she looked and sounded sincere. As sincere as such a woman could be.

She shook any soft feelings from her heart. "You put me to work under a terrible man." Squire Hughes had been her first employer in Brookley, and he was no better than Robin Hood's portrayal of King John.

"I put you to work under a rich man. You were provided for," Merton countered. "And you saw firsthand the evils we needed to fight."

The mention of *evil* brought Elsie's teeth down on her tongue for the hypocrisy. She inched closer. "You took away Ogden's will—"

"That was *your* doing, dear." Her facial features sharpened again. "I would never have known about him if you'd stayed put."

Elsie reeled back as though she'd been slapped. It *wasn't* her fault. Deep down, she knew that. She hadn't placed the spell on Ogden. She hadn't used his secret abilities to plan the murders of aspectors and theft of their opuses.

Yet she *had* led Merton right to him, unknowingly.

Ignorance didn't lessen the sting.

Master Merton brushed off her skirt. "Perhaps you need a little more time to think about it." A pause. "I *do* hope the judge is lenient," she added, tone flippant.

And just as quickly as it had come, the projection of Master Merton disappeared as though it never were, leaving Elsie utterly and helplessly alone.

Again.

CHAPTER 3

Elsie was dreaming of the stocks when a sudden banging on the bars jolted her awake. She'd stuffed herself into the far corner, head against the cool stone, and managed to fall asleep. It took her a moment to orient herself, to remember her surroundings and her predicament, and to recognize the people on the other side of the bars. The guard, who'd rattled the door with his club, was unfamiliar, but the sight of the other two sent her pulse raging, yanking her into complete wakefulness.

"That was unnecessary," Bacchus growled, but his eyes remained on Elsie. Beside him stood Ogden, his lips pulled into a frown, his arms folded tightly across his chest in displeasure.

Lord knew she ought to be embarrassed to be seen like this, disheveled, dress wrinkled, curled up like a beaten dog, but all she felt was relief. She stood too quickly, which made her head swim, and only just avoided smacking her crown on the ceiling. Leaning on the wall to orient herself, she stumbled. "I-I thought I wasn't allowed visitors."

"Not poor ones, anyway," the guard said, eyeing Bacchus. "Five minutes," he added before strolling down the hallway and out of Elsie's line of sight.

Ogden reached through the bars; Elsie crossed the tiny space, stooping, and grasped his hand. "It's not so very terrible," she lied. Then, to Bacchus, "I don't suppose this was the meeting you had in mind."

Bacchus scoffed. "At least they haven't curbed your sense of humor."

Elsie smiled at that . . . until she noticed her chamber pot only a few feet away. Her entire body pulsed crimson.

"I've caught him up," Ogden said, referring to Bacchus. "He knows everything."

Elsie swallowed. "She came, last night."

Bacchus blanched. "Merton? Here?"

"A projection. Practically admitted to everything—finding me at the workhouse, controlling Ogden, turning me in. She offered to get me out if I came with her willingly."

Ogden frowned. "She still wants you, then."

At least somebody does, but the thought sickened her. After all, hadn't Bacchus and Ogden gone to great trouble to be here?

Bacchus, practically squatting to see through the bars, murmured, "No one saw her?"

Elsie shook her head.

He considered a moment. "Your sole witness won't convince anyone. But I've garnered an appointment with the magistrate to discuss your case. There may yet be a way to twist this in your favor."

Elsie's heartbeat skipped. "Truly?"

"There's a forgiveness period for spellbreakers, since their abilities are inherent," he said, his voice warm and quick. "I looked into it."

A sour taste filled her mouth. Elsie had known she was a spellbreaker since she was ten. "How long is the leniency?"

"A year."

She hugged herself. "Bacchus—"

"Let me speak with him," he insisted.

Ogden said, "Have you admitted anything?"

"No." At least there was that. "I haven't said a word."

A long breath passed over Ogden's lips. "Good." He rubbed stubble on his chin, considering. "I can almost picture it, the place I went when Merton made me run. Where the rest of the opus spells were hidden. If I could find it again . . . perhaps there'll be evidence tying Merton to it. At the very least, we'd have spells to arm ourselves with, when she strikes again."

Elsie glanced past the bars, looking for jailers, but Ogden spoke so quietly she doubted he could be overheard.

"Elsie." For a moment Elsie thought Bacchus reached for her—and her heart leapt in anticipation—but instead his large hand wrapped around one of the iron bars. "We'll get you out, one way or another."

Chewing on her lip, she glanced at the small space behind her. "Perhaps, Bacchus. But not even a master aspector can erase the law."

"Elsie, look at me."

She did, the green in his eyes vibrant despite the shadows of the cell. This time it was she who was trapped, not he. For a fleeting moment, she let herself remember what his skin felt like under her lips. But she couldn't run away from him—or what he made her feel—this time. She couldn't do anything.

His gaze was fast and firm. "I will get you out of here, if I have to melt the castle down myself, do you understand?"

She stared at him, wanting so badly to believe him. Wanting to ignore the fear and anxiety festering beneath her ribs and give hope its way, but hoping had always hurt her. Still, she found herself nodding. Not hoping, exactly. Wishing, perhaps.

"Magic-related discipline tends to be swift," Ogden murmured. "I'll need to hunt the opuses down as quickly as I can. Find a way to pin them on Merton."

Elsie nodded. "Go. Emmeline will be fine."

Footsteps closed in on their huddle. "Time's up!" barked the guard.

Ogden ignored him. "I leave it to you, Master Kelsey."

Before Bacchus could say anything, the guard approached, and the two men stepped back from the bars. Elsie felt a thousand threads connecting her to them, a spell in and of itself, and she followed them as far as the heavy door would allow, wrapping both hands around the unyielding iron.

Bacchus put his warm hands over hers, driving back the chill for an instant.

"Be careful," she whispered.

"Come on now." The guard waved his club.

Both Bacchus and Ogden spared her a final look before walking away, and Elsie pressed her face against the slots in the door, watching them until she couldn't see them anymore, then listening to their footsteps until they faded. The prison grew silent once more, save for the sudden, brief wail of a prisoner beyond Elsie's chamber.

Elsie sank to her knees and found herself praying again, hoping God could muddle through her thorny thoughts better than she could.

⁓

Bacchus waited impatiently in the magistrate's sitting room on the east side of Oxford. It was elaborately furnished in reds and creams, and he was sorely tempted to change the color scheme to give himself something to do. Granted, that wouldn't play well. He needed this man to like him, and Englishmen seemed predisposed to think the worst of him. He looked the part of a foreigner, and so he was treated as one.

He tried to sit, first on a posh settee and then on an elaborately carved mahogany armchair, but time ticked slowly and his nerves ran hot, so he stood and paced, first before the unlit fireplace, then by the windows that looked out onto modest but well-kept gardens. Something he might have appreciated, were he not so focused on what to say and how to say it. He hadn't even been this nervous when he'd appealed for his mastership at the London Physical Atheneum. Then again, he'd known precisely what he was doing at the time.

A servant came in, bringing a tray of tea. She set it down on a side table and lifted a cup, but Bacchus waved her off, so she simply poured some for the magistrate and departed. The liquid had to be nearly cold by the time the man finally showed himself.

Bacchus bowed lower than was necessary. "Lord Astley, thank you for seeing me." The man was about Elsie's height, average for a man, and looked to be sixty or thereabouts, with sagging skin on his cheeks and neck that spoke of heavy weight loss, though his stomach was still round beneath his satin cutaway. His hair was curled and receding, a few locks holding on to brown pigment, the rest varying shades of gray. A pair of spectacles rested on his nose.

"Master Kelsey." He nodded toward him. "My butler tells me you're here regarding the Camden case. Forgive my tardiness; I hadn't yet read up on it, and my daughter was rather insistent I attend a picnic in South Park." He rolled his eyes and gestured to the settee. "Please, sit."

The magistrate settled into the chair closest to the tea and picked up the cup the servant had left for him. He made a face as he took a sip, then returned the cup to the tray.

"Then you are familiar with the charges against Miss Camden?" Bacchus didn't have the patience for small talk, not with his mind fixed on the image of Elsie in that awful cell. He'd never seen her look so vulnerable before, so defeated. Those locked bars had completely stripped her of her practiced airs.

The magistrate nodded. "Nasty thing, really. Hard punishments, even for women."

"I believe there's been a misunderstanding. Miss Camden has only recently discovered her abilities. She falls well within the grace period allotted for registration."

Lord Astley studied him in a way that did not instill confidence. "How old is Miss Camden?"

"One and twenty."

The man's brow knit together. "Spellbreakers usually discover their abilities in adolescence."

"But not always," he countered. "Elsie began to suspect only a month ago."

Lord Astley poured a new cup of tea, loading it with sugar. "Then why did she not report it a month ago?"

Bacchus forced his posture to relax; he could feel his muscles tensing with every inquiry. "It was only a suspicion, and of course she hasn't had the time or training to test it. Miss Camden is a working woman, you understand. Her employer keeps her very busy. And there is always a sense of fear attached to such things."

The magistrate met Bacchus's gaze. "Whatever does she have to be afraid of, if she's only just discovered it?"

Choosing to be daring, Bacchus said, "Perhaps that the people she reports it to will think she must have discovered it in her adolescence, and therefore might suspect she is lying."

To his relief, the magistrate's lip quirked. "Touché. But my reports say that she's been aware of her abilities for some time now, even using them."

Bacchus didn't miss a beat. "I believe I know who reported her, and the two met only recently."

The magistrate considered this, but skepticism still weighed on his brow. Master Merton had likely reported the spellbreaking anonymously; how could she not? The accuser would be asked to disclose how he or she knew, and Master Merton was too covetous of her own secrets to risk an interview with a truthseeker. But that very anonymity might give Bacchus's claim more credence. He prayed it would.

Lord Astley took a sip of tea, biding his time, organizing his thoughts. "The charges are not so simple. They're quite severe, you understand."

"Who is accusing her?"

Lord Astley smiled. "I thought you said you knew."

"You make me believe I do not." He clasped his hands together. "I am a witness. I was with Elsie during this entire ordeal. Which is why I'm shocked at the allegation that she knew about her abilities and purposefully concealed them. I know that to be false."

Lord Astley raised an eyebrow. "It's my understanding you arrived in England only six weeks ago."

It took all Bacchus's control to not show his surprise. Had the magistrate looked into his background as well? Had he perhaps read the police report of the happenings at the St. Katharine Docks?

"I met Miss Camden at a market in London shortly after my arrival," he said, adopting the story he had used with the duke and duchess. His mind spun as he attempted to piece together a believable tale that would not result in Elsie's broken neck. "I've been courting her." The duke and his family could confirm that, as they already believed it to be true. Indeed, they'd encouraged him.

"Is that so?" The magistrate returned his cup again to the tray. "A master aspector and a stonemason's employee?"

"I did not have the master title when we met," he pressed. "In fact, I was with her when she detected her first spell. We were both confused. It wasn't until later that I suggested it might be a rune. She didn't believe me, of course."

Lord Astley leaned back in his chair, studying Bacchus for an uncomfortable moment. "And you believe you know her well enough, and you've been in her company long enough, to vouch for her innocence? I find it hard to swallow, Master Kelsey, if you'll forgive my bluntness. Your record is clear, and I believe you have the fellowship of the Duke of Kent, but it's my job to ensure criminals pay their fare and the innocent find their mercy. It's difficult to mete out justice when all of it is 'he said this, she said that' . . . but we must persist in pursuing credible claims."

Bacchus's palms began to sweat. "You must understand that I am an excellent character witness. And that I have no reason to lie to you."

He had every reason to lie.

"Her accuser may have just as much clout as you do, Master Kelsey, if not more. I find it unlikely that you've been so attached to Miss Camden as to witness—"

"We are engaged to be married, you understand." His pulse raced quick enough to make him dizzy, but he held his sure countenance, his confident posture. If a blossoming courtship wasn't believable enough, Bacchus would take it further. "Of course I would spend a great deal of time with her. The wedding is mere weeks away."

Lord Astley paused. Rubbed his chin. Stared at Bacchus as though he could peel away his skin and look into his soul. Bacchus forced himself to stare right back. He'd meant what he'd said to Elsie. He would demolish the entire castle if he had to. What was an audacious lie in comparison to that?

Lord Astley chuckled.

Bacchus stiffened. "Is the matter of a woman's life humorous to you?"

But the magistrate shook his head. "No, no, not at all. I do not *enjoy* handing out sentences of guilt. I would be a terrible magistrate if I did. But I do like you, Master Kelsey. And strangely enough, I find myself wanting to believe you."

A trickle of relief ran down his spine, but Bacchus dared not drop his guard.

"If you deliver your testimony and character witness, and the testimonies of at least three other persons whose statements support yours, I will let her go," he said. "She'll have to register, of course, and receive the necessary training."

A hard sigh escaped him. He could get three witnesses easily. The duke's family made four, Mr. Ogden made five, and perhaps even the maid, Miss Pratt, would be willing to testify. "Thank you, Lord Astley. Truly."

"I am not unreasonable," he said as he stood, and Bacchus followed his lead and rose from the settee. "Tired and busy, but not unreasonable. One of the servants is waiting in the hall and will show you to the door."

Bacchus bowed. "Of course. Thank you." He started for the exit.

"And, Master Kelsey," Lord Astley called, retrieving his teacup once more.

Bacchus paused.

"Do invite me to the wedding," he said, narrow eyes peering over the dish in his hand. "The nuptials between two who have fallen so quickly in love would be very interesting to witness."

Bacchus heard the intonation between words, the kindly veiled threat, the hint that his story was not as watertight as he had hoped. Elsie was not entirely out of danger. Not yet.

Bacchus nodded and stepped out into the hallway.

He found his own way to the door.

CHAPTER 4

Cuthbert knew he needn't travel far from London to find Merton's stolen opuses; he'd been able to make the trip from there to St. Katharine Docks in one night. The problem was, his memory stalled somewhere between cutting clay for future projects in his studio and finding himself on the docks with Elsie. In between, he recalled nothing but a handful of impressions: running through the dark, feeling stone beneath his hands, experiencing the confinement of a cold, starless place. A spiritual aspector could not *erase* his memory—only a rational magician could do that. But she could most definitely make it hard for him to recall what he had been doing, especially in the shadows of night.

Cuthbert had mulled over the puzzle pieces almost constantly this last week. He'd filled up an entire sketchbook with half-finished charcoal drawings. He'd even dreamed about his escape, and while he of all people knew dreams couldn't be trusted, he'd sketched the dreams first thing upon waking, even before using the water closet. And so he was fairly certain Merton had guided him to a cemetery, sepulcher, or crypt, although that didn't narrow things enough, given there were a multitude of them in London.

Were Merton here, he could rip the information from her mind himself. She couldn't manipulate him again without touching him, and he was constantly on guard. A deep, damaged part of him wanted to seize her every thought, force her into a puppetlike state, rip apart her secrets and sorrows and drown her in them. Make her suffer as he had suffered. And yet, when he thought of Merton, he thought of Elsie, and that made him tuck away his anger and his hatred and focus on the task at hand. Because she was in prison, yes, but it was more than that. Despite being tied in with Merton from the start, Elsie made him want to do better, be better. She was the closest thing to a daughter he'd ever had. She'd been with him longer than Emmeline, and as a child, no less. She'd unknowingly brought bondage to him, but in the end, she'd also been his salvation.

She'd been a pawn, too. Cuthbert couldn't dwell on vengeance until she'd had her liberation as well.

Merton's London townhouse was the first place he went after seeing Elsie, and the space was entirely empty, without even a skeleton staff or housekeeper to look after it. She wasn't to be found at the Spiritual Atheneum, either. Cuthbert didn't want to give himself away by asking after her, so he broke his rules and dived into the minds of anyone who might know, pushing past goals and desires, complaints and crudeness, searching for any mark of his enemy. No one had seen her since the dinner at Kent just before his liberation.

Cuthbert could only hope it meant Merton saw him as a threat and sought to save her own hide, not that she was moving on to another portion of whatever mad plan she wanted to unfurl. How many spells did one person need? And what did she intend to *do* with them all?

Rubbing a hand down his face, Cuthbert dropped onto a bench in Burgess Park, considering. Thanks to a decade of church hopping, he knew which cathedrals and the like had crypts. Which had cemeteries large enough to hide away Merton's secrets. Were it Cuthbert, he wouldn't stow away his treasures at a large or frequently visited place, not where they could be discovered. It had to be something out of the way, but not so out of the way that he couldn't retrieve them swiftly.

Closing his eyes, he replayed the night of his escape in his head. He was sure he hadn't gone north, not at first. Would he find his way better if he mimicked the conditions of that night? If he searched in the dark, instead of the light?

Light. He'd been moving toward the light, hadn't he? The moon rose in the east . . .

He needed to find the place now. Before Merton figured out they were on to her and ransacked the place herself.

Rising, he left the park and paid his way onto an omnibus. He'd asked around for the oldest churches and gravesites near East London. His eyes scanned the streets as he rode, as though he could spot *her* among the throngs of people.

He pulled his hat low when he reached the first village on his map, small enough that he might be seen as a stranger. He did not have a large repertoire of spells, given that those he knew had been gathered and adopted illegally, but those he did have were potent. He hopped from mind to mind, learning his way through the streets and alleyways as he did. He found the cemetery and its church easily. Somehow he knew it wasn't right, but he checked anyway before moving on. He had to keep moving if he didn't want to go mad.

It was at the third parish he visited that something raised gooseflesh on his arms. He paused, turning around, his surroundings completely unfamiliar and yet not. A wave of frustration worked through him. If only he could use spells on his own mind, hypnotize answers from his subconscious. But there *was* something.

He could see the spires of the local chapel and began toward it, but that felt wrong somehow. Retreating, he again stood in the place from before, a cobbled road at the crest of the town. It would have been a good view, if not for the thick trees.

Turning slowly, he noticed a narrow staircase to the east, centuries old and laid with stone. A chill coursed down his back. He'd been on that staircase before. The second-to-last step was uneven. He'd tripped on it in his rush . . .

His rush . . .

Clenching his jaw, Cuthbert ran toward the stairs, not out of a desire for speed, but to help him remember. She'd driven him hard; he'd been exhausted upon reaching the docks, which was why Merton had demanded he use opus spells to slow down his pursuers. He sprinted for the stairs, and despite expecting the dip in the stone, he tripped and fell onto his hands and knees at the bottom.

His right knee pounded painfully, the stone striking an old bruise. A bruise he must have gotten *here.*

Standing slowly, Cuthbert closed his eyes, imagining night wind in his hair despite it being midafternoon. He felt a questioning gaze from a passerby and ignored it.

Running downhill, toward a gas lamp. Around the corner. Another stumble at the end of the cobblestone path.

Opening his eyes, Cuthbert jogged down the way, finding an unlit lamp at a crossroads. Left would take him deeper into town, right . . . at the end of the street, the trees were overgrown and the path narrowed, turning to packed dirt.

Cuthbert ran right.

He slowed when he reached the trees, stooping to avoid their branches. He looked around for any broken boughs, any opening in the green. He found nothing. He followed the path for an eighth of a mile before it ended at an old stone wall, flowering weeds poking through its mortar.

He almost didn't notice the steep dip to his right. Sitting, he slid down it five feet and followed the wall. The trees lifted just enough for him to identify three burial chambers, the stone crosses at their heads weathered and nearly indistinguishable from the rest of the stone.

This was it.

Holding his breath, he approached the first sepulcher, scanned for witnesses, and shouldered the heavy door open, the scents of must and mildew rushing at him. The interior was small, but the chill was achingly familiar. He checked the tombs. The first held only bones and remnants of rotted clothes. The next was the same. But the third . . . the third was larger. There was a stone casket in the back, and just behind it a smaller one, made for a child. The moment he touched it, Cuthbert *knew* it. The roughness of the ancient stone, the weight of the lid. This was it. Grasping the lip with both hands, he heaved it up and over, then stood aside so light from the doorway could pour in.

The casket was far deeper than the others, at least four feet, and it was entirely empty, even of bones.

Merton had already been here, and none of the dead could tell him where she'd gone.

∽

Elsie had dozed off again. She startled awake, her stomach cramping as she did so. The jailer kept her fed, but it was food she wasn't used to, as the bucket in the far corner could attest. She wasn't sure if it was a lucky rotation or pity from one of the guards, but they'd let her bathe last night. The water hadn't been fresh, but it had been a bath. She wore the same dress she'd been arrested in, and the hair at the center of her simple braid was still damp.

It was her third day in prison. She hadn't seen either Ogden or Bacchus in a day and a half, although she could have sworn Merton had returned to her cell in the dead of night. She couldn't remember anything else about it—just a fleeting impression—so it may have been a dream. She'd had lots of those here. Snippets of things not quite real, sometimes in the darkness, sometimes in the daylight. She wondered if that was how madness started. Either way, it would make a great plot for a novel reader. Perhaps, if she ever got out of this horrid place, she could sell it to someone.

If she ever got out.

Looking at the bars longingly, Elsie touched her neck, wondering what it would feel like to have it snap. Would she die right away, or just hang there, broken and hurting, until blood stopped flowing to her brain?

Footsteps sounded, and while Elsie longed for company, her heart dropped to her hips and her fingers turned to ice. She stood up slowly, not wanting to upset her stomach, as one of the guards approached the door. He pulled a key ring from his belt and looked up at her through dark eyelashes.

"Miss Camden." He unlocked the door. Her name sounded so *final* on his lips, like it was the only polite thing he could think to say. Pulling the door open, he gestured for her to follow him.

God help her, it was time for her trial. What was she supposed to say? Should she lie and hope, or be completely truthful and pray for a sentence of hard labor instead of death? But not *completely* truthful. She couldn't mention her involvement with the Cowls. That would see her hanged for certain.

Clasping quivering fingers in front of her, Elsie allowed the guard to cuff her before following him out of the cell. Part of her thought she should try to look dignified, but she didn't have the stamina for it. His footsteps were loud in the stone halls; hers were silent. As though she were already a ghost.

Gooseflesh prickled her arms and back. They descended a narrow set of stairs, the air growing even cooler as they did, and wound through massive, ancient stone pillars. Around a corner, down another corridor. Elsie was already lost. Through an open window she saw a small wooden stage, a pole standing just off center. No rope, but she knew death when she saw it.

She tried to swallow and found she couldn't.

Finally, the guard took her up another flight of stairs, past two others in uniform, before shoving open a heavy door with his shoulder. Brilliant sunlight stung Elsie's eyes, and she stumbled blindly for a moment, trying to gain her bearings. She nearly toppled down a set of steps.

She blinked several times, eyes tearing, before the old castle bailey came into view. A few guards walked its perimeter. And there, standing at the base of the steps, was—

"Bacchus?" His name was more breath than voice.

The guard took her wrists and began uncuffing her.

Her pulse sped like a wild horse. "I don't understand."

Bacchus took a step closer. "I spoke with the magistrate about your case and provided him with witness documents. He's released you."

Elsie stared at him, the news taking too long to register in her thoughts. It wasn't until the second cuff dropped from her skin that she understood.

"I'm free to go?" she squeaked.

Bacchus nodded.

In an abrupt burst of anger, she wheeled on her guard and said, "For heaven's sake, you could have *said* something!"

The man shrugged indifferently before heading back inside.

Suddenly weary, Elsie's knees buckled. She sat on the steps, landing hard. Bacchus, bless him, tried to catch her, but he wasn't quite quick enough. Instead, he sat beside her.

"I-I don't believe it." She rubbed her wrists, studied her hands. Was very aware of Bacchus's closeness, for that side of her grew almost uncomfortably warm. "Wh-What did you say? I mean, *thank you*." She let out a short, heavy breath. "Thank you. But what did you say? Has Ogden . . . ?"

"I haven't heard from him." His tone was low and measured, careful. "First, I want to ensure you can easily reach me if anything like this happens again." He reached into the pocket in the lining of his jacket and pulled out two pencils. As he turned one over in his fingers, the wood glimmered and turned a warm shade of green. He focused on the pencils only for a second before handing the green one to her.

Elsie accepted the strange gift hesitantly. Had he known green was her favorite color? She turned it over in her hands, noting that when she did so, the other pencil jerked in his fingers in a similar fashion.

"They're connected by a spell," he explained, carefully returning his pencil to his jacket pocket. Elsie's shifted slightly as he did so. "Leave it home on a piece of paper. If you need to contact me, whatever you write down will transfer to my end."

She blinked. "How smart. And much less expensive than a telegram." She would have to be careful with it so she didn't accidentally stab Bacchus or scribble graphite all over his clothing. There was something reassuring about the gift, about the connection it gave her to him. She ran her thumb over the tiny blue rune only a spellbreaker could see, and a smile touched her lips.

"Second . . . there were some caveats to your release."

She straightened. "I'm listening."

"You'll be required to register."

She nodded. "Of course."

"And train under another spellbreaker."

Elsie paused. Opened her mouth, closed it. She'd been spellbreaking for ten years. She'd broken spells as they were conjured, even! To submit to training . . .

There was a strain in Bacchus's eyes, and her resistance immediately evaporated. "Yes, that makes sense."

Softer, he said, "I convinced the magistrate you discovered your abilities only a month ago. You'll need to act the part."

Only a month ago. "I can play along." A shiver coursed up her spine and tickled her hair. She slouched. "Oh, Bacchus, thank you." She reached for his hand and squeezed it. "I don't know . . . I was so afraid."

His lip quirked in the semblance of a smile, but there was something about his expression that made her uneasy. "What?" she asked, then blanched. "Bacchus, what did you do? Did you pay some unlordly fine?" She would get a second job to pay him back if she had to. Sell anything she had of value . . .

He shook his head and stood, taking her elbow to help her up as well. The delight she felt when he strung her arm through his didn't fully banish her fear. He still hadn't answered her. As he began walking through the bailey, toward the exit, she tried again, quieter. "Bacchus?"

"There is . . . one other caveat." He nodded to a passing guard.

Elsie worried her lip, waiting for him to explain. When he didn't, she pressed. "What?"

They reached the exterior doors and waited for two guards to open them. They passed through, and an invisible weight lifted from her. Everything felt cleaner and greener and more open. But Bacchus still didn't answer. He escorted her over the grounds, short bursts of clover and gravel passing under their feet. A carriage Elsie recognized as the Duke of Kent's waited down at the road, four black horses tethered to it.

Dread filled Elsie like tar. What had Bacchus given up to free her? Money? Lands? His *mastership*? What could it be?

This was it. Surely his silence was out of anger, or maybe distaste. Perhaps the worst had happened, and Bacchus had discovered her flaw—the quality that made her so distasteful to others—or the system had found it for him. This could be goodbye. She'd be free, but Bacchus . . .

Tears stung her eyes, and she forced them back. *Don't think about it. Just smile and nod, understand. Hold it in until you get home. Then Ogden can erase all of it. You won't have to feel a thing. Just last a little longer . . .*

She bit the inside of her cheek.

Bacchus's steps slowed, stopped. He dropped her arm. Turned toward her. Elsie tried her best to look cheery and reposed, but found her acting skills had severely waned during her captivity.

He sighed. Gripped her shoulders, his warmth seeping through her sleeves, then suddenly let her go. A feeling of loss seized her. Would that be the last time he ever touched her?

In a voice too weak for her liking, she said, "Bacchus, you're scaring me."

He barked a chuckle. "That is my main concern, yes."

Confused, she waited.

He drew a hand down his face. "I convinced the magistrate that I was a personal witness to your spellbreaking discovery. Because we've spent a lot of time together."

Elsie blinked. "Nothing wrong with that." It *was* true.

"Obviously I couldn't discuss our work arrangement," he went on. "The witness documents I turned in attest to our . . . courtship. From both the Duke and the Duchess of Kent and Miss Emmeline Pratt."

She felt the heat work its way up her neck and to her cheeks. She desperately wanted to press her cool fingers to her face, yet such an action would draw Bacchus's attention to the color. She cleared her throat. "Not so far-fetched."

He glanced toward the carriage. It wasn't *so* far-fetched . . . was it? Or did the idea of a master aspector courting the employee of a stonemason upset him? Her heart gave a quick, unpleasant thud just before he met her eyes once more.

"Elsie." He looked so uncertain. "I had to sell it, you understand. Convince him of my motivation to be around you. He believes us to be engaged."

Elsie's lips parted.

"And." He hesitated. "Expects to be invited to the wedding."

She stared at him, again struggling to internalize what he was saying. Engaged? But they weren't . . . but there was to be a wedding?

She would not faint. Only dramatic damsels fainted.

Bacchus continued, "He led me to believe that his suspicions remain. We must go through with it, Elsie. That is the only way to assuage his doubts."

Elsie knew she was gawking, but she couldn't stop herself.

Engaged.

Engaged?

Engaged to Bacchus Kelsey. *Master* Bacchus Kelsey.

Her numb lips stuttered, "You didn't . . ." and stopped. *You didn't have to do that,* she wanted to say, but he *did* have to do that if she wanted to walk away from this awful place. And he already had done it. For her.

He was throwing his life away for her.

Oh God, he must hate her.

Her face must have been something to see, for Bacchus notably withdrew into himself. "It won't be terrible. I've already considered . . . We can stay in England, of course."

"I . . . no. What I mean is . . ." She wrung her hands, searching for words. "I-I'm just surprised, is all. I didn't expect—"

"Neither did I."

A laugh escaped her mouth, a nervous sound born of nerves and uncertainty. She tried to reel it back in, but such a thing was impossible. Her stomach growled, and she pressed both hands to it.

"You did it," she tried, unable to meet his eyes. "You said you'd get me out and you did." Her organs twisted inside her. "But, Bacchus—"

"Let's discuss it in the carriage," he said softly, offering his arm.

Finding her wits, Elsie accepted it and let him lead her to the road.

Despite Bacchus's suggestion, the carriage ride to Brookley was rather silent.

CHAPTER 5

Elsie came home to an empty house, unsure if Ogden was still looking for stolen opuses or attending to other business. At first, she assumed Emmeline was simply running errands, but when the maid did not return by nightfall, it became clear she must have left to stay with family or friends. And so Elsie locked up the dark stonemasonry shop and put herself in bed, pretending to sleep and doing a very poor job of it.

She was engaged. To Bacchus Kelsey. Engaged *to be married*.

And he hadn't even proposed.

We'll sort it out, Elsie, he'd said as the carriage pulled down Brookley's high street, his Bajan accent soft. *I promise.*

But he'd seemed tense, so wrapped in thoughts they were suffocating him. Elsie didn't know what she'd wanted him to feel, to say. That he was relieved? That he was actually madly in love with her? That made her laugh.

How funny it was, to have a man who had once nearly thrown her into prison sacrifice his happiness to keep her out of it.

Tears stung her vision, and she blinked them away. *His happiness.* Oh, she wanted Bacchus to be happy. So desperately. She recalled the utter glee that had encompassed him after she pulled that siphoning spell from his chest. How it had buoyed her. Made her feel wanted and important. She wanted him to be like that always.

But this arrangement had practically put the spell back onto him, hadn't it? Elsie would eat up his time, his energy, his money, as any unwanted spouse would.

Rolling over, Elsie pressed her face into her pillow and moaned. How blissful this engagement would have been if it had come about differently. If she'd never been arrested and he'd stayed in England for the want of her and they'd courted in the way a man and a woman were supposed to, without secrets and murderers looming in the background. Yes, Elsie was willing to admit that in that other, perfect scenario, it would be joy keeping her awake. Excitement.

"You'll have to make the best of it," she said into the pillow. "Make him regret it as little as possible. Be the best forced spouse you can be."

And the magistrate might yet lose interest. For all they knew, Bacchus could be let off the hook.

It bothered her how much that thought seared, like she'd swallowed a hot poker.

God help her, she'd be miserable if he stayed, and miserable if he left. The most logical thing to do was to prepare for the pain now. The worst thing about tragedy was being surprised by it. She simply wouldn't let it catch her unawares this time. Not like it had with her family, with Alfred, or with the mysterious American man she'd thought, however briefly, was her long-lost father.

A sore lump formed in her throat, and stubborn tears pushed their way onto her pillowcase. She'd tried very hard not to think on that the last two weeks. The worst of it was how excited she'd been upon receiving a telegram from the Halls, the family with whom her parents had abandoned her. They'd reported that someone had *finally* come looking for her. She'd cashed out her entire bank account and fled for Juniper Down immediately, only to realize the man was not her kin. He wasn't even English. And he thought she'd written a mass of articles to toy with him for a reason she had been unable to surmise.

That horrible disappointment had been followed by the revelation that the Cowls—or, rather, Master Lily Merton—had been using her for years, something that had filled her with shadows that were too poisonous to bear.

She heard the *snap* of the bolt in the back door and sat up, quickly wiping her eyes. The door opened, closed, followed by familiar footsteps. Too heavy to be Emmeline's.

Grabbing her night-robe, Elsie pushed her arms into its sleeves and hurried into the hall.

"Ogden?" she called.

A candle lit at the bottom of the stairs, illuminating Ogden's face. Relief etched his features. "He did it. You're back."

She nodded. "As are you. We need to talk."

He ascended the steps. "Anywhere is fine. Emmeline's not due back until morning."

She stepped aside to let him pass, then followed him into his bedroom, where she perched on the trunk at the edge of his bed. "What did you find?"

"The place she hid the opuses," he answered. Elsie perked up, but he held out a hand, staying her. "It was empty. She's been there. I didn't find her, but I returned to the Spiritual Atheneum in London on my way back. Picked some brains. Apparently she's officially retired and moved from the city, though no one seems to know where."

Elsie's lungs twisted in an unexpected way. Lily Merton must have decided Elsie wasn't necessary anymore. It shouldn't have bothered her—she wanted nothing to do with the murderer—and yet it did.

"I'll be returning soon to try to locate her, keep tabs on her. Someone must know something." He set the candle down and plopped onto his bed, landing hard enough to shake the trunk pressed against its foot. "She's being smart—she knows I could overpower her mind if I found her."

Elsie stiffened. "Could you?"

He hesitated, peering at her with severe turquoise eyes. "Yes, I could."

Elsie licked her lips, considering.

"Does that bother you?"

"Does what?"

"What I am," he clarified. "What I can do."

She shook her head, then paused. "It doesn't *bother* me. I'm just . . . not used to it." *I just don't know if you've ever used it on me.*

She knew he had, in service to Merton, but she had to believe he wouldn't do it intentionally. He'd claimed that their interactions were genuine, that Merton had controlled him only on occasion. She needed to believe that. She needed to believe in *something.*

"I wonder," Ogden went on, "if she's hired new thugs, or if she's choosing to lie low. Perhaps it's over. Perhaps she really has retired."

Elsie gave him an incredulous look that he merely nodded at. People had been murdered, their opuses stolen. A woman did not go through such extensive efforts merely to give up in the end. "The question is," Elsie said aloud, "what is the end?"

"I don't know." He rubbed his hands together. "If she has all those opuses . . . she's the most powerful person in England, if not the world."

Elsie hugged herself, cold in a way that radiated from the inside out, much like she'd been in prison.

As though sensing her thought—and perhaps he had—Ogden asked, "How did he get you out? What did he have to pay?"

The lump in her throat returned, and she swallowed it down. "Not money," she murmured.

And she told him everything, from the moment the guard unlocked her cell to the moment Bacchus dropped her off in Brookley, promising to contact her soon. Everything but the worry and worthlessness gnawing on her insides.

Ogden leaned back. "Interesting."

"That's one way of putting it."

He shrugged. "He's not a bad choice, Elsie. He's titled, wealthy, and virile."

Elsie's cheeks heated. "Did you say *virile*?"

Ogden smirked. "It's hard not to notice."

She covered her face with her hands, hiding her embarrassment.

Until another realization hit her, making her stomach drop.

"Oh no," she whispered.

Ogden tensed. "What? What's wrong?"

Slowly, she dropped her hands from her face and lifted her eyes. "If I marry him . . ."

Ogden leaned closer.

"My name will be *Elsie Kelsey*," she finished, mortified.

Oh, how the Wright sisters would *love* that.

∽

"I *knew* you fancied him!" Emmeline chimed as she picked up the breakfast dishes. Elsie had cooked that morning, early, thanks to her insomnia, but Emmeline had returned home just in time to lend a hand with the morning chores. "How exciting, Elsie! Right out of a storybook. Engaged to a master aspector, and yourself a spellbreaker! The perfect pair. Oh, you're moving up in the world, and so elegantly!"

Elsie brushed crumbs from the table into her hand. "I don't think being arrested is elegant, Em. Prison most certainly is not." She peered out the window. She'd used her enchanted pencil to write to Bacchus that morning, before sunup, after mulling over her options all night long. She needed to know what Merton was aiming for, what she wanted, and why she wanted it, and Bacchus knew three people who might have answers—the Duke and Duchess of Kent and Duchess Morris, a fellow spiritual aspector who'd appeared quite friendly with Merton when Elsie had spied them together on a shopping excursion. Duchess Morris was also a contemptible woman who had put a curse on the Duke of Kent's fields and hired physical and temporal aspectors to make herself more attractive. Elsie knew—she'd unraveled both the curse and the glamour on the woman's nose. Although there was a slim chance the woman might recognize her, Elsie thought it middling. Duchess Morris wasn't the sort to pay attention to those she thought beneath her.

She'd start in Kent, of course. Bacchus was close to the Scotts, even shared their roof. And she'd conjured the perfect excuse to talk to Duchess Morris. As a new spellbreaker, she would be required to interview aspectors in all four disciplines. If she could get Duchess Morris to participate, she could segue into questions about her friendship with Merton.

It was as good a plan as any. She just didn't want to do it alone. Bacchus knew the woman better than she did, and if he helped her, she'd be more likely to get through the front door. Plus, she simply wanted him there.

The kitchen clean, Elsie brushed off her hands and hurried up the stairs, to where the green pencil rested against a piece of parchment. The top of the page read, in her handwriting, *She-who-will-not-be-named has supposedly retired and left London without a trace. I have to find her, Bacchus. I need your help. I know it's wrong of me to ask when you've already done so much, but if she's a friend of the duke's, perhaps he and the duchess could answer some questions.*

She hadn't signed her name. She doubted Bacchus was sharing magicked pencils with a large number of desperate women. Or at least she hoped not.

To her relief, new handwriting had been scrawled under her own, capital letters with small flourishes that made them remarkably handsome. *Of course I will help you. It works out well. The duchess wants to have you for tea.*

That was it. Chewing on her lip, Elsie wrote, *Why?*

The pencil wrenched from her grip seconds later, eliciting a startled chuckle from her. It tilted and scrawled, *Because she wants to help plan the wedding.*

Elsie's stomach clenched. Of course the Scotts would know about the engagement. Seeing the word *wedding* written out so plainly made it feel monumentally real.

When she didn't reply right away, Bacchus added, *Her cousin Mrs. Abrams is visiting and insists on lending a hand. "Six daughters married,"* she says. *Over and over. And over.*

Elsie smiled and took the pencil from his invisible grip. *I will endeavor to rescue you.*

Bacchus waited only a breath before writing, *I'll send a carriage within the hour.*

☙

Mrs. Abrams was a severe woman with meticulously curled auburn hair that parted right at the center of her head in the straightest line Elsie had ever beheld. It oddly matched the duchess's morning room, the chairs and piano of which were all stained cherrywood. The walls were white with simple embellishments around their edges. A painted picture of the estate from a distance hung over a white fireplace, and a rose-colored rug with a fish-scale pattern lay underfoot. Elsie perched, back rigid, on a blush-pink sofa beside Bacchus, while Mrs. Abrams and the duchess occupied a pale-green settee to Elsie's left. A tea tray lay on the table between them, the tea already served, Elsie's teacup cradled in her lap. She'd drunk enough to ensure her nerves would not cause the remainder to spill. Her stomach wouldn't handle any more.

"And it's my understanding you're *employed*?" Mrs. Abrams asked. Her eyes were especially large and seemed to bulge from their sockets, watching Elsie without blinking. She said the word *employed* like it had a sour taste to it.

"Yes, I work for a stonemason." She ached to look anywhere else, but sensed it would be considered rude if she averted her gaze.

The duchess smiled. "It's good for a woman to have a disposition of responsibility, especially going into a marriage." Her gaze shifted to Bacchus. "I really am so happy for you. I must admit my husband is a seer. He remarked on this very possibility the night we had you for dinner, Miss Camden."

An itch rose in Elsie's throat; she sipped some tea to soothe it before leaning forward and safely depositing the cup and saucer on the table before her. "Yes, well, the duke is very, um, perceptive."

The duchess was, of course, referring to the night Elsie had actually been invited to dinner, not the afternoon she'd barged in screaming warnings, after which Abel Nash had emerged from his hiding place behind the curtains and attempted to snuff Bacchus. But they needn't bring that up.

"He is," Bacchus agreed simply. He opened his mouth to say more when Mrs. Abrams barreled in.

"Now, for the wedding. It's good that May is behind us. A very unlucky month to get married."

"Now, Alison," the duchess chided softly.

"It is!" She set down her saucer. "My daughter—I've seen all six of them married, you know, and to good husbands—"

Elsie and Bacchus exchanged a look that had a restrained smile pinching Elsie's cheeks.

"—she married May 27 despite my telling her not to, and she lost her first child!"

Elsie quickly sobered. "Oh my, that's terrible."

"Should have listened to me." Mrs. Abrams's curls bounced as she shook her head, and Elsie decided she did not especially like this woman, let alone want her to play any part in their wedding plans. But she would not voice such a thing here. What she needed was to segue the conversation to Merton.

Mrs. Abrams didn't give her a chance. "It really is a quaint match, isn't it? A spellmaker and a spellbreaker, ha! And you met before Master Kelsey's mastership?"

Bacchus answered, "We did."

"Good, good. That will smooth over any questioning from the peerage." She nodded and sipped her tea.

Elsie stifled a frown. Had the woman just pointed out their class difference, right in front of her?

"As for the wedding party," the woman went on, completely ignorant of the apologetic expression on the duchess's face, "how many are we to expect? There are some large chapels in London, but travel is expensive and will take away from the gifts. I'm sure you will need gifts." She looked pointedly at Elsie, which made Elsie's neck heat. "Are your parents close by, Miss Camden? I assume they are also *employed*."

The warmth crept over Elsie's jaw. "Th-They are not, Mrs. Abrams." She considered saying they were dead, which could be true for all she knew, just to kill the conversation.

"Not? Oh." She nodded. "Then why are you working? Debts, perhaps."

Bacchus's low voice was stern when he said, "Elsie is free of any such things, Mrs. Abrams. Her parents are no longer a part of her life."

"No longer a part . . . ?" Mrs. Abrams looked at the duchess in bewilderment.

"Oh, the details are not so important, are they?" the duchess said, awkwardly trying to smooth things over.

"How so?" Mrs. Abrams protested. "Were you *disowned*, Miss Camden?"

The flush inched up Elsie's cheeks. "I was not particularly owned to begin with. If you must know, I became separated from them at a young age. Which is why I am employed. I care for myself just fine."

"Well." She leaned into the settee's backrest. "That is quite a shock. Your discovery of magic is the only thing that will spare you from the worst of gossip."

Now the duchess flushed. "There will hardly be gossip—"

"There will always be gossip, Abigail—"

"Mrs. Abrams." Bacchus's tone was forceful now; he surprised Elsie by reaching over and taking her hand. The warmth of his fingers sent shocks up her arm and had her blushing for an entirely new reason. "I am grateful for your willingness to assist, but I believe we will have a very small wedding party that will not require much in the way of management. My own parents have passed, and I have no siblings to speak of, so the transaction will be a simple matter. I'm sure your skills would be put to good use elsewhere."

Oh, Elsie could kiss him.

Mrs. Abrams clucked her tongue. "A marriage is a transaction, Master Kelsey. A wedding is not. My second youngest—of six, mind you—had a small wedding, yet it was still the talk of the town. There is the choir to consider, and flowers and guests' attire must be in line with—"

"I hardly think what the guests wear is important," Elsie sputtered.

Mrs. Abrams shot her a sharp look for being interrupted. "It matters a great deal. I would not want to wear the same color as the bride, for instance."

Bacchus set his saucer down. "Then it is fortunate that you will not be invited."

The room seemed to freeze. Elsie held her breath as both a sob and a laugh warred in her throat. She realized she was squeezing Bacchus's hand, but could not seem to convince her fingers to loosen. Bacchus watched Mrs. Abrams with a lowered brow, his green eyes sharp. Mrs.

Abrams's eyes seemed to bulge further. The duchess's mouth was a limp O, but she was the first to regain her composure.

"Alison," she said shakily, "remember how I wanted your thoughts on the geraniums? They're just on the east side of the house. Could I meet you there?"

"You most certainly shall." Mrs. Abrams stood sharply, sticking her nose up in the air. She gave a final hard look to Elsie and Bacchus before turning her back on them and leaving out the door. Given her dignified, self-righteous manner, she likely thought she was being excused so the duchess could reprimand her guests.

A few seconds after she left, the duchess chuckled. "You do have a sharpness about you, Bacchus."

Elsie released the breath she'd been holding. "Thank you," she whispered. When Bacchus's eyes slid to hers, her chest warmed, and she looked away.

"I didn't think she'd be so bold," the duchess went on. "You both have my sincerest apologies."

"No matter," Bacchus said. His hand remained entwined with Elsie's. He must have forgotten he put it there. Would it be awkward to pull away? Elsie didn't want to, but if Bacchus were doing it for mere show, well . . . half of their audience had departed.

Letting herself enjoy the touch of his palm a little longer, Elsie chose to get to the point. "I was curious, Duchess Scott, about one of our acquaintances. I, er, read about her retirement and was sad to see her go."

"Oh?" The duchess smoothed her skirts. "Oh! You must mean Master Merton."

Elsie nodded. "She was very kind to me when we met. I had been hoping to learn something more about her background."

The duchess shook her head. "Honestly, I don't know much. My husband was familiar with her these last couple of years, but we only really got to know her after Ida's promising test with the drops."

Elsie deflated. One dead end.

"I was quite surprised by her leaving. She had taken such an interest in Ida's education . . . granted I didn't think Ida wanted to go the spellmaking route, but she was a little disappointed to lose the attention." She smiled. "I would give you her address so you could write, but I heard she's left London for the country."

Bacchus asked, "Do you know where in the country?"

But the duchess shook her head. "I'm not sure at all." She looked over the teacups. "Here, let me get this taken care of, and we can talk of the wedding in earnest." She stood and moved to the bellpull on the nearby wall.

Bacchus leaned in close. "I'll contact Duchess Morris today and set up an appointment."

Elsie nodded, resisting the urge to turn. He was close enough that their noses might brush, but she wanted to make this as comfortable for him as possible. At that thought, she carefully removed her hand from his grasp and settled it in her lap. "Thank you."

They spoke nothing more on the matter.

∾

Later that night, Bacchus used the magicked pencils to inform Elsie he would be picking her up in the morning to call on Duchess Morris. She woke early and waited by the window for a full forty-five minutes so she didn't miss the stately black victoria carriage when it drove into town and pulled up beside the stonemasonry shop. Stringing her reticule over her wrist, she made sure to secure her hat and smooth her skirt before stepping out the front door. Bacchus was only a few paces away, coming up to retrieve her. Gentlemanly of him.

He offered her a soft smile—"Miss Camden"—and his arm.

She was struck by the formality, but took his arm, allowing him to guide her to the carriage. It was only as she stepped into it that she noticed Miss Alexandra Wright, one of the nosy daughters of the local banker, trotting down the lane from the direction of the saddler. Her eyes were round and curious, her attention directed at Bacchus.

Elsie sighed and stepped up into the two-seater vehicle, wishing it were a closed carriage so she could hide from the town's greatest gossip, but it was not meant to be. Bacchus stepped up after her and took up the reins of two fine-looking hackneys. Elsie ignored the younger Miss Wright as they pulled past her, but she felt the other woman's stare. All of Brookley would be talking by this evening.

In truth, she wouldn't have minded the gossip, were everything playing out the way a normal courtship should. She was hardly ashamed of being seen with an enormous, handsome, *master* spellmaker. It mattered not a whit to her that his skin was deeply suntanned and his hair was long. Indeed, she liked the way the essence of him colored outside the lines, so to speak. Loved to see it rankle prim busybodies like Alexandra Wright.

It was just that, when Bacchus found a way to untangle himself from her mess and sailed home, leaving her behind in England, the gossips would know all about it. Their snickers, whispers, and rumors would only be an infection to Elsie's broken heart, and she dreaded that.

As they pulled out of town, angling westward, Elsie buried the unpleasant thoughts and focused on the present. "I didn't know you could drive."

Bacchus's mouth twitched into a smirk. "Did you presume I was too backward to acquire such a skill, or too refined to take up the reins?" He'd slipped into his Bajan accent.

Elsie smiled, relaxing into the bench a bit. "Is it possible to think you both?"

He slowed the victoria and moved it to the side of the road as a wagon passed, then encouraged the horses back into a trot. "You're welcome to take the reins yourself."

"Am I really?"

He glanced at her. "If you want to."

She smiled and looked ahead. "Perhaps on the way back. I'll consider this a driving lesson. Ogden doesn't own any vehicles."

"The duke has plenty."

Her mind flashed to the carriage house she'd broken into in London. She'd disenchanted one of the carriages at the direction of the Cowls, or rather Merton. The note had indicated she would be saving the lives of poverty-stricken poachers; instead the disenchanted coach had allowed for the kidnapping of Master Alma Digby. Likely her opus was sitting in a trunk in Merton's hideaway, wherever it was.

Mirth fled her.

After a moment, Bacchus noticed. "Elsie? Are you concerned? I wrote ahead to Duchess Morris. It would be more proper to wait for her response, but she'll welcome anything that makes her feel important."

"Oh, yes, I suppose she would." She tugged on her gloves, pulling them tight over her fingers. "I was thinking on how to best approach this. Keep it official sounding at the start, of course."

"Ask her about spiritual aspection before spellbreaking," Bacchus suggested. "Make her think she's the center of the room. She'll be more pliable that way."

Elsie nodded. "She does seem to be a center-of-the-universe sort of person."

Bacchus smiled. It felt so natural, so *wonderful*, to banter with him. So long as they stayed away from the subject of their impending wedding. If she could just cut that out of their story, she could talk to Bacchus forever.

"I shall start with, 'Why did you choose spiritual aspection when you obviously favor spells of a *physical* nature?'" she teased.

He chuckled. "I would love to see her reaction to that."

"But alas, I would love to stay in her sitting room for longer than two minutes." Elsie sighed, her good humor wilting. "In truth, I was pondering over Master Merton."

They drove in silence another few seconds. "Her mistakes are not yours, Elsie."

The words warmed her, or at least the sentiment did. "So you've said."

"You were ignorant."

"I was a pawn," she corrected. "A very well-played one. But that doesn't undo what I did."

"Elsie—"

"It doesn't matter now." She tried to smile and kept her eyes ahead. "What's done is done, and we must do our best to fix what we can. I doubt Duchess Morris will know where Merton is hiding, but perhaps she can help us understand her. Ogden is still searching, but he's found nothing useful yet."

Bacchus nodded. "He informed me about what happened at Juniper Down."

Her stomach pinched, and the edge of the opus spell tucked in her bodice poked her as the victoria went over a bump.

"With the American?"

"Yes. He showed me his sketch, even."

The charcoal drawing of the stranger who'd pointed a gun at her head. For a brief moment, she'd searched the man's features, looking for anything familiar. Anything that might mark him as her father, and then the truth had become clear.

She hadn't really spoken with anyone about that. Hadn't written about it in a journal, hadn't screamed it to the sky. Everything with the Cowls, with Ogden and Merton, with Nash, had unfurled so quickly. Her life had been jerked in a different direction, and she'd barely had a chance to mourn. "I thought he was my father. I mentioned that, didn't I? And why I went . . . or did Ogden tell you? I got a notice from a family in Juniper Down that someone was looking for me. I thought it was my father, come back for me after all these years. It wasn't."

Bacchus's hold on the reins slackened. "Elsie, I'm so sorry. I can't imagine—"

She shrugged and managed a strangled laugh. "Well, that's life for you, isn't it? It would make a very good novel, I think."

The silence that fell between them was awkward. The overcast sky loosed a few drops onto the carriage roof, but perhaps saw that Elsie was miserable enough and held off the rest of its impending torrent.

Elsie took a deep breath. "I'm sorry, I didn't mean—"

At the same time Bacchus said, "The duchess is beside herself—"

They both paused. The steady sound of the horses' hooves cushioned them.

Bacchus recovered first. "What I mean is, I told the duke and duchess about the . . . engagement, of course. Their testimonies helped . . . with the magistrate."

Elsie nodded. "Kind of them."

"The duchess is beside herself with excitement." He sighed. "She turned into a schoolmarm on me today as I was leaving."

Elsie tried to imagine the refined Duchess of Kent in a black dress, a ruler tight in her hand. It made her smile. "Oh?"

"It's only that"—he paused—"Elsie, I don't want to sound insensitive—"

"I know you mean well, Bacchus. You always do." She was tempted to touch his knee, perhaps his hand, but didn't, and her lack of courage made her heart ache.

"She reminded me that an engagement dinner is traditionally thrown by the bride's family." Now Bacchus kept his eyes ahead, though the road was straight for a ways. "I had to inform her that that was not possible, in our case."

Elsie said nothing.

"And so she insists on throwing it herself."

"That's . . . very kind of her. Although I don't find it necessary."

Bacchus leaned back against the bench. "Perhaps not, but it is tradition. That, and I would not be surprised if the magistrate were scrutinizing us." He stopped talking abruptly and winced, but Elsie wasn't sure if it was a reaction to what he'd said or the swaying of the victoria.

But it was a reminder. Their story wasn't watertight, and the law was watching to ensure they carried through on the engagement. Bacchus either had to marry her or send her off to the gallows.

"If you don't object," Bacchus said after a moment, "I would like to post it in the paper as well."

She nodded. "Of course."

And then she laughed.

It was a strained, stupid laugh, and she snapped her mouth shut over it. Some of the pressure between her ribs alleviated, at least, even if she sounded a fool.

Bacchus glanced at her, the overcast sky making his eyes look like the sea. "You'll have to explain the joke to me."

She shook her head. Wished for a fan, but she hadn't brought one. "I don't know. I just . . . an announcement in the paper. It's so official, isn't it? Not at all like I'd thought."

He was ruminating on that, Elsie could tell. She'd learned Bacchus got a certain stoic look to his eyes when he was thinking. "And how did you expect it would be?"

Elsie bit the inside of her cheek. Grabbed the bench on either side of her legs. "I don't know. I didn't think I'd ever marry . . . Well, except I almost did, once."

"Almost?"

She shrunk, embarrassed. "That is . . . I thought I was going to be married before. To another fellow."

He perked. "Oh? Who?"

"No one." Alfred's face popped into her head, grinning, but the grin melted into a sneer. She laughed again, but this time, it hurt. "Funny. The day I thought he was going to propose, he left me. Found a nice, wealthy widow to occupy his time. They're married now. I saw them in town the other day."

"Elsie . . ."

"I'm just a carousel of pity, aren't I?" She straightened, smoothed her dress, adjusted her hat. "You'll have to forgive me, Bacchus. Three days in a stone cell leaves a woman with too much time to think, and I haven't quite recovered yet." She cleared her throat. "I know your parents are deceased, but your mother's family . . . will they be attending?" Bacchus had told her his parents weren't married, that he was a bastard, but she wasn't sure of his relationship with his mother.

"No. I hardly knew my mother. In truth, I'm not sure what Algarve relatives I even have."

"Oh." She rolled her lips together. "I really am making a mess of things, aren't I?"

"No, Elsie." He reached over and ran a thumb over her knee. "You're not."

She didn't believe him, but she managed a tight smile, glad the carriage was dim enough not to reveal the heat that raced across her skin from his touch. He only meant to comfort, she knew, but he pulled away, and the vehicle felt colder for it. Then the rain started in earnest, and she was content with listening to its uneven patterns until they reached Duchess Matilda Morris's estate.

CHAPTER 6

"It's rather unexpected," Duchess Morris said as her maid handed her a cup of tea, "but I am formally trained, of course. I know the atheneums do a poor job at upholding the bounds of propriety."

Duchess Morris's parlor was large and bright, full windows letting in gray, rain-choked light. On one wall hung an enormous portrait of the duchess herself, and on the opposite wall hung a markedly smaller portrait of an older man Elsie assumed to be her husband. The floor and fireplace were marble, the drapes and carpets navy, the ceiling painted with fleur-de-lis. Duchess Morris sat in an elaborate armchair, while Elsie and Bacchus occupied a stiff velvet sofa. Elsie had worn her best dress today, but it didn't feel fancy enough in this posh house.

At the mention of propriety, Duchess Morris's eyes raked between Elsie and Bacchus, even dropping down to Elsie's hand. All the temporal and physical runes lending to her beauty, some of which Elsie had jarred loose some days prior, were firmly back in place. "Are you overseeing her training, Master Kelsey? Does this mean you're secretly a spellbreaker?"

Secretly a spellbreaker hit a little too close to home and stoked Elsie's nerves.

Bacchus, thankfully, smoothly accepted his tea—Elsie refused hers, worried she'd fumble it—and answered, "Not exactly. Miss Camden is my fiancée."

My fiancée. The words washed over her like an autumn breeze.

"Is that so?" Duchess Morris perked up, examining Elsie again. "Why, what an interesting pair."

Elsie wanted to demand what she meant by that, but thought it best to hold her tongue. So far, Duchess Morris had *not* recognized her as the clumsy woman in the millinery, and she needed to stay on her good side if she was to uncover any information about Master Merton.

"I was fortunate," Elsie said, tasting the falsehoods in her mouth, "to have an aspector so close by during my time of discovery." Granted, she *worked* for an aspector, but Duchess Morris didn't know that.

"I imagine so. To think, waking up one day and . . . magic!" She chortled. "To not have to work with it day in and day out from youth up. How lucky you are, Miss Camden."

Elsie forced herself not to grit her teeth. "Very lucky, indeed."

"But, Master Kelsey"—she turned her attention to Bacchus—"I don't know how you tolerate Kent. I hear the place is falling apart with rot."

Elsie could *feel* Bacchus tense beside her. After all, it had likely been Duchess Morris who had placed the rot curses on the Duke of Kent's fields—curses Elsie had since unraveled. She placed a hand on Bacchus's forearm and answered on his behalf. "Oh, it's a modest place, for sure. Very cozy. Though I am rather stunned by your own estate, Duchess Morris. It's so . . . fashionable. I would love a tour if you have time for it."

Duchess Morris smiled. "I might be able to arrange one. You have good taste, Miss Camden. Now"—she set down her tea—"what questions do you have for me?"

Elsie went through the interrogation she'd rehearsed that morning, questions she thought would sound official and scholarly, pertinent to a spellbreaker. She started with simple ones, about the spiritual discipline and its effects, then went personal. Why had Duchess Morris chosen that discipline? How had magic affected her life? And then brought it back around—when had Duchess Morris needed a spellbreaker, and how efficient were they?

"I don't often hire them. I'm essentially retired from magic. A lady of my stature doesn't work." She twisted a dark curl around her index finger and released it. Bacchus had once said Duchess Morris had burned out, which meant she'd reached the peak of her learnable spells and could no longer progress, but Elsie knew better than to mention it. "But on occasion a hired hand will make a mistake. The usual."

Or you need to change the shape of your nose, she thought. Feeling the duchess at ease, Elsie tried, "If you'll excuse the interjection, Duchess Morris, something about you is very familiar. You're not the kind of woman who can be mistaken for anyone else."

She seemed pleased by the assertion. "Is that so?"

"Yes." She glanced to Bacchus. "Is it . . . Are you chummy with Master Merton, by chance?"

Her face lit up. "I *am*! How did you know?"

Bacchus said, "Master Merton has dined with the Duke and Duchess of Kent on numerous occasions."

Duchess Morris rolled her eyes. "Oh, I'm not surprised. She's all about recruitment, especially for women, for whatever reason. She'll go just about anywhere. She doesn't have an estate or family of her own to attend to, so she has the time."

Elsie squeezed Bacchus's arm, as if to say, *I know, she's ridiculous. Just wait it out a little longer.*

Picking through the duchess's words, Elsie grabbed on to what felt most useful. "No estate? Has she not been in her mastership for some time?"

"Oh, yes. Shortly before I earned mine." Duchess Morris again toyed with her hair. "But she has no natural inheritance. She's not even English, you know."

Elsie started. "She's not?" She looked English, sounded English.

"Oh yes." She waved a bored hand, as though the conversation had lost her interest now that the focus had drifted from her. "Fled Russia with her parents during that war. They died off somehow, and she wound up in a workhouse somewhere around here. She mentioned it once a long time ago, in school."

Elsie's mind was racing enough to kick up dust. Russia? Did Duchess Morris mean the Crimean War? Merton was certainly old enough; she had to be nearing sixty. She would have been . . . what, Emmeline's age when that happened?

"I'm very sorry to hear that," Bacchus said, covering for Elsie's silent stupor.

"Oh, yes." Elsie nodded. "That is tragic."

Duchess Morris shrugged. "It was a long time ago. She never talks of it anymore. You know how some people are, bringing up their sad stories over and over again for attention. Not Lily."

Pressing her luck, Elsie asked, "Do you remember how she made it to the atheneum? Workhouses . . . are hard to leave behind." She knew from experience. And spellmaking was expensive, besides.

The duchess sighed. "The only way poor riffraff can, Miss Camden. She made the sponsorship lottery."

Bacchus said, "And you took her under your wing. How very kind of you, to reach out to someone so below your station."

A surprising shock of sadness flashed across Duchess Morris's face. "Oh, of course. There was a time when . . ." She sat up straighter in her chair. "Well, it doesn't matter now. Do you have any more questions for me?"

"Oh please, Duchess Morris." Elsie clamped her hands together in the folds of her skirt. "I would love to hear your tale of charity." *Tell us everything you can,* please.

The duchess pursed her lips and studied Elsie. For a moment, Elsie worried she had gone too far. But the kind words must have had the intended effect, for Duchess Morris's shoulders relaxed a fraction. "It was so long ago. Let's just say my fool father took it into his head to humble the entirety of his family." She sniffed. "So I suppose Lily and I took each other under wing, until I made my match." She gestured weakly to the portrait of the duke on the wall. "Lily is a good person. Quite the Christian, donating to peace efforts and, I don't know, feeding the poor or some nonsense. Always was dedicated to her sponsor more than anyone else. She even supported him financially, in his old age. Very distraught when he passed on. I haven't seen Lily since . . ."

Duchess Morris tapped her chin. If she was thinking back, she might be considering the hat shop and the incident there—

Elsie tapped Bacchus's shoe with her own.

"Thank you for your time, Duchess Morris," he said without missing a beat. He stood and offered his hand to Elsie for her to do the same. He looked especially large in this room, somehow, or perhaps that was because Duchess Morris was barely over five feet. The way she carried herself, one would think she wasn't aware of her petite stature.

"Oh, my pleasure. Always happy to help." She smiled. Elsie didn't mention the tour, and Duchess Morris seemed to have forgotten, for she didn't initiate another invitation. She saw them into the hallway, where a smartly dressed servant escorted them to the door.

Elsie barely noticed the passing of distance between the house and the victoria. *Crimean War. Lost mother. Charitable donations.* Master Merton seemed to fit the mold of a serial murderer even less, knowing all of that.

It wasn't until Bacchus pulled the carriage around that Elsie said, "Do you think it bothered her, swearing allegiance to Britain? I would never have thought her Russian. She speaks so elegantly, wears all the English fashions—"

"Elsie," he said, nodding as another servant opened the gates for them. "When you are an outsider, you do what you have to do to fit in, or people will ostracize you. Sometimes without even realizing it. If

Master Merton wanted to succeed in spiritual magic here in London, she would have had to assimilate so thoroughly that others would forget she was ever different. It is a necessity, for people like us."

That gave Elsie pause. She studied Bacchus, the darkness of his skin, the length of his hair, his height and breadth. He'd held on to his English accent, not slipping into his natural one, like he had before. His father was English, but his mother was Algarve, and he'd been raised in Barbados. He dressed like an Englishman, spoke like an Englishman, but he didn't look like one. Elsie had forgotten he was different.

No wonder Alexandra Wright had been staring.

"Have I offended you?" She found herself holding her breath, waiting for his response.

"No." He slipped the reins into his left hand and reached over with his right, covering her fingers with his palm. "No, you haven't." She wondered if his Bajan tones came through naturally or if he let them in to reassure her. "But it is easy to miss the pain of being different when you fit in so well with the standard."

She nodded. Dared to lift her other hand and place it atop his. "I suppose you're right." She thought of Ogden, of his confessions. He was different, too, and hid it remarkably well. "I wonder what sort of pains Master Merton has borne in her lifetime. And why they've made her behave the way she has."

Because if Lily Merton wanted *peace*, as Duchess Morris claimed, why was she killing so many people? Why the grab for power?

And what did the American have to do with any of it?

Elsie felt closer to finding answers. The only problem was that she seemed to acquire more questions at every turn.

❧

It was oddly difficult to get back into a daily routine after being imprisoned.

Elsie managed it anyway, ordering materials for Ogden, who had blessedly gotten two more commissions. One was from the hateful squire, who had decided to commission a bust of himself, as if the people who visited his home didn't know perfectly well what he looked like. The other was from out of town. Ogden needed the distraction just as much as Elsie did. When he wasn't slinking around London, prying into strangers' minds, he was quiet, unlike himself, sketching and murmuring under his breath.

Elsie was more than happy to spend her morning trekking to the squire's estate, for while she didn't like the man—it really was a pity *he* wasn't the murderer—she quite enjoyed his steward, Mr. Parker. Polite and to the point, he passed along the measurements and other information she needed with admirable efficiency. Elsie wondered if Ogden would notice if she altered the sculpture before it set—giving the squire an unseemly mole or a crooked tooth. Then again, if she got Ogden put out of his job, she'd be put out of hers, too.

Fortunately, she'd have a husband to support her if that happened.

She tripped on nothing as she trekked back through town, catching herself and managing not to drop the satchel with her employer's papers in it. *Husband.* It all seemed like a very odd dream, didn't it? The worst part was that they still hadn't discussed their plans. How would Bacchus balance Barbados and England? Or perhaps he wouldn't balance them at all. For all she knew, he intended to let her live in a townhouse in London, while he fled to Barbados and grabbed a mistress or two. That would be a fair compromise, wouldn't it?

If only the thought didn't form such a deep pit in her stomach. It would have been rather nice to be engaged after a pleasant courtship. To be sure of wanting.

"Oh, Miss Camden!"

Elsie winced at the sound of the familiar voice behind her, and kept walking as though she hadn't heard. Increased her pace.

"Miss Camden!"

Gritting her teeth, then relaxing her jaw, Elsie turned around, shielding her eyes from the sun despite her bonnet already doing it for her. "Oh, Misses Wright. How are you today?"

Rose and Alexandra Wright scrambled to her, kicking up dust as they went. "We are absolutely beside ourselves with glee," the latter said, bouncing on her toes.

Elsie adjusted her satchel. "Whatever for?"

"Whatever for?" Rose Wright repeated, a hand pressed to her breast. "Why, your engagement!"

It wouldn't have been in the papers already. Not that Elsie had to ask, for Alexandra Wright pushed in, "We spoke to Emmeline after you left yesterday! Quite a *fine* carriage, if I say so myself."

"Of course you did," Elsie said.

"A very fine carriage," her sister agreed. "And quite a man."

"A foreigner," Alexandra piped in, as though Elsie didn't know.

"Yes," said Rose, "tell me, is he Turkish?"

Elsie resisted the urge to tell these women that they had no right to any of her personal information, especially since they couldn't care less about her well-being when she wasn't at the center of gossip. "He's from Barbados."

"Barbados!" Rose repeated, and her sister said, "Where is that?"

"Near Turkey," Elsie lied.

Alexandra turned to Rose. "Well, that makes sense, doesn't it? You were right, again."

"Is he an officer?" Rose asked.

Elsie glanced around, wishing someone would come interrupt them. "An officer? In the army?"

"No, in the police force," Alexandra said.

"We saw them at the stonemasonry shop last week," Rose added.

Elsie blanched. "S-Something like that."

"But," Alexandra said, more to her sister than to Elsie, "an officer wouldn't have such a fine carriage, would he?"

Elsie cleared her throat. "If you'll excuse me, I have work to do."

"Oh yes!" Rose cried. "A working woman. I forget sometimes. Won't that be nice, to have your support taken care of?"

Elsie frowned. "Indeed."

"Do invite us for tea," Alexandra pushed in. "It would be so wonderful to catch up."

Pasting on a smile, Elsie said, "I shall have to do that."

The sisters giggled in delight and waved their goodbyes, and Elsie hurried away from them. She'd rather be spoon-fed the dry leaves than waste tea on those two ninnies. She sighed.

It will all sort itself out, don't worry.

If only she believed that.

She started for the shortcut to her house, behind the post office, when she saw a woman standing outside a curricle, holding a piece of paper to her face, spying around near the bank. She looked to be in her early thirties, with pale-brown hair pinned up from her face and a smart hat on top. The sun glinted off a delicate pair of silver spectacles on her nose. Elsie didn't recognize her. She wouldn't be from Clunwood, Brookley's neighbor to the south. She was dressed too genteelly, and there was no driver in the carriage behind her, which suggested it might belong to her.

Checking the road for passersby, Elsie quickly crossed and approached her.

"Pardon me," she tried, "but are you lost?"

A look of relief washed over the woman's features. "Indeed I am, thank you. I've already asked for directions twice, and I swear the gentlemen told me differing things."

Elsie smiled. "Men will do that. Where are you headed?"

The woman showed her the paper in her hand, upon which was scrawled a familiar address. "To the stonemasonry shop. There is a stonemason, isn't there? Otherwise I'll have to head back to London and start all over again."

She chuckled. "There is, in fact. I'm on my way there now."

"Bless you." She tucked her paper away and followed Elsie down the road. "I hear he's an aspector."

Bells of alarm rang in Elsie's ears, until she remembered the ruse about Ogden's aspecting. "He is, a physical one. Only a novice, but the spells he does know aid his handiwork, which is quite excellent."

"Glad to hear it. Oh, look at that." She pointed at the narrow road leading off the high street. "I think I walked right past that and didn't notice."

They passed the cobbler and continued down the road. The clouds were parted today, letting the heat of the sun press down fully. Elsie was relieved to step out of it, and held the door open for the stranger.

Emmeline looked up from the other end of the studio, broom in hand. She noticed the woman. "Oh, hello."

"Hello!" she called, and stepped around the desk and into the studio, offering a hand to Emmeline. "My name is Irene Prescott. You must be Elsie Camden?"

Emmeline shook her head. "You just walked in with her, ma'am."

Miss Prescott turned around. "Oh my, I should have introduced myself."

Elsie's wrists itched as though she'd broken four dozen spells. "I should have done that myself." *What do you want?* "How might I help you?"

Miss Prescott crossed the room once more, extending a hand to Elsie, which she hesitantly shook. "Did you not get my letter?"

"Post is late," Emmeline said.

"Ah, well." Releasing Elsie, Miss Prescott continued, "The board sent me. I'm to register you and start your training as a spellbreaker."

Elsie gaped, caught herself, and closed her mouth with a click of her teeth. "O-Oh, I see."

Opening her parcel, Miss Prescott pulled out a sheaf of papers and set them on a cabinet. Turning to Emmeline, she said, "My dear, do you have a pen on hand?"

Emmeline nodded and set the broom aside, hurrying to the cubbies beneath the desk to retrieve a pen and ink.

"I'll just need you to fill this out." Miss Prescott slid the papers to Elsie. A quick flip through the pages revealed they were filled with personal questions, about her age, appearance, height, et cetera, as well as her family history. Well, she couldn't tell the board what she didn't know.

Licking her lips, Elsie took the pen, reminding herself she needn't be nervous; this was all part of the plan. Register, train for a while, be free. It might be nice, using her abilities openly. She'd make more money, certainly. Wouldn't be as much of a burden on Bacchus.

Bacchus.

Elsie found herself writing his name on one of the lines and hurriedly scribbled it out, replacing it with her age.

Miss Prescott smiled. "I often forget my own years."

Elsie nodded and moved on to the next page.

"Your family history will help us track magical lines," Miss Prescott pressed.

"I'm an orphan," Elsie said, unsure if it was true. She began filling out the second page.

Miss Prescott at least was polite enough to sound embarrassed. "Terribly sorry."

She finished the paperwork and signed her name at the end. Miss Prescott signed hers as well, then organized the papers into a neat stack. "Could have called you in, but I know this is all new, so I thought I'd make the trip out here."

Elsie straightened, rubbing at a spot of ink on her hand. "Thank you. That's kind."

"Though we'll have to travel a bit for your training," she continued. "To the atheneums, of course, so we can gather the spells you'll need to practice breaking. On occasion we'll have a spellmaker come to us, but they're a busy lot."

"I do work, Miss Prescott."

She clucked sympathetically. "I understand that, though unfortunately this takes precedence. Magic, even simple spellbreaking, can be dangerous if unchecked."

Simple spellbreaking. Elsie almost snorted. In her opinion, dismantling spells was far more complex than laying them. Spellmakers didn't even know what their runes looked like. Couldn't see them, smell them, nothing. But Miss Prescott *was* correct—the abilities could be dangerous if left untrained. Elsie's ignorance of spellbreaking had indirectly led to her workhouse burning down when she was ten.

Her thoughts slid to Master Merton.

"Of course," she said, trying to stay present. "It's just that, well, I'm getting married within the month." Her stomach clenched. They hadn't actually set a date. Had she just pushed Bacchus into a tighter cage?

"Oh! Congratulations. Well, we can work around that."

Emmeline added, "He's a spellmaker, too. A master physical aspector."

Now Miss Prescott's eyes went wide. "Is he really?"

"Recently promoted." It sounded more believable that she'd win the heart of an advanced aspector over a master aspector. The class difference wasn't as stark. Though now that she would be a registered spellbreaker, her own status would improve. A spellbreaker would never merit a title, but the role carried prestige, nonetheless. Spellbreakers were necessary. But being a spell*maker* . . . that term alone meant one had money.

"Well, perhaps we'll be able to use his services." She put the papers in her bag. "I'll be contacting you shortly. I saw a post office, so I presume a telegram is fine?"

Elsie nodded.

Miss Prescott extended her hand once more, and Elsie shook it. "Lovely again to make your acquaintance, Miss Camden. And don't worry—in a few years, you'll be ready to take on the world."

Elsie smiled, trying not to make her grip too tight. A few *years*?

God help her, this would be the longest ruse she'd ever pulled.

God help her.

CHAPTER 7

Late that night, after Emmeline went to bed, Elsie rapped on Ogden's door.

She waited a long moment before he opened it, his hair mussed. "Sorry to wake you," she said, "but I have an idea."

Ogden sighed. "You didn't wake me. I don't sleep like I used to." He glanced down the hallway to Emmeline's room. "Let's go downstairs."

Shielding her candle, Elsie led the way to the kitchen. She understood Ogden's predicament—she was pulling later nights and earlier mornings as well, kept awake by tumultuous thoughts with no end, wondering what happens if and what happens now. Yet she still felt sorry for him. His will was freely his own after nine years, and he seemed only to be suffering for it.

She lit two more candles in the kitchen before settling down, pulling a shawl tight over her robe. Ogden sat across from her, rubbing the thick stubble on his cheeks.

"I keep playing it over and over. Juniper Down, I mean." She kept an ear attuned to the stairs, listening for any creaks in the wood that would signal Emmeline was up and about, but the house remained quiet. "The American said he knew my name from newspapers and magazines. Articles I'd published. But I've never published a word in my life."

Ogden nodded. "I remember."

Leaning closer, she asked, "Is there a way to look up newspaper articles by author?"

Ogden straightened.

"He said they were in Europe and the States. Some of them had to be published in England, surely."

To her relief, Ogden nodded. "Yes, in Colindale. There's a repository there with newspapers dating back decades. If they've been well archived, we should be able to look up your name."

Excitement pricked her like needles. Perhaps they could unfurl another part of this mystery. "That's not far from here." North London, if she was right.

He nodded. "We can go in the morning."

She bit her lip. "I can go. You have the squire's deadline—"

"I'll go with you," he reaffirmed. "If the squire complains, I'll just make him think he extended."

Elsie paused. "You can do that?"

Ogden simply looked at her.

"All right." She stood, careful not to let her chair scrape on the floor. "It will be a good place to start. First thing in the morning." She turned from the table, paused, and turned back. "Ogden?"

He snuffed one of the three candles. "Hm?"

She debated with herself a moment, but it was better to risk offense than to keep on wondering and fearing. This was one worry she could kill here and now. "I need you to promise me you will never make me think differently than I do. Not without my asking." It was a bold statement to make to one's employer, but in all truthfulness, Cuthbert Ogden was much more than that now.

His lip quirked. "I don't think I could, without you noticing."

"But you could make me not notice, couldn't you? Like before."

He pressed his lips together and leaned his chin on his hands. "Perhaps. But you've grown in strength, Elsie. Your skills are . . . impressive."

"Still," she pressed, trying not to preen with the compliment. "I need you to promise me."

"I promise you." A sliver of volume leaked into his voice. "I promise you, Elsie, over my parents' graves, and my own. I'll never influence you with magic."

The hidden opus spell tucked beneath her sash grew heavy. She thought about the horrible things Merton had manipulated her into doing, and about Bacchus, whose understanding and patience surely had limits—limits she was pushing. But she had no idea how much of her life such a spell would erase . . .

"Unless I ask you to," she added in a soft voice.

He raised an eyebrow. "Unless you ask me to."

Content, Elsie retrieved her candle and made her way back upstairs, leaving Ogden to ponder alone in the light of only one.

〜

The British Museum's repository for newspapers was an unremarkable and unassuming building, lacking in any refined architecture or color, but Elsie was hardly interested in its exterior. Ogden held the door for her, and she slipped inside, almost immediately being greeted by rows and rows of books, drawers, and shelves. At least they were notably organized.

After a moment, Ogden pointed. "This way."

Elsie followed him. "Did you spy into a curator's mind for that?"

Ogden gave her a flat look and pointed to a sign indicating newspapers and their dates. Feeling foolish, Elsie followed.

Only problem was, she didn't know precisely what dates she needed. How long had it taken the American to sniff her out? Still, if the articles weren't indexed by name, it would be a nearly impossible task to sort through even a year's worth of newspapers. Especially since she doubted the curators would permit her to simply take whole stacks of newspapers home to rifle through.

An older gentleman strode by, glancing once at her and Ogden before continuing on his way.

"Here." Ogden pointed in the direction from which the man had come, to a wall full of tiny wooden drawers. Elsie had to remind herself not to run as she approached. There were drawers organized by date, by region, and—

"By author," she whispered, touching the handwritten surnames on one of the drawers. She quickly reviewed the display, dropping to her knees to reach the *C*'s. She pulled out one that read, *Calladine–Cook*.

Ogden crouched beside her. The drawer was much longer than she had thought. Hundreds of cards were crammed into it, all handwritten, some in different penmanship and colors of ink. It made her think of aspecting, but there were no spells to be found here. She carefully separated the cards with her nails, one by one. She found what she was looking for fairly quickly, thanks to the magic of alphabetizing.

Her name, *Camden, Elsie*, was scrawled along the top. She pulled the card out. It wasn't very full, boasting only three article titles. But locations were listed for each, and she and Ogden quickly divided them and began their hunt. Elsie ended up in a section for Irish newspapers, and in the time it took her to find the correct one, Ogden had already pulled both English papers. Instead of moving to one of the tables near the entrance, they set the papers atop the card cabinets.

"Here," Ogden said, pointing to an article. "It's on the front page."

Elsie leaned close to him, reading, *Valuable Items Stolen from American Estate*.

"Hmm," she hummed.

Ogden glanced at her.

"Why would that make the front page of a London newspaper?" She pointed to the large letters spelling out the *Manchester Guardian*. It was dated April 5, 1887. Eight years ago.

Both of them hushed as they read the article. It was short, not even continued on a later page. And it was incredibly vague, never actually stating *what* had been stolen from *which* estate. One line was curious, however: *The inquirer would gladly pay a high price for the black birds.* It felt like it meant something. There was nothing else about birds in the article. The effect was jarring.

Ogden pulled out the other newspaper, the *Daily Telegraph*, in which Elsie's name was printed on the second page, under a headline reading, Spiritual Aspecting Across the Pond. Again, the article was brief unto the point of meaningless. It had been published last year and had a typo in it: *A shame if things were to take a Turner and end entirely.*

"I could have written something better than this," Elsie commented, flipping back to the front page.

"For such bad journalism written by a nobody—no offense," Ogden offered, "the author, presumably Lily Merton, must have paid a good sum to have the articles put at the front. To make them more noticeable."

Elsie pulled up the *News Letter*, the Irish paper, and sure enough, the article with her name was on the front. The Dangers of Intercontinental Travel, it read, the headline accompanied by a photo of a wealthy person's home, though the photo had no caption. This article was the briefest of them all. It spoke of dangerous voyages from Boston, but there was little else of substance. It was four years old.

Elsie tapped her fingers against the cabinets. "This isn't helping at all."

Ogden pulled a sketchbook from the satchel at his hip. "Let's copy them down." He tore out a page for her and then took the Irish article for himself, going as far as to sketch out the faded photograph of the house. Elsie copied the aspecting article in pencil, reading over it thrice to make sure she hadn't forgotten anything, and then transcribed the American estate article beneath it.

"There have to be more." She carefully folded the page, not wanting to smear the graphite. "There has to be *something* that made him come find me. Some kind of code. Something we're not seeing."

"We need to look further. American newspapers, perhaps."

Elsie shook her head. "It will take a month for a letter to reach a repository over there."

"I'll use the spirit line." Ogden closed his sketchbook.

The spirit line was a messaging system developed by spiritual aspectors in the seventeen hundreds, shortly before the American Revolution. Aspectors across the sea—Iceland, Greenland, Canada—could link up with one another, casting spiritual projections that could carry news faster than a ship, or even a telegraph network.

"It's so expensive, Ogden," she whispered.

But Ogden shook his head. "It's an expense I'm happy to make. You just might not be getting much pin money this month."

Elsie let out a long breath. "I'm more than happy to contribute. Thank you."

$\backsim$

They returned home later than planned, as they had to stop in London to make arrangements for the spirit line. Ogden sent messages to the Library of Congress in the United States, as well as libraries in a few select European countries. Elsie winced at the number of pounds he exchanged for it; they might be eating cabbage for dinner the next few weeks. *The sooner I become a profitable spellbreaker, the better,* she thought.

And it seemed Irene Prescott agreed, for Elsie found a telegram from her on her bed when she arrived home. Miss Prescott wanted to meet in London tomorrow—she really didn't heed the fact that Elsie had to work—to begin their training. There was a second message on her nightstand from the enchanted pencil. Her stomach did a little flip at the familiar penmanship.

I'm hoping to interest you in dinner tomorrow at Seven Oaks.
More interrogation from the duke and duchess is to be expected,
but I guarantee Mrs. Abrams will be conspicuously absent.

Elsie smiled.

"Emmeline, would you do me a favor?" The newspaper articles weighed on her, and she ached to examine them again, more closely.

"Sure, what is it?"

"Run to the post office and reply to Miss Prescott." She handed Emmeline the telegram. "Ask her if she'd be willing to meet me at Seven Oaks in Kent for training. Tell her I can provide an aspector."

Emmeline grinned knowingly. "Gladly. And what about that?"

She pointed at the newest novel reader sitting on Elsie's pillow. Elsie had completely missed it.

She paused, thinking of the story of the baron and his rubies. "You take it, Em," she offered, and the maid's eyes lit with delight. "I have a few personal things to see to first."

CHAPTER 8

Bacchus, being the gentleman he was, sent a carriage for her just after lunch the following day. Elsie put on her second-best dress, as Bacchus had last seen her in her best dress, and she certainly couldn't repeat the fashion twice in a row. She polished the buttons down the front and put on a smart hat, hoping she would look presentable for the evening's dinner with the duke and duchess. She had bumped up in society—or she would once she completed her spellbreaker training—but the promotion still felt pathetic when cast in the light of the true peerage. She still worried over bumbling the details of the engagement as well. What if she said something contrary to the story Bacchus had laid out? What if the duke and duchess discovered Elsie was marrying their dear Master Kelsey only to spare herself from the gallows?

Guilt gnawed at her as she rode to Seven Oaks, and she did her best to push it down. The housekeeper escorted her to a drawing room, where Miss Prescott and Bacchus already awaited her. Their small talk ceased upon her entrance. Elsie's eyes went first to Bacchus, who stood from his chair, polite as always. He was wearing the same blue waistcoat he'd stripped off in Ipswich so she could remove the temporal and physical spells embedded into his chest. Her cheeks warmed at the memory. The sun was high and not coming directly through the windows, and the lighting made his skin look darker. His hair was pulled back into a folded tail just above the nape of his neck.

Miss Prescott wore a smart violet visiting dress that was notably finer than what Elsie had donned, and her light hair was meticulously curled and pinned.

"I do hope I'm not late." Elsie spared another glance to Bacchus.

"Not at all," Miss Prescott replied. "I was early. I always am." She clapped her hands together and turned to Bacchus. "Master Kelsey, where would you like to begin?"

He simply gestured to the low table between them. "Here is fine."

"Excellent." Miss Prescott dug through a large bag on the floor, and Elsie, feeling awkward, crossed the room to stand beside Bacchus.

"Thank you," she murmured.

"I'm interested to see what you can do," he replied, and though he didn't laugh, she could hear the sound of it edging his words.

Elsie rolled her eyes. "I beg your pardon, but this is hardly funny—"

"Here we are." Miss Prescott set a small tin dish and a bottle of water on the tabletop, then knelt beside it. Bacchus pulled up a chair for Elsie, who gratefully sat, before kneeling across from Miss Prescott.

"Master Kelsey and I have discussed his repertoire, and I think we're set." Miss Prescott poured a third of the bottle into the dish. "Now, Elsie, I want to discuss runes with you. You see, every spell has a rune." She reached down and pulled out a thin book, passing it to Elsie. She flipped the cover open, and an assortment of runes peeked up at her. They were organized by color: blue for physical, red for rational, yellow for spiritual, and green for temporal. Elsie recognized nearly every single one—hardening spells, softening spells, emotive manipulation, luck, aging of plants, and so on.

And then remembered she had to act like this was all new to her.

"Aspectors can't see these runes"—Miss Prescott gestured to Bacchus—"and technically we can't, either, unless it's a physical rune. Each discipline of magic has its own flavor, so to speak. Physical runes you can see, which makes it that much better for our first lesson to be with a physical aspector. Spiritual runes are auditory, temporal runes are olfactory, and rational runes are tangible, in a sense. You'll understand what I mean when we get to those."

Elsie glanced at Bacchus, who seemed interested in the lecture, but perhaps he was simply better at pretending. *I know,* Elsie wanted to say, yet she forced the words into her stomach, where they boiled and popped. Miss Prescott was going to cover *every single* basic premise of spellbreaking, and Elsie would have to take it all in without complaint. Because if she complained, then her story was flawed, and she would go to prison.

"Miss Camden?"

Elsie's eyes shot to Miss Prescott. "Oh, yes, it's incredibly interesting!"

Miss Prescott smiled. "Now, I'll show you what I mean. Master Kelsey, if you would freeze this."

Bacchus leaned over and touched his hand to the dish. Magic tickled Elsie's senses as the water froze and pulsed with a glimmering blue rune. Changing the state of water was a novice-level spell. Bacchus could have placed a stronger enchantment on it—a more complicated rune that would be more difficult to break—but he'd gone for the simplest option, knowing Miss Prescott would expect to start with something elementary.

Elsie could have untied that rune with a sneeze. Instead, she said, "It's so lovely."

"Isn't it? I've always thought so." Miss Prescott slid the dish to Elsie and then began explaining how the rune held, and how spellbreaking could be applied to it, and how all spells were like an algebraic equation—

Algebraic . . . what? What nonsense. Elsie had always seen runes as knots to be untied, not numbers to calculate. Miss Prescott was making it far more complicated than it needed to be. The sum of this and the division of that to determine where to start . . . Elsie just tugged at the thing until she found a loose end. She highly doubted counting and equating would make the process any faster.

She's still talking, she thought with dismay. She was overexplaining. Even Bacchus would know how to pull the spell apart at this point.

"Now, find the same rune in the book," Miss Prescott said.

Trying not to grit her teeth, Elsie opened the book. She found the novice freezing rune right away, but acted like it took her a moment. "Here it is."

"Very good. Now, I want you to study the rune, do the calculation, and tell me where you think you should start."

Elsie resisted the urge to grumble. *Top right,* she knew. But she paced herself, her remaining patience slowly unraveling, and played along.

It took another quarter hour, *a quarter hour,* before Miss Prescott let her try breaking the rune. And again, Elsie purposefully made a mistake and started over before turning the ice back to water.

And then she had to do it again. And again. *And again.*

Elsie was going to lose her mind.

The lesson lasted two hours, with Bacchus hardening a tea cake and turning a coin translucent, all novice physical spells. Each and every time, Miss Prescott explained how it all worked, and each and every time, Elsie played the unknowing yet fascinated child, enough so that Miss Prescott praised her as she cleaned up her supplies. They bid farewell, and Elsie waited several minutes after the spellbreaker's footsteps left the room before crossing to the far corner, where a tapestry of a field of sheep hung along the wall.

Bacchus followed. "Bravo," he said.

"That was the most maddening thing I've ever had to do," she hissed. "Even as a child, I would have thought it ridiculous."

His lip quirked into a smile. "But you performed well."

Elsie folded her arms, annoyed at the way her wrists were starting to itch. They hadn't broken any large spells, but she'd unwoven more small ones than she could count. "She said *years*, Bacchus. That I'd be training for *years*. I can't do this for years."

"Perhaps you will be a very quick learner."

"But I can't." She dropped her arms. "I can't be a quick learner, Bacchus, because I can't give them any reason to suspect."

The smile faded. "I suppose that's true."

Sighing, Elsie looked out the window. There was a nice walking path down below, along with a garden sporting orange and pink flowers. Beyond that, Elsie knew, were the woods she had crept through the night Bacchus had caught her in an act of illegal spellbreaking. The assignment had been to break a spell on the servants' door. She'd thought she was freeing them from an oppressive master, but in truth Merton had sent her there to strip the house of protections, probably with the intention of killing Bacchus. Thank God he'd stopped her. Thank God he'd given her a chance to redeem herself instead of turning her in to the authorities.

"But why did she want you?" she wondered aloud.

"Pardon?"

"When the Cowls—Merton—sent me to dis-spell the servants' door." She gave in and scratched her wrists. "You were only an advanced aspector, and a new arrival. You didn't know her previously. So why was she after your opus?"

Leaning forward, Bacchus set his elbows on his knees. "Perhaps she wasn't. The duke has an opus. Passed down from . . . his great uncle, I believe. A temporal one, in a locked glass case in the library. If Merton was collecting opuses to strengthen her hand, that might have been her target."

Elsie nodded. "She must have seen it when she was visiting with Miss Ida."

"Perhaps. All opuses are documented by the atheneums; she might have viewed the records there. We may never know for sure."

She rolled her lips together, trying to imagine an alternate history to the one that had played out. Would she still be a pawn beneath Merton's thumb if Bacchus hadn't stopped her that day? She shivered at the thought.

"I'm glad you caught me." She studied a vase on a nearby table, so she didn't see his reaction. "Even more so that you let me barter my way out."

He snorted, drawing Elsie's eyes back. "You were certainly unexpected. And wily."

She smiled at him.

He waited a beat before carefully saying, "The other option for your spellbreaking predicament is leaving."

Elsie glanced at him. "What do you mean?"

"I mean we could hire a spellbreaking tutor in Barbados. Fudge the timeline. Wait a few years for your certification. Skip the rudimentary stuff."

Elsie blinked. *Barbados.* She'd never been anywhere tropical. What would it be like to live there?

What would it be like for Bacchus to have her live there? *With* him? In truth, she'd never considered it. She'd never allowed herself the fancy of marrying Bacchus before the whole jail conundrum unfolded; she'd been sure he'd sail off without her and that would be that. And now . . . now she was so concerned about their ruse and about the possibility that he might hate her for it that she hadn't considered anything beyond the marriage ceremony.

"We couldn't." She turned away. "Not while Merton is still at large."

He nodded.

She rubbed the bridge of her nose, a sudden headache starting there. Now she was keeping him from his home, too. "Bacchus, I'm so sorry. I didn't mean—"

But the door opened just then, revealing the butler. "If Miss Camden is ready, the duchess would like to meet with her."

Elsie threw an apologetic look to Bacchus. One she hoped read, *I'm so sorry I dragged you into this. I'm so sorry I'm a burden. I'm so sorry you're stuck with me.*

But Bacchus said, "She is," and took Elsie's hand in his. Her stomach warmed in response. "I'll see you when you're done."

He kissed the back of her hand, the press of his lips sending sparks like a fire spell up her arm. Her voice got lost somewhere between her throat and her tongue, so she simply nodded and allowed the butler to see her out, her hand pulling too slowly from Bacchus's.

Once in the hallway, she checked the back of her hand for a spell; she could swear she felt something powerful pulsing against her skin, but there was nothing. She rubbed it, hoping to diffuse the aching that had begun just over her breastbone, but it was no use.

The duchess greeted her kindly and had her sit on a plush settee, an assortment of menus scattered across the table before them. "I wanted to secure everything and have the dinner right away, since I understand you two are in a hurry." She winked. "No cousins this time."

Voice still caught, Elsie nodded yet again.

"Oh, my dear"—the duchess reached toward her—"has something happened to your hand?"

Realizing she still clutched the appendage, Elsie dropped both hands to her lap. "No, nothing." She flushed. "Nothing at all."

∾

The duchess had not been fibbing when she'd said she wanted to move things along, for the weekend following Elsie's training with the spellbreaker, Bacchus and Elsie's engagement dinner was served.

Or it would be shortly.

Bacchus found himself walking the grounds of Seven Oaks, around and around the mansion, his hands clasped behind his back, or fidgeting with his waistcoat, or combing through and rebinding his hair. The last few weeks had gone by in a blur, and he was still trying to orient himself. Plan. Make the road ahead as straight and easy as possible.

He had made the offer to take Elsie to Barbados, but she wouldn't be able to give him an answer until Merton was taken care of. He knew that women raised in English households and English weather might not take to the sunny, humid climate, especially when wearing English fashions. But he hoped Elsie would succumb to the beauty of the island as he had. Would the island grow in her heart the way it had in his? Would she be willing to take off her shoes and walk its beaches, or watch the sun set over an endless sea?

Yet it was just as likely that they would stay in England. Perhaps not indefinitely, but for a while. Master aspector work was far more plentiful here than the islands, unless he wanted to take frequent commutes to the States, which he did not. In truth, he'd wanted the master ambulation spell only so he could continue to care for his plantation and its employees, but his future had changed in unexpected ways. He would have a wife, and eventually a family to rear. He had been mistaken about his polio. He had new options, and new responsibilities.

That, and Elsie's entire life was in England. Not family, no, but friends, colleagues. She was close to Mr. Ogden and Miss Pratt; she'd even inquired about inviting them to the dinner tonight, but there was a certain decorum about these things, and in the end, she'd feared overstepping her bounds.

He'd glimpsed the dark side of her heart, the fear and sorrow left by her family's abandonment and the callow treatment of this former beau of hers. Bacchus had no wish to extend the shadows. No, he wanted to lift them entirely. He wanted to see her smile and hear her laugh. Genuinely, as she had not done since that disastrous dinner when Abel

Nash had tried to take Bacchus's life, and Merton, the secret crook, had run free.

The sound of the duke's carriage reached his ears as he came around the west side of the house. From his vantage point, he could see it coming down the road, and his stomach tightened. Straightening, he made his way toward the gates, though the carriage beat him to it, horses trotting up the lane and pulling in at the front of the house. Two servants came out to intercept, but they spied Bacchus and he waved them away so he could open the door himself.

Elsie gave him an uneasy smile, then let him take her gloved hand in his. She was wearing his favorite dress, the light cerulean one that almost matched her eyes. He thought that was a new hat with it and wondered if he should comment on it.

"Was your ride agreeable?" he asked instead, escorting her to the house, linking her arm through his.

"Wonderfully uneventful." She brushed off her skirt. He could feel her pulse through her elbow, however, and it wasn't precisely calm.

"You've dined with them before, Elsie."

She let out a false laugh, then sucked in a large gulp of air and let it all out at once. "I know that." She stuck her nose up in that proud way of hers, as though she could convince herself and all the world that she didn't possess a single nerve or worry.

He guided her up the stairs, where one of the servants opened the door for them. Elsie pulled toward the dining hall—the smaller one, as the first was still under repairs—but Bacchus guided her off to the right, where the hallway curved. He stopped near a painted replica of the queen's gardens, shadows dancing on the image as the candles flickered in their sconces.

Elsie looked at him, wide-eyed and curious.

He cleared his throat, his own nerves suddenly making themselves known. "I wasn't sure when to give you this, but you might as well sport it, given the night's event." He fished into his pocket and pulled out the green ribbon in there, tied around a ring. As he began to unfasten it, Elsie grew very still.

"B-Bacchus, I don't need a ring." Her voice was barely above a whisper.

He slid the ring off the ribbon—it was a golden band with a large, circular sapphire, surrounded by a braided loop that made it look almost like a flower—and held it up between them. "Every bride needs a ring, Elsie."

She lifted her hand as though to touch it, but her fingers cowered at the last moment, curling inward like a dying insect's legs. "It looks expensive." Now she *did* whisper. Heaven forbid a passing servant discover Bacchus wasn't cheap.

"I would give you my mother's ring," he said, reaching for her left hand, "but she never had one."

Elsie didn't resist as he took her hand. He slid the small ring onto his pinky finger, down to the first knuckle. Then he tugged on her glove, one fingertip at a time, loosening the lace until it came free. It was only a glove, he knew, but something about it felt deeply intimate. Her hand was soft against his, her nails neatly trimmed, her fingers quivering so slightly he almost didn't detect it. But he did.

He slid the ring onto her fourth finger. It was a little large.

A soft chuckle came up her throat. "I'll eat seconds at every meal until it fits."

He smiled. Gently pinched the ring and let a novice spell flow through him with master control, a spell that, little by little, shrunk the band of the ring until it fit snuggly around her finger. Turned her hand over so that the sapphire sparkled in the candlelight. "It suits you."

She flushed in an oddly provocative way, and Bacchus forced himself to step back and turn his thoughts elsewhere. "I believe we're expected."

Elsie nodded, her eyes still on the ring. She looked so guilty Bacchus almost felt as though he'd done something wrong.

He hadn't. Yes, the circumstances were unconventional, but he intended to marry her. He *wanted* to marry her. The magistrate simply . . . complicated things.

Surely he wasn't a fool for thinking she felt the same way. If she didn't give a farthing for him, she wouldn't have pushed herself in front of a bolt of lightning pointed at *his* person. She wouldn't have refused to abandon him in that warehouse on the docks. Surely the kiss she'd given him on his cheek hadn't been merely in farewell.

And yet she'd become so stiff around him lately, so apologetic, Bacchus had started to question it. Perhaps he wasn't what she'd expected—he was aware he didn't fit the mold of a typical English gentleman. But he could make a comfortable life for her. Protect her. Laugh with her.

He just hoped she realized it as well.

He guided Elsie to a sitting room, where the other guests awaited them—the Duke and Duchess of Kent and their daughters, Ida and Josie. The duchess had also invited the duke's brother, the Earl of Kent, and his family to even out the numbers. Bacchus introduced Elsie to all of them: the earl himself, Lady Lena Scott, Mr. Allen Scott, and Mr. Fred Scott, the latter two being Ida and Josie's cousins and roughly of an age with Elsie.

Elsie took the introductions quietly and graciously, and then they walked in to dinner, Bacchus taking the seat to the duke's right, and Elsie sitting beside him.

As kidney soup was served, Bacchus found himself recounting his and Elsie's false meeting story to the duke's family. When that conversation grew stale, Elsie asked after Miss Ida's pursuit of aspecting. Given what the duchess had said about the unlikelihood of such a pursuit, he suspected she'd mentioned it only for lack of anything else to say.

"I think I might give it another year before I decide, which I know isn't best," Ida said. "I'm a little old to train already. But, Elsie, I hear you're a spellbreaker! Do tell me all about it."

Elsie faltered only once before spinning a half-true story about seeing spells on the duke's stone walls, and then launched into the details of her lesson with Miss Prescott. When the attention turned to the earl's latest hunting expedition, Bacchus leaned over to her and said, "At least Miss Prescott provides you with ample dinner conversation."

She smiled at her plate, twisting the sapphire ring on her finger. The servants brought out a roasted forequarter of lamb beautifully wrapped in pastry. Elsie did a poor job of keeping the surprise from her face, though it was Bacchus's understanding that she'd helped select the menu.

When the meal was finished, the duke announced, "I think we might enjoy some port and sherry."

The duchess clicked her tongue. "Not for long; tonight is about Miss Camden as well."

Miss Josie suddenly choked on her wine, barely getting a napkin up to her face before spewing it over the table.

"Josie!" the duchess exclaimed. "What's come over you?"

The poor girl mopped herself up. "I'm sorry. It's nothing, really."

The duchess's stare was penetrating.

"It's just . . ." She looked sheepish and glanced at her cousins. "It's just . . . well. Mrs. *Elsie Kelsey.*"

Elsie touched her forehead and sighed.

Bacchus paused as the cousins tittered. "I hadn't realized."

Recovering, Elsie pasted on a smile and stood, the men quickly following her lead for etiquette's sake. "It's fine. I shall simply go by my middle name."

Miss Ida asked, "And what's that?"

She rolled her lips together, and so quietly that Bacchus was sure he was the only one who heard, she answered, "I don't remember."

Fortunately, the duchess came around the table and clasped Elsie's elbow. "I think it's marvelous. Come now, ladies, let's leave the gentlemen to a *short* bout of port, shall we?"

Bacchus let out a breath, grateful for the duchess's reprieve. However, as Elsie came around the table toward the exit, she froze suddenly behind the duke's chair, causing the duchess to stagger back a step. Her gaze shot immediately to the back of the duke's head.

"Whatever is wrong?" the duchess asked.

Elsie cast a somewhat alarmed look at Bacchus, which made him tense. *What?* he mouthed, but she didn't respond. Instead, she shook her head and said to the duchess, "Forgive me. New shoes."

The duchess laughed. "Always a bother, aren't they?" and they continued on to the sitting room.

Once Elsie left, Bacchus forced himself to sit down, but his thoughts were firmly fixed on her and whatever she'd sensed.

"No worries, lad," the Earl of Kent said beside him, pouring himself a drink. "She's not going far."

Bacchus did not drink, and indeed was relieved, fifteen minutes later, when the duke honored his wife's request to keep the men's visit short. "Let's go entertain them, shall we?" he asked, and started the march for the sitting room.

Bacchus found Elsie immediately upon entering. She stood by the mantel, having a conversation with Lady Lena Scott and one of her sons. Upon seeing him, she said, "If you'll excuse me, I've just decided what flowers I would like at the wedding, and I must tell Bacchus while he's in a pleasant mood."

It was obviously a rehearsed excuse, but her companions chuckled and let her go. She met him in the corner of the room, out of earshot of the others.

"What's wrong?" Bacchus asked, lowering his head to hers.

She bit her lip, glanced over her shoulder. "What spell is the duke wearing?"

Bacchus lifted his head, brows drawing together. "Pardon?"

"The spell on the duke. What is it?"

Bacchus shook his head. "The duke doesn't have . . . ," but he stopped himself. Elsie of all people would know. "What did you sense?"

"Something strong," she whispered. "Not a smell or a sound, so it's rational or physical. I mean, physical spells are visual, but sometimes I just *feel* them anyway, like with you, but not like a rational spell, of course, just something else deep down—"

He placed a hand on her shoulder, stopping her spiraling explanation. His thoughts swam as he considered. "Are you sure it's not a temporal spell? He had a temporal aspector here recently, if you recall."

Temporal aspectors could alter time's effects on things; they could strip the rust from iron or the wrinkles from skin. But Elsie shook her head. "Temporal spells have a certain . . . *flavor*, to quote Miss Prescott. It's not that."

"Then what—"

Bacchus suddenly felt sick. Enough so that he put his hand out against the wall to steady himself.

Worry flashed across Elsie's face. "Bacchus?"

The duchess noticed. "Are you quite well?"

Catching himself, Bacchus stood to his full height and straightened his waistcoat. "Of course. If you'll excuse us a moment."

The earl's wife gave them a knowing look, which Bacchus promptly ignored as he ushered Elsie into the hallway. He strode down it, nearly too quick for her to easily keep up, and around the corner.

"Bacchus—" Elsie was growing breathless.

He stopped suddenly, standing in the sliver of shadow between two sconces. "The duke was recently ill."

She studied his face. "Yes, you mentioned it."

"He was recently ill immediately following our trip to Ipswich. Extremely ill. His recovery was nothing short of miraculous."

It took only a moment for Elsie to understand his meaning; he knew when she did, for her face lit with sudden horror.

"Elsie"—he gripped both of her shoulders—"could he be receiving energy from a siphoning spell?"

She worked her mouth. "I . . . I don't know. I-I'd have to see it to be certain."

Releasing her, Bacchus stepped back and wiped a hand down his face.

"Bacchus, he's like a father to you. Do you really suspect he might be the one behind it? The . . . 'polio'?"

It hadn't been polio, of course. Bacchus had merely spent a decade thinking it was. Someone had placed the physical siphoning spell on him without his knowledge, hidden beneath a temporal spell he had mistakenly thought was keeping him well. "The timing is suspect, and I don't know of any other spell he could have that isn't temporal." His hand formed a fist, and he pressed it against the wall, resisting the urge to burst through it with his knuckles. "I need to know."

"I can try getting closer," she suggested, "but if I can't see it . . ."

Bacchus let out a long breath. What would he do if his suspicions were true? If the man who had been like family to him for so long had actually been robbing him of his health and vitality since his adolescence?

"Bacchus." Her voice was soft as smoke, and her hands came up to his face, gentle but firm, cradling his jaw. He looked down, meeting her eyes.

"Be patient," she pleaded. "Don't jump to conclusions. Maybe I was wrong."

"Do you really think you were wrong?"

She didn't answer. "I'll figure it out. Get closer if I can. Just . . . distract yourself in the interim, all right?"

Distract myself.

Her hands still lingered on his jaw. They were close together, half a pace apart, the hallway quiet, empty.

His gaze dropped to her lips. He could certainly think of one way to distract himself.

She flushed again, searching his face, then promptly removed her hands, self-consciously touching her mouth as though she'd left food there. Misinterpreting him, likely. She'd done that often, ever since being arrested. Like her confidence was still imprisoned in Oxford.

Damn Merton. She'd made it so much harder to straighten Elsie's crippled wings.

Sighing, Bacchus straightened. "Do what you can, but don't risk yourself on my behalf."

She looked at him apologetically. Fidgeted with the ring on her finger.

He offered his arm. "We'd best head back before they think I'm robbing you of your maidenhood."

Elsie blushed redder than the carpet.

It was a comely sight, yet Bacchus could not bring himself to smile.

CHAPTER 9

Two days after the somewhat awkward engagement dinner at Seven Oaks, Elsie was still wondering what it would be like to kiss Bacchus Kelsey. She'd chided herself many times and even tried to start her novel reader, but the pleasure of it had faded—she found she couldn't care about the fictional baron nearly as much as the real-life master spell-maker, and it made her miserable.

For the briefest moment, she had thought Bacchus might try, there in the duke's hallway. Kiss her, that was. But that had just been bread crumbs on her chin. Thinking of it made her coil in embarrassment, and pining for the man only flared an uneasy depression. She'd only ever kissed Alfred, unless one were to count that boy at the workhouse when she was nine. His name was . . . Matthew, if memory served her right.

At least Bacchus still tolerated her. He hadn't yet discovered she was disposable. And if she knew him at all, he might be noble enough to keep her around even once he did.

"Miss Camden?"

Elsie jerked to attention. She sat at the dining table in Ogden's kitchen, barely a sixth of the size of the one at Seven Oaks, Miss Irene Prescott just across the corner from her. *Blast, I missed what she said.*

"Hmm?" she inquired sweetly.

Miss Prescott smiled patiently, a small iron rod in her hands. "Do you detect the points of this rune?"

Miss Prescott had brought temporally enchanted items today, as the Temporal Atheneum was all the way in Newcastle upon Tyne, and it was easier to have a local aspector enchant items than take the long trip north. The spell was a reverse aging spell, meant to remove rust. The rod in the spellbreaker's hands looked fresh and new, but it had the telltale smell of mushrooms.

Elsie touched the rod, detecting the points of its knots. "I think so," she lied. She knew exactly where they were. She could untie them while standing on her head. Assuming she still had that skill. She hadn't tried since she was a child.

Miss Prescott went on to discuss the rune for the next fifteen minutes, followed by the assurance that even though Elsie couldn't see the rune, she could still untie it.

Elsie's cheeks were beginning to hurt from all the forced smiling, and she was so relieved to untie the bloody thing, she didn't bother making any mistakes.

"Wonderful!" Miss Prescott set the now-rusted rod on the table. "What a quick learner you are, Miss Camden! It took me a month to feel out temporal runes."

A *month*? Elsie tried to remember the first temporal rune she'd come across, and found she couldn't. "Beginner's luck," she offered. She'd need to stall her learning next time. The last thing she wanted was Miss Prescott announcing to important people that Elsie was talented, lest the magistrate determine she'd had more practice than Bacchus had let on.

Thoughts of Bacchus had her fiddling with the ring on her finger. She'd need to procure one for him as well. A nice band . . . But what would Bacchus like? Something simple, most likely. She wouldn't have much time to look until . . . She wasn't sure. After the wedding, certainly.

The wedding.

They were going to keep it simple, yet Elsie still had two sheets of paper upstairs filled with discussions on it, mostly inquiries from the duchess, though Bacchus always wrote them out himself. Having a duchess as a guest made her almost as nervous as having Bacchus as the groom.

"Rational spells are the trickiest, in my opinion. We'll get to those last," Miss Prescott said, and Elsie became aware once more of the opus spell tucked beneath her dress. "I'll set up an appointment for us at the Spiritual Atheneum so you can get a feel for that type of magic before we start focusing on individual disciplines. It shouldn't be hard—the atheneums are always in need of spellbreakers. They'll be happy to have us."

Elsie perked up at this. Perhaps she could learn something more of Lily Merton at the Spiritual Atheneum? Could she have left any tracks uncovered? So far, Ogden had had no success in tracking her down, but maybe he'd been looking in the wrong places. "I would very much like that."

They chatted for another quarter hour, blessedly not about spellbreaking, before Miss Prescott took her leave. The moment she did, Elsie went upstairs—careful not to disturb Emmeline's hanging laundry—and slipped into the sitting room, where she'd left the copies of the newspaper articles penned under her name. Sitting on the sofa, she spread them out before her, reading each of them in turn. The newspapers from the spirit line still hadn't come in. She nearly had these ones memorized. The only thing of interest she could find were two lines: *The inquirer would gladly pay a high price for the black birds,* from the *Manchester Guardian.*

It sounded like a bribe, or it did to Elsie's mind, which arguably had been made fanciful from novel readers. Then there was the line that stood out in the more recent article, which was a sight less cheery: *A shame if things were to take a Turner and end entirely.* That sounded like a threat.

Emmeline had set the day's newspaper on the side table. With a sigh, Elsie opened it, eager to read something sensical.

What she found made her blood run cold.

"Again?" she whispered, setting the pages on her lap. The main headline read, Master Rational Aspector Missing Three Days, Believed to Be Victim of Opus Thief.

Her thoughts jumped to Ogden, but she'd seen him last night. Not that she'd ever report him as a master aspector were he to get lost.

She read the article, which detailed a Mr. Kyle Landon Murray, who was forty-eight years old, a popular aspector in Oxford.

> *"He has a very strict schedule," his daughter said. "He's meticulous. He wouldn't have just run off."*

> *Police are still investigating.*

"Merton." Elsie said her name like a curse. Was she so bold as to continue her scheme while in hiding, or was this simply an unrelated disappearance?

No, the coincidence was too great. But this meant Elsie, Ogden, and Bacchus *really* needed to find some clues or else more people would get hurt, and Merton . . . Merton would do whatever it was she was planning to do.

Merton. *Merton.*

Elsie's chest tightened.

Sitting at the edge of her seat, Elsie looked over the last article again. *A shame if things were to take a Turner and end entirely.* It wasn't just a misspelling; the word *Turner* was capitalized.

One of the murders had happened at a Mr. Turner's home in London.

Elsie held her breath. It couldn't be happenstance. That line *had* been intended as a threat. Whomever the articles were intended for . . . Merton had been informing them of what she would do if they didn't cooperate. Had she gotten impatient, moving from coercion to threats, and then to outright murder? But what did she want?

Elsie pulled up the *News Letter* article and pored over it, searching for something similar. The vapid writing went on and on about traveling via ships and trains—

And then she finally saw something that stood out. Not a name or a threat, but something else. Letting herself breathe, she read again.

> It is difficult to maneuver ships when a neighbor seeks a conversation back home. We must analyze the situation and come together.

Elsie pressed her finger beneath the last sentence and glanced over the rest of the article. Yes, this was different.

For whatever reason, the author had switched to American spelling for those two sentences. *Maneuver* instead of *manoeuvre, neighbor* instead of *neighbour,* and *analyze* instead of *analyse.* The words themselves didn't seem to fit, rendering the writing subpar and clunky. As though Merton really wanted that line to stand out.

Elsie took a pencil and underlined the passage, then returned to the article from the *Manchester Guardian,* carefully reading that one as well. To her delight, she found a similar passage.

> The owner has traveled away, though he is wanted in London. "There is no pretense," a neighbor said. "We merely want to open a dialogue about the spell."

Traveled, pretense, and *neighbor* were all in American English. What spell this neighbor referred to was not detailed. Elsie underlined it and moved on to the *Daily Telegraph*, finding this line: *This behavior is unnecessary; let us labor together for a better end.*

Behavior and *labor* were both American English, while the rest of the article was British.

Getting a new piece of paper, Elsie wrote down all the irregular lines. A neighbor—Merton?—was trying to contact someone who had traveled away from America. One of the other headlines mentioned a spiritual aspector—the American Elsie had met in Juniper Down, surely. So Master Merton wanted to talk to him . . . about a spell? And she was trying to convey that his behavior, the traveling he'd been doing, was unnecessary.

Was he hiding from Merton? Had she paid to publish these articles across random papers in the hopes that he'd take notice? Was that why she'd used American spelling?

Astonishingly enough, it had worked, because the American *had* come to England. He'd looked up the articles' author—Elsie Camden—and met her in Juniper Down, her last known residence prior to the burned-down workhouse.

That had happened while Ogden was still under Merton's spell, but because Ogden hadn't witnessed it himself, Merton had no way of gleaning the information from him.

Which meant she likely didn't know the American had come at all.

Elsie tapped her pencil against her lips. She had so many questions, but this was progress. With luck, Ogden would return home tonight with news from the spirit line. Finding more of these articles might reveal more truths, about both Merton and the unknown man from Juniper Down.

"Elsie?" Emmeline poked her head into the room.

Lowering her pencil, Elsie said, "Hmm?"

"Do you want help getting ready?"

Elsie looked up, confused, before understanding dawned on her and she leapt off the sofa. "Emmeline, thank you. I'd nearly forgotten."

She was to dine at Seven Oaks again tonight. Bacchus had arranged it—in a storybook, he would have done so to spend time with her because they were blissfully in love. In reality, he needed her to get close to the duke again so she could uncover the truth behind the mysterious spell hidden on his person. She hoped she didn't make a fool of herself, but more so, she hoped she was wrong. That she actually hadn't sensed a spell, or that the spell was something else entirely. Bacchus was so close to the duke . . . Elsie didn't want anything to estrange them. Nor did she want Bacchus to taste betrayal. The acrid flavor was still familiar on Elsie's tongue, and she didn't wish it upon anyone, least of all the man she lov—

She cleared her throat, reining in her thoughts. At least she'd managed to convince the duke and duchess that she was fine company.

"Do you want to wear my pearls?" Emmeline asked as Elsie stepped through the door. "They look real."

She was about to say no, but paused. This was a duke's home, and there was only so much she could do to her dresses to make it look like she belonged. "Yes, Emmeline," she said, running her thumb over the sapphire on her finger. "That would be wonderful."

⌒

Elsie was especially nervous riding to Seven Oaks this time, and not merely because a bout of rain threatened to unwind her meticulously placed curls. The problem was this: while the duke seemed happy enough to welcome her into his home—he'd always been welcoming, even before her forced engagement to Bacchus—they weren't chummy. Getting close enough to the *duchess* to uncover a spell would be trying enough, but to her husband? Elsie had to find a way to do it without looking like she'd gone mad. And even then, if it was a physical spell, she wouldn't know for sure unless she *saw* the bloody thing. Perhaps if she tripped while carrying a knife just so, she could slice through the buttons of the duke's shirt without actually injuring him . . .

Do it for Bacchus, she reminded herself. She didn't want him to doubt people like she did.

She twisted the ring on her finger until the skin beneath grew raw.

When the carriage pulled through the gates and around the drive, Elsie searched for Bacchus, but he wasn't there to meet her. Something inside her sank.

A servant opened the carriage, and Elsie hid her discomfort somewhere near her diaphragm, where it bubbled and mewed little enough for her to ignore it. "Miss Camden," the young man said, "allow me to escort you to the sitting room."

"Thank you." Elsie tried her best to sound refined. The servant walked two steps ahead of her, guiding her down an increasingly familiar path to the elaborate sitting room. The duke and his entire family were inside; a harp had been brought over, and Ida played a lovely tune upon it. Bacchus was nowhere to be seen.

Her anxiety sharpened. Was he well? Worried? Should she find him?

"Miss Camden!" exclaimed the duchess, who rose from her chair and crossed to her, grasping Elsie's hands gently in greeting. "It's so wonderful to have you with us again."

Elsie put on a smile. "It's always wonderful to be here, Your Grace."

The duchess chuckled. "Please, you must call me Abigail. Come take a seat. I apologize for Bacchus; it's not like him to be late."

Elsie glanced back to the way she had come. "No, it's not."

The duchess guided her to a settee. Elsie was about to sit, but the duke was leaning against the mantel, watching his daughter play. Sensing her opportunity, she offered up an excuse about stretching her legs and went to stand by him, taking up a place a little too close for comfort.

She could feel it, the spell, with something beyond her five senses. Maybe if she got *very* close, she would be able to tell whether it was the siphoning spell.

She cleared her throat. "Lovely woods you have." It was one of her many rehearsed lines. "Do you hunt often, Your Grace?"

The duke chuckled. "Not for some time now. Perhaps you have not noticed, Elsie, but I am beginning to lean toward old."

Behind her, Miss Josie chuckled.

Elsie smiled. "I hadn't noticed." Though, in fact, the Duke of Kent was perhaps the oldest man she knew, short of Two-Thom from Clunwood. "You seem to have recovered from your illness nicely, if I may say so."

He smiled. "I try my best."

This was getting nowhere. Elsie racked her brain for something else to say.

"How is your training coming along?" the duke asked.

"Oh fine. Lovely. Quite lovely. Keeps me busy." She studied his face, that spell pulsing just beyond her reach. An idea struck. "Forgive me for saying so, but I believe your cravat is crooked." She knew nothing about fixing a cravat, but if she could just reach for it—

The duke raised a hand before she could, his slender fingers tracing the knot. He adjusted it slightly. "It's actually a new design my valet introduced me to. Not sure how fond of it I am."

Blast.

The duke looked at her expectantly, so she said the first thing that came to mind. "You haven't by chance heard from Master Merton, have you?"

He blinked. "No, she hasn't—"

The door opened, calling Elsie's attention away. Curse her heart for how it quickened at the sight of Bacchus, looking smart, well groomed, and tired.

The duke straightened. "I suppose we can all head in now. Abigail?" He held out his arm for the duchess.

Bacchus spied Elsie and came toward her, his strides long and purposeful.

Elsie swallowed. "Where were you?"

"I lost track of time."

She wilted. Touched his elbow. "It's understandable."

He rewarded her with a soft smile before rubbing his eyes. "Forgive me, I haven't slept well."

"I see that, too. And it's no wonder," she added quietly. "But I will forgive you for anything and everything as long as you forgive me for anything absurd I do in that dining room."

Because she *would* make a fool of herself, one way or another. If it meant Bacchus's happiness.

"Anything and everything, hm?" There was a sparkle in his gaze that made her belly warm. She couldn't muster a sensible reply.

The others had started for the dining room, so Bacchus offered his arm. Elsie took it, relishing the feel of the strong muscles under his sleeve, wishing for . . . everything.

But it was no use feeling sorry for herself. She had a job to do.

They had nearly reached the dining room when Bacchus whispered, "You seem uneasy."

She scoffed. "I'm about to accost a duke. Of course I'm uneasy."

Bacchus's lips pressed into a line, and he said nothing more until they were seated, the first course served. Elsie sat around the table from the duke this time, though not close enough to feel that otherly buzz of his spell.

She considered, as Miss Josie recounted her day shopping in town, what actions she needed to take. She swallowed spoonful after spoonful of white soup as she debated and was surprised when her spoon hit the bottom of the empty bowl.

"What flowers did you decide upon, Miss Camden?" the duchess inquired as a servant took her dish away.

"Flowers?" Her brain remembered too slowly her excuse for pulling Bacchus away at the engagement dinner. "Oh! Well, roses, of course."

The duchess smiled. "A good, traditional choice."

In truth, Elsie couldn't care less about what flowers decorated the chapel when she got married. It seemed so inconsequential, so abstract, compared with her other worries.

"It's too bad laceleaf doesn't grow here," Bacchus added. Elsie could detect the very slightest hint of tension in his voice, something she might not have noticed if this were their first meeting. His English accent was especially crisp. "It's quite lovely, especially the red variety."

"Is it native to Barbados?" Elsie asked.

He nodded and took a sip of water.

Elsie's gaze narrowed in on that glass, and a perfect, mortifying plan sprung into her head.

"What a lovely name," Miss Ida said. "Laceleaf. Do tell us what it looks like."

Bacchus set the glass down. "It's a variety of lily." The servants came around with the second course, serving the duke first. Elsie waited until they moved away so there would be none to lend aid but herself. "The entire flower is made of a single petal wrapped around the tip of the stem, and the spadix—"

Elsie swiped her arm out and tipped over her full water glass, spilling it over the table and, subsequently, onto the duke's lap.

No one could say she hadn't tried.

"Oh no!" she stood immediately, seizing her napkin and coming to the duke's aid. The spell on his person called to her, but she still wasn't close enough to read it. "I'm so clumsy. Oh, forgive me." She needn't fake her embarrassment.

The duke scooted back, shaking water off his hand. Elsie moved closer. Her initial impressions held out—there was no smell, no sound, and now that she was closer, she didn't feel the tingle of a rational spell. It *had* to be physical—

"It's quite all right. It's not the first time." The duke stood.

Now if only he would be so kind as to change his clothes right there in the dining room and allow Elsie a good look at his naked torso.

"Elsie." Bacchus stood, fingers grazing her elbow.

"I've almost got it," she replied. The others would think she meant the mess, which the servants were now hurrying to clean up. She dared to reach for the duke's chest with her half-soaked napkin—

Bacchus's grip tightened, holding her back. Frustrated, she turned to him, but the set of his brow and jaw, like they'd been crafted by a blacksmith, gave her pause.

"Why don't you change," the duchess offered. "We'll wait for you—"

Bacchus's voice carried over hers. "What spell is on your person?"

The room silenced. Even the servants hushed. Elsie's lips parted. *That's one way to do it . . .*

The duke froze. "Pardon?"

"The spell on your torso," Bacchus specified. "Is it or is it not the recipient enchantment for a siphoning spell?"

The duke blanched. "I don't know what you mean."

"Be straight with me, Isaiah," Bacchus pressed. "She's a spellbreaker."

Elsie guiltily set down her napkin.

The duke glanced at his wife, then settled on the tabletop. "It's not what you think, Bacchus."

Bacchus tensed. "Explain it to me, then. Explain why I had a hidden spell on my person *since my youth*, and why you grew ill immediately following its removal."

The duchess looked shocked. Had she not known? "Isaiah?"

One of the servants gestured to the other, and they quickly exited the room.

Miss Josie looked back and forth between Bacchus and her father. "What's going on?"

Bacchus merely waited.

The duke sighed. "I was growing frail, and you were such a strong, healthy boy."

Bacchus's hold on Elsie tightened.

"Please"—the Duke of Kent lifted a hand—"I did not mean to *take* it from you. Your father—"

"My *father* knew?"

The knob in the duke's throat bobbed. "Your father gave his consent."

Bacchus glowered. "It was not his to give."

"Strictly speaking—"

"I thought I had *polio*." Bacchus leaned over the table, finally releasing Elsie so he could press both hands against its surface. "For *years* I thought I had polio. I thought I would lose the use of my legs. I went to *countless* doctors."

"Girls," the duchess murmured, "let's wait for your father in the parlor, hm?" She hurriedly ushered them to the door. Elsie's pulse raced, but she didn't try to join them. She needed to be here. She needed to stand by Bacchus's side. Her hand strayed to his triceps, her touch featherlight.

Chagrined, the duke repeated, "Your father knew."

"And so did you," Bacchus replied darkly. He straightened, seeming to almost double in size. "Who did it? My father was no spellmaker."

The duke turned away. "I swore that I would not—"

"*Who?*" Bacchus pressed. "You owe me at least that much."

The duke's shoulders slumped so deeply Elsie thought his fingertips might brush the carpet. "Master Enoch Phillips performed it while you slept."

Elsie gaped. Wasn't Master Phillips the head of the London Physical Atheneum?

Bacchus said, "I don't suppose you'll share whose vitality you're drinking from now."

The duke looked ready to cry.

Elsie started as Bacchus's hand gripped hers, and suddenly she was being pulled away from the table toward the door, barely able to keep up with his long strides. A maid swept by the passageway, and Bacchus barked, "See a carriage pulled around immediately and ensure Miss Camden is taken care of."

His presence and his baritone emanated both authority and restrained rage, and the maid didn't hesitate to respond. "O-Of course. Miss Camden." She curtsied and, abandoning whatever chore she was about, quickly led Elsie to a cushioned bench in the vestibule by the front door. Meanwhile, Bacchus burst up the stairs, taking the steps three at a time.

The maid bolted in the other direction.

Elsie let out a long breath as she lowered herself onto the bench. This was not how she had expected the evening to go. Peering up at the stairs, she longed to follow Bacchus, to see if he was all right. But of course that was silly. He *wasn't* all right. Why would he be? The duke's revelation had made everything a thousandfold worse. Bacchus's own father had betrayed him.

She twiddled her thumbs, uneasy. What if one of the family stopped by? What would she say? It was obvious *she* had told Bacchus about the spell. Surely they'd never want to see her again. Perhaps she should start walking home. Let the carriage catch up, or see if she could find a cab farther into the city. It was raining—pouring, really—but a cold wouldn't *kill* her, now would it?

Embarrassment might.

She was just about to rise from the bench when she heard the heavy clamor of hooves outside. A moment later, a man in a very wet driver's uniform burst in. "Miss Camden? I'm ready for you."

She nodded and followed him out. A heavy black carriage awaited her, pulled by four horses. An awful lot for a single person, but she wasn't about to complain—it had a roof. Holding her hands over her head as though they could protect her from the downpour, Elsie hurried to it, grateful for the driver's assistance as he opened the door. He was so swift he nearly closed it on her skirt.

Leaning back on the bench, she blew a damp curl from her face. What would happen now? Surely Bacchus wouldn't continue to stay with the duke and duchess. Would he want to return to Barbados? And if so, what would it mean for their plans? She didn't truly think he would leave her to the magistrate—to the jailers—but her hand moved to her neck at the thought of hanging. Emmeline's pearls offered a sliver of comfort.

The carriage rocked as the driver took his seat, but before the horses could pull forward, her door ripped open, shooting a cold, wet gust her way. To her surprise, Bacchus stepped in and sat across from her, slamming the door shut behind him. The carriage dipped once more as someone secured a trunk to its back.

"I'm coming with you," Bacchus announced, and banged his fist on the carriage roof.

CHAPTER 10

"We're making a detour," he added as the carriage pulled down the drive. Elsie glanced out the window at the darkening estate, but didn't see any of the family.

"Detour?" she asked.

"Master Hill once offered me a room in her home," he explained, pulling the tie from his hair and leaning back against the wall behind him. "I'm going to accept it."

"At this hour?"

Bacchus didn't reply.

Elsie worried her hands. Hadn't she brought gloves with her? Had she left them inside? "Will . . . Will the duke be all right with you taking his carriage?"

Folding his arms, he answered, "He won't stop me."

She swallowed. "And . . . your men?" John and . . . Rainer, wasn't it? "They have instructions to follow."

She turned the ring around on her finger. "I'm sorry, Bacchus. I was hoping it was something else."

Bacchus relaxed into his bench. "I was as well. But I was prepared for it not to be." He reached into his jacket and pulled out two lace gloves, folding them in half before handing them to Elsie. "I believe these are yours."

Her lips parted as she took them, their fingers just brushing. Such a simple, silly thing, but it got her pulse hurrying along well enough. "Thank you. That was considerate of you." She set them on her lap.

They rode for some time in silence, heading into London. Elsie glanced outside, seeing nothing beyond the rain pelting the window. "How much of that trunk did you pack?"

"About half."

"Leave it to a man to be able to throw his things together and travel on a whim." She folded her hands in her lap. "It's much more difficult for a woman, you know."

A ghost of a smile touched his face. "I'm sure there will be many wrinkles in my clothing come morning." He'd slipped into his Bajan accent, and she was glad for it.

"You fill out your clothes well enough that I don't think it would matter." Her ears heated at her own comment. She picked at the handle of her reticule. "What now?"

He rubbed the half beard around his mouth. "I'll lean on Master Hill's hospitality until I can find a reasonable house in the city. I intend to join the atheneum as a free agent."

Her stomach tightened. "Even with the . . . revelation about Master Phillips?"

"He will have the last say, regardless of his past deeds."

A flicker of hope lit her. "You're staying in London?"

"Until we decide to sail to Barbados. I have lands there, Elsie, but forwarding profits will be complicated. It would be more sound for us to have a steady income here."

Us. God help her. "I'm tethering you here," she whispered. "To a city you hate, with a duke who's used you, under a hateful employer, to a place without any laceleaf."

He lowered his hand. "I don't hate England. I've spent a good deal of my life here. The laceleaf was merely a suggestion."

"But you prefer Barbados," she pressed.

Frowning, he nodded.

Elbows on her knees, Elsie sunk her head into her hands. "I'm so sorry, Bacchus. This is all my fault. I've ruined your relationship with the duke. I've forced you into this marriage. I've taken you away from your home."

"Elsie—"

"We could probably call it off." She lifted her head but couldn't garner the strength to look him in the eye. "Couples split up all the time. I should know." Her gut twisted like it was trying to wring out all her dinner. "It will be . . . awkward, with the newspaper announcement already published, but I'm not well known in any aristocratic circles. We just need an excuse. Maybe we can even tie it to the duke. The magistrate can't *really* revoke his clemency once he's given it, can he? And Miss Prescott truly thinks I'm a beginner, so we'll have her as a witness. Emmeline, too—"

"Is the thought of marrying me so terrible?"

The question knocked the air from her. Her ribs cinched together as she met his eyes. They were dusky emeralds, narrow and unforgiving. They reminded her of the night they met, when she had begged him not to turn her in to the authorities.

Her next words caught in her throat like fishing hooks. "That's not what I said."

"That is precisely what you are saying," he argued. "You are finding every excuse you can to break the engagement." He gripped the edges of his seat. "I know I am not what a woman has in mind when she thinks of matrimony—"

"Oh, Bacchus, no." Tears slipped into her voice, and she hated every one of them. "Don't you see? You're going to regret helping me. I'm already a burden to you and we haven't even met with a priest."

Shadows drew across his face as they passed a gas lamp on the street. "You are not a burden. Why would you think that?"

"How could I not?" she shot back. "I'm a burden to *everyone*." She blinked her eyes dry. "Even as a child I was a burden. Why else would my family just up and leave in the middle of the night if not to get rid of me? And Alfred ran from me the first chance he got. Even Ogden had to be practically possessed to take me in—"

Bacchus leaned forward, almost enough to knock heads with her. "You are *not* a burden, Elsie Camden. You merely have an unfortunate number of complete imbeciles in your life."

Leaning back, she hugged herself. "You'll see, soon enough. I'm not a good person, Bacchus. Master Merton—"

"We are not discussing something you have already been acquitted for."

"You're not my judge." The carriage turned. "You can't acquit me. If they knew—if that magistrate knew—I would be shown no mercy, and you know it. I just . . . There's something about me, Bacchus. Something unlovable."

"You are not unlovable."

"You are not listening."

"No, *you* are not listening." Frustration weighed his voice, and he flung out a hand toward the opposite window. "Do you think I did this just to save you? That I'm some gallant prince from a fairy tale, selflessly trying to save the young maiden from certain doom? No. I did not expect your arrest or this magistrate's games. They merely sped up the process. And I have spent hour after blasted hour, day after day, trying to find a way to convince you that I am genuine in my affections, but it's like throwing darts at a stone wall."

Elsie simply shook her head at his attempts to reassure her, too miserable to examine them closely.

"Am I so untrustworthy?" he asked, and he might as well have stabbed her through the heart with a kitchen knife. "Do my actions seem so completely false to you?"

"No." A tear slid down her cheek. "It's not you. You are wonderful and perfect. You have been nothing but wonderful and perfect. But I'm a regret waiting to happen." She fumbled to open her reticule, seeking a handkerchief. "I only want to save you, Bacchus. I only want you to be happy."

"You are a foolish woman."

She nodded, found her handkerchief. Looked up to apologize. "I—"

But Bacchus was there, so close to her, risen off his seat. She barely had time to register his closeness before his hand slipped around her neck and he gruffly pulled her toward him, his lips finding hers.

A storm burst out of Elsie, electrifying her limbs, sending her heart into her throat. She gasped, and Bacchus took advantage of it, tilting his head and claiming her fully. His lips were warm and moist and *demanding*. He called her very soul out of her body, and it flew up to meet him, dancing beneath his touch, sending shivers across every inch of her skin.

And then her hands were in his hair, his beautiful, thick hair, tangling with the waves as she kissed him back with enough passion to put even her favorite novel reader to shame. The carriage fell away, and she was floating, utterly enraptured by his touch, his taste, the way he smelled like oranges and rain. Heat crawled across her tongue and down her throat, warming her from the inside out, growing hotter until it was a fire. She took his bottom lip for her own, and thought she heard the faintest moan trapped between their mouths. It awoke something utterly enticing within her, a spell in a class all its own.

This wasn't happening. But she certainly could not deny that it *was*, most definitely, happening.

Alfred had *never* kissed her like this.

And then the bolt shifted on the door beside them. Bacchus pulled away, leaving Elsie dizzy and longing, only barely aware that the carriage had indeed stopped, that they'd reached their destination, and that their driver was half a second away from discovering them in a very compromising position.

Bacchus wisely grabbed the handle and beat the man to it, making it look like he had left his seat merely to open the door. "Thank you," he said, forgetting to paste on his English dialect. "If you would knock on the door and inform Master Hill, I'll see to my trunk."

The driver nodded and sprinted toward the looming house across the drive, a few of its windows still alight.

Bacchus put one foot out on the step, but the other remained planted in the carriage.

Struggling for her voice, her wits, and her composure, Elsie managed to say through tingling lips, "Is that how all Bajan men kiss?"

He smirked, the insolent man. "I wouldn't know. I've never kissed any of them."

Elsie laughed, and it hurt, yet relieved the pressure building in her chest.

Reaching a hand up, Bacchus pushed away that same soggy curl from earlier before cupping the side of her face. "I want you to trust me, Elsie."

She nodded against his hand. "I do."

He looked like he might kiss her again, and Elsie's entire body thrilled at the prospect, but the driver was already running back to the carriage. So Bacchus dropped his hand to hers, squeezed it, and said, "Write me," before stepping out into the rain.

Elsie barely noticed the ride back to Brookley, the storm and the bumps. She had completely forgotten the debacle at Seven Oaks, as well as the articles waiting for her at the stonemasonry shop.

She arrived home as though in a dream, and found she had the most intense craving for oranges.

CHAPTER 11

Master Ruth Hill was surprised to see Bacchus on her doorstep, but she accepted him into her home with the utmost generosity. He was upfront about the situation revolving around his arrival, at least as far as the Duke of Kent was concerned. He'd been concerned that Master Hill might sympathize with the duke—after all, Bacchus was a healthy, strong individual who certainly had some vitality to spare—but she did not. She had a room ready for him within the hour, and he poured as much gratitude upon her as the woman could take without drowning in it.

Bacchus rode with Master Hill to the London Physical Atheneum the following morning, though they parted ways almost immediately upon entering the large stone fortress. Bacchus had not written ahead; the assembly was not meeting today, as far as he knew. But he didn't need the assembly so much as he needed Master Phillips, and Master Hill had told Bacchus exactly where the man's office was located.

The guards posted throughout the atheneum didn't stop him, though a couple looked ready to try. The golden pin affixed to his lapel—a token of his mastership—halted their steps. He traipsed through hallways and up stairs to Master Phillips's office. It was strange to think that, only a month ago, such a trek would have wearied him. If not for Elsie, it still would.

He couldn't stop the smug smile that came to his lips as he took a winding set of stairs to the third floor, slipping by a maid carrying an empty bucket and mop. *Perfect*, was he? Granted, he hadn't meant to bring the woman to tears, but Elsie was so attached to this bizarre concept that she was worthless, tears seemed inevitable. He felt fairly confident that he had begun to prove her wrong about that. And he'd happily show her again and again, as many times as she needed the reminder.

Indeed, as Bacchus approached the door at the end of the corridor, he found himself very much looking forward to his nuptials. But for now, he had to put thoughts of Elsie aside and deal with the matter at hand.

He knocked loudly on the heavy wooden door, hard enough for it to shudder on its hinges.

After several seconds, an annoyed voice said, "Come."

Bacchus shouldered open the door and stepped inside. Master Phillips's office was just like the rest of the atheneum, built of ancient stone, but hickory wood had been laid over the floor. A single window let in sunlight from the outside, while large glass baubles in each corner of the ceiling glowed with enchanted light to brighten the space. Master Phillips's large desk sat atop an Indian rug, and a large tapestry depicting running horses occupied the wall behind him.

The spellmaker did not appear pleased to see him. Setting down his quill from a letter he'd been drafting, Master Phillips tugged his sleeves down and leaned back in his chair. "Mr. Kelsey. No, it's Master now, isn't it? You are aware I take meetings only by appointment."

Pulling on the dwindling politeness within him, Bacchus nodded. "I hoped you would forgive the intrusion."

"Intrusion indeed." He folded his arms. "Whatever have you disturbed me for?"

They would skip the empty pleasantries, then. Good. Bacchus didn't know if he had enough serenity to ask after the man's health and family. He noted there were no chairs in the room other than the one Master Phillips occupied. Either he didn't take meetings in his office often, or he insisted his guests stand. Fortunately, Bacchus preferred standing. He liked having the height advantage, not that he would have lost it upon sitting.

"I have decided to join the atheneum as a free agent," he said, clasping his hands behind his back. As it was, he was technically still registered as a student, something that barred him from doing aspector work for pay in England.

Master Phillips raised an eyebrow. "There is a formal way to go about this."

"I was never one for ceremony."

He pushed his half-finished letter aside. "You don't merely walk in and declare yourself part of the London Physical Atheneum, Master Kelsey. You must have a sponsor, for instance—"

"Master Hill is my sponsor," Bacchus slipped in. "And I've acquired the appropriate paperwork as well. In truth, all I lack is approval of the head."

Master Phillips considered this for a moment, his mouth sour. He picked up his pen, tracing circles on his desk with its uninked end. "I thought you'd sailed back to that island you hail from. What was it again?"

Bacchus's shoulders tightened. "Barbados."

"Right, right. I think it might be better if you returned to your holdings, Master Kelsey. I'm sure Barbados is in dire need of spellmakers."

The comment grated down to his bones. He wondered if Master Phillips would be so bold if Bacchus *had* called a meeting of the assembly. Then again, others of the assembly might have agreed with Master Phillips, which would have made Bacchus's path forward more difficult.

"My intention is to stay in England," he said, tone even. Some travel back and forth to Barbados would be necessary, but Master Phillips needn't know that.

Irritation twitched along the sides of Master Phillips's eyes. He seemed to be a man who was not accustomed to being told no. "And why ever would you do that?"

"Because I'm marrying an Englishwoman." He leaned his weight to one side. "A spellbreaker, actually."

Master Phillips smirked. "Is that so? You managed to coerce someone into matrimony? Congratulations are in store, then. But I'll not be accepting your request at this time."

Bacchus glowered. "Or at any time, I dare say."

"Now we're getting somewhere." He straightened in his seat. "I'm not fond of you, Master Kelsey."

"We hardly know each other," Bacchus interjected.

Master Phillips merely shrugged. "I'm not fond of what you represent. An . . . otherness, so to speak. Master Hill is enough of a pain in my side. I needn't have a second. Do you understand?"

Bacchus's stomach tightened, but he nodded. He had been preparing for this conversation since his meeting with the magistrate, and even more so since last night. "I do. But I think you will approve it. Especially if you insist on these games."

He looked incredulous. "Are you threatening me, Master Kelsey? You might best me in size, but my magic is far superior."

"I have no intention of harming your person," he clarified. "But I recently came across quite the revelation. You knew my father, yes?"

Master Phillips eyed him. "I vaguely recall the man."

"And I suppose you vaguely recall performing a siphoning spell on his son to preserve the welfare of the Duke of Kent?"

Master Phillips's forehead creased. "You're twisting the wrong arm. Such a spell is perfectly legal with parental consent. You were underage."

"Ah, but you must also recall that my father has been deceased for some time." Bacchus took a single step closer to the desk. "And therefore you've no witness to say he consented."

The man's brow lowered. "You forget the Duke of Kent."

"*You* forget that I am as a son to him, and he will not speak out against me. Especially considering that the siphoning spell has since been removed."

His eye twitched again. Bacchus needn't tell the man that the duke had found a new pawn to suck life from, likely a commoner boy looking to make extra coin for his family, not that Bacchus had ever seen a farthing for his own unwilling contributions. The duke was old; he wouldn't last forever, with or without magic to aid him.

Bacchus closed the distance between himself and the desk, placed both his palms on the wood, and leaned forward. "There are no laws that would forbid you from denying my enrollment in the atheneum based on my ethnicity or nationality, Master Phillips. But there are also no laws to keep me from involving you in the court system for illegally bespelling a minor. I believe the jailtime for such an offense is significant, and even if you're not convicted, I can't imagine what it would do to your reputation."

Master Phillips looked like a dog protecting his bone. "So you do intend to threaten me."

"I don't intend, Master Phillips." Bacchus enunciated every word. "I am."

～⌾～

Bacchus waited at the carriage for Master Ruth Hill later that afternoon, softening and hardening a rock in his hand to pass the time, occasionally molding it into a tree or a fish, though his artistic skill was somewhat lacking. When she came out, she asked, "How did it go?"

He smiled. "Quite well, actually. I think we may have misjudged Master Phillips—he is far more reasonable a man than I had expected."

Master Hill did not hide her disbelief. "Really? You'll have to tell me about it on the way."

And Bacchus did, though only the slivers of truth regarding Elsie he kept safely to himself.

∽

Bacchus hunched over a monstrous desk in Master Hill's study late that night, scrawling letters across paper with rich black ink. His cramping fingers were making his handwriting sloppy, but he'd rather get these letters finished while they were on the forefront of his mind than leave them until morning. That, and he wanted to be out of Master Hill's way as much as possible. She had told him she had no use for her study at midnight. Granted, it was now an hour past.

The letters were destined for Barbados, some for his steward and others for his land managers, dictating what he wanted to see done with his house and his holdings, as well as asking for updates on his finances. He liked being current, and he hadn't been since his initial arrival in London. Fortunately, thanks to his loss at the auction house, he still had the savings he'd intended for the master ambulation spell, and those alone would see him and Elsie comfortable for some time, even if his holdings flooded and Master Phillips could not be swayed. The letter he penned now was meant for his housekeeper. He didn't know when, exactly, he'd be visiting again, but he wanted to make sure everything was adequate for his new wife. He chuckled to himself, imagining the frenzy the woman would go into upon reading *that*.

A soft knock sounded on the study door. "Come," Bacchus said, setting aside his pen and flexing his hand. He set the letter down on the finished paperwork for his atheneum registration.

Rainer, one of Bacchus's friends and servants from Barbados, stepped in, and the poor lighting—only two candles—made him blend with the shadows. He noticed the paperwork and asked, "Do you want me to make sure that gets posted tomorrow?"

Bacchus nodded. "Thank you, but you should be in bed."

Rainer smiled. "Never have gotten used to the time change."

Over their heads, a woman gasped. During the day, Bacchus might not have heard it. But with the house quiet as it was—

Something shattered against the floor.

Bacchus stood, knocking his chair back. "Get help."

Rainer dashed into the hallway. Bacchus followed on his heels, but turned the opposite way, bursting up the stairs to the bedrooms. Wasn't Master Hill's suite over the study? He hadn't been in the house long enough to be sure.

Dim light came from under her door—a single lamp. She hadn't turned in yet, either. Bacchus grabbed the handle and shoved, but the door was locked. Ignoring decorum, Bacchus utilized his master spell and converted the brass handle into gas, which, in turn, combusted half the door and sent a sour tang into the air. Splinters shot into Bacchus's arm, but he ignored them as he shoved his way inside.

Large bed, still made, sheer curtains flapping over an open window, a lamp set on the vanity.

And Master Hill collapsed on the floor, her nightgown stained red.

"Ruth!" Bacchus shouted, rushing to her. She was still alive. All aspectors turned into opuses upon their death, and she hadn't yet made the transformation. He dropped to his knees beside her. "Ruth!"

And then a wire came around his neck and pulled taut.

His air cut off instantly, and the strength of his assailant hauled him back. Bacchus's hands leapt up to the wire, but he couldn't get a grip on it. Spots danced in his vision. Reaching back, he found and clasped his assailant's wrists, then heaved forward, throwing the blasted man over his shoulder. The man slammed into the floor, narrowly missing Master Hill. Bacchus gasped as the wire pulled free. He blinked stars from his sight.

The man, darkly dressed, with a full face mask pulled over his head, rolled to his feet. A dagger was ready at his hip—the cause of Master Hill's injury, no doubt. The only part of him exposed was his hands.

Bacchus found his feet, but not before the black-clad man rushed for him so swiftly he blurred. A speed spell, then. Such spells, when used on living things, were not transferable.

He barely had time to register the attacker as a physical aspector before they collided, the man's fist striking him like a cannonball. They tumbled onto the cream carpet, Bacchus's air rushing out of him. The man pulled out his bloodied dagger and aimed for Bacchus's chest.

Bacchus caught his forearm, the point of the dagger hovering only an inch from its target. A drop of Master Hill's blood slid over the point and dropped onto his cravat.

The attacker pushed down on the dagger with both hands. He was strong, but not as strong as Bacchus.

Bacchus's other hand flew up, catching the man's wrist, and he rolled until he had the dagger pinned to the floor, whereupon he bound it with a fuse spell. When the man tried to pull it up, the dagger remained stuck to the carpet.

Bacchus bucked him off, but the assailant wasn't stupid. He left the dagger and danced back, stepping on Master Hill's outstretched arm. The air in front of him shimmered, and although Bacchus could not see the rune, he recognized it as a density alteration spell. He pushed through it, his movement slowed by half. As he cast a spell to lighten the air, the black-clad man grabbed a post of the bed and, with two quick state-changing spells, pulled a three-foot length of it free, while the rest liquefied and splashed against the floor, steaming.

The air thinned, and Bacchus charged.

The wooden pole gleamed as it hardened into something as deadly as steel in the attacker's hand. He raised it to strike—not Bacchus, but Master Hill.

Bacchus leapt and grabbed the pole before it made contact, and the force behind it radiated up his arm. He gritted his teeth and wrestled with the man. Tried to liquefy the pole, but the blasted spellmaker kept hardening it, canceling out his spell.

So Bacchus changed tactics and made it radiate heat instead.

The man cursed—the first Bacchus had heard his voice, although he couldn't place it—and dropped the scalding wood. It threatened to light the carpet on fire, but Bacchus couldn't take his attention away from the aspector. He didn't dare try to summon static and create lightning for risk of hurting Master Hill.

But *this* man didn't care about Master Hill's well-being. The air crackled.

Bacchus reeled back and punched the spellmaker in the face. The man stumbled, but as Bacchus moved to swing again, his arm slowed, the air suddenly too dense to carry his momentum.

An unexpected gust spell collided with him, whisking him off his feet and across the room until his back slammed into the half-demolished door. It cracked under his weight, and he fell to the floor in a burst of splinters. His head spun, and by the time he reoriented himself, the assailant stood over him, armed with a nine-inch splinter shaped like a stake. The wood gleamed with a hardening spell.

The air crackled. Lightning sparked across Bacchus's vision. He waited for a fiery burn that never came. Blinking his eyes clear, he saw two things at once: the attacker's clothes smoking and Ruth Hill falling from her propped elbow, her hand outstretched. The spell she'd used to save him had clearly zapped her remaining strength.

The man groaned and dropped his weapon. He cast another thickening spell to the air, so strong it became hard to breathe. In the few seconds it bought him, the assailant leapt for the window and disappeared between the curtains, fleeing.

Bacchus reverted the air density to normal and bolted after him, stopping at the edge of the balcony. He thought he saw movement down below—the aspector could have easily slowed his fall with more density spells—but Master Hill was gravely injured. Bacchus couldn't risk leaving her side.

Rushing back into the room, he grabbed an afghan from her bed and raced to press the thick cloth against her torso, where at *least* one stab wound bloomed.

Perhaps sensing safety, one of Master Hill's servants peeked into the room.

"Get a doctor!" Bacchus barked.

"H-He's on his way." The maid's round eyes took in Master Hill's supine form.

"Call for a surgeon," Bacchus said, trying to remain calm. The muscles in his arms quivered, and his heart pounded like that of an overworked horse. "She needs a surgeon."

"I-I will, but the doctor, he's a temporal aspector, sir. He should be able to slow it down."

"But not stop it. Get a surgeon."

The servant nodded and fled down the hall.

Master Hill moaned under the pressure on her torso.

"Hold on, Ruth," Bacchus murmured, refusing to let up. "Hold on a little longer."

CHAPTER 12

Thus far, Ogden had received two articles through the spirit line from the United States: one from the *Boston Herald* and another from the *New York Times*.

Elsie sat with him in his sitting room, looking over the information under the guise that he was helping her with her wedding finances. Emmeline remained innocent of the situation they were in, and they intended to keep it that way. Like with the British articles, Elsie had found the lines she wanted via their spelling, only this time, the articles were predominantly in American English, with the coded lines in British English.

The first, The Intrigue of Bespelling Ravens in the Spiritual Alignment, had the line *It is critical to recognise the need for organising ravens, either in the United States or Britain itself.* It referenced spiritual aspecting just as the *Daily Telegraph* had, which was surely no coincidence.

The second article, titled A Letter to My Colleague, read, *Humour me and come; open a dialogue. We are but neighbours, are we not?*

Ogden had come to the same conclusion Elsie had. Merton was after this American man, who was a spiritual aspector, because he had a spell she wanted—a rare spell that was, so far, not in any of the spiritual opuses she had collected. He was hiding from her, and the articles were her attempt to bait him out. Ogden suspected she'd published more articles, possibly hundreds of them, although finding them might not be helpful.

"Merton is unlikely to show her hand more than this." Ogden set down his sketchbook, which was opened to the drawing of the American Elsie had described. "Whoever this man is, he understands her meaning."

"But this isn't her end goal." Elsie tapped the end of her pencil against the article on ravens. "Because she's taking more than just spiritual opuses. She's attacked aspectors from every alignment."

"To gain power, perhaps," he replied. "Or to weaken those who would oppose her."

"But oppose her in *what*?" Elsie asked, and not for the first time. She picked up the *Daily Telegraph* article and murmured, "What are you after, Merton?"

Could they track down the American to *ask*? Elsie doubted he would come after her again. Perhaps she could—

The sitting room door opened. Ogden grabbed his sketchbook and closed it. "Yes, Emmeline?"

"Visitor for you." She opened the door wider, and Bacchus strode in.

Elsie leapt to her feet, but her heart soared higher than that, and a flush of remembrance rose to her cheeks. "Bacchus! We weren't expecting you." *I would have done something better with my hair—*

Then she noticed the angry red line around his neck and gasped.

"What happened?" In her haste to get to him, she nearly tripped over the short table in the center of the room. She moved to embrace him, but stopped short under the gazes of Ogden and Emmeline.

Instead she clutched his forearms, and he cupped her elbows. "Bacchus, you look like you haven't slept."

"I did on the way over." His lilt was caught somewhere between feigned British and natural Bajan.

Ogden gathered up the articles and set them aside. "Please, come sit."

"Thank you." Bacchus offered a weak smile to Elsie and sat on the couch; Elsie resumed her earlier seat. Before she could ask more questions, Bacchus said, "Master Hill was assaulted last night."

"What?" Elsie blurted at the same time Ogden said, "Good God."

"She's alive," he added. "In serious condition, but the doctors believe she will recover. She was transferred to a hospital in the city late last night after a temporal aspector slowed her bleeding."

Elsie pressed a hand to her chest. "That's . . . terrible. Was she shot?"

"Stabbed."

Elsie blanched and reached for Bacchus's hand. "You fought him, didn't you? The attacker."

Ogden turned to the door. "Emmeline, would you make us some tea?"

The maid hesitated, obviously wanting to hear the conversation, but she curtsied and left.

Bacchus's nod was severe. "Briefly. But this was no Abel Nash. He was a physical aspector. A master one."

Ogden cursed. "She's found another pawn."

"My thoughts precisely," Bacchus agreed. "It was a man of average build, perhaps a little taller. He wore black entirely, even on his face. I had no means of recognizing him."

Elsie said, "We could get a list of registered spellmakers in London and weed it down from there—"

"Who is to say he's registered?" Ogden asked. "I wasn't."

"She never used you to kill spellmakers directly," Elsie whispered.

Ogden frowned. "Not that I can remember, at least."

Elsie reached for him as well, squeezing his hand before shifting her attention to Bacchus. "Where else are you hurt?"

"It's nothing serious. Only bruises."

Elsie sighed, pulling both her hands back to herself. "I want this to end. I want this to be over."

"Soon enough it will be, one way or another." Ogden picked up the stack of articles and handed them to Bacchus. "We should catch you up on our research. We've deciphered Merton's code, though we've found only five articles under Elsie's name." He went on to explain everything they knew, which, unfortunately, did not take long.

"I see." Bacchus flipped through the papers. "This is good. The information, I mean."

Elsie's eyes dropped to the line on his neck. "Are you sure you're all right?"

Lowering the papers, Bacchus gave her a soft smile. "I am. In truth, it is fortunate I was there. I don't think Merton, or whoever this attacker was, expected a second aspector to be in residence. He must have come upon her suddenly to avoid retaliation. She'd been stabbed three times . . ."

Elsie considered that. Bacchus had likely saved Master Hill's life. That made one more opus that Merton didn't have, and surely the attacker wouldn't risk attacking a patient in a public hospital to finish the job. Not where there were so many witnesses . . .

Emmeline returned, and the conversation went silent under her watch. She set a silver tray on the table to Bacchus's left and poured three cups, filling Ogden's only half full with tea, then adding cream to bring the liquid up to the top. "Master Kelsey, how do you like your tea?"

A knock sounded downstairs.

"Oh." Emmeline set down the cream. "I'll answer that."

"Thank you," Ogden said.

Emmeline scurried from the room, wiping her hands on her apron as she went.

A moment passed before Bacchus said, "The vicar is available July 16."

Elsie had forgotten the date they had discussed at the engagement dinner. "Oh. But . . . is Kent the right place?" She initially hadn't wanted the ceremony in Brookley. The whole town might expect to be invited, and if she didn't invite them, they might invite themselves. The last thing she wanted was the Wright sisters tittering over Bacchus.

But with the recent break from the Scotts . . .

His eyes turned downcast for a moment. "I also inquired of Mr. Harrison."

Elsie nodded. Mr. Harrison was the vicar for Brookley. Nice enough man. And really, moving the ceremony to Brookley was the sensible thing to do, was it not? It would make things easier on Bacchus.

She rubbed her arms. "You've not heard from them."

Ogden, clearing his throat, stood from his chair and moved to the window, peering down at the street below. It wasn't the subtlest attempt to give them privacy, but Elsie appreciated it all the same.

"From the duchess, yes. I received her letter as I was leaving this morning." Bacchus reached into his jacket and pulled out the folded missive. He handed it to her.

She glanced at his face, ensuring he did in fact want her to read it, before unfurling the message. It was rather long, the penmanship even finer than Bacchus's. It was an apology interlaced with kind words regarding Bacchus . . . oh, and Elsie.

> *She really is a marvelous find. I only wish we could have resolved this in a better way. Please believe me when I say I had no idea, Bacchus. Isaiah didn't want me or the children to know. He didn't want us to worry. I'm not condoning his choice. Of course I want my husband to live a long life. Of course I want his health to be pristine.*

*But I fear the cost has been too high. You are already
greatly missed. All of our consciences are heavy over this,
Isaiah's especially.*

Elsie folded the letter in her lap. "How are you?" she murmured.

Bacchus stretched his arm over the back of the couch, running a
finger along one of the curls at the nape of Elsie's neck as he did so.
Shivers rained down her spine. "I believe her, of course." He sighed.
"It's too much to sort out right now. I've not yet replied to her. I don't
know if I will. So perhaps Kent . . ."

When he trailed off, Elsie supplied, "I really don't mind having it
in the church here. It's smaller. Fewer flowers, smaller bill."

His lip quirked. "I don't mind purchasing you flowers."

"And what am I to do with them after?" She sat up straighter.
"Who's even going to see them? Besides, all eyes should be on the bride
anyway."

He tugged that curl again. "They will be."

Her cheeks warmed. Goodness, July 16 was very close—only six-
teen days away. *To be married . . .*

Elsie's thoughts flew back to the conversation they'd had in the
carriage, which naturally made her think of that kiss, and the warmth
flooded into her ears. Bacchus must have noticed, because he chuckled
softly beside her, and it took all of Elsie's willpower not to swat him.

Emmeline returned, poking her head in. "Someone for you, Elsie.
I don't know who he is. He wouldn't tell me his name."

Elsie's breath caught. "He's not in uniform, is he?"

But Emmeline shook her head. "Normal-looking bloke if you
ask me."

Elsie exchanged a glance with Ogden. It couldn't be the *American*,
could it? Surely they wouldn't be so lucky. Or unlucky, depending on
his approach.

Standing, Elsie smoothed her dress and hurried to the door. "I'm getting a little tired of surprise visitors," she said flippantly, though her stomach was in knots. Perhaps Miss Prescott had sent an aspector to her home? Elsie couldn't recall any appointments, but she'd been so flustered as of late, she might have forgotten.

Ogden and Bacchus followed Elsie as she wound her way down the stairs, through the kitchen and hall, into the studio. Emmeline hadn't exaggerated—the man waiting just beside the counter was a normal-looking bloke, indeed. He appeared to be a couple of years Elsie's senior, and he wrung a cap in his hands. He was as well dressed as a working man could be, in all shades of brown, though his jacket was olive. He had a mop of wavy hair atop his head. He looked up when Elsie entered, and there was something oddly familiar about his blue eyes, but Elsie couldn't place what. She was sure she'd never met the fellow before.

"Elsie . . . that is, you're Elsie Camden," the man said immediately.

Elsie hesitated, but nodded. "I am, but I'm not the artist here." Ogden and Bacchus came in, and she pointed to the former. "He is."

"Oh, uh . . ." He laughed awkwardly. "Not here about art. It's just. Well." He put his cap on, rubbed his hands together, then took his cap off again. "Well, this might sound a little strange."

I assure you it's already strange, Elsie thought with apprehension, glancing sidelong to Bacchus.

"But, uh, I saw your wedding announcement in the paper." His eyes moved between Bacchus and Ogden before returning to her. "And, well, if I could ask you a personal question . . ."

Elsie frowned. "I'm not sure I should agree."

"Please, Miss Camden."

Emmeline met her eyes, and she looked so hopeful that Elsie consented with a nod.

He wrung that hat like it was a chicken's neck. "It's just that . . . Do you know your parents, Miss Camden?"

Her stomach tightened. "That *is* a personal question. And an odd one at that."

"I know. It's just . . ." He finally had mercy on the cap and set it on the counter. He took one step forward, no more. "It's just that, you see, my parents . . . they were real poor, you know? Had a hard time keeping us. Left me with a family in Reading." A soft chuckle passed his lips, but Elsie's stomach tightened further. "And it's just . . . I had a sister named Elsie. Haven't seen her since I was eight. And you . . . you're the right age. Haven't been able to find an Elsie Camden until I saw the announcement last week, you see."

Elsie's hand moved up to her mouth. It couldn't be. It *couldn't* be.

"Lad," Ogden started gently, "what did you say your name was?"

"Reggie," he answered, now wringing the hem of his coat. "That is, Reginald. Reginald Camden."

And just like that, Elsie knew why his eyes looked familiar. Because she'd seen them every day in her mirror.

They were *her* eyes.

Tears blurred her vision. In a weak whisper, she said, "D-Do you know where they left her?"

Reggie shook his head. "I don't. Somewhere near Reading. A small town. We lost her first, although I'm not sure why. I didn't know they planned it for all of us. Ma and Pa . . . they never explained it to me. I didn't understand until I was older."

A sore lump pressed into Elsie's throat. How could he know that? How could he know that, unless . . .

"You're my brother," she breathed, and a sob escaped her lips.

The man smiled, his own eyes watering. "Yeah, Elsie. I'm pretty sure I am."

CHAPTER 13

"You really don't remember?"

They all sat at the dining room table, Ogden at its head, Reginald—
Reggie—in the chair across from Elsie. Bacchus sat beside her. Emmeline
took up the other end of the table, silent and fascinated. Decorum
meant one of them ought to be serving tea, but who could focus on tea
at a time such as this?

Elsie was soaring and hoped to never come back down. She shook
her head in wonder. "I knew I had a mother and a father, and I remembered a brother. I *knew* I remembered a brother!"

Reggie smiled. "That you did. There were four of us in all. Maybe
you remember John. He was older than me. Found him, too, about six
years ago."

Elsie's heart flipped. "You did? Where—"

Reggie stayed her question with a hand. "Don't get too excited,
Elsie." His face fell. "I'm real sorry, but he's not . . . not around anymore.
Died of measles a few winters back."

Elsie felt heavy in her chair. Beneath the table, Bacchus's hand found her knee. The weight of the simple touch anchored her.

"I see. Where is he buried?"

Reggie was manhandling his cap again. It was a wonder it still held its shape. "Little town north of London a ways called Green Knoll. I could take you there if you'd like."

"I would. I would like that. But . . . you said there were four of us?"

Reggie snapped his fingers. "A sister, younger than you. Her name was Alice, I'm sure of it. But I haven't been able to find her. Don't know if our parents kept her or left her somewhere, too. Could be anywhere."

A sister. Elsie had a sister out there somewhere. A sister who probably didn't remember her last name was Camden, which would make her that much harder to locate. Pressing her palms against the table, Elsie said, "I just don't understand why they would do that. Why they would abandon their own children."

"As I said, we were poor," Reggie offered softly, while the others listened in silence. "Real poor. I remember being hungry a lot. We traveled quite a bit, our pa always looking for work, though I don't remember what he did. We lived off the hospitality of strangers. Which is where they got the idea, I guess."

Elsie nodded, solemn. "Did you go to the workhouse, then?"

Reggie looked abashed. "Uh . . . no, I didn't. See, they left me with a family that couldn't take me on. But there was an older couple in the same village, the Turnkeys, who weren't able to have a child of their own. They took me in. Made me work for every stitch I wore, but they gave me a place to stay."

Elsie nodded. "That sounds nice."

"I suppose it's better than a workhouse. But it looks to have worked out for you." He glanced around the room, then to Ogden, Emmeline, and finally Bacchus. To the last, he said, "You probably get this a lot, but where are you from?"

"Barbados," Bacchus answered patiently.

Reggie whistled. "That's far. I would have guessed Turkey."

"Reggie, that is, Mr. Camden"—Emmeline sounded suddenly eager—"what is it you do? Are you a farmer?"

Reggie laughed. "Could say I used to be, but nah, I repair letterpresses. Sell the parts, too. Just up in London." He pointed north as though they didn't know where the sprawling city was located.

"Sounds like good work," Ogden chimed in.

Reggie nodded. "I like it well enough. Don't own my own shop like you do, but the bloke I work with is a good man and fair."

Wondering if there was more family she had yet to meet, Elsie asked, "Are you married?"

To her surprise, Reggie colored slightly and glanced to Emmeline. "Ah, no. Not yet. Can't say I haven't worked on it."

Emmeline blurted, "Elsie is a spellbreaker!"

It was still strange to her, having that information public.

Her brother—*her brother!*—looked at her with wide eyes. "Are you really?"

"In training," she said, and Bacchus squeezed her knee. It would have been utterly inappropriate were they not engaged, and Elsie had to continually remind herself she was engaged.

For what had to be the thousandth time, she found herself thinking of what Bacchus had said in the carriage before kissing her. *They merely sped up the process.* Had he planned to court her in earnest, then, and not sail for Barbados right away? Elsie wasn't sure how else to interpret such a confession, so she clung to the hopeful answer.

First Bacchus, and now Reggie . . . maybe she *had* been wrong. Maybe it was simply misfortune—and imbeciles—that had carved her life into what it was today. Perhaps she wasn't as terrible as she thought.

Perhaps.

Reggie whistled again, and it made Elsie smile. "Ain't that something, Elsie. You can do a lot being a spellbreaker. They make good coin. And yer a spellmaker." He looked to Bacchus as he said it. Then, sheepish again, followed up with, "After I saw Elsie's name in the paper, I looked you up, too. Master physical aspector. Bang up the elephant, you two have it made."

Elsie flushed. "I suppose we do. And you'll stay for lunch, won't you?"

Her brother grinned. "Took the whole day off, and I'm not one to say no to a free meal." He glanced at Emmeline again. "If you don't mind me sticking around."

"Of course not!" Remembering herself, Elsie waited for Ogden's nod of approval and exhaled when she got it. This was *his* house, after all. "And, Bacchus, you'll stay as well." She bravely set her hand atop his.

Bacchus nodded. "After, I would like to return to London to see after Master Hill."

"Of course." Reality, nearly forgotten, crashed down on her. They still had to find Merton, to stop her from whatever she was attempting to do.

But for now, she could ignore those pressing matters and focus on her brother, if only for one day. She had a brother! She still couldn't wrap her mind around it. "Now, tell me about where you grew up. About this couple who took you in."

Reggie leaned back in the chair, getting comfortable. "Well, we lived right by a stream that had the name of St. Patrick, but we all called it Pattie's Water, which maybe was a bit sacrilegious . . ."

Elsie and Reggie got on so swimmingly, like true siblings, she didn't want him to leave. Ever. But they were adults, and they both had jobs and lives, and so leave he did, with the promise they'd see each other again soon. All in all, it was one of the most pleasant days of Elsie's life.

The following day, however, was far less cheery.

A clash of thunder echoed within the dressmaker's shop, reverberating through the walls as it clamored its way into the earth. Elsie flinched at the sound, and the seamstress nearly stuck her with a pin.

Emmeline stood at the window, admiring a white dove pin, occasionally peering into the murky gray beyond the fat and fast raindrops pelting the glass. It had been raining all day, since before Elsie woke. Raining with a vengeance. But it did provide her with rare privacy for her pursuit of bridal necessities. Brookley was quiet all around, and therefore there was no one at the dressmaker's to witness her being measured, or to ask her questions about Bacchus, or to gossip about her personal life.

She had intended to get married in one of the dresses she already owned, just as any frugal woman would. Perhaps splurge on some extra lace and ribbon to elevate her church gown. Bacchus had inquired about it yesterday after lunch, and she'd told him as much.

While I *think that's perfectly suitable,* he'd said carefully, *if we'd been engaged as long as the magistrate thinks, there would be plenty of time to order a dress. It might be better to have one.*

He'd then handed Elsie a banknote. It was now in the dressmaker's possession, but the guilt of it weighed on her, nonetheless.

She looked at herself in the mirror. The seamstress had her measurements on file and was fitting some muslin around her waist. A wedding gown. A simple wedding gown, given the time constraints. Elsie truly had thought she'd never wear one, after Alfred. She'd had *everything* planned with him. The gown, the flowers, the guest list, the honeymoon. She'd thought it all out, giggled about the details with Emmeline late at night. Sketched an assortment of hats in one of Ogden's books. So when Alfred had cast her aside like an old flour sack, she'd felt completely and resolutely foolish. She'd hated everything about weddings. Everything white. Everything romantic.

She brushed her thumb over the ring on her finger and sighed.

It can't happen twice, Elsie, she chided herself.

Yet part of her was sure this unexpected betrothal with Bacchus still wouldn't pan out. That the church would burn down, or Merton would interfere, or he'd simply change his mind.

If that happened . . . She touched her bodice, reassuring herself the paper was still tucked within it.

Think about happy things. Her brother would be at her wedding. Her *brother*! And despite her worries, she smiled at her reflection.

Returning from the window, Emmeline practically sang, "You'll need some white shoes and ribbon, kid gloves, and silk stockings. Oh! And a silk handkerchief."

"It's just a small ceremony," Elsie insisted, and the dressmaker waved to indicate she was done. Elsie carefully stepped out of the muslin and off the stool she'd been perched on.

"I'll start on this right away." The dressmaker set the skirt on a chair. "Without the embellishments, I should be able to get it ready in time."

Feeling childish, Elsie said, "I suppose we could do some embroidery . . . or lace on the sleeves." She peered toward the dove pin in the window.

The woman smiled. "I thought so. Come back in a few days and we'll see where we are."

Emmeline clapped. "So good, Elsie! You'll make such a lovely bride."

She'd said so before, back when she'd thought Elsie would marry Alfred, but it wouldn't do to point it out. Instead, Elsie grabbed their umbrella. "Shall we brave the winds and spare our shoes, or make a run for it and suffer the mud?"

Thunder groaned again.

Emmeline swallowed. "I say we run like we're mad."

They gripped the umbrella together and pushed open the door. The wind nearly wrenched the umbrella from their hands as they made a half-blind dash for the stonemasonry, soaking their stockings with mud. Emmeline squealed, which made Elsie laugh, and they were barely capable of breathing by the time they reached home. At least the empty streets meant no witnesses to their tomfoolery.

Elsie wiped rain from her eyes, pulled off her gloves, and unpinned her hat, which was wet despite the umbrella. "At least we got some good exercise."

"I expect so."

Both Elsie and Emmeline jumped at the new voice. None other than Miss Irene Prescott stood in the door leading to the kitchen.

"M-Miss Prescott!" Elsie paused, shoes making a muddy puddle on the floor. "I didn't think you'd be coming! What with the storm and all."

Indeed, she'd hoped for a reprieve.

"I am always punctual," she said with good humor. "That's why I employ my own vehicle. And I've been waiting only a few minutes. Come along, I've brought something exciting today."

I doubt it. Elsie exchanged an uncertain glance with Emmeline. Should she change? But the woman had already been waiting . . .

"I'll make tea," Emmeline said, doing her best to clean off her shoes.

Sighing, Elsie slid hers off, cut through the kitchen, and entered the dining room in her wet, stockinged feet. Miss Prescott sat at the table with a shriveled plant, a rabbit's foot, and a cage—

Elsie started, hand flying to her breast. "My goodness, where did you get *that*?"

A long-tailed rat sat in the cage, turning about, checking and rechecking the wires for a way out.

Miss Prescott grinned. "We're going to study a few spiritual spells today! Rational we'll really have to do at the atheneum, but I managed to get my hands on these bespelled items."

Elsie sat down, hearing a pitch coming from all three items. She'd seen the first spell recently—the sad-looking flower was cursed, just as the Duke of Kent's farmland had been. The rabbit's foot carried a charm of luck, and the rat would have some sort of communication spell on it, just like the post dogs did.

Setting her chin in her hands, Elsie halfheartedly said, "Do tell."

And Miss Prescott did, in her usual long-winded way. Elsie didn't know how a person could find so much to say about spellbreaking, but Miss Prescott always managed it. Perhaps, were Elsie truly a novice, she would need the explanations. Maybe they would have helped in her younger years. Everything she knew had been self-taught, guided by bits of advice written on silvery paper and stamped with a raven's foot. Had those early messages come directly from Ogden's mind, or from Merton's?

Ogden walked through just then, using a cloth to wipe paint off his fingers. Elsie straightened in her chair—it was good to see him working again. He'd been so beside himself since the docks.

Ogden dropped an opened telegram envelope on the table. It was crinkled, as though it had been rained on and left to dry. "From Kelsey. Says Master Hill is recuperating and expected to recover."

Elsie unfolded the note and checked for herself. He must have meant the message for everyone, or he was away from his enchanted pencil. "That's good news."

"Oh dear, Master Hill." Miss Prescott set down the rabbit's foot. "What a relief that she pulled through."

"Indeed," Ogden agreed. "I'll leave you two to it."

He slipped away as Emmeline came in with a tea tray.

And then Elsie . . . sensed something.

She paused, catching her breath. A physical spell . . . and yet she didn't see the glimmer of the rune anywhere. She couldn't explain how she felt it, exactly, but it had happened before, with the siphoning runes on Bacchus and the duke. It was as if . . . something within her had sniffed it out. But this one was farther away, like something caught on the wind.

Ogden was capable of physical spells, of course, but none that were this strong.

"Miss Camden?" Miss Prescott asked.

Elsie shook herself. "Thank you, Emmeline. I'll pour it."

Emmeline nodded and stepped into the kitchen.

Picking up a teacup, Elsie turned it over, half expecting to spy a rune glimmering against its bottom. But there was nothing. Nothing on the tea tray, or the table. Just an inkling that she couldn't place.

"One moment." Elsie stood. "I think I heard the door."

"I'll help myself." Miss Prescott reached for the teapot.

Elsie slipped away, down the hall and into the studio. A canvas was set up in the corner, base paints streaking across it, drying. No spells on them.

Thunder rolled. A ways off, a horse whinnied.

Uncomfortable, Elsie returned to the kitchen, unsure whether the sensation was actually getting stronger or her own mind was magnifying it. She barely heard Miss Prescott ask after her welfare.

Hadn't Bacchus said a physical aspector had attacked Ruth Hill?

Without excusing herself, Elsie hurried up the stairs, grabbing the handrail to propel her steps faster. She noted with surprise that her feet were silent on the last three steps. They made no sound at all. Nothing did.

Her heart surged into her throat. She shouted Ogden's name, but her voice was sucked away by a spell. Running, Elsie burst into his room just as his bed slid across the floor of its own volition, pinning him to the opposite wall.

And there, just inside the window, stood a gray-clad figure, dressed to match the storm but dry as a wood fire, his hand outstretched.

Elsie screamed soundlessly.

This wasn't a staged attack arranged with Nash. This was real.

And what person could Merton want dead more than the master rational aspector who knew her secrets?

Grabbing the closest thing to her—a tin pitcher—Elsie threw it across the room as hard as she could. The instant she released it, she saw a glimmer in the air a few feet in front of her, about nose height:

the sound-dampening spell. At the moment it benefited her as much as it did the assailant, for the man had neither heard nor seen her. The pitcher flew true, colliding with the side of his skull.

Clutching his head, the assailant whirled around, his face, save for his eyes, covered. Beyond him, Elsie could see Ogden was yelling something at her, but she could no more hear him than she could anything else.

She bolted forward and grabbed the spell, pulling apart its fibers—

"—do it!" Ogden bellowed as the spell came apart. An invisible fist slammed into Elsie and threw her back. Had she not been even with the doorway, she would have struck the wall, but her feet touched down where the hall started and she merely stumbled down onto her backside, bruising her tailbone.

"Ogden!" Elsie screamed. *"Do something!"*

"There's a barrier!" he shouted back, then groaned.

Leaping to her feet, Elsie rushed inside. The bed was pushing hard against Ogden's thighs, pinning him to the wall. The intruder came toward him with a knife.

Elsie's progress slowed like she was walking through pudding. The spell hung between her and the aspector. She wormed toward the rune, movements painfully sluggish, and finally reached it and yanked it apart, tumbling forward as gravity reoriented itself.

The assailant raised his knife. Elsie had no weapon, no spells, save the one tucked securely in her corset.

But she would not let any harm come to Ogden. So she ran at the gray-clad man and jumped on his back, wrapping both arms around his neck.

The man danced back, trying to fling her off. His spell must have been one of concentration, for the moment Elsie leapt on him, Ogden shoved the bed back and jumped up and over it, bolting across the room to help her.

"Remember, there might be a compulsion spell on him!" Elsie shouted, letting go of the man when the knife point sailed for her arm. Ogden grabbed the intruder's wrist and twisted it, but the other man formed a fist with his free hand and collided it with Ogden's teeth, forcing him to release his hold. In the same movement, the curtains came alive over Elsie's head. The aspector grabbed the edge of them and elongated them, stretching them beyond their woven limits, enchanting the fibers to grow.

That was when Elsie noticed the gun tucked into the man's waist. A thorough way to murder someone, especially if they couldn't hear his approach.

She leapt for it. The man twisted, flinging the former curtain toward Ogden. Elsie missed the firearm and fell into his legs instead. She grabbed his knees. They both toppled over. Elsie grappled for the gun, and this time she got her fingers around the handle and tossed it across the room. Then, snaking around the man's legs, she felt for a spell. Tried to listen for the hum of the eighteen-point spiritual spell that had been Ogden's parasite for so long. Did she detect it on his torso, or were her ears ringing?

The man threw back an elbow, hitting Elsie square in the breast before throwing her off. Quick to his feet, he spun away as Ogden ripped the curtain rod from the wall.

Wincing, Elsie barely had a moment to stand before the floor came up around her feet, holding her in place. Then the attacker held out his hand, and Elsie recognized the shape and glimmer of the rune before the magic even started.

Wind.

Elsie lifted her hands just as the rune burst toward her in a hurricane-sized torrent, ripping paintings off the walls and books from the shelves.

It stopped the moment it met Elsie, her fingers tearing the magic apart.

And the aspector's eyes . . . they weren't surprised at all. They were . . . nothing. Like they weren't his.

He was Merton's puppet, for sure.

He sent out the gust again, even stronger than before. Oddly enough, the spell holding Elsie to the floor helped her keep her footing as she broke the rune, just as she had with Nash's lightning. The aspector didn't let up, but continued casting, again and again and again, a continuous loop of torrents. He threw pens and papers around the bedroom, but the projectiles only rustled Elsie's hair and clothing as she untied each and every one. If anything, it got easier—the rune never changed.

A shot rang out, opening up a wide gash in the gray-clad man's arm before embedding itself in the wall. Ogden. Ogden had reached the pistol.

The wind stopped instantly, and the man ran back for the window, *liquefying* it as he passed through, the glass no different from the pouring rain save for how it steamed against its frame.

Elsie bolted to the window, looking into the town. She couldn't see him—

But she did spy someone in her peripheral vision, and when she turned toward the doorway, Miss Irene Prescott stood there, eyes wide, her mouth a perfect O.

Elsie froze. How long had she been standing there?

Behind Miss Prescott, Emmeline ran for the stairs.

"Em, stop!" Elsie shouted. "Don't call the police!"

The maid paused, unsure. They *couldn't* call the police, not again. Certainly Ogden would be able to clear the way, but the more people involved, the trickier it became. They couldn't risk any more suspicion on either of them.

"I couldn't get in," Ogden murmured, picking himself off the floor. "He had a barrier on his mind, another's rational spell. I couldn't read his thoughts, learn who he was, nothing."

"Ogden," Elsie hissed, and he turned to see their witnesses.

Miss Prescott licked her lips. "You're not a novice, are you?"

Elsie opened her mouth, closed it. Rain pattered the window ledge, cooling the melted glass into twisted, reaching fingers.

"I can explain. That is . . ." She glanced to Ogden. "It's not what it looks like."

Miss Prescott shook her head, but seemingly more in wonder than disdain. "I've never seen anything like it. Please, Miss Camden. You must *show* me."

Ogden tapped his head. Elsie felt a rational rune moving toward her, and because it was from Ogden, she didn't stop it. Inside her mind, his voice said, *<I can erase her memory.>*

Elsie responded. *<Then do it . . . after I see if she's an ally.>*

Because judging by the expression on the older spellbreaker's face, Miss Prescott might be more *fascinated* than anything else.

Ogden moved toward the window, searching the ground below.

Rubbing coldness from her hands, Elsie said, "All right. Downstairs. Both of you."

Overhead, thunder groaned.

CHAPTER 14

The problem was, Elsie couldn't explain *how* she knew a thing about spellbreaking without revealing how she'd learned, which involved the Cowls. And she couldn't explain the Cowls without mentioning the crimes they—and she—had committed.

Knowing Ogden could wipe Emmeline's and Miss Prescott's memories at the drop of a hat gave her courage. Emmeline was so loyal and kind Elsie didn't actually worry that she'd act against them in any way. But Miss Prescott was a wild card. Elsie still understood her only as well as one might understand a painting viewed from across a room.

And so, Elsie chose her words very carefully. She began with the workhouse, where she discovered her abilities for the first time. She discussed the Cowls, but left off the victims' names—it seemed more tasteful to do so, less *real*. By all means, if Miss Prescott really wanted to know, all she need do was read the papers. She ended with what had happened upstairs. She used Lily Merton's name, feeling no need to protect a murderer, but didn't specify Bacchus's role in anything.

"And I believe strongly that he is the same person who attacked Master Hill." Each syllable was pronounced. Elsie clasped her clammy hands together atop the table. Ogden twisted his head back and forth like a bird, ensuring no sudden customer would interrupt or overhear them.

Emmeline, at the table's head, was wide-eyed and pale as a porcelain doll. Miss Prescott had been entirely animated during the story, as though it were a wholly fictional tale reenacted with hand puppets. Now, with the explanation over, a stiff silence fell over the room. It was so hushed Elsie would have heard an ant crawl across the floor. That is, it was quiet until Miss Prescott started tapping her fingers against the tabletop, slowly at first, then quicker and quicker. She worked her mouth, tightening it, relaxing it, pursing it. Her eyes crinkled, then her forehead. She seemed to be having a rather intense conversation with herself.

Emmeline worried her lip and stared at the ceiling, perhaps trying to work out a response.

And so Miss Prescott took the honor for herself. "That is utterly marvelous." She shook her head. "It's genius, really . . . not that I support murder or crime in any fashion. But when you think about it objectively . . ." She cleared her throat. "But you must tell the authorities! Then Master Merton will be out of the way—"

"Miss Prescott," Elsie interrupted.

"You really should call me Irene, after all that."

Elsie paused, considering. This was going strangely . . . well. "You're not under a spell, too, are you?"

The fellow spellbreaker laughed. "No. I'll let you check if you'd like."

Elsie considered it for a moment. "No, thank you. But the point is that we *cannot* tell the authorities without condemning both Ogden and myself. We surely wouldn't live through it."

Irene blanched. "I suppose that's right. But you might be granted clemency."

Ogden said, "*Might* is not a guarantee."

Frowning, Irene's fingers tapped with yet more fervor. "Yes. The laws of aspecting are very strict. I don't think it's a risk I would take."

"And . . . you two are just fine with this?" Elsie blurted, gaze shifting from Irene to Emmeline.

Emmeline peeped, "I-I am. It makes sense of some things, really. I think . . . I won't tell, I promise."

Elsie offered Emmeline a faint smile. She wholeheartedly believed the younger woman. Besides, if Ogden were turned in, Emmeline would be out a job.

"I suppose you could just take it right out of me, hm?" Irene glanced at Ogden. "That's why you risked telling me at all."

Ogden paused, then nodded.

Irene quieted a moment, save for her drumming fingers. "Miss Camden—Elsie, if I may—is one thing, but an unregistered rational aspector with master spells . . . that is a little harder to stomach. There are reasons rational magic is so strictly regulated."

Ogden said nothing.

"He wouldn't harm anyone," Elsie pressed. "That is, he wouldn't do it unless someone forced him to, and Merton no longer has any control over him."

Irene considered this a long moment, taking her time as she always did. The kitchen was beginning to grow uncomfortable by the time she asked, "Might I see the articles?"

Ogden slipped from the room to retrieve his sketchbook. Meanwhile, Elsie explained, "We just have copies of them, not the actual articles themselves."

"Good enough."

Ogden returned, and Elsie felt a slight pulse in the air as a spell moved out from him. Irene took the sketchbook, then stiffened.

"You needed merely to ask," she murmured.

Ogden didn't look at all chastised. He studied her a moment before saying, "She's genuine. I think she's trustworthy." He sounded surprised. The pulse happened a second time, directed toward Emmeline, who didn't react to it whatsoever. After several seconds, Ogden confirmed, "Emmeline is as well."

"I told you so," Emmeline said, then jumped in her chair. "Did you just magic me?"

Elsie wrung her hands together, trying to think of a way Irene could tamper with Ogden's spell. But even if the woman possessed an opus page like Elsie did, she wouldn't be able to use it without pulling it out and saying the word *excitant*. Yet Elsie struggled to believe that someone could simply be *all right* with what they'd confessed, or that the woman she'd seen as an obstacle had become an ally so easily. Even Bacchus had needed to be persuaded to keep her secret when he'd first learned she was an illegal spellbreaker.

Could it be that God, the universe, or fate was finally showing them a kindness?

It felt too good to be true, but she would simply have to trust Ogden. And, somehow, trust Irene as well.

Irene looked over the articles. "Interesting. And it's spelled exactly this way in the original?" She turned the page.

"Letter for letter." Elsie searched her face for clues, but she *did* seem genuine.

Irene flipped to the last article, the one from the United States, and turned back to the beginning, reading them through a second time. She turned one page too many at the end, landing on the half-finished sketch of Lily Merton. Continuing on, she came face-to-face with the rendering of the American.

"The one who stopped me in Juniper Down," Elsie said.

Irene bit her lip and tilted the sketchbook closer to her face. She scrutinized him, tilting her head one way, then another. "I know him."

Elsie's heart leapt into her mouth. Ogden must have had a similar reaction, for he suddenly bumped the table. He said, "You do?" at the same time Elsie exclaimed, "Truly?"

Irene nodded, eyes still on the page. She chewed on the inside of her cheek as she contemplated. "Let's see . . . Boston . . . Raven. Something Raven . . ."

Ogden stiffened, his pale eyes shooting to Elsie's. "The articles. One of them mentioned ravens."

Numb, Elsie recited the title of the article from the *Boston Herald*: The Intrigue of Bespelling Ravens in the Spiritual Alignment. "And the *Manchester Guardian* mentioned black birds."

Ogden looked weak in the knees, and he pulled out a chair and sat down. "She called him by name."

Swallowing, Elsie worked to recall what else had been in that article. She'd read it so many times it wasn't difficult. "'It is critical to recognize the need for organizing ravens, either in the United States or Britain itself.' That means she wants to meet him and she doesn't care where."

"Quinn!" Irene shouted, dropping Elsie's heart back into her chest. "Quinn Raven. I'm sure that was it.

"I knew of him during my time in America—I lived there for a short while," she explained. "He vanished suddenly about eleven years ago. I remember because he left nearly everything behind, outside of emptying his bank account. It was quite extraordinary. No one knew where he went. They still don't, I believe.

"I was working under Maurice Barre at the time—he was the head of accounting at the Boston Spiritual Atheneum. He was in charge of sorting through Raven's estate. In fact . . . yes, I believe that's where I first met Master Merton."

"She was in the States?" Emmeline leaned over the table with utmost interest.

"Mr. Barre brought me along in case anything was, well, rigged or baited," Irene explained. "Aspectors, especially master ones, tend to use

149

grave security measures to protect themselves and their property. The place was in utter disarray." She set the sketchbook down. "His notes were scattered, many of them burnt or half so. We believe he was in a deep study of some theory or another before he vanished. He was a very secretive fellow. Eccentric and reclusive."

Ogden gripped the edge of the table. "Is there anything else you remember?"

Irene pondered a moment while Elsie's pulse pounded through her entire body. She snapped her fingers. "Drops. There was a large amount of drops in the steward's records that were never found. It would have been surprising if he'd left something so valuable behind. Mr. Barre was quite put out about it."

Elsie considered this. Spellmakers tended to purchase drops—the quartz-based "currency" needed to absorb spells—as they needed them, because they were painfully expensive and every spell required a different amount. The more powerful the spell, the more drops necessary to absorb it.

"Perhaps he used them," Ogden murmured. When the others looked at him, he continued, "We've deduced he has a *spell* Merton wants. Think on it. A spiritual aspector, working on some great theory, vanished, only to be hunted down by *another* spiritual aspector. His theory likely pertained to a master spell. A spell that would require a large amount of drops. Many do."

Elsie wondered how Ogden obtained the drops for his spells. Likely not by legal means, but she thought it best not to ask in front of Irene. Her willingness to overlook their illegal activities might go only so far.

"Perhaps," Irene considered. "But the spells of aspection have been solidified for centuries. One does not merely make up a new one."

"It may not be made-up," Ogden countered. "It might merely have been lost." Opuses saved aspection from the throes of time, but there was no evidence that all the spells mankind knew now equaled all the spells mankind had known a millennia ago.

"Master Merton knows." Elsie took a deep breath and let it out slowly. "She knows what he found, spell or theory or whatever it may be. And she wants it."

Silence again filled the dining room until Ogden asked, "Anything else?"

Irene shook her head. "I don't recall. I'm sorry. I didn't know him personally. I might not have remembered him at all, but the mystery revolving around his disappearance was . . . noteworthy."

Elsie clasped her hands together. This was so much more information than they'd had before. They had a *name*! He was no longer "the American," but Master Quinn Raven. They also had a motivation: Merton wanted something he had, likely a spiritual spell. And they had a new partner, who in the matter of an hour had already proven herself incredibly useful.

Closing her eyes, Elsie transported back to Juniper Down, remembering the man's stance, his scowl, the gun in his hands. *I know what you want, but I'll kill you before I utter the words,* he'd said.

Utter the words. It *had* to be a spell. But what spell had he discovered that Merton wanted so badly? So badly that she'd devolved into a thief and a murderer?

Irene broke Elsie's train of thought. "Will you tell me how you did it? How you stopped the gust spell before it had a chance to start?"

Elsie opened her eyes. "I . . . I don't know how I did it. I mean, I can try? We can simulate it later, with Bacchus." Her focus shifted to Ogden. "We need to reach out to Raven. Let him know he has allies to stand with him against Merton."

"How?" Emmeline asked.

"The same way Merton did." Ogden folded his arms. "Through the newspapers."

Elsie nodded. "Irene said Master Raven vanished eleven years ago. We can't wait another eleven years."

Ogden interjected, "He knows that's how she's trying to reach him. He also knows your name. If we publish under your name, he'll likely take notice. He might even still be in Europe."

Elsie considered this, then perked up. "Reggie said he repairs letterpresses. He must have connections to newspapers all over London."

Emmeline grinned. "What a wonderful idea! He could help us!"

"Who is this person?" Irene asked.

"My brother." Those words still felt so singular passing her lips. "We'll invite him here and tell him—it will be easier if we don't have to tiptoe around him. Ogden, you can ensure he's trustworthy. I'll start writing up articles to publish. We might need to be more direct than Merton was if we want to do this quickly." She'd write to Bacchus straightaway and let him know. He needed to be kept in the loop, and Elsie didn't mind the excuse to contact him.

Closing the sketchbook, Irene said, "Will Master Merton notice?"

Elsie shook her head. "I don't know. Maybe not, if she's in hiding. But we'll have to risk it."

"I'll send a telegram." Emmeline hopped up from her chair. Reggie had left his contact information before leaving yesterday.

"Good. And I'll write to Bacchus. Perhaps he can fund us if the newspapers insist we pay." She winced at the idea of asking him for more money. She still felt guilty about the dress.

"I can fund it," Irene said. "And I'll help you write the articles, too."

Elsie nearly crumbled with relief. Irene smiled, and for the first time, Elsie saw the bright possibility of friendship with her tutor. "That would be wonderful."

Irene nodded resolutely. "And I'll keep checking off on your lessons. None will be the wiser."

Elsie could have hugged the woman. "I am in your debt."

"As am I," Ogden added. "Let's get started."

Reggie's eyes widened as Elsie greeted him in the studio with a stack of twelve handwritten articles, all brief and stylized like the ones she and Ogden had found in the British papers. "You weren't having a laugh about this, were you?" Reggie said. Each article had a clue buried in the headline, and each one mentioned ravens. Reggie glimpsed at the first.

"Don't worry about what they say," Elsie insisted. Like Merton's articles, they were vague unto the point of meaninglessness, the messages hidden within. "Just get them published. Front page if possible."

Beside her, Irene handed Reggie an envelope. "In case you need to purchase the space."

"As soon as possible," Ogden pressed.

Reggie didn't know everything, not in the way Irene and Emmeline now did—they'd told him an aspector crook was at large and Quinn Raven might be able to help find her.

"Don't give them any reasoning if you don't have to," Elsie added.

"And be careful," Emmeline interjected.

Reggie managed a lopsided smile at the last request. "Makes me feel sort of like a vigilante. But a good one." He counted the individual papers. "I'll see what I can do. Couple might need to be in the same paper, but I can do different dates."

"Perfect." Elsie kissed him on the cheek. "It will be such a help to us. To me."

Reggie shrugged. "Not a problem. Anything for my sister."

Elsie beamed as brightly as if a gas lamp burned behind her smile. She saw Reggie back out to his mount—he'd ridden on horseback instead of taking a cab—and hurried back in to find Irene pinning her hat into her hair. She always had on a different hat. Perhaps when Elsie became fully certified, she'd have a plethora of hats of her own.

"With luck, they'll be in Monday's paper." Irene hung her umbrella over her arm, though yesterday's storm was long gone.

"With luck," Elsie repeated. They'd had plenty of it, hadn't they? She still struggled to believe they'd found such a friend in Irene, but

Ogden had declared her trustworthy. And Elsie so desperately wanted to believe it. "I'll repay you."

Irene waved her hand. "I might not be a spellmaker, but I've a good salary in my own right and no family to spend it on." There was a sad note at the end of the confession, but the spellbreaker merely smiled. "I'll check in with you on Tuesday."

"Perfect." Elsie saw her to the door, then went up to her room to rest. She heard the scratching of a pencil as she opened the door, and spied on her table the enchanted green pencil dancing as though held by a ghost. Hurrying over, she read the script pouring out onto the blank page she'd left beneath it, noting that the pencil was in need of sharpening. She and Bacchus had been corresponding for much of the day about the attack on Ogden and its aftermath, plus Master Hill's health. The tail end of their last conversation took up the top quarter of the paper.

His message from earlier caught her eye first: *It would not be a problem for me to stay there.*

Her reply: *Why, so he can have two opuses if he returns? Ogden is looking into it. I don't think he'll try again. Especially not with Irene here so frequently.*

Bacchus's script had turned dark, as though he'd pushed on the pencil too hard. *Assumptions like that are how villains get the upper hand.*

She skipped the material she'd already read and focused on the new words still writing themselves down: *Elsie,* Bacchus's fine script spelled, *I've been contacted by the duke. He wants to talk, but*—the pencil paused for a moment—*I'd prefer to have you with me. I do not believe the duke or anyone in his household intends me harm. Nor do I think there will be any nonsense with spells. But I've not yet sorted through my feelings regarding the revelation about the siphoning spell, and I believe your presence will help me remain steady.*

Elsie's heart softened like butter. *Help him remain steady.* Smiling, she reached for the pencil, but it moved again, and she stayed her hand.

He wishes to see me tonight. I do not expect you to rearrange your plans for this. I'm prepared to reschedule. I believe he will do as I wish; if the duchess's letters are to be believed, Isaiah feels guilty for the part he has played in this. I am happy to provide transport—

Elsie grabbed the pencil and wrenched it out of Bacchus's invisible hand. She felt the moment he let it go, and beneath his half-finished sentence, she wrote, *Of course I'll come, you lummox. You don't need to beg me. What more important thing could I possibly have to do?*

She set the pencil down and waited. A few seconds passed before it rose and tilted, nub pressing to the paper.

Lummox?

She chuckled. *It's a term of endearment.*

The pencil jerked in her hand—Bacchus had started writing before she could set it down. *Then you find me endearing.*

He'd underlined the word. Something about the smooth stroke brought heat to her face. Taking the pencil, she touched its tip to the paper, ready to scrawl out a snarky response, but something held her back. Pulse quickening, she found herself glancing up at what he'd written earlier: *Your presence will help me remain steady.*

She reflected on their conversation in the carriage, before Bacchus had kissed her. With her free hand, she tentatively touched her lips.

He cares for you, she carefully admitted, keeping the thought far from the paper. It was still hard to believe, hard to swallow, hard to *feel,* but she wanted to feel it. She'd spent her whole life wanting to be wanted. To be . . . loved.

Biting on the inside of her lower lip, building her courage, she wrote, *I do.* And set the pencil down.

Several seconds passed before the enchantment took hold of it again. *Perhaps I could see you sooner?*

Warmth bloomed in her breast. She wrote, *I would love a stroll in Hyde Park.*

His reply, *I can be there within an hour.*

It would take her an hour to get there herself. *I'll find a cab in Brookley.* Her hand shook a little on the letters, and she halfheartedly chided herself for letting her excitement get the better of her. She needed to talk to him about the newspapers—she'd been very round-about when writing to him before, unsure if someone else might read it—but she didn't want to ruin the mood by insinuating she merely wanted to talk shop.

Bacchus took the pencil from her grip and simply scrawled, *Thank you, Elsie.*

In her mind, Elsie replied, *I love you, Bacchus,* and it startled her hand from taking the pencil up again. Her pulse galloped; she pressed suddenly cool fingers to its rhythm. She stared at the green pencil, waiting for it to move—afraid that it would, terrified that it wouldn't. But the conversation would continue only if she wrote something, and she didn't dare pick up the pencil with that thought echoing so loudly within her skull.

She took a deep breath, then another, to calm herself before taking the paper and folding it carefully, stowing it away in her drawer for later reading. She replaced it with fresh parchment and gingerly lay the green pencil atop it. Antsy for distraction, she moved to the small mirror on her wall and tidied her hair, pinned on her hat, and readied her reticule before finding Ogden in the sitting room.

"I hope you don't mind," she started carefully—he had his sketch-book in hand and was staring at the sketch of a more youthful Lily Merton. "We don't have a lot of orders ready . . . Bacchus was hoping I could go to London to take care of some . . . affairs. Regarding the Duke of Kent." She'd mentioned the situation to Ogden last night after the attack.

He glanced up. "Of course. I should probably work on something, shouldn't I? Income is a fairly important matter."

Elsie smiled. "I can't imagine why you aren't jumping at the chance to finish the squire's likeness." She shrugged. "I don't mind the free time."

"Your purse might mind its lightness soon enough." He set down the sketchbook. "You'll return late?"

"I think so."

He nodded. "Take care."

Offering a wave, Elsie closed the door to a crack and forced herself not to skip down the stairs, opting for the back door and taking the shortcut into town. She went to the hotel, where she found a coach just dropping off a few of its passengers. She hailed it, confirmed it would stop at her destination, and hopped inside. The coach pulled away as soon as the horses were watered.

There were only two other passengers on the coach—a middle-aged woman and a young girl, who, through idle chatter as the coach pulled onto the main road, Elsie learned had just turned twelve. They exchanged small talk until the coach pulled off toward Welsbury, delivering her company to the post office there. Alone, Elsie sighed, leaned back, and closed her eyes, feeling the bumps of the road pass beneath the carriage wheels. After a moment, she leaned forward and opened her reticule, counting the notes in it. She'd spent a large percentage of her life savings on her trip to Juniper Down and Reading. The rest, save some change, had been returned to her account at the bank. She had just enough for this trip.

Ogden's earlier comment about income surfaced in her thoughts. Was it too early for her to take on spellbreaking assignments herself? Perhaps if Irene came with her . . . Of course, she'd be a married woman soon. *Her* finances would be taken care of, and Ogden would have one less mouth to feed until he hired her replacement. Still, Elsie itched to make her own way in the world. She adored and trusted Bacchus, but given that she had a lucrative gift, she didn't *need* to be dependent on him. Or she wouldn't need to once the bother with this "training" was finished. Then she could help him, Ogden, Reggie, Emmeline, and anyone else occupying space in her heart.

Her thoughts quickly turned to Bacchus. Soon she would be *Mrs. Kelsey*. It had a nice ring to it, so long as her first name was omitted. She should ask Reggie if she had a middle name! Perhaps it was her mother's given name. Did he remember that? He hadn't been able to find them, so perhaps not. Or maybe they had changed their names, or wandered so far that no one could find them. Who knew if they were still in Britain at all.

She frowned at the familiar ache that always accompanied thoughts of her parents, but she pushed it away. *Elsie Amanda Camden. Amanda Kelsey,* she tried. That sounded well. So did *Elsie Elizabeth*. Was that too many *E*'s for a name? *Elsie Mary.* Hmmm . . . no.

Perhaps Bacchus had a name he was fond of. Though he was just as likely to tell her *Elsie Kelsey* wasn't silly at all and she should keep it. Elsie rolled her eyes. *He would.*

Her gaze fell to the sapphire ring on her finger, and she tilted her hand, letting it catch a wink of sunlight coming through the window. It sparked patterns across the carriage wall, like a cluster of fairies.

Did Bacchus love her? She couldn't imagine it. She tried to picture the words coming from his lips, honest and earnest in his Bajan accent, but her mind refused to stitch the daydream together. She couldn't be the first to admit it. What if they went years without saying it, even after they married, and she finally mustered up the courage to tell him how she felt, only for him to look at her with pity and say something ridiculous, like *You're a good woman* or *I'm glad,* and Elsie was left feeling like a fool for the rest of her years, exposed like a half-healed wound, a stranger in her own house?

She thought of Alfred. He'd told her he loved her. Multiple times. But he'd never once meant it.

Elsie covered the ring with her other hand, snuffing its sparkles.

She dared to hope, but hoping hurt. It was only wise to keep it in check. To let no more than a thin trickle seep in until she found better footing.

But whatever Bacchus felt for her, whether it was affection and friendship or something more, *she* loved him. She knew it, and it hurt like she'd drunk too-hot tea that had scalded her throat. Like her heart was somehow too big and too small for her body. Like it pulsed his name, and anyone who listened would be able to hear it.

Sighing, Elsie glanced out the window just as a man on horseback rushed toward it, perpendicular to the road. A dark-brown cloak billowed behind him, and a dark mask covered his face.

Then he raised a pistol and fired.

Elsie screamed. The horses whinnied and jerked, and the carriage bucked, as though rolling over something large. It took a moment for Elsie to realize the rider had shot her driver. He must have fallen from his seat and . . . and . . . God help them, if the bullet hadn't killed him, the trampling would have.

It felt like Elsie's spirit had abandoned her body, leaving her skin and bones numb, like they were someone else's. She barely registered the highwayman whisking by her window to slow the horses, but she had enough sense to push herself to the other side of the carriage, feeling for a door handle. Of course there was only one door, and the highwayman, still mounted, was already wrenching it open.

Elsie gathered herself enough to throw her reticule at him. Part of her feared he was no simple thief, but she had to try. "Take it, please! Just leave me be!"

The highwayman's eyes—the only part of his face she could see—narrowed. And in that moment she knew for sure. She'd last seen those eyes in Ogden's bedroom. The glimmer of a spell caught her attention as the air froze around her, forbidding her to move.

Nausea turned sharp in her stomach. Her lungs weakened, and she strained to breathe.

The man's gloved hand picked up the reticule, weighed it, and tossed it onto the bench. "She wants *you*," he said simply, his voice low and gruff. He closed his eyes for a moment, the lids creasing, as though he was in pain. It reminded her of the way Ogden had acted on the docks, fighting his own spell. Then the man's glare hardened, and briefly Elsie was sure she heard the faint pitch of a spiritual spell, like the magic was flaring, forcing him back under its thumb.

The man leveled his gun at her. "Can't spellbreak a bullet, Elsie Camden. Come quietly."

Elsie needn't agree; the stiffened air around her shifted, carrying her to the door. "Please, I can help you. I can break the spell she has on you—"

His other hand whipped out and pressed a foul-smelling rag to her face, and the world around her went dark.

CHAPTER 15

The gray-cast sky finally gave in to a miserable, misty sort of rain. The kind that caught on the breeze and got everything wet. It was cold rain, despite the summer. English rain was one of the things that made Bacchus miss home.

He had no jacket and no umbrella. Instead, he cast a spell on the air around him, curving the rain away from him. Scanning the park, he spied a few people running for the shelter of trees. A barouche passed by, its driver quickening the steps of its horses.

Bacchus had been here two hours, with no sign or word from Elsie.

After the carriage passed, he crossed the narrow path and approached a chestnut tree. Leaning against the trunk, he pulled out his bespelled blue pencil and a piece of parchment, which he laid across his raised knee. If he leaned it against the tree, the pencil on Elsie's side might end up scrawling across her wall or furniture instead of the paper she was supposed to leave beneath it.

Are you well? he wrote simply. Then he waited.

And waited.

The magic on the linked pencil didn't take—no grip touched its bespelled wood. Bacchus was a patient man, so he remained in that stance for several moments longer, the rain increasing in power, then decreasing until it was little more than fog. Still no response. She usually didn't take this long to respond.

And so Bacchus strode out of Hyde Park, feeling uneasy. His mind circled around some irrational fears, some personal doubts regarding Elsie's affections for him, but he cast them aside. He would not feed them. No use in torturing himself over what was likely a misunderstanding.

He'd driven himself here in Master Hill's cabriolet, thinking perhaps Elsie would enjoy a ride before they headed to Seven Oaks, where he was due shortly. But after Bacchus cared for the horse and pulled out onto the main road, he drove to the post office rather than Kent.

"I'd like to send a telegram," he said upon opening the door. The young man behind the counter, no older than fifteen, gave him a look that was half fear and half awe; Bacchus was a head and a half taller than he and darker than the heavy freckles bespattering the lad's nose. No matter. Bacchus was used to being received in such a manner.

Fortunately, the boy gave him no problems and handed him a pad of paper and a pencil. "Write it out here. The cost is—"

"I don't care." Bacchus scratched out, *Is Elsie well? She was meant to meet me at Hyde Park. Kelsey.* Below it, he wrote the address of the stonemasonry shop.

"Send it to the Brookley post office." He slid the paper to the boy and dropped his coin pouch beside it. "To anyone present in the household."

The lad nervously smiled and took the requisite coin and the letter before disappearing into the back room where the telegraph was kept. Bacchus took his purse back and stood at the door of the post office, peering down the road in the direction of Hyde Park, as though he might catch Elsie running up it at any moment. He thought to return there to wait for her, but with luck someone at the stonemasonry shop would send a swift reply.

The postal employee returned a few minutes later, but after acknowledging Bacchus with a nervous nod, he continued to sort through a stack of letters. Bacchus waited at the door for another quarter hour before sitting in one of two chairs crammed into the small foyer.

Leaning back, he folded his arms and continued to watch the road through the window. It felt later than it was, thanks to the rain. He watched a drop on the pane grow heavier as others joined it, until it could no longer cling to the glass and wound its way down the window.

Another quarter hour passed before he heard the telltale clicking of the telegraph. He stood, and the lad rushed into the back and out of sight. Bacchus massaged his knuckles anxiously. When the employee returned, he said, "I didn't write it down. Thought you'd just want to hear it."

Bacchus nodded.

"*'E left over three hours ago. Not seen?'* Sorry, the cost is per word, so sometimes people aren't very specific—"

Bacchus didn't wait for the boy to finish. He swung open the post office door and rushed into the rain, not bothering to enchant it away.

⌒

Bacchus burst into the stonemasonry shop just over an hour later, his hair dripping from the ride. Emmeline squeaked and dropped the broom she was carrying, then turned toward him with a hand over her heart.

"Oh, Master Kelsey!" she exclaimed. "You scared me . . ." She watched him shut the door behind him. "Elsie isn't with you?"

The question strummed a chord of fear within him. "You sent the telegram?"

She nodded. "She left"—she glanced to the clock on the wall—"coming on five hours ago, now."

Bacchus pulled the tie from his hair and shook it out. "Did she say where she was going?"

"She told Ogden she was doing something with the Duke of Kent." Emmeline's voice grew quieter.

Mr. Ogden strode in just then, his expression tight. "You haven't seen her."

"No. We were to meet at Hyde Park. I waited two hours. I wrote her before sending the telegram."

"Oh," Emmeline chimed in, "with that magic pencil?" She picked up the broom and hurried out of the room, taking it with her. A moment later, she returned. "She didn't take it with her. Your message is on her bedside table."

Bacchus worked his hands. "Did she seem upset? Did she take anything with her as though planning for a longer trip?"

Emmeline and Mr. Ogden exchanged a glance before the latter answered him. "No, just her reticule."

That chord of fear began to sing, spreading cold prickles across Bacchus's skin. He'd seen nothing of her on his hurried journey to Brookley.

Mr. Ogden said, "I'll send Emmeline to check locally. This isn't like her. And with Merton . . ."

He didn't finish the thought, only left to grab his coat.

⁓

The first thing Elsie observed was the stone beneath her—the coldness of it against her cheek and its hardness beneath her shoulder and hip. The second thing she noticed was the darkness, save for a single enchanted light in the middle of a low stone ceiling. The third was the awful taste in the back of her mouth, followed by the dryness of her tongue and rawness of her sinuses.

She pushed herself up, head pounding. For a brief moment, she thought she was still in prison and everything else had been an oddly detailed dream. But as she blinked and gained her bearings, swallowing to moisten her throat, she realized her surroundings were completely new to her.

It looked like a cellar, all dark stone walls, about fifteen feet across and ten feet wide. When she stood on shaky legs, the ceiling pressed against the top of her head. No windows.

"Hello?" she asked, and the stone swallowed her voice. She peered at the small, bright light in the center of the room. The ground beneath it was packed dirt, but closer to the walls it turned to stone. In the back of her thoughts, she noted she probably wouldn't be able to dig herself out.

Which was when she realized she was trapped.

"Hello?" Panic grazed her voice. She walked to one corner, her legs weak, then to another, where she found a small loaf of bread and a bottle of water. She stared at them, memories from her incarceration pushing to the front of her mind. Then she crossed the room again, looking about more carefully this time, and found a cellar door in the ceiling.

Elsie pushed on it, gingerly at first and then as hard as she could. She heard heavy chains rattle from the other side. She slammed her fists into it once, twice, three times. It still wouldn't budge.

"Help!" she screamed, cupping her hands around her mouth. "Someone, anyone!"

Was it night already? No light seeped around the edges of the door. She screamed at the door again and again.

"Help!"

"I'm trapped! Someone help me!"

"Please, anyone!"

She screamed until her throat grew raw and her voice choked. Coughing, she crossed the small space to the bottle of water, sniffing it before raising the cool liquid to her lips. Before she took a single sip, the faintest buzz prickled her ears. She paused, straining to hear it. It was barely there . . . incredibly well hidden. So much so that she had to turn the bottle over in her hands, ear pressed to the glass, to find the spiritual spell attached to it.

She didn't recognize it. It was so tightly wound, so small . . . What was it for? Something to make her feel full, or maybe hungry? Something to calm her?

She pressed her hand to the spell and suddenly felt fatigued despite her forced rest. Her eyes drooped . . .

Wrenching her hand away, Elsie ground her teeth. *Really, Merton? A spell against a spellbreaker?* But it had almost worked. She considered taking the spell off, but perhaps it would be better if her captors thought she hadn't noticed it. After all, she hadn't noticed Ogden's spell for years. Let them think they had the upper hand.

Tentative, Elsie took a sip of water, but the liquid itself wasn't enchanted, only the bottle—right at the base of the neck where she was most likely to grab it. Gripping the bottle's bottom instead, she drank half of its contents.

"It's no use, so you might as well save your strength."

Elsie whirled around at the voice, nearly dropping the bottle. A ghost stood near the light—no, not a ghost, but a projection. A fuzzy projection, lacking detail and color, which meant the spiritual aspector casting the spell was some distance away.

Even so, Elsie would have recognized this particular aspector anywhere.

"Merton," she spat, setting the bottle down and standing, pressing her crown into the stone overhead. If Merton was fuzzy, that likely meant Elsie was fuzzy to her, too. So Merton probably couldn't see clearly enough to know whether Elsie had touched her sleeping spell or whether it was working. Elsie would have to talk carefully to avoid giving herself away.

"Are we dropping titles now?" the apparition asked. "I worked very hard for that *master*, I'll have you know."

"Yes, all the way from the workhouse." That gave the projection pause. Good. "What do you want?" Elsie grasped her anger, preferring it infinitely to fear, then tried to make herself sound tired. "Where am I?"

"I'm giving you another chance, dear," Merton replied. "I really would love to have your company. I've grown so fond of you."

Elsie shook her head, disbelieving. "You say you're *fond* of me, and yet you've had me incarcerated, drugged, *abducted*, and now caged in some . . . some *cellar*?"

The faded ghost shrugged. "I didn't think you'd listen if I came to you in person." The words were a little garbled, but Elsie understood them.

She rubbed a chill from her arms. Merton must have noticed, because she said, "There should be a blanket in there. I don't want you catching cold. Why don't you rest? You must be exhausted."

Elsie choked back a scoff, then feigned a yawn. "Who is your puppet now? The physical aspector?"

The features on the blurred face shifted just enough for Elsie to detect a frown. "That's the problem with the powerful ones. They so like to fight back. Your artist did the same for the first few months, you know. Until he finally gave in and cooperated." She sighed. "Although he didn't have the dexterity necessary to accomplish all I needed. I never was fond of that ruffian you left all over the Duke of Kent's dining room floor."

Stomach acid burned in Elsie's gut. She referred to Nash, Ogden's "business partner" and the man who had carried out Merton's murders. "You talk about murder like it's a cup of tea."

"Oh hardly, my dear. But it is necessary. You'll understand soon enough."

Elsie paused, sensing an opening. "Couldn't you help me understand now? If you want me to come with you." She barely remembered to sound sleepy.

Another frown. "No, dear. I don't trust you just yet, and I've been planning too long to have it all upset now. But a few deaths are nothing compared to the lives I will save, I'll say that much."

Elsie wanted to goad her, and Quinn Raven's name danced on her tongue. But any advantage they currently had—and it didn't feel like they had much of one given she was once again a prisoner—would be demolished if Merton learned Elsie had met the very man Merton had been pursuing for years.

No. If Merton wanted Raven so badly, Elsie could not help her find him. And who knew what sort of methods Merton—or her puppets—might enact to get the information from her. Or from Bacchus, Ogden, Emmeline, or Irene.

So many are involved now, she realized. She had to keep them safe. Thank the Lord Reggie was still in the dark.

"Let me out," Elsie pleaded, clasping cold fingers against her breast. "I'll talk with you, face-to-face. I'm not armed."

The projection laughed. "Oh, I know."

It was then Elsie realized her reticule was gone. Her pockets were empty. Even her hat was gone, and her hair fell freely in uneven curls about her shoulders, every last hairpin stolen from it.

Panic seized her as she pressed her hands to her corset, but the slight rise of the opus spell gave her some relief. Relief that she still had the spell, however useless in this situation, and relief that the man who'd taken her hadn't undressed her. Then again, who would think an unsuspecting woman would hide anything beneath the boning of her underthings?

Straightening her spine, Elsie repeated, "Please."

"Not yet, dear Elsie," Merton said, familiar. Elsie wondered how much of her life Merton had witnessed through Ogden's eyes, if any. She didn't understand how the control spell worked, only how to untie it. "I'll keep you safe until I'm ready for you. You'll have ample time to consider my offer. It's not like you'll be giving anything up. A lousy job working at a stonemasonry shop? A family who left you behind? An unwanted marriage?"

Elsie did not feel the need to correct the woman. She merely scowled, hoping the expression came through their murky connection.

"You won't starve," the spiritual aspector promised. "With luck, it won't be long now."

Elsie's chest tightened. Won't be long? Until what? What did Merton plan to do? As close as they'd come to piecing the puzzle together, she still didn't know.

The ghost began to fade. Elsie had to keep her talking. "Which workhouse was it?" she blurted.

Merton paused.

"Which one did they take you to?" she reframed.

Several seconds passed. Elsie was sure Merton would refuse to answer, but she said, "Abingdon-on-Thames, of course."

Elsie stiffened. Same workhouse as herself.

"Is that how you found me?"

Merton sighed, but it sounded weary rather than exasperated. Until now, the woman had chosen her words carefully. But perhaps Elsie could convince her to talk more openly. If she managed to create the illusion of a bond between them, something Merton might want if she'd truly wished to adopt Elsie, she could use it to her advantage.

"I'm a spiritual aspector, of course. I have the ability to help those with less." She cupped her hands together. "I visited all the local workhouses, leaving blessings where I could. Where I was *allowed* to." She scoffed. "And of course I went back to Abingdon. I know what it's like, dear Elsie."

"I never saw you."

"If you did, you wouldn't remember. They rarely let me interact with the children. As for *finding* you"—she tilted her head—"you nearly found me. I was nearby when that fire lit. I came quickly to help. I asked questions. Your name came up."

Elsie bit her lip. She'd told two children about the rune. She'd always assumed they hadn't tattled on her. Then again, a spiritual aspector could elicit the truth from anyone with a spell.

"I saw myself in you." She spoke quietly. "Young and impoverished, no one to turn to, with untapped talents."

Elsie dared to reveal her hand—if Merton thought she could trust her, perhaps she'd release her. "Duchess Morris said you won sponsorship in a lottery."

Merton frowned—or at least Elsie thought she did. It was hard to tell, blurry as the projection was. "Yes, there was a selection for aspectors nearby. I walked nearly eight miles to get there. I had promise, but not as much as the postmaster's son." She scoffed again. "A boy who had more than anyone else in the village. Whose profession was guaranteed. I didn't even have a pair of shoes to wear."

Elsie held her breath, waiting for the story to unravel.

"The recruiter took me in, but I had to *beg* the sponsor to choose me, Elsie." Merton looked her squarely in the eyes. "He easily could have sponsored two, but such a thing was absurd to him. It was so obvious I was destitute, that I had nothing, but he made me beg for his help. For his money. Even then, he only relented because I agreed to siphon a portion of my pay to him after I reached my mastership. Of course I agreed. I would have agreed to nearly anything. I hadn't eaten all day. I was desperate."

A portion of her pay. Duchess Morris had said Merton had supported her sponsor in his later years. Had that support been forced?

"That's terrible." And it was. Elsie needn't pretend.

Merton nodded. "The rich are entitled, Elsie. They always will be. He was entitled, and his children were even more so. When he died, they took me to court to try to force me to continue paying the estate. So they could live off my earnings in addition to their inheritance."

Elsie's chin dropped.

Merton waved a blurry hand. "It didn't take. I could afford a good solicitor by then. But you must understand, Elsie. The problem is so much greater than what you've seen. We are at war. Not across country borders, but in our very streets. The lower classes must fight for everything. Food on their table, employment, right of way, their very dignity." Her voice was strained. "We even fight each other. If there's one pattern history teaches us, it's that the rich start the wars and force the poor to soldier them."

Elsie took a deep breath, then another, processing all of it. She didn't want to agree with Merton about anything, but there was no denying the cruelty of the class system. She'd experienced the pain it caused firsthand. It didn't surprise her that Merton saw it as war. Merton had grown up in war. And seeing it that way would help her to sanction violence. Murder.

"Once you marry that spellmaker, you'll become just like them. Complacent to others' struggles. It saddens me that I have to explain this to you," she added.

Mention of Bacchus made her stomach clench. Was that why he'd been one of Merton's targets? "No, I understand." She approached. "I do understand you. Please, come speak to me in person."

But the projection shook its head. "I know you do, dear, but not enough. Not yet. All you need is a little more time, hm?" The image began to fade.

Pulse racing, Elsie ran to her. "Merton, wait! Lily, listen to me—"

The projection puffed away like smoke, leaving Elsie alone once more.

Setting her jaw, Elsie moved to the far wall, running her hands along the stone, searching for anything—gaps, loose rocks, spells. She searched high and low, then scoured the next wall, finding a knit blanket tucked into the shadows beneath it. She ignored it. Investigated the third wall, then the fourth, and finally picked over the floor.

Nothing. *Nothing.*

So she returned to the locked basement door and screamed as loud as she could, deep into the night, until she tasted blood.

CHAPTER 16

It was late evening by the time Bacchus jerked back on the reins of Master Hill's horse, slowing the cabriolet on the main road to London. He and Mr. Ogden both were speckled with rain and mud thanks to their speed. The enchanted lights fastened to either side of the carriage swung wildly as the horse staggered to a stop—in the dark they spotted the shine of red police lights down a narrower road leading to Welsbury. Bacchus rode toward it, his own lights highlighting an obstruction in the road and the handful of people around it, two of whom wore blue police uniforms.

Two carriages, a growler in the middle of the road and a cabriolet pulled off to the side. The latter appeared to be occupied; two men, one in a driver's livery, lingered nearby, talking quietly. As his eyes adjusted, he noticed a third vehicle, a coach, several feet off the edge of the road. One of the policemen waved his hand and approached Bacchus, who slid from the cabriolet into the rain.

"Turn around or go around," the policeman said. "This is a crime sce—"

"Was there a woman in that coach?" Bacchus interrupted.

The policeman paused. "Are you missing someone?"

"Elsie Camden," Mr. Ogden interjected, pulling his coat closer. "She would have taken a coach to go into London hours ago and hasn't been seen."

The policeman pursed his lips. Wiped rain from his upper lip. "No woman here, only a dead driver."

A chill colder than the rain sank into Bacchus's bones. "Dead driver?"

He nodded. "Shot through the neck and trampled." He tilted his head back. Thanks to the storm, the night was especially dark, but Bacchus spied a blanket-covered mound near the growler.

He stepped forward only to have the policeman splay a hand on his chest and urge him back. "This is a crime scene."

"Is there any evidence of a passenger?" Bacchus pressed, impatience bubbling up. "A driver's log, a shoe—"

Mr. Ogden, without looking at Bacchus or the policeman, said, "A reticule."

The officer stiffened. Emmeline had mentioned a reticule, but judging by the policeman's reaction, Bacchus had to wonder if Mr. Ogden had searched his mind for clues. "There *is* a reticule," the officer said, hesitant. "We found one in the grass."

"With gray blossoms printed on it," Mr. Ogden guessed.

The officer set his jaw, then nodded.

Bacchus cursed loudly enough that the other witnesses broke from their conversation to gawk at him. Mr. Ogden said quietly, "I take it they're the ones who found the body and summoned the police?"

The policeman nodded. "Indeed."

Bacchus stepped forward, his sheer size causing the officer to back up. "That reticule belongs to Elsie Camden, my fiancée. Please. Let us take a look."

The man sighed and glanced to the other policeman on duty. "Wait here," he said, before returning to his partner.

Bacchus put a hand on Mr. Ogden's shoulder. "I don't care if you listen in, but wait for them to answer before you start twisting their minds. Let's do this legally."

Mr. Ogden didn't answer, merely stood there, a glowering stone of a man.

Several minutes passed before the first officer waved them forward. Bacchus rushed to the abandoned coach, taking one of the enchanted lights with him. It was empty. He searched for signs of struggle and found none. Any prints leading away had been washed out by the rain.

He felt sick enough to empty his stomach.

Mr. Ogden had retrieved the reticule from the officers and searched through it. "Nothing of use." He tucked it into his jacket.

Grabbing fistfuls of hair, Bacchus turned a slow circle, peering into the darkness for any sign of her, any clue, any*thing*. "Do you have any evidence of where the murderer might have gone?"

The second officer said, "Not yet. Perhaps there will be more in the daylight, but with this rain . . ." He shrugged. "We'll do what we can, but the weather will stall us."

Bacchus tried not to let their response throw him into a rage. It wouldn't benefit Elsie for him to lose his head now.

Quietly, Mr. Ogden murmured, "They don't know anything. None of them do." His voice was a hammer against a rusted nail.

Bacchus growled and turned to the officers. "I'm a master physical aspector. Is there anything I can do?"

The policemen glanced at each other. The first said, "Not unless you can stop the rain and make the sun come up, but even that will be of limited help."

Cursing again, Bacchus stepped off the road into the wild grass, searching with his enchanted light. He walked east, then south, coming around to the west, then north. Moved about in larger and larger circles, searching futilely for any sign of her.

Soaked through and shivering, he shouted her name into the night. No one answered.

⁖

Back at the stonemasonry shop, Bacchus's body was tense from crown to heel, like wet leather pulled taut over a frame, left to cure in the blistering sun. It was well past the hour of retiring, but he sat at the dining room table with Mr. Ogden and Miss Pratt, who had stoked the fire and the oven to warm them. Bacchus's jacket lay drying near the latter, but he hadn't changed out of his damp clothes—Mr. Ogden owned nothing that would fit him. He flexed and relaxed his fists atop the table, stopping only after he saw Miss Pratt staring at them, wide-eyed.

"No one has a motive but Merton." Bacchus tried not to let his voice growl. "You're sure you saw nothing notable about the man who attacked the house?"

Mr. Ogden shook his head, looking over his sketch work for the twentieth time. He'd drawn the attacker on multiple pages, from different angles, but the sketches were all alike, all next to useless. Each one depicted a man of slightly above-average build, clad in gray. Blue eyes. Physical aspector. That was all they knew.

All they knew.

Bacchus lifted a fist and slammed it on the table, making Miss Pratt jump. If they couldn't find Merton, and they couldn't find her goon, then they would never find Elsie.

Where was she right now? Tied up in some back room, or on her way across the Channel?

Bacchus's stomach shifted. He really was going to be sick.

Sucking in a deep breath through his nose, he said, "Tell me everything about that night. *Everything.*"

"He was guarded." Mr. Ogden leaned against the stove. "Mentally. I think Merton used one of her opus spells on him before sending him our way."

"Which means they've been in recent contact," Bacchus said.

Mr. Ogden nodded. "Or she simply directed him to where she left it. She's well hidden. I don't know if she'd risk . . . not that it matters. Point being that I couldn't fight him myself. My attempts bounced off him. I got close to breaking through once, but I lost my concentration."

Miss Pratt added, "It was so quiet at first. Then all of a sudden a loud ruckus came from upstairs. Elsie was shouting."

"Sound dampening," Mr. Ogden clarified. "Elsie broke it."

"I thought Mr. Ogden had fallen," the maid went on, "but . . . the thumping happened over and over again."

"He came in through the window." Mr. Ogden closed his eyes. "Slammed me back against the wall, then shot the bed at me, pinning me there. That's when Elsie came in and took down the dampener. Then"—he chuckled—"she jumped on him."

Bacchus shook his head. *She would.*

"I got free. The man drew a knife—"

"Wait." Bacchus straightened. "You said he threw you into a wall? With what? Wind?"

Mr. Ogden shook his head. "He simply flung his hand out, like he pushed me without touching me. Same with the bed."

Bacchus's breath hitched. His mind moved through every spell he knew, but nothing else fit. "Ambulation."

Mr. Ogden pushed off the stove. "Pardon?"

"An ambulation spell. The ability to move a physical object without touch. I had occasion to research it recently." He stood, needing to move, needing to expel the energy building in his limbs. "It's a very rare, very powerful *master* spell. Few people would have it."

Mr. Ogden looked hopeful. "And you know who does?"

"I know where to look," he said. "The London Physical Atheneum. No doubt someone on the assembly there has it, and they will know who else does. What time is it?"

"A-About half past two," Miss Pratt said. "None of the atheneums will be open."

Bacchus ground his teeth. "Then we'll knock on the doors of each assembly member, one by one."

"You know where they live?" Mr. Ogden seemed intrigued.

Bacchus rubbed his eyes. "I . . . have an idea on a few. Master Hill might have some of the locations in her study."

Mr. Ogden sighed. "By the time we find them, the atheneum will be open. Eight o'clock, is it not?"

Bacchus nodded. "It's worth a shot."

The rational aspector rubbed his eyes. "Perhaps it would be best for us to get a few hours of rest before heading into London. We can be at the Physical Atheneum's doors the moment they're unlocked."

Bacchus shook his head. "No. I'll not sleep while she's in danger."

"Whoever took her is likely resting, too." Mr. Ogden turned to Miss Pratt. "Would you get Elsie's bed ready? Master Kelsey will be staying here tonight."

Shaking his head, Bacchus snatched his damp coat from its place by the fire and pulled it on. "I'm going to London."

"And you'll be too weary to be of any use to anyone," the stonemason countered. "Rest only a few hours."

"I will not—"

"I can force you to, and I will." He stifled a yawn. "There is nothing we can do now. We'll leave the moment the clock strikes six."

Bacchus glowered. "You wouldn't dare."

Mr. Ogden met his glare. "I am a practitioner in the rational arts, Master Kelsey, however unlicensed. When a man is not being rational, I must force him to be."

Bacchus's jaw was so tight he feared he'd chip several teeth. Buttoning his coat, he stepped around Mr. Ogden and headed for the back door.

He had almost reached it when his mind suddenly felt fuzzy, his thoughts dripping like wet paint. He couldn't think straight . . . He was so tired . . .

"Blast you," he muttered, leaning hard against the wall, sliding to the floor.

And then, against his will, he slept.

$\sim$

Elsie leaned against the cold wall of the cellar. The chill had seeped into all of her, down to her bones, despite the fact that it was summer and she had a decent blanket. Even prison had been warmer than this. She didn't shiver, just felt frigid through every inch of skin and muscle. Even her teeth were cold.

Every now and then she got up and walked the perimeter of the space—at least she had the option to do that. In jail, she hadn't. Then again, she'd at least had some idea of what might happen in jail. Here, she hadn't a clue.

She'd woken to a new loaf of bread and some cheese. Their mere existence shocked her. *No one* had come in last night. She hadn't slept . . . not really. She'd tried to, after a time. But food and water couldn't just spell themselves into a room. She was sure of that. And surely no physical aspector could open a hole in the wall willy-nilly, slide the food through it, and seal it up again. Or at least it sounded like a terrible amount of effort.

She'd missed something. Something important.

Her tailbone was sore, but she didn't move. She was tired but not sleepy, weak but not hungry. She listened to her breathing, thinking half-formed thoughts that slid away before they had any real meaning.

That was, until one pressed on her.

She felt something.

A *sensation*, hard to describe, but she'd felt it before. In the kitchen, with Irene. And with Bacchus and the duke. Spellbreakers identified physical spells by sight, but she'd *sensed* all those spells without ever glimpsing the runes.

Closing her eyes, Elsie tried to focus on the sensation. It felt like an itch on bone, too deep to scratch. It wasn't terribly close—not in this room—and for some reason she got an earthy taste in the back of her mouth. A temporal spell? It made sense. There was probably a wine cellar, or a cellar used for actual food nearby. A temporal spell would keep it from wasting. It was . . . above her and behind, she thought.

Interesting. Had Irene ever sensed spells this way? Elsie would have to ask when . . . if . . . she saw the woman again.

She dwelled on the temporal spell a little longer before trying to push out her awareness. She imagined herself as one of the Tibetan monks she'd read about, meditating, seeking enlightenment. The room around her was silent, still, cool. Not even a rat to interrupt her.

There was a distant whisper of a spell, higher up, near the door. A physical spell. Was that . . . a sound-dampening spell? So no one could hear her scream? She shuddered and sensed another farther away, a feather brush across her mind. She couldn't quite tell what it was. A color-changing one, perhaps. Something to keep mortar hard or cork-board soft? Actually . . . it felt like two of them, close together.

Physical and temporal. Not opus spells—judging by Merton's projection, she'd contacted Elsie from some distance, so this couldn't be *her* residence. It would have been foolish for her to bring an enemy to her hideaway anyway.

Perhaps this was the enslaved physical aspector's home, but spells were expensive. If he had multiple classes of spells, he was probably rich. Granted, all master aspectors were well-off, so it wasn't surprising that he should be.

Elsie suspected she would find more spells if she were to escape her prison. Opulent ones, excessive ones. Perhaps there was a great manor overhead, stretches of green speckled with gardens. That's how it looked in her mind, at least.

Her head began to throb, and her wrists itched as though she'd been spellbreaking. Elsie opened her eyes, and the faraway sensations of spells slowly receded.

So she crossed the room, sat down, and tried again.

⌒☉

Bacchus woke to a spell in his brain at a quarter to six, his shoulder stiff from lying on the floor. But any hard words he had for Mr. Ogden were quashed when he said, "Emmeline has the horse ready."

As promised, they were on the road by six, the dawn only a whisper of promise on the horizon.

When Bacchus entered the London Physical Atheneum this time, it was Mr. Ogden who got the looks. Bacchus was an increasingly familiar presence, whereas Mr. Ogden was a nobody—as far as anyone could tell.

They'd gone over the names of everyone in the assembly, as well as their descriptions, though Bacchus was fuzzy on a few of them. Only Master Hill was not a suspect. The plan they'd formed was simple, and completely dependent upon the rational aspector's abilities.

Once they entered the library, Mr. Ogden nudged Bacchus with his elbow and tilted his head toward a heavy smattering of bookshelves. Bacchus followed him there, the light dimming as the expansive shelves blocked the glow from the high windows. Mr. Ogden paused near the back and walked to the middle of one shelf.

Then he closed his eyes.

Nothing extraordinary happened, but Bacchus knew spells were being cast. He had never considered rational aspecting—he had enough issues getting people to trust him without the threat that he could rip all their secrets from their brains—but its usefulness was becoming more and more apparent.

He wondered what this would look like—feel like?—to Elsie if she were in his place. Listening to Miss Prescott explain runes during Elsie's lessons somewhat fascinated him, but he preferred the more colorful descriptions Elsie shared with him in quiet moments afterward. Knots and glitter and mushrooms. He hadn't asked her what rational spells felt like.

Chest tightening, Bacchus feigned an interest in the book spines in front of them. The embossed lettering might as well have been in another language. *Dear God, please help us find her before it's too late. Please.*

If she died . . . Bacchus didn't know what he'd do. Lock himself away in Barbados and never cross the ocean again. Too many reminders . . .

Several minutes passed before Mr. Ogden opened his eyes. "I think I found someone useful. Come."

He left like he owned the place, though it was apparent he'd never stepped foot in it, since he tried to walk through a wall more than once. Making his way to the "someone useful," no doubt. Paying more attention to thoughts than to reality. Questions flitted about Bacchus's uneasy mind, but he didn't voice them.

They stayed on the main floor. Passed through a study hall before entering another chamber crammed with books. Mr. Ogden paused once, then took a sharp left.

A young man, probably a little younger than Bacchus, sat at a small round table in the corner, the enchanted disk on the table giving off enough light to illuminate the old book clutched in his hands. He didn't look up when they approached.

Judging by his appearance, age, and the book he was reading, Bacchus guessed him to be an advanced physical aspector.

"My good sir," Mr. Ogden said with authority, but quietly enough to keep his voice from carrying, "I have questions for you."

The man looked up, forehead crinkled with irritation at being interrupted. Before he spoke, however, his entire expression changed, and he slammed the book shut and tried to stand, knocking the enchanted light off his table. "Master Bennett! What brings you here?"

Bacchus scooped up the light and replaced it as Mr. Ogden said, "No need for exclamations, young man. Sit."

He did, admiration in his eyes.

Master Bennett? Bacchus eyed his companion. Had he planted a false memory in the man, making him think he was speaking to a venerable master aspector?

He's even more powerful than I thought. Which put Bacchus on edge. Had *he* ever been enchanted in such a way? Rational aspectors were very closely monitored because of the nature of their spells. But Mr. Ogden was not a member of any atheneum—there was no oversight for his use of the magic. And while it was possible to purchase a rational master spell protecting the mind, not unlike what Ruth Hill's assailant had worn when attacking Mr. Ogden, Bacchus certainly would not delay Elsie's rescue in order to acquire one. Which left him with little choice but to push his misgivings aside and go with the plan.

"Tell me." Mr. Ogden waved his hand. "I need to speak with the assembly about an ambulation spell, but it's very private, involving the queen and all. I don't want everyone knowing until I learn a few things for certain."

Then, in Bacchus's mind, <*This one's being groomed by the assembly for greatness.*>

Bacchus nodded, never taking his eyes off the advanced aspector, whom he noted was as English and male as they came. Mr. Ogden had chosen this man because he was favored enough to know things, while also unimportant enough not to break the trust of someone he thought more senior.

It was only then that Bacchus truly understood how dangerous this all was. Elsie might not be the only one sleeping in a jail cell.

"Oh." The man looked uncomfortable for a moment. Mr. Ogden subtly waved his hands again.

"You can trust me, lad," he pressed.

After a few seconds, the aspector nodded. "Well, you know only Master Phillips and Master Ulf know the master ambulation spell."

Bacchus cut in, "Tell me about Master Ulf." He was one of three men in the assembly that Bacchus knew very little about.

"Master Johan Ulf." His gaze slid back to Mr. Ogden, as though entranced by his presence. "German scholar, the one with red sideburns. He lives just down the street in the gated neighborhood." The aspector shifted in his chair. "Doesn't like me much."

"And Master Phillips doesn't like anyone," Bacchus muttered.

Mr. Ogden shifted suddenly, his gaze on the younger man. "What was that?"

The aspector blinked. "I . . . didn't say anything, sir."

Another wave of his hand. "Yes, you did, son. About Master Phillips?"

The man fiddled with a button on his waistcoat. Bacchus intuited that Mr. Ogden had heard a thought and was forcing the aspector to verbalize it. "Just that he's been acting strangely lately. He hasn't been to the atheneum in a couple days. He missed a meeting I was taking notes at. Very unlike him."

Bacchus's pulse quickened. He pressed his hand to the stone wall for balance. "Where does Master Phillips live?"

"In London, on the east side," the man said. "Never been there, but his estate is called Wide Springs."

Mr. Ogden turned to Bacchus. "So one of us will go there, the other to Master Ulf."

Bacchus nodded.

"Though," the man added, "he does have a country estate over in Childwickbury. He had a Christmas party there a few years back."

Bacchus tensed. "Childwickbury? Where is that?"

"Northeast," Mr. Ogden said. "Several hours' ride, if I'm not mistaken."

Bacchus swallowed, his throat constricting. Whispering, he said, "If it's him, then that would be a good place—"

Mr. Ogden stalled him with a raised hand. "Thank you, lad. What is that on the wall?"

The man turned to look. "I don't see any—"

His voice cut off, and Mr. Ogden pushed Bacchus away. They walked, somewhat leisurely, away from the space. Bacchus glanced over his shoulder, only to catch the advanced aspector opening his book again, seemingly unaware of them.

"You made him forget us," he whispered once they were a good distance away.

"It's easier when someone's attention is diverted elsewhere. But yes." Mr. Ogden's tone had a dark edge to it. "My spells are strong, but they are few. I've learned how to use what I have the best I can."

Bacchus didn't dare speak again until they'd cleared the front door of the atheneum, and when he did, it was hushed. "Childwickbury. I'm sure of it."

"You're not sure of it," Mr. Ogden stressed, then massaged tension from his forehead with his fingers. "None of us are. But it's a good lead."

"We'll go together."

But the artist shook his head. "Master Ulf is nearby. I'll see to him, then find Master Phillips's London home, just to be safe. If they're dead ends, I'll meet you in Childwickbury. If it's dangerous, *wait for me*, do you understand?"

Normally, taking orders from an illegal spellmaker would rankle Bacchus. But this was no ordinary situation, and Mr. Ogden was no ordinary spellmaker. "Of course."

"Don't let him see you," Mr. Ogden warned. "I won't be able to erase his mind."

Bacchus nodded.

With nothing else left to be said, they went their separate ways. Mr. Ogden hired a cab, and Bacchus returned to their carriage, where he unhitched Master Hill's horse and barked at a stable hand to get him a saddle.

Elsie sensed a new spell.

She was nearly ready to fall asleep when she did. Her only way to tell time was through the slim crack between basement doors, which let in a hair of light—which she could see only if she stood directly under them. So she knew it was night, but she didn't know *when* in the night. It could be the tenth hour. It could be nearly dawn, for all she knew.

But she sensed a new spell, farther out, and it was *moving*.

She bolted upright, breath catching, and listened. Yes . . . it was only the slightest itch of sensation, something she wouldn't have noticed had she not spent all day reaching out for the house spells above her. This one was moving. Definitely coming closer.

Throwing off her blanket, Elsie ran to the basement doors, ready to scream for help at a volume even a sound-dampening spell couldn't temper—but stopped. Closing her eyes, steadying her breathing, she *reached* for the spell, trying to get a better feel for it. After several seconds, she determined it was moving straight for her, not meandering. Like it had a purpose. No, this wasn't some innocent passerby who might help her. In all likelihood it was her abductor, headed straight for her, and she was sensing Merton's spell!

Terror woke her limbs and pricked gooseflesh along her skin. What to do, what to do?

Backing away from the doors, Elsie tried to calm down. She was losing the sensation. *Focus.*

She couldn't still her racing heart, but she closed her eyes and reached for that spell. Closer, closer . . .

Physical.

What did he want now? Was he going to take her away from here? To Merton? Or had Merton decided Elsie was too much of a problem? Or was Merton *busy* and this crook had something entirely different up his sleeve. Torture, or . . .

She swallowed, her corset too tight. She planted a hand over the opus spell there. She couldn't lose it. But she could use it if she had to. She could make this man forget his intentions. It might give her the opening she needed to break the spell.

Then she noticed the empty tray and bottle of water.

The bread and cheese. Someone had to replace those, didn't they?

Either way, Elsie intended to put up a fight.

The spell was practically screaming at her with its nearness, though she heard nothing. Bolting across the room, Elsie grabbed the bottle—it was about the length of her elbow to the tip of her middle finger—and stretched back onto the floor, pulling her blanket over her, careful not to touch the spiritual spell embedded in the glass. Worried her expression might give her away, she turned her back to the small enchanted light on the ceiling.

Breathe. Breathe! she urged herself, trying to deepen and slow her breaths as the spell came ever closer.

She lay there, counting heartbeats, focusing on deep breaths and the spell . . . which was so close now. *So* close. She hadn't heard a single footstep or the creaking of the doors, but Elsie could have sworn the carrier of that spell was in the cellar with her—

Mute spell. She thought she could sense it now. Just like the spell that had sucked all the sound from Ogden's attack.

Her heart flipped, and it took all her effort not to let her breathing hitch. *He's in here right now. And I can't hear him.* Was *this* why Merton wanted to keep her unconscious?

Closer, closer. Over to the tray. Did he notice the missing bottle? The spell stalled for just a moment. Elsie's heart lodged firmly in her throat. Then the person passed by her.

Gritting her teeth, Elsie pushed herself up off the floor and whirled around, colliding into another body. She barely registered it as a man before she swung the bottle with all her might into the side of his head.

He crumpled to the ground, soundless.

Her hands slick on the bottle's neck, Elsie gasped for air, her hair wild around her face and shoulders. He wore all black, along with a high collar that might have been pulled up over his mouth if he'd had the mind. A large nose, slender shoulders . . . he looked to be a little younger than Elsie.

She took a step back. His build was wrong, and his eyes. This wasn't her abductor.

There was bread on the tray, and a tin pitcher beside it.

A servant of some kind. Another Nash. She swallowed and, keeping one hand on the bottle, knelt next to him, searching for . . . yes, a rune glimmering through his black sleeve.

Cringing, Elsie grabbed his wrist and pulled back the cloth. She untied the spell, and suddenly the lad's breathing touched her ears. A little strained, but even. There was a sizeable goose egg growing behind his ear. But no compulsion spell, and he wasn't armed.

And the left basement door was open, a ladder set against it.

"Sweet merciful heaven." Abandoning the servant, Elsie bolted to the ladder, picking up her skirts so she could climb it. It was difficult with the bottle still in hand, but it was her only weapon, and she wasn't going to give it up anytime soon.

A cool night wind caught her hair as she climbed out. The first thing she noticed was the untamed grass nearby, and the dark silhouettes of tall trees. Then the light in a window not far from her.

She'd been right—there was a house. A *big* house, belonging to some nobleman or another. She might have scoffed at it at another time, but right now she needed to *flee* before the servant woke and spread the alarm.

Setting the bottle down, she grabbed the ladder with both hands and hauled it out of the basement, then carefully shut the door so it wouldn't slam, just in case the mute spell she'd sensed earlier wouldn't cover that noise.

Taking the bottle in hand, she ran.

Away from the house. She didn't care where she was going as long as it was *away*. The terrain was smooth enough, the moon high but partially shielded by clouds. She carried the front of her skirt in her arms in a very unladylike manner, pumping her legs, running, *running*—

She nearly ran into the stone wall, it was so dark. She skidded to a stop right before it.

"No," she whispered, pressing a hand against it. It was about ten feet high.

Cursing, she followed the wall in one direction, then the other, but she couldn't see where it ended. So she dropped the bottle and wedged her fingertips between layers of weathered stone, but there wasn't enough of a lip for her to get a strong hold. She tried in several spots, her fingers always slipping.

So she jumped, trying to reach the top of the wall to pull herself over—but she didn't come close to breaching it.

Her breaths were hoarse now. "Oh God, help me," she whispered, turning back, the partially lit mansion looming in the distance. If she kept moving away from it, who knew how long she'd be wandering around. Many houses this large had extensive properties.

Gate. There had to be a gate somewhere closer to the house. Retrieving her glass weapon, Elsie hurried along the wall, keeping one hand to it as she went. A physical spell glowed ahead of her—a fortification spell, just like the ones she'd unbound at Seven Oaks. Hope swelled in her. She untied it, but no, the wall didn't crumble in the absence of magic. In fact, it looked entirely unchanged. Able to be taken out by a sledgehammer, perhaps, not a woman's bare hands.

So Elsie hurried on, quickening her pace, ignoring the next fortification spell when she reached it. *Gate, gate, gate.*

The moon snuck out from behind a thick cloud, casting her in darkness. She stepped in a rabbit hole and fell forward, biting her tongue to keep from crying out. The bottle flew from her grasp.

Groaning, she got her knees under her and stood. Her ankle throbbed—it hurt to put weight on it, but it wasn't broken, thank heaven. So she continued, hobbling as she went. She lost her shoe almost immediately, but didn't stop to retrieve it. Or the bottle. If the foot was going to swell up, it wouldn't fit in the shoe anyway. And as much as she needed the bottle, she also needed time.

She reached a junction in the wall. Tried again for handholds, with no luck. She scanned the dark yard—perhaps she could find . . . oh, a stump or a bucket or *something* to give her a lift. But she saw nothing. No back gate, either.

So she followed the next wall, eyeing the mansion she was slowly moving closer to, praying for a hidden door, a latch, *anything*.

And then, moments later, she found one.

And it was locked.

Stay calm. She ran her hands over the wrought iron gate, the moon peeking out to help her. The gate started close to the ground and rose just as high as the rest of the wall. It wasn't locked by magical means—no, that would be too easy. It had a thick steel contraption on it.

But there *were* crossbars on it. So, ignoring the pointed tips of the gate, Elsie set her good foot onto the first crossbar, which was just below the height of her hip, and lifted herself up. The gate shifted on its hinges. Elsie held on tightly, hissing through her teeth when she put weight on her sore ankle. Using as much upper-body strength as she could to relieve it, she swung over the top of the gate, her skirt catching as she did.

She jumped down the rest of the way, a sharp whine trapped in her throat when she landed on her sore foot, a loud *rip* sounding as the tip of an iron bar tore through her skirt.

She was a spellbreaker, for goodness's sake. She could buy another bloody dress.

She had only just gotten back on her feet—her right ankle throbbing anew—when she heard her name.

"Hello, Elsie."

She whirled around, first to the gate, which was still locked, then to the silhouette a few paces . . . north, was it? She recognized his voice from the carriage. And his stature . . . it was the same.

She limped backward, stumbling. "I-I can help you. I can take it off."

The man took a step forward. The moonlight highlighted his pointed chin and the gray strands running through his short, side-swept hair. He didn't have on a mask. He wore normal, tailored clothes. Like he hadn't had time to disguise himself before Merton had sent him to check on her.

And then he stopped suddenly, like the air had hardened around him. He trembled.

Just like Ogden had.

He was fighting back.

Suppressing her instinct to flee, Elsie hurried toward him and grabbed the front of his shirt. She . . . yes! She could hear Merton's spell humming—

The man grabbed her wrists. "I don't think so," he said, then worked his mouth, a puppet refusing to obey its strings.

Sharpness entered his blue eyes. Merton had won control.

Elsie pulled against his grip, but it didn't relent. So she kneed him in the groin instead.

The man let out a wheeze, and Elsie twisted her arms, breaking his hold. She turned and ran, stumbling on her aching ankle. Limped to a dark tree line. She could barely see, but it didn't matter. She had to get *away*.

Her abductor was following her, feet swift and sure. And truly, what hope did she have of escaping this man on his own property?

Tears flew from her eyes and caught in her hair. *God help me. Help me!*

She stumbled over a tree branch. Changed direction and rushed south, or what she thought was south. She barely made out a dip in the earth and managed to get over it without tripping. She could feel her foot swelling. Every other step was torture, like glass had wedged into the joints. Her skirt caught on something else, and she yanked it free, tearing more fabric. The trees grew thicker to the east, so she hobbled that way, trying to keep her steps light but knowing she was making a ruckus. She ducked behind one tree, changed direction, pushed between two more. Her pulse thundered in her ears. She couldn't feel the toes on her right foot.

The ground evened a little, and she picked up speed, feeling like an injured deer with beagles on its tail. She grasped trees as she ran, trying to keep her balance as her foot screamed at her—

Two hands grabbed her.

"No!" she screamed, beating away at them. *"Let me go!"*

"Elsie!"

Everything stopped.

That voice.

That accent.

She blinked, tears running freely now. "Bacchus?"

He crushed her to him, and the scents of citrus and fresh-cut wood filled her senses. She clung to him, shuddering, weeping—

Then she ripped away and turned around, nearly falling to her knees. "He's here. He was just here."

Bacchus's arm wrapped around her, his hand splayed across her stomach. He searched the dark wood around them. Elsie strained to hear.

Nothing but crickets and the breeze.

She swallowed. "I got out of the cellar, but he f-found me—"

"Let's go," he whispered, the words heavy and sharp. "While we have a chance."

He tugged her south, and Elsie hissed, grabbing him for support. "I-I twisted my ankle—"

Bacchus bent down, and in one effortless swoop picked her up, holding her like a small child. She gripped fistfuls of his shirt—he didn't have on a jacket or a waistcoat—and frantically searched the forest beyond his shoulder. There was no sign of her abductor. Had he managed to thwart Merton's will after all, or had he seen Bacchus and determined it best to stand down?

Bacchus's footsteps were long and swift. The ground turned downward, sloping into a hill, and she saw a road at the base of it, with a large horse tied across the way. The relief that burst through Elsie was nearly enough to make her lose consciousness.

"Thank you," she breathed. "Thank you, thank you."

He was tense and silent as he strode across the road, glancing over his shoulder as he did. He mustn't have seen anything, because he simply lifted her onto the saddle.

Elsie swallowed against a tight throat. "I'm so sorry. I didn't know—"

"Elsie." His tone was dark. "If you apologize again, I'm going to rip out my own beard." Grabbing the horse's neck, he swung up behind her, quick to take the reins and pull the horse away. They went straight into a gallop, taking off down the dark road, not even a lamp to guide their way. It wasn't safe, especially not for the horse, but Elsie didn't complain.

Finally, he said against her neck, "I was so scared I'd find you dead."

The hairs on her arms stood on end. She leaned against him, head pressed into the valley between his neck and shoulder. She was so utterly terrified and so blissfully happy she barely knew how to feel at all.

"I saw him," she said, just loud enough to be heard over the horse. "I saw his face. It was narrow, pointed—"

"Master Enoch Phillips."

She stiffened. "What?"

"This is his estate," Bacchus practically growled. "Blue eyes, severe features, gray hair?"

She nodded.

"Merton has perhaps the most powerful physical aspector in England under her thumb," he said. "But she no longer has the element of surprise."

"What will we do now?" she asked.

Bacchus's arms tightened around her. "I don't know."

His breath was warm against her ear. Words pushed against her tongue—*I love you. Thank you. I love you*—but she swallowed them back down. She clung to his arms with both hands as they sped into the shadows, leaving her nightmare behind them.

For now, at least.

CHAPTER 17

They rode through the night, meeting Ogden on the road. It was late—past midnight, Elsie learned—and they were exhausted, but no one suggested stopping. They continued on to Master Hill's house in London.

To think, the man who'd attacked Master Hill was the head of her own atheneum, Master Enoch Phillips.

Elsie still struggled to absorb that one.

After sleeping a few hours in Ruth Hill's quiet home, they hired a carriage to take them the rest of the way to Brookley in the early-morning hours of Monday. Elsie, having no hairpins, settled on a braid over her shoulder and offered a prayer that none of her neighbors would notice her. She'd slept with her foot up, and the swelling of her ankle had receded, but she still couldn't walk on it normally.

She was surprised to see a large trunk sitting in the middle of the studio upon entering the house.

"Ah," Ogden said behind her, "Master Kelsey, it seems your things arrived while we were away."

"Your *things*?" Elsie asked as Bacchus, fatigue marking his face, entered the room. Was that why he hadn't changed after their visit to Master Hill's home?

Ogden answered, "After your abduction and the attack, we decided it might be better to have two aspectors here instead of one. He'll stay until the wedding. You will, unfortunately, have to give up your bedroom."

Elsie blushed, though she really ought not to. It wasn't *technically* improper.

Her second thought was relief that she'd decided not to keep her stolen opus spell under her mattress.

"Elsie!" Emmeline shrieked as she bolted into the studio and threw her arms around Elsie's shoulders. Elsie nearly tumbled over, unable to properly balance with both feet, but she embraced her back, another wave of relief engulfing her. It brought her attention to the sleepiness in her joints. "Oh, I'm so glad you're back! What happened?"

"Too much." Elsie pulled away and glanced to the men. "But what about Phillips?"

"Phillips?" Emmeline repeated.

"We'll sort it out." Bacchus ran his hand over his half beard.

Emmeline tugged on Elsie's hand.

"I'll tell you over a bath," Elsie said, forcing a smile. "That is, if I might use it first."

Ogden nodded. "Go on."

Elsie allowed Emmeline to help her up the stairs, grateful for the care and affection of the younger woman. Sure enough, in her absence, Emmeline had already moved all of Elsie's things into her room, which was the smallest of the three bedrooms the house boasted. Her bookshelf was crammed into the corner, the few items from her desk set neatly on top of it. Her clothes were in Emmeline's wardrobe, her decorations on Emmeline's shelves. The furniture—bed, desk, wardrobe—would stay in the other room for Bacchus.

Bacchus Kelsey was going to sleep in her bed.

Soon enough, she would be sleeping in his.

Her face heated. But the idea felt strangely hypnagogic, like it was still just a hope, not something that was actually going to happen.

Emmeline, blessedly, lugged in the copper bath and filled it. Elsie didn't wait for all the water to heat on the stove downstairs—lukewarm was fine with her. She stripped off her clothes, careful to conceal the opus spell in the boning of the corset. All the while, she told Emmeline everything. It was so liberating, being able to just speak the full truth to another human. She'd been keeping secrets for so long they'd become a part of her.

As she dried off, Emmeline told her what had happened at the house while she was away, and how worried she had been. Touched, Elsie kissed her on the cheek.

Once she was dried and in her dressing gown, Elsie stifled a yawn. "Let's heat some water for the others. They'll be wanting to bathe, too."

Emmeline smiled. "I'll do it, Elsie. You should rest."

Elsie looked around the room, all her things mingled with Emmeline's. "You've done so much already."

"Just let me. You're limping, besides. I don't mind. It's, well, it's the only way I feel useful. I don't have any magic or money." She pulled back the linens on the bed that she and Elsie would be sharing for the next two weeks.

Elsie let out a sigh. "Emmeline Pratt, I'm going to buy you chocolate for all this."

Emmeline beamed. "A fair trade."

And so Elsie let her friend maneuver the tub while she lay down.

She tried her best to sleep, and she did in short spurts, a minute here or there, but her mind kept replaying last night over and over— *What if I seriously injured that servant? What if he was under Merton's control, too?* After a time, her thoughts shifted to her confessions to Irene and what Elsie would do if the other spellbreaker blew the whistle on them. To Ogden and what he must think of all of this. To Bacchus and what he might be thinking of her.

Eventually she gave up. Her hair was nearly dry, so she combed it through and let it hang loose. When she stepped out of the room, she noticed the door across from her—the one to her room—was closed. If the sounds she'd heard coming back and forth in the hallway while she snoozed were any indication, the tub had been taken to Bacchus next.

She hesitated in the doorway, then turned back to get dressed. Paused. Glanced at the door again. Down the hallway. She heard Emmeline in the kitchen downstairs.

Biting her lip, she crossed to the other door and knocked. "Bacchus?"

"Yes?"

She hesitated. "Can I talk to you?"

A pause. "I'm a little indecent at the moment."

Her cheeks warmed. "Just through the door, then."

She thought she heard movement in the water. "What's wrong?"

"Nothing." Well, *that* was a lie, but Bacchus knew about all the wrong things, so there wasn't much point in reiterating them. Her ankle was a little better, but not wanting to push her luck, she slid down the frame so that she sat parallel to the door. Tucking her good foot beneath her, she asked, "What happened at Seven Oaks?"

"I didn't go to Seven Oaks. I came straight here after I learned you were missing."

Emmeline had mentioned a telegram. "Are you going? To Seven Oaks, I mean."

More shifting in the water. "I'm not sure. Not immediately. There are more pressing matters at hand." A second of silence, then, "I should probably write to the duchess, if only for propriety's sake." He was slipping into his Bajan accent again.

Elsie's lip quirked. "Yes, you probably should." Weaving her fingers together, she asked, "What about your servants?"

"John and Rainer will continue staying at Master Hill's."

"Oh." She pulled her hands apart, weaved her fingers again. "I didn't see them this morning."

"I spoke with them briefly. They're well." A shuffling sound followed.

"Bacchus"—she leaned her head on the door—"tell me about Barbados."

Another pause. "What do you want to know?"

"The things no one else does. I know it's hot and tropical and full of sugarcane. But what else can you tell me?"

The floor creaked. "The air tastes good."

A chuckle crept up her throat. "What?"

"It's a mix of sweet and salt, from the plants and the ocean. Here the air smells like smoke and rain. In Barbados it's like a delicate dessert. Sweet and savory. Unless you're too close to the fish market."

She smiled.

"It's green. The sugar plantations are green"—a hint of disdain slipped into his voice at that—"but the rest of the island is green as well—what the European settlers didn't destroy. There are palm trees and thick grasses. They seem to sing when the sun goes down."

She tried to imagine it. "How do they sing?"

"It's hard to describe." Now his tone was wistful. "The insects, the breeze in the blades . . . it's not something I've heard on this side of the ocean."

"Do you live by the ocean?"

"All of Barbados is by the ocean." Another creak. "It's not a large island. But I live in an old plantation house. Jacobean style, if you know it."

Elsie considered a moment. "The sloping roofs."

"Indeed." He sounded pleased.

Elsie adjusted the picture in her mind—a place full of sunshine, green, and ocean, where the air tasted like the first bite of dessert and the night sang. It portrayed a fairy tale. "I would like to see it." She spoke a little quieter. "That is . . . I would go to Barbados. We don't have to stay here."

A few seconds flitted by before he answered. "You have family here, Elsie."

"I don—" She paused. *Reggie.* She had just found him, hadn't she? And Ogden and Emmeline were almost family. "We could split our time."

He didn't reply.

Wringing her hands together, Elsie added, "Are you . . . Are you sure it's worth all of this, Bacchus?"

The floorboards creaked, and suddenly the door opened. Bacchus stood there in breeches and a long-sleeved white shirt, the collar loose. His dark hair, lighter at the ends, hung wet over his shoulders, leaving speckles of water along the fabric that turned it translucent.

He looked down at her, tired but not angry. "Are we really going to have this conversation again?"

Elsie rolled her lips together. "I think it's a valid question."

He extended his hand, which she took, allowing him to help her up. She adjusted her dressing gown, ensuring her modesty.

Bacchus lifted a hand and ran the pad of his thumb along her cheek, sending a wave of heat coursing over her skin. "You are very much worth it, Elsie Camden."

She stared into the beautiful green of his eyes. Right now they didn't look like a stormy sea, or jade, or anything she could pinpoint. Perhaps they were the green of Barbados. They were just as fanciful as the place he had described, and she struggled to believe either of them were real.

She realized she was just standing there, staring at him—in her defense, he was doing the same—but she couldn't bring herself to look away. She memorized the slope of his nose, the shape of his hairline, the curve of his beard. His cheeks were newly shaved. He smelled like soap, but the faintest hint of citrus lingered under it.

Her heart danced beneath her breast, and before she could check herself, she whispered, "Kiss me."

His eyes bore into hers.

And then his mouth was gliding across hers, tentatively at first. But when Elsie pressed her hands to his chest, he gained confidence and kissed her as he had in the carriage, with intent and meaning. A thrill coursed through her jaw and down her neck, not unlike the heat of a candle flame when pinched between two fingers, snuffed just before it could burn. Elsie's hands took on a mind of their own and crawled up to his shoulders, then to his neck, the skin wet from the drape of his hair. His palms pressed into either side of her waist. She didn't remember how they'd gotten there, but their weight invigorated her. Lent her courage.

He was a tall man, and Elsie desperately wanted to be closer to him, so she rose onto her toes and tilted her head a little more to the right, fitting her lips against his just so. An invisible string pulled taut between her heart and her hips when the kiss deepened, a slip of heat crossing her bottom lip. She only loosely recognized it as his tongue, but the sensation of it made her knees weak. He must have noticed, for his grip on her waist tightened. When Elsie parted her lips for breath, Bacchus claimed her, seeking entrance to her mouth, which she readily gave him.

Aspecting be damned, *this* was real magic. Physical, spiritual, rational, temporal . . . all of it rolled into a blissful ball of sensations she was only just beginning to pick apart, ever so eager to find what lay at its center.

Bacchus's left hand lifted from her waist, leaving a chill in his wake. She heard it *thud* against the door frame, gripping it. Elsie's fingers had journeyed into Bacchus's wet hair, tangling with the waves. She nipped at his lower lip and heard the faintest sound escape his throat, though she sensed it more with her mouth than her ears.

His lips slowed, and he pulled back, his eyes dark. A long breath escaped his nose before he said, "We need to stop before you make me think unchristian thoughts, Elsie."

She could feel her lips swelling. She licked them.

For the first time since learning of their surprise engagement, Elsie found herself greatly looking forward to her wedding night.

Footsteps on the stairs had Elsie stepping back, forgetting about her ankle and wincing when she put weight on it. Bacchus reached forward to steady her just as Emmeline popped up with a basket of linens on her hip. Elsie's entire body warmed, but Emmeline—dear, sweet, innocent Emmeline—did not seem to notice anything amiss about Elsie and Bacchus standing so close together, neither nearly dressed enough for proper decency.

"Dinner will be ready in a few hours." She grinned and set the basket just inside her bedroom door. "Though I think Mr. Camden may arrive before that. He said he might finish early."

It was still enormously strange to hear that name. "Oh! I'd completely forgotten Reggie was coming . . ." He would have updates about the newspaper articles. If he'd managed to get them published, he might even have some replies.

Emmeline pulled a long linen bandage from her apron pocket. "I'll wrap your ankle for you and help you change." She glanced at Bacchus. "I'm happy to take your laundry from you as well, Master Kelsey."

Bacchus cleared his throat. "I'll see to it myself, thank you."

Avoiding Bacchus's gaze because she knew she'd turn red as a beet if she didn't, Elsie leaned on Emmeline and limped back into their shared room, where Emmeline snuggly wrapped her ankle. The dress Elsie had been wearing when Master Phillips—that was still hard to process—abducted her was ruined. A pity. Emmeline helped her into her Sunday gown, her best one. Fitting, since she'd obviously missed church yesterday.

But what to do about Master Phillips? Elsie's and Ogden's anonymous tips regarding Merton had gone nowhere. Would it be the same for him? Elsie had no proof save Bacchus's eyewitness account. They might be able to explain the kidnapping—and the way Bacchus had turned up at the perfect place and time to save her—but it would be difficult to do so without admitting to their own loose relationship with the law. Then again, it *wasn't* Master Phillips at all. He needed to be stopped, of course, but why should he have to suffer because Merton had chosen him as her pawn?

Reggie did indeed arrive early—Elsie had only just finished pinning her hair. Emmeline had also changed into her Sunday best and curled the strands of dark hair that framed her face, something that caught Elsie's attention. No matter who the guest, Emmeline never bothered with the curling iron. Not for herself. Elsie was intrigued, but she'd wait for a more private moment to inquire about it.

"Got 'em all in," Reggie said as he took a seat across from Elsie in the dining room. The meal had already been brought out, and Elsie's stomach grumbled. She sat beside Bacchus, who was also fully dressed and dry, his hair pulled back into a half-hearted tail. Ogden sat at the head of the table, and Emmeline was across from Bacchus, next to Reggie. They needed only one more guest to have a full party. "Last one goes out in tomorrow's *Daily Telegraph*, then they're all set."

Elsie breathed out a sigh of relief. "Thank you."

"Can you keep tabs on them?" Ogden asked as he carved the pheasant. "Find out if they get responses?"

Reggie worked his mouth. "I can ask, at least. Don't hurt to ask."

After helping serve everyone, Emmeline smoothed her skirt and asked, "Tell me how the printing presses work. Do the letters go in backward?"

"Indeed they do." Reggie sat a little straighter in his chair. "They have to be set a certain way, like this—"

<Someone is here.> Ogden's voice sounded in Elsie's head, sending a shiver down her spine. Bacchus startled, so Elsie guessed he'd heard it, too.

Sure enough, a moment later, someone pounded on the front door.

They'd had two unexpected visitors of late: first the police come to arrest her, then Reggie . . . Did that mean this one had to be bad, to keep the pattern?

Emmeline moved to stand. Elsie held out a hand. "You're talking, I'll get it."

Bacchus sighed. "They'll be gone by the time you limp over there." He stood from his chair.

Elsie's mouth opened, working on a retort, but she couldn't find a decent one. She was used to doing things herself; she was quite capable, usually. Yet she found herself more appreciative than put out. So she relaxed into her chair and allowed Bacchus to answer the door. She wondered how often he'd had occasion to answer doors. Given he usually spent his time at estates like Seven Oaks, Ruth Hill's home, and his plantation in Barbados, he likely always had a servant doing it for him.

Elsie heard Irene's voice almost instantly and stood, ankle be damned.

The spellbreaker's rushed footsteps sounded through the hallway, and she appeared in their kitchen dressed head to toe in pale violet, one hand on her hat to keep it atop her head. Her cheeks were flushed and her chest heaved with each breath. Bacchus appeared behind her.

Ogden stood as well. "Miss Prescott, what's happened?"

She swallowed, wetting her tongue. "I came as soon as I heard."

Elsie offered a weak smile. "As you can see, I'm quite all right."

Reggie glanced between the two spellbreakers. "You mean yer ankle?"

But Irene shook her head, trying to catch her breath. "No, not . . . your ankle?" She licked her lips and refocused. "I was at the London

Physical Atheneum today. I—" Eyes straying back to Reggie, she hesitated.

Elsie felt the air shiver with a rational spell. A moment later, Ogden said, "Tell us. He's safe."

Elsie bit the inside of her cheek. Seemed that her brother would be involved in this after all. A relief in a way; she wanted to be open with him, but she didn't want to endanger him.

"The police came to arrest Master Phillips." Irene grabbed the back of the free chair. "He's an accomplice."

Elsie exchanged looks with Bacchus and Ogden. "We know. We didn't know how to proceed."

Reggie began to say something, but Irene talked over him. "You know? When?"

Bacchus said, "As of last night."

"He's being controlled, too," Elsie offered, passing a sympathetic look to Ogden.

Irene's brow furrowed. "But that can't be right."

"She need only touch him," Bacchus reminded her. "She's had plenty of opportunities to find him and do so."

But Irene shook her head. "No, you must be mistaken. He must have acted of his own accord."

Hard lines creased the skin around Ogden's eyes and mouth. "What are you saying?"

Irene's eyes flitted to each of them in turn, her confusion obvious. "I stayed for the aftermath, after they took Master Phillips away. I was there when the message came in to the constable."

"What message?" Bacchus asked.

"About Merton," Irene clarified. "She's dead."

CHAPTER 18

The woman might as well have slapped Cuthbert in the face.

"Pardon?" A mind-reading spell—an intermediate one, subtle, skimming the surface—went out almost of its own volition, scanning her for truthfulness. But that was exactly what he got. Honesty. Shock. Emergency. Her emotions were strong. Her information rang true, at least to her.

"Master Lily Merton is dead," Miss Prescott repeated, and this time, instead of a slap, it felt like a bullet to his chest, right where that bloody spell had been all those years. "I . . . They didn't know much. I was eavesdropping. She was an older woman, yes, but seemingly in good health. Still, it might have been natural causes, or the murderer could have struck again—"

"*She* is the murderer!" Cuthbert slammed his hand on the table hard enough to make the plates rattle. Elsie gaped at him. Emmeline squeaked, then touched Reggie's shoulder and whispered to him. The two left the room, giving the others blessed privacy. Hopefully Emmeline would explain what the boy needed to know so Cuthbert wouldn't have to. He was sick of reviewing what they already knew without adding to it.

"Many of the stolen opuses were found in Master Phillips's London home—"

"Of course they were. But they didn't find *all* of them, did they?" Cuthbert pulled his hand back and ran it down his face, feeling old. "There is *no doubt* it's a ruse, Miss Prescott. What better way for Merton to hide herself, to assuage any guilt, than to fake her own death?"

Miss Prescott looked as though she might cry. "But, Mr. Ogden. She left an opus."

"What?" Elsie blurted.

"That's what I heard. She had a summer home she recently purchased in Rochester—"

Rochester. So she hadn't been far.

"—and her neighbors heard a clatter while passing by. Called the local police, and they found her opus . . . along with shattered windows and"—she grimaced—"well, signs of a struggle. Blood. There will be an investigation, of course."

Master Kelsey growled, "If someone murdered her, they would have taken the opus."

Cuthbert nodded, frustration boiling beneath his skin.

"Unless she had fortifications to stop him, or defended herself before giving up the ghost." Miss Prescott met Cuthbert's eyes. "I-I'm sorry, I don't wish to cause you grief. I'm merely repeating what I heard."

Elsie hugged herself. "Master Phillips in jail and Merton dead? But surely she's the one who arranged his arrest, just like she did with me!"

"Yes, it's far too convenient." Cuthbert gripped the table edge and leaned over his barely touched dinner. "Are we truly to believe she met with some unfortunate fate less than a day after we found Elsie and unmasked her pawn?"

"Found Elsie?" Miss Prescott was baffled. "What?"

Elsie sighed. "I was the unfortunate victim of an abduction by Master Phillips. That's how we know about him. I will tell you all of it momentarily. But this . . ." She glanced to Cuthbert, her blue eyes bright and afraid. "I agree. This is too easy."

"There's only one way we can know for sure." Cuthbert's fingernails dug into the wood. "We have to see that opus."

They were silent for a moment, until Master Kelsey spoke.

"It will not go to auction," he said, his tone low and dark, reflecting Cuthbert's feelings perfectly. "But Master Merton has no family, from what we understand." He gestured to Elsie. "Which means the London Spiritual Atheneum will do her rites for her."

Miss Prescott nodded. "There may be an estate sale, like there was for Master Quinn Raven. Whatever happens, the opus will be heavily guarded for a viewing before being taken to the atheneum."

"Unless they skip the viewing and take it straight to the vaults," Master Kelsey said. "There's no family to complain."

Cuthbert grabbed both sides of his head. Pain bloomed under his skull above both temples. "She's not dead. Damn it all. She's acquitting herself."

And he wouldn't let that happen.

Pushing off the table, he went to the back door to retrieve his coat.

Elsie limped after him. "Where are you going?"

"To Rochester."

She glanced out the window. The sun had nearly set. *"Now?"*

"Yes, *now*." His tone was sharp, but he couldn't reel it in, even for her. "I have to know. I *have to*, Elsie." He sighed. Set his jaw. "Don't wait up for me."

He wrenched the back door open and stepped into the cooling night, thankful that Elsie had twisted her ankle.

It was likely the only thing that kept her from going after him.

Reggie knew now. That made six of them.

Bacchus graciously helped Elsie up the stairs to the sitting room, where Emmeline had taken Reggie. Elsie refused to lose her dignity and be carried, but she did allow him to keep a firm grip on her elbow. Irene followed behind.

Once they were seated comfortably, Elsie filled in the holes of the story, though in the interest of saving time—and face—she was somewhat less forthcoming than she'd been with Emmeline and Irene. Neither woman corrected her, thankfully. Irene, in turn, gave full details of Master Phillips's arrest and the announcement of Merton's supposed demise, though those details pertained more to such logistical concerns as what she had been doing and where she had been standing. Nothing that would help Ogden, in the long run.

Ogden. Elsie prayed he'd be all right. If he was caught snooping around . . . well, Bacchus couldn't marry both of them.

"I didn't see him myself," Irene said, concluding her story, "but I saw the prison wagon pull away. They had aspectors to keep him in line."

Because a master physical aspector could easily decimate any vehicle that tried to apprehend him.

Leaning back against the settee, Elsie said, "Thank you, Irene, for everything."

The woman nodded, and it seemed like she wanted to say more—to ask for details on Elsie's abduction, perhaps. But she must have sensed the mood in the room, for instead she said, "I should probably go. I'll be in contact."

"Your efforts are appreciated," Bacchus said. He sounded almost as tired as he had while under the influence of the siphoning spell. Another thing they needed to address.

Irene left first, followed by Reggie, who insisted he had to get back to London for work in the morning—his days started early—despite the necessity of riding back in the dark. Once Emmeline saw him out, the candles burning low, Elsie said, "Seven Oaks."

Bacchus sighed. He sat beside her on the settee, his arm draped across its back, a few inches above Elsie's shoulders. She hoped it would lose its balance and plop down on her.

He rubbed his eyes. "I need to write to the duchess and explain. She's likely worried. First thing in the morning. You'll have to show me where the post office is."

"It's not hard to find."

Emmeline slipped in, stepping carefully as though they were sleeping. "Do you think he'll be all right?"

"Reggie is smart and good with his horse," Elsie answered. "He'll be fine."

Emmeline smiled, but it soon faded. "I meant Mr. Ogden."

Elsie's heart sank. "I . . . yes, I'm sure he will be. He's made it fifty-five years yet. I would be shocked if he had anything less than another fifty-five in him."

Emmeline seemed comforted and dropped into a chair across from them, thumbing listlessly at the edge of yesterday's newspaper. Bacchus asked after her family, and Elsie was filled with a keen awareness of how close he sat—his voice in her ear, his body inches away from hers. A halo of warmth emanated from him, and she wondered how a man could burn so hot and still be comfortable in a frock coat.

Which of course made her think of the last time she was very close to him. Her body flushed, and her heat in addition to his was nigh unbearable.

She'd been forward. *Very* forward. How reckless she'd been! And yet Bacchus hadn't seemed put off by it. Quite the opposite, in fact . . .

What would happen if she were to be forward a second time?

But Emmeline chatted about the views in Aylesbury, and her familiar, cheerful voice was a stark reminder that Elsie and Bacchus were not alone in the room. For the better, of course. Yet Elsie found herself wanting to reach over and touch his knee, just to see how he would react. To pull on his fingers and coax his arm around her. To feel his beard against her mouth, because she liked the idea of him having unchristian thoughts about her.

But then she thought of Ogden, of Merton, of Master Phillips, and the awareness of her own selfishness crashed down on her, banishing the heat beneath her skin so thoroughly she shivered.

Bacchus glanced at her, and his arm *did* come around her shoulders. He pressed his fingers and palm into her upper arm, and a splendid warmth emanated from them—too strong to merely be from the contact. It was a novice temperature spell. To keep her comfortable.

Of all the things that had happened the last few days, *this* was the one that made her want to weep.

Finding her voice, she asked Emmeline, "Did you visit Waddesdon Manor on this last trip home?" The manor was a local house often opened up for tour to the public. Emmeline talked about it often enough that Elsie felt she'd taken a tour herself.

She shook her head. "No, there was so much to do at the house. But you should come by sometime, Elsie, and take the tour with me. I might know enough to give it myself." She grinned.

The candlelight held, and so the three of them talked quietly for a while longer, Elsie listening for Ogden despite his admonition not to wait up. Bacchus fell asleep first, his head against the backrest. Elsie studied his face in his slumber as Emmeline caught her up on the events of the novel readers she'd failed to read. Bacchus looked younger, peaceful, beautiful in repose, and had Emmeline not been there, Elsie might have had the courage to whisper the truth of her feelings to him, and let him think he'd dreamed the entire thing.

∽

Ogden did not return home until a quarter past ten the next morning. Fortunately, Elsie was hale enough to take the stairs down on her own.

It was obvious he had not slept; dark circles rimmed his eyes, and there was a hunch to his shoulders that betrayed his age. His overall presence was haggard, though that might have been due to the thick disappointment dripping off him like undercooked caramel.

"The entire place is under heavy guard." His voice was twenty years too old. "But there *will* be an estate sale. Four days. The opus will be on display on the first day only." He rubbed his red-rimmed eyes. "The question remains *when* it will happen. None of the men standing watch appeared to know, either. I . . . I couldn't get inside. Too many people."

Elsie set a light hand on Ogden's shoulder, relieved when he didn't shrug it off. "Then we'll wait. I'll send a message to Irene. She has the best chance of finding out first, what with Bacchus staying here instead of London."

Ogden nodded. He seemed like a man at a funeral for a loved one. "I'm going to go rest."

"Breakfast?" Elsie offered.

But he waved it away and dragged himself up the stairs.

♈

Wednesday, the question arose of whether or not Elsie and Bacchus's wedding date should be postponed, given the turn of events. It was only ten days away. Bacchus gave a firm no, saying he didn't want to allow Merton that power over them. But Elsie also heard what he didn't say: better to keep Elsie from the noose. Invitations had already been mailed, and Lord Astley, the magistrate who'd overseen her case, had received one. He'd already sent his confirmation that he would be in attendance.

Bacchus had claimed he would have courted her regardless of their unique situation. But how? Would he have started showing up at the stonemasonry shop more often? Invited her to more dinners at Seven

Oaks? Or would he have sailed home and mulled it over longer, not seeking her out until his next trip to England?

Where would Elsie be right now, had the justice system not forced his hand? Certainly not standing on a stool in a cream-colored gown while the seamstress measured her hem. Elsie pressed her palm against her stomach. *Remember how he kisses you. He doesn't* not *want this.*

Chewing on her lip, Elsie dared to look in the nearby mirror. The dress wasn't quite finished, but all the important bits were there. The sleeves, the collar, the gathers in the skirt. Three kinds of lace trim were spread over Emmeline's lap, and her friend touched each one gingerly, reverently. Elsie hoped she'd be in that chair when Emmeline found someone worthy of her. In truth, she dared to hope her friend's eye had already been turned to a certain family member of hers.

"You can choose," Elsie offered, turning a smidge when the dressmaker indicated. "I like all of them."

Beaming, Emmeline picked up the center strip. "This one will be perfect."

She prayed Bacchus thought so, too.

Thursday, Reggie returned. He had copies of all the newspapers their articles had been printed in, and though Elsie knew exactly what the articles said, she looked them over anyway, trying to imagine what Quinn Raven's reaction would be when and if he saw them. She wondered if Reggie could pull in a few favors and get the articles published more than once.

With Elsie occupied, Reggie handed the last paper under his arm to Ogden, whose sleeves were rolled up from pottery work, a few flecks of gray clay clinging to his dark arm hair. "Wasn't sure if you saw this one."

Ogden unfurled the paper. The headline font was large enough that when Elsie glanced up, she could easily read it from where she sat at the dining table. Master Enoch Phillips Found Guilty of Opus Thefts, Murders.

Her mouth went dry.

Sighing, Bacchus rubbed his beard. "At least there should be no more, not if Merton wants him to be her scapegoat. The stonemasonry shop should be safe."

He said nothing about moving out, for which Elsie was grateful. Not only did she feel safer with him there, but she'd come to depend on his steady presence, their late-night talks, his astute nature. He made her feel seen in a way she'd never been seen before.

But this wasn't right. They couldn't let Merton get away with it.

"What if it was Ogden behind bars?" She felt the chill of her Oxford cell on her skin, and shivered at the sensation. "Master Phillips . . . he was terrifying, and he was made to do some awful things, but it wasn't *him*. I saw him fight it. This isn't right."

Ogden lowered the paper. "What would you have us do, Elsie?"

She worried her lip, thinking as Reggie took a seat beside her. "I'll write to Irene. Perhaps she can bring me to see him before the sentencing. If she says there's a spell on him, they'll listen to her. We can prove he was used."

Bacchus considered. "He would make a powerful ally."

"I'll do it now." She stood, pushing her chair back.

"Careful how you word it," Ogden warned.

Elsie cast him her best attempt at a withering look. "Really? Ten years of hiding what I am, and you think I'll make a mistake now?"

Ogden's lip quirked. He waved, gesturing for her to proceed. "See if she's heard about the estate, please," he said, quieter.

Elsie nodded, but she knew Irene would have nothing for her. The spellbreaker had promised to contact them the moment she found out, and thus far, no messages had arrived at the house.

⌒༄

Friday, Irene and Elsie set out before dawn for Her Majesty's Prison Oxford, where Master Phillips was being held. The same place where Elsie had spent three days herself.

Elsie described the points of the knot of the spiritual spell on the way there, and Irene explained how they would work this trip into Elsie's studies. Aspector prisons were the most secure jails in the country, and they employed spellbreakers to keep prisoners in line. "It's a grim job, but a well-paying one," she offered.

Elsie had no desire to step into Her Majesty's Prison Oxford again after today, let alone make her living there.

The ride seemed to carry on forever, though the journey had felt even longer in the back of a prison wagon. Her nerves danced when they finally arrived at the stone behemoth, her mind inventing scenarios of being found out and caged once more. But surely Merton wouldn't surface now, when she was supposed to be dead, and Irene . . . she trusted Irene. The woman had no reason to sell her out.

A guard led them to the prison warden, who wore the pin of a physical aspector himself. Not a master's pin, like the one Bacchus had, but a blue one that indicated his specialty. Elsie wondered briefly how experienced he was—Intermediate? Advanced?—but didn't ask. His office was as gray and stony as the rest of the prison, with a single barred window facing south. He sat behind a simple desk nearly empty but for a hibiscus plant sitting on the corner, along with a large magnifying glass and a cup of cold tea.

Irene introduced them, referring to Elsie as her apprentice. She had already telegrammed ahead, so their arrival was expected. Leave it to Irene to not miss a detail. Despite what Elsie had once thought of her, Irene Prescott was one of the most competent people of Elsie's acquaintance. Elsie did not like to think where she would be had the London Physical Atheneum assigned her a different tutor.

"And you believe this spell to be on his person?" The warden, who looked about Ogden's age, sounded skeptical.

"I know Master Phillips," Irene assured him. "From what I've studied of the spell . . . well, he exhibits the symptoms. You must let me check. Send as many guards with me as you wish."

"I found your telegram very interesting." The warden leaned back in his chair, folding his arms across his chest. "Because he, too, claims there was a spell on him."

A shock jolted up Elsie's spine. Of course Master Phillips knew. He'd been actively fighting it that night on his estate, just as Ogden had been at the docks.

Irene kept her composure. "Then surely the truthseekers have confirmed it."

The warden frowned. "I don't know of any way a physical aspector could get around a truth spell, but yes, they have. You're welcome to look, Miss Prescott, but we've seen no evidence as to a spell, and he can't tell us who placed it. Unless you know."

Irene glanced to Elsie. "That is yet to be determined."

The warden's gaze shifted to Elsie, but he didn't complain about her presence. Irene had told him she wished to expose her student to all aspects of spellbreaking. He shrugged. "Very well. He's in our highest-security holding, but I'll send a few extra guards with you just in case, myself included." He stood and gestured for the exit. Once in the corridor, he spoke quietly to a nonspellmaking guard on hand, who left to collect three men to attend them. Elsie noted two were spellbreakers and one was a spiritual aspector.

Had the prison's own spellbreakers attempted to confirm Master Phillips's claims, or were they simply there to prevent him from using his magic? Elsie glanced to Irene, whose face was a stiff mask.

The warden, keys in hand, led them to Master Phillips's cell.

Elsie set her jaw to keep her teeth from clattering as the warden led them deeper into the castle, and then down, down, down, each stair growing darker, until sunlight vanished completely. Simple aspected lights hung from the walls, but not nearly enough to brighten the place or add the slightest bit of cheerfulness.

The warden had not lied: the cells were heavily guarded. There were two armored men to each one, plus more who stood guard at the exits or simply paced back and forth, ready to spring into action. Several of them nodded to the warden as they passed, eyeing Elsie and Irene curiously. They were the only women on the floor.

Master Phillips was in the second-farthest cell from the exit. His hands were gloved with enchanted mail, and his wrists and ankles were tied. He wore gray prison clothes and looked haggard, his beard growing in like someone had seasoned him unevenly with pepper and salt.

It struck Elsie viscerally that she'd been lucky to come here as a spellbreaker. Spellbreakers had no power over iron and stone—they were no more dangerous than the average prisoner and were treated as such. But spellmakers could warp their environment, physical aspectors especially. Master Phillips lacked even the simplest freedom of movement. He eyed them without recognition until he spied Elsie. Afraid he might say something, she hung back and let Irene take charge.

"Spellbreaker, Phillips," the warden said, handing his keys to a guard, who unlocked the heavy door. "Looking you over for a project. Don't try anything. I'd hate to bind you further."

Phillips said nothing, but glanced at Irene with such sorrowful eyes Elsie's heart hurt. The prison spellbreakers entered first, coming to stand on either side of Phillips. Irene stepped in next, pulling her skirts beneath her so she could kneel before the master aspector.

Elsie pushed forward, watching. Irene dipped her head, placing her ear on Master Phillips's chest as if she were a doctor and this were a perfectly normal examination. Phillips murmured something to her, and it took a moment for Elsie's brain to put the sounds together.

"You won't find it," he'd said.

Elsie held her breath. Irene investigated him, his front and back, his legs, even going so far as to lift his shirt. Then she turned, bright eyes first finding Elsie, then the warden.

"I'm afraid I was mistaken." Her voice was fragile, uneasy. "I must further my studies, it seems. There isn't a single spell on him."

Elsie wrapped a hand around the bars, needing something to balance her. There were only two ways a spell like that could be vanished from Master Phillips's person. First, if Merton had truly thought of everything and arranged for it to be removed before turning him in. The second . . .

Lily Merton might be truly dead.

CHAPTER 19

It was hard, pretending everything was normal. To walk to Squire Douglas's home to have a bust design approved, to fill out Ogden's ledgers, to greet customers when they came. Their worlds kept spinning even though hers had stopped.

Master Phillips would almost certainly be executed, in the end, but the truthseekers' findings were delaying the inevitable. He had said, and meant, three things—that he wasn't the killer, that he hadn't stolen opuses, and that he'd been under a spell. But there was no evidence to support Master Phillips's claim other than his own words . . . which was not enough to exonerate him. A person could *believe* something to be true that wasn't—a selfish person might think themselves kind, or an ugly person think themselves beautiful. And so truth was a sticky thing of wavering substance, not enough to acquit a man, especially when so many of the missing opuses had been found at his home.

With no evidence to support Master Phillips's claims, he would probably be ruled as insane and his trial would proceed. Though surely there were alibis from others to show he wasn't near, say, Viscount Byron or Alma Digby when they met their ends. Perhaps the confusion would keep Master Phillips safe long enough for Elsie to figure out what on earth Merton was up to, if she was even *on* Earth anymore.

If Elsie had been less devout to the Cowls, none of this would have happened. Not to Master Phillips, not to the deceased, and not to Ogden.

Which was part of her newest worry. Something Irene had said on the ride home yesterday evening had stuck in Elsie's mind like a rusted knife, and she struggled to wrench it free.

Who knows who else she's controlled. Irene had clucked her tongue and stared out the window, hopelessness on her face. Meanwhile, for Elsie, the trip from Oxford turned out to be the longest one yet.

Lily Merton was friendly with the Duke and Duchess of Kent, and Elsie had met her for the first time—officially, at least—the night she'd first dined at Seven Oaks. Back then, of course, she'd had no idea who Lily Merton was, but the woman had already sent her to Seven Oaks on Cowls duty twice before that. Either for the duke's ancestral opus or for Bacchus's. Perhaps for both.

Looking up from her path—she was coming back from the squire's now, with Mr. Parker's signature of approval in hand—she spied Bacchus waiting outside the stonemasonry shop. His arms were folded across his tight chest, and the way he squinted in the sunlight made him look menacing, or at least it might to one who didn't know him. His dark hair glimmered in the light, and when he turned and saw her coming, recognition lit up his face. He walked to meet her, passing the well, crossing Main Street.

Elsie's chest hurt as she met him near the dressmaker's. "What's wrong?"

He offered his elbow, which she took, and handed her a thin paper. There weren't many out in the street, so Elsie needn't worry about onlookers.

He'd given her a flyer for the Merton estate sale.

"Tuesday." Bacchus spoke quietly as they walked down the lane leading to the stonemasonry shop. "Ogden's information was good. The estate sale runs until Friday, but the opus will be on display only on Tuesday, for the memorial, before it's taken to the atheneum."

Elsie read over the paper, though it merely reiterated what Bacchus had said. "Irene?"

"She's inside, speaking with Mr. Ogden."

Elsie nodded. Folded the paper. "I don't know how we'll get to it."

"He feels confident we can, if we go early." He let out a breath. "He thinks he can turn the minds of the guards so I can access the opus."

Elsie's steps slowed. "You?"

He nodded. "It's in Latin; it's my understanding you're not fluent."

Elsie frowned, but nodded. "And if there are spells?"

"You'll be in the room with us, and Irene will be nearby. He wants to bring Reggie and Emmeline along in case a distraction is needed."

Elsie's stomach tightened. "If they see you with the opus . . ."

"We're all taking risks." His elbow squeezed around her hand, reassuring her.

It *was* a risk. Ogden would have to slip into the minds of multiple guards . . . Elsie had never been to an estate sale before, let alone one for a master aspector. How many guards would there be? How far could Ogden's spells stretch?

How far could Merton's?

They approached the house, but Elsie tugged on Bacchus's arm. "Can I . . . talk to you, for a moment?" She knew it would kill her to keep her fears to herself, letting them simmer in the back of her mind. With so much happening, she wouldn't survive another problem.

Bacchus raised an eyebrow, but nodded, and Elsie guided him around the stonemasonry shop, to the wild land behind it. There was a copse of dogwood back there that offered some shade—the same place she had once argued with him about the propriety of traveling together to Ipswich.

Bacchus paused, unwinding her hand from his arm and cupping her elbow instead. "What's wrong?"

Elsie laughed. "That is the question of the year, isn't it?"

His lip quirked, but his eyes were sober. He waited patiently, a wavy strand of hair falling from its tie. Elsie wanted to tuck it behind his ear, but she felt suddenly self-conscious. As though that simple touch would be more intimate than what they had already shared.

"Merton," she began quietly, glancing around to ensure their privacy, "did she ever . . . touch you?"

"Touch me?" He thought a moment. "I did lead her into the dining room once." His eyes softened. "She never set a spell on me. You would have found it, with the others."

"Time has passed since we visited Master Pierrelo's home," she replied, her voice soft.

Bacchus put a knuckle under her chin. "For better or for worse, I haven't seen the woman since Abel Nash tried to kill me."

The words weren't as reassuring as they should have been. Doubt was a long-term companion to Elsie, present in all her thoughts, all her conversations. She'd trusted the Cowls so blindly, and the debacle with Master Phillips had her questioning her own truths. "She could be making you say that." She twisted the ring on her finger.

Bacchus considered a moment before stepping closer to her, his strong arms wrapping around her shoulders. There was no one to see, but embarrassment tickled Elsie's spine regardless. Bacchus put his chin on her head. "Listen."

Relax. It's all right, she chided herself, and, muscle by muscle, loosened in his grasp, letting her hands curl up to his shoulders. She turned her head, ear near his collar, and listened. Crickets hummed in the nearby grass. Bacchus's heartbeat was strong and steady beneath her cheek. There was no song outside of that—no spiritual spells.

Still in his embrace, she murmured, "Ogden hid his for nine years."

"I could take my clothes off, if you insist."

Elsie stiffened, and Bacchus laughed, which made her laugh, which made her realize there was not enough laughter in her life. Merton was controlling her even without a spell.

Stepping back, Elsie rubbed her neck, hoping to hide her pinkening cheeks. "I don't think that will be necessary, Master Kelsey." A flash of memory—of her hand on his shirtless chest—only made her skin flame brighter. Yet relief blossomed in her breast; surely all of their relationship had been genuine, from his initial manhandling of her at Seven Oaks to his insistence of her innocence to the proposal that never really happened to that kiss in the carriage to now. It was real, it *had* to be real, and yet it felt no more real to her than a novel reader. Any moment now Elsie would turn the page and the story would be over because that's how fairy stories like this worked.

"Dogwood."

She pulled from her reverie at the word and met Bacchus's gaze. "What?"

He gestured to the bright-green bushes that stood even taller than he did. "Dogwood. Ogden had some control during those nine years, yes? To leave you those clues about the spell. If Merton really is alive, and she ever tries to bespell one of us, that's how we'll know. It will be a password, of sorts."

"Dogwood," Elsie repeated. A small smile pulled on her mouth. "But what if we're sitting in this very spot and I insist on talking of the landscape?"

"Then we must refrain from speaking of the landscape, or horticulture in general. In truth, it is not my strongest subject, so you'll have little to regret."

She smiled fully at him, then brought herself back to the present. "We've a few days before the estate sale if you want to visit Seven Oaks."

Bacchus planted his hands on his hips and sighed.

"They were invited to the wedding," he said. "The duchess even picked out the invitations. But I do not think the duke would come, even if I forgave him." He looked into the dogwood. The wind rippled its leaves, and one could almost imagine fairies hidden among them.

"Will you let him die with such guilt on his shoulders?" He glanced to her, and Elsie held up her hands in mock surrender. "I am not pardoning him. But he's been like a father to you for many years."

"And my own father had his hand in it," Bacchus replied gruffly. He shook his head. "The further I get from it, the more civil I feel. But then I remember all the challenges and fears I had for my entire adult life and several years of my adolescence, and forgiveness seems . . . not impossible, but far away." He paused, swallowed. "I wonder, if they'd approached me, if I would have offered to help of my own volition. I'm not sure; there's no way to know, in the end."

"Don't hold yourself accountable for it." She said it in the serious tone it deserved, then found herself chuckling. "Now where have I heard that advice before?"

Bacchus pressed a kiss to her forehead. She wished they could stay there in the spotty shade so Elsie could hold on to that fairy-tale-like respite, but it was not to be.

They had a caper to plan.

༄

The opus was in the second-floor parlor.

They split up, Bacchus taking Elsie on his arm, Mr. Ogden wandering with Miss Prescott, while Miss Pratt and Mr. Camden toured the gardens. They did not want to draw attention to themselves as a large group, and they did not think it wise to head straight for the opus. This was an estate sale; they needed to present themselves as interested buyers. The flyer Miss Prescott had given them had been handed out at the atheneums, giving spellmakers—and breakers—priority with the event. In order to look the part, Bacchus had donned his garish master's pin, and Irene wore a similar one depicting her as a licensed spellbreaker.

They had a plan, but there were many things that could go wrong. Bacchus was worried about Mr. Ogden, who was too emotionally invested in this matter. He hadn't been sleeping well—Bacchus had seen him up late in the sitting room with his sketchbook more than once, and his left eye had taken to occasionally twitching. Hopefully the drive to protect the others would overpower his personal need for closure. And if the opus *was* Merton's . . . then this entire venture was more or less over. Truthfully, Bacchus hoped for that outcome, even if it robbed justice. It would be nice to have peace, for once. Though it might leave Master Phillips in dire straits. Despite Bacchus's personal dislike for the man, his sense of justice insisted that he not suffer for another's crimes.

He and Elsie had looked over the paintings, feigning interest in some, though a depiction of the English countryside did appeal to his aesthetic. A few rooms were closed and roped off. One of the windows that had been broken was boarded up, and there was a pale spot on the carpet where a rug used to be—a rug that had supposedly been stained with blood from the "attack." Other rooms still needed sorting or were being used for storage.

Merton's home was quaint but spacious, more room than a single woman would likely need, especially since the only servant she had kept on hand was, apparently, a cook. The parlor sat at the end of a large hall, and great windows leading to a narrow veranda let in the early-morning light, illuminating the space. Two rooms lay on either side of the parlor—the library and Merton's study—where a few other early risers were perusing books, perhaps hoping to find aspecting secrets between their pages.

The parlor's walls were stark white and simply adorned, the carpet burgundy, and in the back of the room, several feet off center, stood a white-painted podium of wood, surrounded by taupe cords to dissuade the passing public from touching. Atop that podium sat a thick opus, its cover marbled mauve and cream, its thick pages lined silver, its corners rounded. A rather feminine opus. And, of course, it was closed.

More importantly, there were five guards in the parlor alone, each armed with a sword and rifle. One stood between the podium and the veranda. One lingered near the library entrance, another near the study entrance, and two watched from where the hall opened up into the parlor. One of those men wore blue lapels, labeling him as a physical aspector. His lack of a pin indicated he was likely an intermediate spellmaker who had burned out and taken a position in law enforcement instead of staying with the atheneum.

Elsie squeezed Bacchus's arm as they approached to pay their respects, just as one would at a coffin. She looked beyond the opus, her eyes going out of focus.

"It's the real thing," she whispered, then blinked in surprise. "I thought . . . I thought it might be an astral projection, and the real book would be in one of those locked rooms. But there are no active spiritual spells here."

Bacchus, pointedly not looking at the guards, walked Elsie around the podium slowly. Anyone watching would think they were just admiring the opus. "What else?"

She closed her eyes a moment. "There's a rational spell on the podium. An emotional one."

"Perhaps fear, to dissuade those who are too interested."

She nodded, still unfocused, trying to perceive any other spells they might face. A few faint freckles dotted the bridge of her nose. For a moment, Bacchus let his thoughts wander elsewhere, to Barbados, to Elsie strolling along the beach, freckles blooming across the entirety of her face. She would hate the notion, he was sure, but the image his mind conjured was rather beautiful.

"There's a spell thickening the air around the opus, and I think it's also fused to the podium. And"—she sniffed—"possibly a temporal spell to keep the pages well, but that might just be the opus itself. I . . . I haven't smelled a lot of opuses."

Bacchus chuckled and led Elsie away before they could garner too much of the guards' attention. It was unfortunate none of the others could do the job; Bacchus tended to rouse suspicion no matter his behavior, as he had at Christie's Auction House. At least the pin helped. He'd seen more than one security detail's eyes drop to it.

<Is Elsie still with you?> Mr. Ogden's voice pushed into his head.

Elsie perked, sensing the spell. Bacchus guided her into the study.

<Yes,> he thought back. *<The opus is in the parlor. It's defended by a few physical spells and a rational one.>*

<Can you replace the physical spells if she unwinds them?>

All the spells Elsie had mentioned were in Bacchus's repertoire. *<Yes. But I don't know about the rational one.>*

<Do your best.>

They wandered about the study, Elsie and he taking turns glancing out the door. Another pair entered the parlor, an older couple, neither wearing a pin. Possibly a local baron and his wife? Regardless, they needed to act quickly. The crowd would only grow.

The people who'd gathered in the library also stepped into the parlor, but they must have already looked at the opus, for they turned back for the hall.

Bacchus ran his hand over the smooth oak desktop. A price tag on it read, *£100.*

"Ogden," Elsie whispered, so faint Bacchus barely picked up on it. His pulse picked up, but he forced himself to continue to wander through the room, looking over a few things, writing down, *silver candlesticks, £2,* on his bid card so he would not leave entirely empty-handed. Elsie's grip on his arm tightened, but otherwise she hid her nerves well.

When they finally returned to the parlor, they spied Ogden on the veranda and Miss Prescott studying a grandmother clock on the far wall. The couple from before stepped into the library.

<*Now.*> Mr. Ogden's voice forced its way into Bacchus's skull.

And suddenly the guards all looked up at once, squinting at something on the ceiling. Something only they could see.

Elsie rushed to the podium, her fingers picking at the air as though they spun a web. Bacchus hurried after her. It didn't matter if the opus was fused with the podium. They didn't need to take it, only look at it—

He jerked his hand away as though the book had bitten him.

Elsie reached for what he assumed was the rational spell.

"Don't," he whispered, gritting his teeth. Ogden was pushing himself to the limit, distracting five men at once. He might not have the chance to replace a rational spell as well.

Hand shaking, Bacchus grabbed the cover of the book and flipped it open. His heartbeat soared until it rattled in his skin. At least his clammy hands made turning the pages easier. He flipped to the back of the book, where the master spells were penned in surprisingly sloppy handwriting. Did Merton have an uneven hand? He couldn't recall.

Heaven help him, the fear spell was like dipping his hand into the mouth of a snake. Elsie's grip on his bicep helped steady him, even as his breaths came too fast. As long as her hand was there, he knew the guards were still distracted. His job was to read.

The fear helped him read faster.

He had to read several lines of each spell to assess what they were. A slew of curses and blessings, communications spells for plants and animals—

"Oh, I absolutely love your dress!" Miss Prescott's voice rang out from the library. The couple must have been on their way back into the parlor. She was distracting them. "Wherever did you get it? The color looks so well on you."

Bacchus's shaking hands tore one of the opus pages. He winced, flipping past astral projection of oneself, and then a very similar spell allowing astral projection of another person.

Which was when he reached the back cover.

He slammed the book shut and reeled back, breathing hard as the fear spell released its grip. Wiping his forehead, he said, "It's not hers." There was no spell that controlled another person. Merton had faked her death with another spellmaker's opus.

The sound of vomiting brought Bacchus back to the present.

"You! Stop!" Two of the five guards rushed to the veranda, where Mr. Ogden was doubled over and retching on the marble floor.

"Oh, you poor man!" Elsie exclaimed, acting a hair on the excessive side. "Here, now." She handed him her handkerchief. Ogden's skin was pale, his eyes hollow. "You should know better than to go out when you're ill. At least it's on stone, hmm?" She put an arm around Ogden's shoulders. "My name is Elsie. Let me help you outside."

Bacchus wiped the perspiration from his face with his own handkerchief and hurried over. Elsie's hands were trembling. In addition to the vomit, Mr. Ogden's nose was bleeding profusely. He'd extended himself too far.

Had Bacchus paged through the master spells any slower, he would surely have been caught with his hands on the opus.

He rushed forward, helping to steady Mr. Ogden as well. "Let's get you home," he said, then whispered, "It's not her."

Mr. Ogden shut his eyes as though overcome by heavy exhaustion. Validation. He had been right. But it also meant Merton was out there, somewhere, pursuing the heinous plans that had brought them all together.

"Oh dear, he's with me. I've got him." Miss Prescott gently took Elsie's place. She apologized profusely to the guards, one of whom remained with them as they escorted Mr. Ogden out of the house. Bacchus pressed Elsie's handkerchief to Mr. Ogden's nose so he would not bleed on the carpet. It ruined the cloth, of course, but it hardly mattered. Elsie would need an updated handkerchief soon besides. One that read *EK* instead of *EC*.

Miss Pratt and Mr. Camden were near the front of the house when Bacchus and the others emerged. Mr. Camden rushed to the stonemason's side, and Miss Pratt paled nearly as much as Ogden had.

"I'll get 'im a carriage," Mr. Camden said, and ran for the lane. Meanwhile, Bacchus and Miss Prescott led Mr. Ogden to the grass and sat him down. He looked ready to vomit a second time.

"Take her away," Miss Prescott murmured, tilting her head to Elsie. "It's best we're not seen together too long, just in case."

Elsie's lips parted as though to protest, but she closed them again, pressing them into a thin line. Bacchus took her hand and guided her away. They would hire their own carriage home.

"He'll be fine," he assured her. "It will pass."

Elsie glanced over her shoulder as they neared the lane her brother had darted toward. A small carriage was pulling around, hopefully for Mr. Ogden. It couldn't pull too close; as the morning wore on, more and more people were arriving for the memorial-turned-estate-sale, and those who owned their vehicles left them parked as close to the house as they could get. At least the clutter made it easy for Bacchus and Elsie to vanish from sight. The guards outside the home were likely watching Mr. Ogden like a hawk.

Elsie somehow managed to take in a deep breath; Bacchus wasn't sure how women breathed in those contraptions they wore around their waists. Perhaps sometime he'd ask her. "He'll be fine," she repeated. Then, "I suppose we won't be getting those candlesticks."

Bacchus had forgotten about the card in his pocket. "I suppose not."

She squeezed his arm, drawing closer to him, which Bacchus didn't mind in the slightest. "You're sure it wasn't . . . ?"

"The pages were thick and easy to turn. I saw every spell. That opus is not Master Merton's."

Elsie nodded, looking straight ahead. They'd reached the main road, and Bacchus turned them west to keep the sun from their eyes. They could walk off the morning's events before finding transportation. Even Bacchus needed a moment, his body still recovering from the rational spell.

"What next?" he asked.

Elsie shrugged. "More newspaper articles? Perhaps once Ogden is recovered, he can search for clues around Rochester . . . but I'm honestly not—"

She stopped—speech, movement, everything—her eyes glued to a couple coming across the street. There was nothing special about them; they were well dressed, but not to the extent an aristocrat would be. The man appeared to be close to Bacchus's age, with coiffed ginger hair that was beginning to recede from his forehead. The woman looked older, perhaps Miss Prescott's age. Her hat was so wide it nearly hit the gentleman in the head while they walked.

"Someone you know?" Bacchus inquired.

Elsie nodded. "That is Alfred Miller."

It took a second for Bacchus to place the name; Elsie had mentioned the man only once.

This was her old beau.

Bacchus altered their course slightly to be sure they'd cross paths with the couple.

Elsie didn't object, but her hand tightened on his arm. For a moment it seemed the couple wouldn't notice them, so Bacchus cleared his throat.

Mr. Miller looked up first, noticing Elsie at once. His countenance was first that of surprise, which he quickly tucked away with a too-wide smile. "Oh! My dear, look. You remember Miss—"

And then his gaze shifted to Bacchus, who stood a full head taller than he and nearly twice as broad. Bacchus made a point of keeping his chin up so he could look down his nose at the man. Here was another reason to be grateful for that gaudy aspector's pin.

Elsie leaned into Bacchus as they paused on the side of the road. "Oh, Alfred. You're looking well." She said nothing to his wife. "What are you doing way out here?"

"The estate sale, of course . . ." Mr. Miller's eyes kept jerking over Bacchus, like he was trying to ignore him and having a hard time. In that moment, Bacchus found great joy in standing out like a cat in a crow's nest.

"Oh, I didn't think you would be interested." Elsie smiled. "Do stay clear of the veranda; I hear a man lost his breakfast there, looking at the prices of everything."

Mr. Miller flushed slightly. "And what are you doing here, Elsie?" He eyed the pin on Bacchus's lapel.

Before Elsie could answer, Bacchus said, "Have you not heard? Mrs. Kelsey is a spellbreaker. She has priority."

The flush faded to a blanch. "Are you really?"

His wife tugged on his arm. "Alfred."

"We'd best be going." Bacchus offered only a nod in farewell before escorting Elsie farther down the street. Neither of them looked back. Elsie walked with a straight spine until they turned the next corner.

Then her flat affect slipped, and she broke out in laughter.

"That was brilliant," she said, releasing his arm and clapping her hands. "Did you see the look on his face? Just brilliant. You're so direct, Bacchus. It's quite menacing."

Bacchus smirked. "Is it?"

She softly jabbed his ribs. "Do not pretend like you did not mean it to be. This was so much more satisfying than the trick we played on Duchess Morris." Her laughter softened, and she took in their surroundings. A few shops pocked a narrow road. A few boys chatted with one another, one holding a dog's leash.

"Perhaps I should have asked," he tried, seeing her expression shift.

But she waved his words away. "Oh no, not that. It's just . . . you called me Mrs. Kelsey."

"More or less accurate," he said. "It has a certain ring to it."

She smiled, though she seemed to be fighting it. "It does, doesn't it?"

Four more days. One bright thing in the midst of so much darkness.

Bacchus offered Elsie his elbow, and they slowly made their way back to Brookley.

CHAPTER 20

Some ginger tea and a lot of rest set Ogden to rights again.

After returning to Brookley, Elsie barely left his side. When she did, Emmeline took over, keeping an eye on him, listening to his breathing, checking for fever. Elsie couldn't imagine how much spellbreaking she'd have to do to exert herself to the point Ogden had. The worst she'd ever experienced was fiercely itchy wrists. Bacchus had told her he'd never suffered anything more than a headache. How much had Ogden struggled on that veranda, casting spells to distract five different guards? And thank goodness for Irene. If she hadn't distracted the rogue couple, they might have been caught anyway.

Still, when Ogden declared he was going back to Rochester, it made Elsie uneasy.

"Perhaps wait until after the wedding," she pressed as they ate lunch in the dining room, Emmeline up and about and mothering them per usual. "To make sure."

"I'm fine." Ogden tore into a piece of buttered bread. At least his appetite had returned. He'd barely eaten since coming home from the estate sale yesterday. "I need to do it now, before the estate sale ends, in case someone there knows something."

"If a spellbreaker is present," Bacchus said, "they might detect you."

Ogden frowned, picked up his knife, and cut into his pie. "Then I will endeavor to not get caught."

"What was it that you said the other day, about being the rational one?" Bacchus asked. Elsie wasn't sure what he meant, but Ogden ignored him.

Elsie worried her lip, but there would be no stopping him, she knew. He was proving himself to be a positively stubborn man. Yet, in a way, he had earned the right to be stubborn.

"One of us should come with you," she tried.

Ogden rebuffed the statement with a wave of his hand, eating too quickly to give a proper reply. When he finished, he pushed his plate away, wiped his mouth, and stood. "One thing before I go." He gestured to Elsie to follow, then started for the stairs.

She passed a curious look to Bacchus before following Ogden to the second floor, to his bedroom. He motioned for Elsie to step in, shut the door behind them, then went to the trunks under his bed. He must have rifled through them earlier, because what he was searching for sat at the very top.

A wooden ring box.

"Ogden?" Elsie asked.

"It occurred to me last night that Master Kelsey has not been outfitted with the appropriate matrimonial jewelry." He held the box in his palm, as though weighing it, before turning to Elsie. "I want you to have this."

Hesitant, she took the box and gingerly opened it. Inside was a thin gold ring delicately carved to look like a winding snake. The symbol of eternity.

Her lips parted. "O-Ogden—"

"It was my father's ring." He shrugged. "I highly doubt I'll be able to use it myself."

Closing the box, Elsie shook her head. "I can't take this."

"You can." He closed the gap between them and placed his hand on top of hers, keeping the ring box pressed between her fingers. He looked her in the eyes. "Elsie, you are the closest thing to a daughter I have."

Tears sprang to her eyes.

"I know you may think otherwise, especially given Merton's involvement in our lives. But I cherish you, and nothing would make me happier than to pass down this heirloom to my rightful family."

Elsie pressed her lips together. Sniffed. Wiped her eyes on her sleeve. Nodded.

Ogden smiled and embraced her, his arms encircling her shoulders. Warm and strong, just as a father's hug should be.

"My father was a sturdy man," he murmured. "So that ring might even fit that man you have down there."

Elsie laughed. "He can adjust it either way." When Ogden pulled back, she added, "I wouldn't mind being Elsie Ogden. At least for a few days."

She thought she saw a glimmer of wetness in Ogden's eyes as well. "I would like that very much."

～❦～

Ogden set off shortly after that. Emmeline packed him a dinner, and Elsie packed him a valise, just in case. Bacchus offered him an enchanted pencil, but he'd declined, saying he'd be moving about too much for it to be of any use.

"They have telegrams in Rochester." It was the last thing he said before donning his hat and leaving the stonemasonry shop.

There wasn't much to do with Ogden gone, and since the upcoming wedding was so simple, there wasn't much left to plan. Elsie took to wiping down the counters in the studio and sweeping and mopping. She even took a putty knife to some paint drips on the floor. She had just finished when a dog barked outside. Opening the front door, she saw a post dog panting with a satchel hanging off its side, containing three letters. She took the envelopes and patted the dog's head. Poor thing was probably sweltering in this July weather.

The dog trotted away, off to the next house, and Elsie stepped inside. The first letter was from Ogden's mortgager, reminding him of the month's upcoming payment. The second and third were addressed to Bacchus.

"Oh," she said, turning the first letter about. It bore the seal of Seven Oaks. The second missive she didn't recognize.

Setting the bill atop the counter, Elsie hurried upstairs, finding Bacchus drafting a letter of his own in the sitting room. He did that a lot—writing missives to establish himself in London, or sending instructions back home to Barbados. It was all very official sounding.

"You know you're well and settled in Brookley when you get more mail than we do." She offered a smile as she crossed the room, handing the mail to him.

Bacchus set down his pen and accepted it. He opened the unfamiliar letter first and read silently. A sigh escaped him.

Elsie took a seat beside him. "What is it?"

"Good news, we're not homeless." He handed the letter to her. "Our offer on that townhome in London was approved."

Mice scurried about in Elsie's stomach. "Oh." It was official, then. They would be living somewhere else, together. It was a stark reminder that all of this was actually happening. Hopefully happening. Admittedly, she was sad to say goodbye to the stonemasonry shop. She couldn't keep her job if she lived so deep in the capital, though without an occupation, she could fully dive into her pretend training as a spellbreaker and earn the official title that much faster. Still, she would miss seeing Ogden and Emmeline every day. At least she would be closer to Reggie.

And much closer to Bacchus.

Ignoring the warmth climbing up her neck, she said, "The other is from Seven Oaks."

Bacchus, his expression slack, turned the letter over and ran the pad of his thumb over its seal. "So it is." He handed it to her.

"It's addressed to you."

"I know you're curious." He offered her a weak half smile.

Chewing on the inside of her cheek, Elsie broke the seal and opened the letter. It was brief, the penmanship fine. She glanced at the bottom. "It's from the duchess." Then she read slowly.

"Oh."

Bacchus quirked an eyebrow. "Oh?"

She read to the end of the letter, then set it on her lap. "The duke feels terrible about what happened."

He leaned his chin on his fist. "So she's said."

"He took off the siphoning spell."

Bacchus straightened in his seat. "What?"

She held out the letter to him, but he didn't take it. "It says he canceled the new one. The one he got after I broke your end. She says they're going to take what life will give them."

Now Bacchus did take the letter, and looked it over. "I'm . . . surprised" was all he said.

Elsie drew a hand down the length of his back. "How are you doing?"

He shook his head. "I'm not sure."

A scream pierced the air, and something shattered.

Elsie shot to her feet. "Emmeline!" She ran for the door, Bacchus close behind her. She nearly toppled down the stairs for how swiftly she took them.

She swung around into the kitchen, seeing first the broken pieces of a serving tray littering the floor, then Emmeline pressed up against the wall, wide eyes staring at the far corner. At a person. No, an astral projection. But the one casting it was so far away it was little more than a wisp of a ghost. No discernable facial features, smeared colors of brown, gray, black, and peach.

Elsie's stomach hit the floor, and her throat constricted. She managed to croak, "M-Merton?"

"I'm not familiar with him," a gravelly *male* voice replied, as though he were speaking through a wall. But more importantly, he spoke with an American accent.

A chill passed over Elsie's everything.

He'd come.

Master Quinn Raven.

"It worked," Elsie whispered.

The image shifted. "You'll have to speak up."

She stepped closer, and Bacchus's hand found her shoulder, stopping her. Turning to him, she said, "A projection of him can hardly hurt us."

Bacchus's mouth thinned to a line, but he nodded, and Elsie crossed the room, ceramic shards cracking under her shoes.

"My name is Elsie Camden. I'm the one you met in Juniper Down."

"Yes, I know," he barked, still garbled, but there was nothing to be done about that. "You said you didn't pen them, but now they're everywhere. Explain yourself."

"I didn't pen the originals. That was Master Lily Merton."

Raven didn't answer right away. "Isn't she the one who just died?"

"She faked her death. We checked the opus."

Behind her, Bacchus said, "Do you know her?"

"Vaguely." He offered nothing else.

"Merton is the one who wrote those articles, goading you," Elsie went on. She needed to relay as much information as she could, as quickly as possible, given Raven's obvious lack of patience. They *needed* him as an ally. This moment meant everything. "She bespelled my employer for nine years to control him, and he controlled me. She's been murdering aspectors for their opuses. And searching for you, apparently."

Raven spat something that sounded like a curse, but it was too garbled to determine which one he'd chosen. "First she tried to buy me; then she tried to goad me, threaten my acquaintances." He paused, and when he spoke again, his voice was strained. "So many of them are books now. Never thought she'd go for Alma." He cleared his throat. "I had to put an end to it."

That's why he had finally come, then. Why he had tracked down Elsie. Turner and the others, they were people he knew. Merton had forced him out of hiding in the cruelest way possible. "Why does she want you so badly?" Elsie tried.

He snorted, or so Elsie thought he did. "Why does anyone *want* me? They want what I know! Years of research, thrown in the fire. You whisper it to one person and the entire community dogs you. They stopped when I 'died.' All but one."

"Please," Bacchus said. "We're trying to find her. To stop the madness."

"But we don't understand *why*," Elsie added. "The opuses . . . She must have been trying to lure you out, and strengthen herself in the process. But to what end?"

"And why should I trust you?" Raven's voice was like chipping mortar. "You're goading me just as she has. You'll use me, too."

"I'm a *spellbreaker*!" Elsie snapped. "You know that. I showed you!"

"But the others."

Elsie glanced over her shoulder. Bacchus nodded. Emmeline just stared at Raven openmouthed, like he truly was a ghost. "We've no spiritual aspectors here," she said. "I'm with Master Bacchus Kelsey of the Physical Atheneum and our maid. My employer is Cuthbert Ogden, also of the Physical Atheneum." He clearly didn't trust them, and it wasn't likely to win them any favor that Ogden was an unregistered rational aspector.

"How do you know that matters if—"

"It's a spell, isn't it?" Elsie interrupted. "That's what she wants from you."

Raven hesitated. "Do you want me to be impressed?"

"I want you to be my ally." Her anger was rising. "Do you think you're the only one who's suffered?"

He was silent a moment.

Elsie pushed, "Don't you want it to end, too?"

He let out a loud sigh. "You are a pestering woman."

Bacchus said, "Come here in person if you don't believe us. Cast a truthseeking spell."

"I'm not so foolish." He paused. "I know Miss Camden was truthful in Juniper Down."

Emmeline chirped, "Then y-you'll help us?"

The projection groaned. Shifted slightly to the right, slightly to the left. Either the magic was wavering or Raven was struggling to stand still. "It's a contagion spell."

Elsie furrowed her brow. "What?"

"A contagion spell. I discovered it."

Bacchus shook his head. "Spells cannot be discovered. They have been set in stone since their creation."

"Don't talk to me like I'm a fool, boy," Raven snapped. "Spells are like any form of knowledge—they can be forgotten. Who knows how much magic died with our ancestors, swallowed by history? I found evidence of it twenty years ago." He paused, then added, "If you're churchgoers, I expect you're familiar with the mass-blessing spell."

Indeed, Elsie *was* familiar with mass blessings. Often spiritual aspectors assigned to a church cast them at the end of a sermon to help the congregation feel good about their decision to worship. Often it was a blessing of peace, a facsimile of the feeling bestowed by the Holy Spirit. While a blessing of peace by itself was a novice-level spell, a master spiritual aspector had the ability to cast it in such a manner that it would affect a small crowd, letting the blessing carry through multiple persons the way the flu would.

"I found evidence that there was once a spell that acted similarly, but with health. Something that might cure a pandemic. A journal from the time of the Black Death. I devoted my life to researching it. To finding old works, retranslating them, putting the missing pieces together. And I found my answer. But it surprised me.

"The spell is not specifically a cure—rather, it's a master contagion spell. Like a plague. A spell of exponential growth that doesn't stop after thirty heads. Only the very strongest aspectors could hope to cast such a thing."

Which meant Quinn Raven was one of them. "Go on," she whispered, then cleared her throat. "Go on."

"That's it. It takes something and multiplies it *indefinitely*. Do you not understand the repercussions of a spell like that finding its way into the wrong hands? *Indefinitely.* Disease, blessings, curses, ideals—"

"Ideals?" Elsie repeated.

"That's what I said, isn't it?" The sharpness of his tone pierced the room.

Elsie hardly noticed. Her mind was spinning. Merton had been displaced from her family. Raised in a workhouse. Reduced to begging and coercion in order to improve her station and become a spellmaker.

She'd visited workhouses to offer blessings before all this. *Quite the Christian, donating to peace efforts,* Duchess Morris had said.

She'd railed against the rich, likening the differences in class to a war.

Raven was talking again, but Elsie wasn't listening.

What if she and Merton both wanted the same thing?

"Can it force people to cooperate?" she asked. "To share their resources and get along?"

Raven growled. "I told you, you have to speak up—"

"The contagion spell," Elsie said. "Can it spread peace, like a mass-blessing spell?" She thought of Ogden. "Or perhaps force obedience?"

Bacchus gave her a curious look.

Raven hesitated again. "Theoretically, yes."

"What if your spell were used to disperse a spiritual spell capable of controlling others?" Bacchus murmured. "What then?" Before Raven could rail against him for speaking too softly, Elsie repeated the sentiment, louder.

Raven was quiet for nearly a minute. "That would be a terrible way to use it."

Emmeline said, "Why? What's so awful about forcing people to share and get along?"

He scoffed. "You English and your ideals. Why? *Freedom.* Can you imagine forced pacifism spreading like a plague across cities, countries, continents? Stripping people of their free will?"

"Guaranteeing equality no matter what the cost." Elsie rubbed a chill from her arms. That might not be it, but based on what Merton had related to her over the years . . . it *felt* right. Yes, Merton could have been lying about her ideals, her aims, but there'd been such unity to the messages, and some of the earlier tasks she'd been given had indeed helped the less fortunate. Ultimately, it didn't matter—it would be a disaster if a serial murderer in the possession of dozens of opuses got hold of a spell like that.

And only Raven knew it. He had absorbed it, hence the missing drops. It would be the only way for an aspector to know, definitely, that a spell was legitimate. If the drops didn't absorb, the spell was fraudulent or the aspector wasn't powerful enough to cast it. If they did . . .

"Meet with us." Bacchus stepped up to the projection. "Talk with us. Help us find a way to stop her."

"I think not."

"Yes, you will," Elsie pressed. "Because you have to. Because if you didn't care, you wouldn't have been in hiding so long. You wouldn't have sought me out. You wouldn't be talking to us now. Because some day you *will* die, and you can't allow your opus to be found by someone like Lily Merton."

The colors of the projection shifted, and Elsie could almost feel Quinn Raven staring at her.

Then it winked out entirely.

Emmeline squeaked.

"He'll be back." Elsie hugged herself, staring at the corner where the American had been. "He has to come back."

Because he was part of this, and even if Merton's "death" had limited her in some ways, she wasn't going to stop anytime soon. That was a truth Elsie understood without the aid of any spell.

CHAPTER 21

Ogden returned from Rochester on Thursday with a grim look on his face. As Elsie had expected, he'd found no leads on Merton. Every mind he'd pierced believed her to be dead.

Granted, updating him about Master Raven's visit had instantly lifted his spirits. Which was a very good thing come Saturday, as he was giving Elsie away.

Today.

She was getting married today.

She leaned against the wall beside the door in Emmeline's room, which had been restored to its original appearance. Rainer and John, Bacchus's servants from Barbados, had already taken her belongings to their new London home. Her cream-colored dress draping her perfectly; her hair coifed, curled, and pinned; both hands pressed to her stomach as she struggled to breathe. And her corset wasn't even that tight.

Emmeline stepped into the room, carrying a basket of flower petals that would be used for the aisle in the chapel. One look at Elsie had her mouth and eyes forming perfect O's.

"Everything will be fine!" Emmeline assured her, rubbing a hand up and down Elsie's arm.

Elsie shook her head. Everything would not be fine. She'd barely slept last night. She hadn't been able to stomach breakfast. She couldn't breathe.

A frown curved Emmeline's lips. "Really, I think Master Kelsey will make a fine husband—"

"It's not *Master Kelsey*." Her response was airy. "Believe me, Em, I want to marry Bacchus with everything I am. But something terrible is going to happen. I can feel it in my bones. I won't be allowed this happiness."

Emmeline laughed. "You're too young to feel it in your bones! And everything will be perfect. I've prayed for you every day this week."

Elsie couldn't help but smile at the kind sentiment. "Thank you." She swallowed. "They're not all gathering around the church, are they?" They were to have a very small wedding. Elsie wouldn't have agreed to announce it in the paper if not for the need to make a show for Lord Harold Astley, the magistrate who had agreed to release Elsie from prison. She couldn't regret that they'd done so, of course, for it had brought Reggie to her.

Emmeline looked away. "Well, they *are* curious. Oh, Elsie. Deep breaths."

Elsie did as told. A few gulps of air later, she said, "Merton is still out there. Master Raven could decide to pop in at any time. Master Phillips has been released from his spell . . . Surely Merton has taken over a new lackey by now. And he or she will show up and murder us all."

"Elsie—"

"He's not going to be there," she said, throat constricting. "I'm going to show up, and they'll ring those church bells, and he won't be at the end of the aisle. And the whole town will see, and I'll be humiliated."

Emmeline set down the basket and took both of Elsie's hands in hers. Elsie's fingers were ice; Emmeline's were as warm as freshly baked bread. "You are a silly woman. The way he looks at you . . . There's no way he won't be there. I saw him leave for the church myself this morning."

Elsie squeezed her friend's hands. "There's still time for him to change his mind." It would wreck her if he did. She'd become a recluse. Never leave the house. Perhaps adopt a cat.

Her hopes had gotten so high, despite her best efforts to contain them. She wouldn't survive the fall this time. Not with Bacchus.

Emmeline kissed Elsie's cheek. "It will be a beautiful wedding. And short."

Elsie filled her lungs to bursting and nodded. It *would* be brief. The customary dinner was to have taken place at Seven Oaks, but they'd cut it from the program given the uncertain situation with the duke and duchess.

"You look beautiful, and the dress is perfect," Emmeline assured her.

A soft laugh escaped Elsie's mouth. She pushed off the wall, standing of her own accord. "I suppose if something horrible does happen, staying in here isn't going to stop it."

"It will only stop good things from happening. Come, now. They're waiting for you." She grinned. "*He's* waiting for you."

Elsie nodded and let Emmeline pull her from the room.

Please let it be so. Please. Please. Please.

The church wasn't far from the stonemasonry shop, so there was no point in hiring a carriage, though Elsie did not like walking down Main Street garbed like a bride. She hadn't yet put on her veil, and she ignored the few looks she got, keeping her eyes straight ahead. The light exercise helped steady her. Maybe Emmeline was right. Maybe this would all go off without a hitch. Maybe she'd get a happy ending like in her novel readers. Maybe.

They entered through the tower, and the church bells began ringing as Emmeline pinned Elsie's veil to her hair. Elsie's nerves cooled and ran from her shoulders to her feet, raising gooseflesh beneath her dress.

Emmeline gently pinched Elsie's cheeks, bringing some color into them. Then, with an encouraging smile, she hurried into the nave to spread her flowers before sitting down. It was tradition, ensuring a happy path for the bride.

Elsie licked her lips. Took another breath.

The church bells ceased, and the church sounded eerily silent in their absence. She hadn't asked for a choir to fill the empty space. She'd been too convinced something would happen to prevent . . . well, this.

She gripped her simple bouquet, made of twelve white roses. The flowers had been nearly as expensive as the dress.

If he's there, everything will be all right, she thought, approaching the door to the nave. *If Bacchus is there, then even if Merton appears, or a spellmaker with a knife, or Raven himself, it will be all right.*

Please, God, let him be there.

Surely Emmeline would have rushed back out to warn her if he weren't.

The organ music started. Heart thudding against her ribs like a battering ram, Elsie waited until a boy no older than ten opened the door to the nave. The aisle leading to the altar was lined with white rose petals. Most of the pews were empty, as was to be expected. Her gaze traveled down it, finding Ogden, the clergyman, the parish clerk, and—

Bacchus.

He stood to the left of the altar, dressed in blue, his hair pulled back more neatly than she'd ever seen it. Elsie walked toward him, down the aisle, which seemed painfully long given all the eyes on her. She glanced over them. The Duchess of Kent had come and smiled at her sweetly. There was no sign of her husband or daughters. Across the aisle from her stood Lord Astley; he'd come to witness the event, as promised. Ahead of him, Emmeline, Reggie, and Irene. By the duchess, in a wheeled chair and unable to stand, was an older woman with gray-streaked blonde hair. It took a second for Elsie to place her. That had to be Master Ruth Hill! Her color looked well, and that was a relief.

And then her gaze found Bacchus again. His green eyes hadn't wavered from hers, and in the chapel lighting they reminded her of an evening in the forest. He was beautiful in every sense a man could be beautiful. Her nerves lightened to a buzz. Let Merton come. She couldn't hurt Elsie so long as Bacchus was near. No one could.

The way he looked at her warmed her center. Was Emmeline right? *Did* Bacchus look at her a certain way? Was it just the dress? But Bacchus's eyes hadn't so much as strayed to the dress.

She reached him, heart still drumming as though she were marching to war. The congregation sat. The clergyman started saying something. Elsie couldn't process it.

She was getting married. She was getting married. *She was getting married.*

God, please don't let me cry.

"Who gives this woman away?" the clergyman asked.

Ogden stepped forward, a gentle smile on his face. "I do."

Elsie grinned at him. She would miss seeing his mussed hair in the morning, sharing meals with him and Emmeline, arguing over how old he was. Heaven knew she would miss that.

Ogden sat, and Elsie found herself glancing at the doors, the windows, looking for shadows, listening for sounds. But she found nothing out of the ordinary.

She caught sight of Reggie's ear-to-ear grin, and realized she was mirroring it when her cheeks began to hurt.

And then her gaze shifted to Bacchus, who was still watching her with those forest eyes, and Elsie felt suddenly undone, like she was falling and flying at the same time. Like her heart beat somewhere besides in her body.

And then he spoke, his Bajan accent genuine and rich.

"I, Bacchus Kelsey, take thee, Elsie Camden, to be my wedded wife, to have and to hold from this day forward, for better for worse, for richer or poorer, in sickness and in health, to love and to cherish, till death us do part, according to God's holy ordinance, and thereto I plight thee my troth."

Her vision blurred, and she blinked it clear. Her spirit turned within her. The clergyman spoke to her, and it was by some miracle she was coherent enough to repeat what he said.

"I, Elsie Camden, take thee, Bacchus Kelsey, to be my wedded husband, to have and to hold from this day forward, for better for worse, for richer for poorer, in sickness and in health, to love, cherish, and to obey, till death us do part, according to God's holy ordinance, and thereto I give thee my troth."

And then Bacchus reached for her hand. She'd given the ring back to him last night, and when he slid it on her finger, it felt like she was seeing it for the first time. For a moment, as his fingers slid up hers, time stopped.

"With this ring I thee wed, with my body I thee worship, and with all my worldly goods I thee endow. In the name of the Father, and of the Son, and of the Holy Ghost. Amen."

Placing the ring—Ogden's father's ring—on Bacchus's fourth finger was the most reverent experience Elsie had ever had. "With this ring I thee wed, with my body I thee worship, and with all my worldly goods I thee endow. In the name of the Father, and of the Son, and of the Holy Ghost. Amen."

To her right, the clergyman closed the *Book of Common Prayer*. "I pronounce you man and wife."

Elsie's heart slammed back into her, nearly knocking her from her feet. This was it. It was done. She and Bacchus were married.

"You may kiss the bride."

Her thoughts snapped to attention as Bacchus leaned down and touched his lips to hers. It was the most chaste kiss he'd ever given her.

And then, despite herself, she laughed.

The rest passed in a blur. The cheers, the applause—Elsie barely registered Lord Astley leaving, his witness done. She and Bacchus were swept into the vestry, where their marriage license awaited them. The clergyman signed it first, followed by Bacchus. Elsie, with trembling fingers, scrawled her name: *Elsie Amanda Camden.* She hadn't realized she'd settled on a middle name until that moment. It looked well, she thought. *Elsie Amanda Camden . . . Kelsey.*

Congratulations were heaped upon them from their small wedding party. Cheeks kissed, hands shaken. Elsie pulled Emmeline aside after receiving the vicar's well-wishes.

"I know you're not formally a bridesmaid, but you should be," she confessed, and pulled a small broach, in the shape of a dove, free from her gown. "I wanted you to have this anyway."

Emmeline gasped. "Oh, this is the one from the dressmaker's shop! Oh, Elsie, it must've been expensive."

"I'm a spellbreaker, don't you know?" Elsie prodded her shoulder. "I am quite employable. I want you to have it so you'll think of me when I'm not around."

Emmeline drew her into a tight hug. "I'll remember you besides, you ninny! Thank you." She pulled back, then tipped her head to something over Elsie's shoulder. Elsie turned to see the Duchess of Kent approaching shyly. Emmeline squeezed Elsie's hand before leaving them. Bacchus noticed as well, for he stepped over and placed a hand on Elsie's shoulder.

"I'm so, *so* happy for the both of you." She held something in her hand—an ornate box tied up with ribbon, dried flowers delicately glued under a glass lid. "Isaiah and the girls wanted so badly to be here, but given the circumstances . . ." She shrugged.

Smiling, Elsie reached out and clasped the duchess's arm. "I'm honored that you came, Abigail."

The woman brightened at the sound of her Christian name. "And I'm honored to be here." Her gaze flitted to Bacchus. "And this is a wedding gift, from us to you." She handed over the box. Bacchus took it, his brow furrowing.

"This isn't . . . ," he began, eyeing the duchess.

Elsie blinked. "Isn't what?"

The duchess smiled softly. "In truth, Bacchus, the duke intended to bequeath it to you. You've been like a son to him. And it is an adequate gift, for a magical pair."

Curious, Elsie took the box from Bacchus's hands and pulled the ribbon free, peering beneath its lid. Inside was a book with a leather cover dark as onyx, with inlaid, gemlike flowers not dissimilar from those in the box's lid. The corners were cut into soft fringes, and the thick pages were lined with a glimmering orange that made Elsie think of a sunset.

Her chin dropped. "Th-This is an opus, isn't it?"

Reaching forward, the duchess took Elsie's hand and placed it firmly on top of the box. "Take care of it. It's the least we can do." She eyed Bacchus. "Receive it graciously. It is not given out of guilt, but love."

Bacchus nodded, his eyes moist. "Thank you."

Though they were not having a dinner, Bacchus had made sure some traditions were kept. Outside the church awaited a carriage—a closed carriage, thank goodness—pulled by two gray horses, Rainer at the reins. White roses adorned the carriage—surely half of them would fall off during the ride into London, but the impracticality of it somehow made the gesture sweeter. As Bacchus took her hand and led her to the vehicle, the wedding guests threw nuts in the air. Elsie felt herself blush—it was tradition, yes, but she didn't miss that the nuts symbolized fertility.

She caught a glimpse of curious townsfolk around them as she slid inside the cab, spying briefly the amazed looks on the Wright sisters' faces. She wondered what sort of gossip they'd be spreading today, then realized she didn't care.

Bacchus came in after her, taking a seat beside her instead of across from her. When he slid his hand in her direction, she wove her fingers between his.

"We did it, Mrs. Kelsey." He had a roguish expression on his face.

The name really did have a rather pleasant ring to it, especially in his Bajan accent. "You've decided not to be English today?"

He ran his thumb along hers. "I've decided to be myself."

And if that didn't spread a warm glow through her . . .

The carriage pulled northward, heading into London. Although they were moving into their new home, they'd agreed to spend the majority of their time at the stonemasonry shop until they stopped Merton. Bacchus had moved in to protect Elsie, yes, but also to protect Ogden, who was just as likely to be attacked or waylaid by the spiritual aspector. But it was also their wedding day.

Wedding day. How surreal.

They arrived at the townhome without fanfare; it was about five miles west of Parliament Square and had a small garden walled off from the street. The irony wasn't missed on Elsie. She had once thought such nasty things about the wealthy and their walls, and now she was going to live behind one. She still wasn't sure how she felt about that.

They stepped through the veranda, and Bacchus unlocked the door. Rainer pulled away with the carriage. It seemed, for now, they were to be alone.

Elsie's nerves returned in full force. She clutched the temporal opus to her chest.

The door opened onto a short hallway, a set of stairs to its left. Bacchus gestured to the room on the right. "The parlor," he said, then, taking her arm through his, led her down the hallway. "The dining room, and the kitchen is through here."

The rooms all held appropriate furniture—the parlor could do with another chair—but the walls were scant and in need of decoration, as was the mantel. Bacchus led her back through the hallway.

"I think this wall could do with a portrait," she said.

He nodded. "I leave all of that to you. Decorate however you see fit."

Elsie scanned the wall, unsure what to say. She certainly wasn't going to ask about the budget. Not now. All the better when she'd be able to contribute to it properly.

They walked upstairs, where Bacchus continued the tour. He pointed to an empty room. "I thought this could be a study, unless you'd like it for the library. There's a larger space this way if you want a sitting room like the one at the stonemasonry shop. It has west-facing windows."

He showed her the spaces, and together they walked the perimeter of them. There were a few trunks, but these rooms were bare of furniture—an empty canvas for them to paint together. The walls bore outdated wallpaper. Elsie tried to imagine something more floral, with a fine settee and perhaps even a gaming table, but the cylinder of her imagination wasn't firing. It was far too distracted by the man on her arm, and the rooms that lay upstairs.

They reached the third floor. There was a small chamber near the stairs.

"A guest room, or a servants' quarters," Bacchus suggested. "I do think it would be prudent to have a maid. Perhaps Emmeline would hire on?"

Elsie shook her head. "I couldn't possibly steal her away from Ogden." And leave him alone in that house. "And I would think your study could be here, and any help we bring in could sleep downstairs. For . . . privacy."

Bacchus nodded and showed her a second chamber, then a third at the far end of the house, which was larger than the others. This room was furnished, a bed with a sea-green coverlet already made up, side tables beside it, a glass-top breakfast table nearby. It boasted a large wardrobe and additional dresser, as well as a white bookshelf. Elsie's trunks sat at the foot of the bed, which was most definitely large enough for two. She set the opus gingerly on top of one.

Bacchus rubbed the back of his neck. "John got drapes that matched the coverlet. I hardly mind if you change them."

Elsie crossed the room and ran her hand down the drapes, which were closed over the window. "Fortunately I know a spellmaker who can easily change the color for me. It's one of his favorite pastimes."

Bacchus chuckled. "He sounds like a dandy."

When he said nothing more, Elsie turned around. His expression had grown serious, and he absentmindedly traced his beard.

Before she could say anything, he dropped his hand and said, "Elsie, I'm more than aware that our union has not been . . . ordinary, or at all conventional. Of course there are expectations between a man and wife . . . What I mean to say is that I will not require anything of you, if you want time to acclimate."

Elsie's nerves danced under her skin like fairies. She felt her pulse in her stomach. "How utterly respectful of you, Bacchus." Her chest felt too light as she garnered courage. "But you cannot kiss a woman the way you have and then not expect her to be fully prepared for her wedding night, even eager for it." She feigned interest in the windows, ignoring the burning of her cheeks. "Even if it is still daylight."

"I see." His voice was lower, seductively rich. She dared a glance at him and saw his eyes looked darker than usual.

Elsie ran her hands down her bodice. The secret page was not beneath her corset today, but stowed in the lining of her smaller trunk. She turned her back to him. "I would greatly appreciate your help with this dress."

Her heart flipped when Bacchus crossed the room, his fingers grazing the base of her neck, pushing aside a few curls there. She could feel his breath in her hair as his fingers deftly unhooked the first button, then the second, then the third. For better or worse, the dressmaker had sewn a great many buttons onto this dress.

Elsie pressed her hands to her chest, both holding up her dress as it loosened and attempting to calm her racing heart, which seemed to quicken with each brush of his fingers against her chemise. Surely Bacchus could feel it. This time it wasn't anxiety that made it race, but excitement. Not once since arriving in London had she worried about Merton or Master Raven or any of it.

She clung to her courage as Bacchus reached the small of her back. Squeezing her eyes shut, she murmured, "I love you."

His fingers stilled. Silence settled.

Panic rose.

Elsie held her breath, keeping the anxiety at bay. Waiting, listening, hoping. It was hardly wrong, making such a confession now, of all times! Yet the seconds felt like minutes, felt like hours, and her stomach tightened in fear and anticipation, so much so that they quickly became unbearable.

"Bacchus?" she whispered.

His strong arms encircled her, pulling her against him. His mouth found the groove of her neck, its presence shooting shivers up her skull. His hair tickled her cheek.

"Of course I love you, you precious, wonderful woman."

Tears sprang to Elsie's eyes.

"I love you more than Barbados, more than magic, more than myself. You are all I think about. And now you are mine. I love you, Elsie."

With those words, he helped her out of her dress, out of her corset, and out of her chemise.

And showed her.

CHAPTER 22

There would be no honeymoon, of course. Not yet. Not while everything else in their lives was so unsure.

But they certainly made the best of their first night together.
Enough so that had they employed servants—that was, servants besides
the men Bacchus had brought from Barbados—Elsie might never have
left the bedroom. But such was not the case, and things needed to be
done. The world would still turn even if Elsie didn't want it to.

She wanted to hold on to this intoxicating bliss for as long as the
universe would allow it.

Bacchus, ever the responsible one, faced the day first. Watching him
dress was nearly as tantalizing as watching him undress. It was evident
he'd made a full recovery from whatever the siphoning spell had taken
from him. With his hair still loose and his cravat dangling on either side
of his neck, he returned to the edge of the bed and kissed her, slowly and
sweetly. All of it was genuine, for true to his word, he had not a single
spell on him. Elsie had checked. Thoroughly.

"If we want to eat, we'll have to venture out of doors," he said.

"I've heard fasting can be a healthy practice," Elsie countered. That earned her a smile and a second kiss, but Bacchus moved toward the door anyway.

"I'll see that we hire a maid and purchase a curricle this week." He ran his fingers through his dark waves, still sun-kissed on the ends, before pulling the locks back into a tie. "We'll need both, with all the travel back and forth to Brookley."

Elsie sat up, holding the sheet to her, her own bed-mussed hair falling over her shoulders. Without Emmeline's help, she'd be wearing it simply today. Nothing a good hat couldn't hide. "Perhaps it's for the best. Another, oh, three years of falsified training will see me contributing to the expenses."

Bacchus smirked. "I'll remind you it's unnecessary. I'm perfectly capable of keeping a wife."

She loved the way that word sounded on his lips. *Wife.* "And I'm perfectly capable of keeping a husband."

His eyes dropped momentarily to her half-covered breasts. "Indeed you are."

Elsie flushed.

Chuckling, Bacchus excused himself to the privy. With a yawn and a stretch, Elsie let herself out of bed and padded to her larger trunk, finding in it a clean chemise. She picked up her corset off the floor. It laced in the front, so she pulled it on herself. Then, from the smaller trunk, she retrieved her crinkled opus spell and tucked it into the boning.

With her new life situation, a corset might not be the smartest place to hide the thing. Did she need to keep it at all? The worry that had compelled her to carry it around for so long had faded, but it wasn't as though she could sell it. Perhaps Ogden could make some use of it, if he didn't already know the spell—

The sound of scratching drew her attention to one of Bacchus's trunks, as though a mouse had hidden beneath its lid and was desperate for escape. She moved toward it and lifted the lid, listening for the scratching. She moved two shirts and a pair of shoes before the sound stopped, but she managed to find the culprit.

It was a pencil, a tiny, silvery rune glimmering on its end.

She'd left its green partner with Emmeline. Pulling the pencil free, she searched for parchment, but couldn't find any. Sighing, she took it to the white-painted window ledge. She'd clean it later. In small print, she wrote, *Please repeat. I didn't have paper ready.*

Two seconds ticked by before Emmeline's familiar script wrote, *Raven appeared again! He agreed to come back in three hours' time. He wants to talk to* you.

The door opened behind her. "I would say the purple dress, but I rather like this look on you."

Elsie, clad solely in her underthings, turned about. "We need to go to Brookley right away. Master Raven has agreed to meet with us."

◦◦

When Quinn Raven appeared this time, his image was much clearer. This was a phenomenal sign, for it meant he dared to move closer to the stonemasonry shop. Admittedly, Bacchus wasn't entirely sure how far an astral projection spell could stretch. It likely depended on the strength of the person casting it. And given Master Raven's previous revelations, he was in the top tier of spellmakers.

"We've been unable to locate her," Mr. Ogden was saying. They'd all pulled up chairs to watch the somewhat murky middle-aged man in the corner. He hovered a few inches above the floor and wore dark clothing. He had a beard coming in and wore a hat. His features were just sharp enough that Bacchus could make out a large nose above a firm scowl and narrow jaw.

"Then you're not looking hard enough," spat the American.

Mr. Ogden, arms folded across his chest, kept his temper. "I assure you that is not the case."

"She's been hiding for some time," Elsie said, picking at the hem of her sleeve. She did that when she was nervous, but Bacchus didn't think she was aware of it. "First she retired, then she moved, then she faked her death. She won't reveal herself unless absolutely necessary."

Bacchus said, "We'll need to bait her."

Master Raven scoffed. "She wants the woman, doesn't she? Perhaps you should dangle her from that enormous clock of yours."

Ogden leaned forward. "I believe you would be a more enticing target."

Master Raven didn't miss a beat. "Absolutely not."

"You're the one she truly wants," Elsie pressed. She sounded desperate. Bacchus ran his thumb along her forearm before settling a hand on her thigh.

"Do you know what I've sacrificed?" The image shifted as Master Raven moved his weight from one leg to the other. "I have been running for over a decade. I've never stayed anywhere longer than a month. I forfeited my property, my livelihood, my studies—"

"Don't you want to rest?" Bacchus risked interrupting him. "We will protect you. We will work together to disarm her, and then you can settle wherever you'd like."

The spiritual aspector didn't seem convinced.

Miss Pratt, softly, said, "It would make a wonderful story."

Elsie perked. "It would. That is, if you wanted it, Master Raven. An esteemed spellmaker, returned from the dead, saves the world!"

Master Raven clicked his tongue. "Preposterous." And yet, despite Miss Prescott's testament that the man was a recluse, Bacchus thought he detected a hum of interest in the American's voice. Eleven years alone was a long time, particularly for a man who must have been accustomed to acclaim and recognition.

"How would we use him?" Mr. Ogden rubbed his chin, speaking as though Master Raven had agreed to play the lure. "How do we get through to Merton? Would she notice newspaper articles geared toward her?"

"She might not get the paper where she is," Elsie said. "She hasn't responded to anything we've published to get Master Raven's attention. She doesn't know he came to England."

"Mr. Ogden," Bacchus said, "do you happen to know the spell for visual illusions?"

Mr. Ogden's gaze narrowed. "I do, but it's only an intermediate spell. I . . . was never able to find or purchase anything more."

"Illusions?" Master Raven repeated. His blurry eyes shifted to Elsie. "You told me he was with the Physical Atheneum!"

"He is," Elsie shot back. "Legally."

Master Raven laughed. "What am I going to say about it? Heaven forbid there be some competence in this group."

Bacchus tried not to take the comment to heart. "How big of an illusion can you create?"

Mr. Ogden looked around. "Perhaps something the size of this room, if it were simple enough."

"How simple are birds?"

The artist's forehead crinkled, then smoothed. "You want me to make ravens?"

"If we put on enough of a show in the right place, people will talk," Bacchus offered. "Master Merton may be in hiding, but if she's still searching for Master Raven . . . she'll find out, one way or another."

"Where?"

Bacchus considered. "I can think of a few places where a sudden flock would draw attention."

Miss Pratt said, "But won't they know he's the one doing it?"

"Not if he never leaves the carriage," Elsie chimed in. "In fact, we had plans to purchase one, didn't we?" She passed Bacchus a conniving smile that made her blue eyes brighter.

"Indeed."

Master Raven grumbled something under his breath.

"Pardon?" Elsie asked.

"Fine." The word was a bullet. "But don't be stupid and get caught ahead of time. And don't move. I'm coming to you."

Elsie shot up from her seat. "You are?"

"Don't get your skirts twisted. But if you're going to announce me to the world, I intend to do my part. I have a few tricks up my sleeve."

Spells of luck and blessings, most likely—they were the most popular spells requested of spiritual aspectors.

Mr. Ogden said, "But we don't just want Merton's attention. We want her. We need to draw her out to a safe place, somewhere we can apprehend her. Without witnesses."

Quiet settled for several seconds before Miss Pratt said, "What about the Thornfield barn?"

"Pardon?" Mr. Ogden turned in his chair to better see her.

Miss Pratt flushed. "That is . . . it's a large, run-down barn on the road to Aylesbury. I pass it on my way home. The owner died some ten years ago, and only half his farm is still being run. The barn isn't on it."

"We could start in Rochester, perhaps." Elsie's hand covered Bacchus's, and she gripped his index finger, perhaps seeking courage. "Send up the ravens near the estate, and again in London. Until they make the papers."

Bacchus added, "And then start over again, making a trail toward the barn."

"Where I'll be hanging on a meat hook," Master Raven grumbled.

"I'll stay with you," Elsie offered. "Bacchus could drive the curricle."

"Leave me with an amateur spellbreaker while the two useful people are far away?"

Elsie's brows drew together. "I'm not an amateur." Her expression relaxed. "But if you want spellmakers"—she glanced to Bacchus—"then Master Kelsey can guard you as well. I happen to know someone who is rather adept at driving a carriage."

"Who?" Mr. Ogden asked.

"Irene, of course." Elsie grinned. "And then we'll have *two* spell-breakers ready to thwart Merton's magic. And if Miss Pratt can alert the local police near the end, we'll have their assistance as well. Ogden and I will make ourselves scarce before they arrive."

Miss Pratt nodded eagerly. "I can do that."

"Let's think on it, and speak in person." Mr. Ogden looked to Master Raven's projection. "We'll be waiting for you."

CHAPTER 23

The Thornfield barn was visible from the main road but not close to it. Wild grass and weeds swept Bacchus's knees as he walked to it; he couldn't imagine how bothersome it would be in a skirt. Elsie kept a firm grip on his elbow as they headed toward the run-down, abandoned building, which looked to have been blue at one time but had faded to a shade of gray that matched the overcast sky. Master Raven walked a few paces ahead of them, his strides sure. He expected the terrain to yield to him, not the other way around.

He was shorter than Bacchus had expected, but then again, Bacchus had only before seen him hovering three feet above the floor.

Two days ago, Master Raven had arrived at the stonemasonry shop and bestowed blessings of luck like a curmudgeonly Santa Claus. Miss Prescott and Mr. Ogden had ridden out that night and the following day, spreading illusions of ravens in unlikely places where bystanders were sure to pay attention to the birds rather than the spellcaster. Sure enough, the sightings had been reported in this morning's newspaper. Not wanting to lose their momentum, they intended to strike tonight.

The sun was starting to set, and Mr. Ogden and Miss Prescott were on their way here, casting ravens as they went, hoping to draw Merton from her hiding place. If it didn't work, they would repeat the maneuver in a few days. If it never worked . . . Bacchus wasn't sure what they would do then, or how long they'd be able to convince Master Raven to stay with them.

Miss Pratt was poised and ready to alert the local police force the moment Master Raven told her to via astral projection. Mr. Camden accompanied her.

They were silent entering the barn. One of the loft doors was crooked, hanging on its topmost hinge. The walls leaned slightly to the north. Not enough for Bacchus to be concerned about the soundness of the structure, but a strengthening spell certainly wouldn't hurt it. The paddock doors were all locked, but the alley doors on either side of the building opened with the pull of a simple barrel slide. Bacchus found an old lamp hanging from a timber bolt and lit it with a spell. Something scurried away when he did. He glanced at Elsie, but if she heard the sound of rodent feet, it didn't bother her.

She lifted her skirts as she walked over the filthy flooring, which covered about two-thirds of the ground. Some of the boards had rotted through or bent as though weighed down by something heavy. The hay store was empty, and the place smelled of winter and mold. There were two stall walls still standing, about four feet high, strewn with spiderwebs.

"Cozy." Master Raven's arms were folded tight across his chest. He spun in a slow circle, taking in the rafters and the narrow windows.

Looking to Elsie, Bacchus said, "They should be here soon. I'm going to walk the perimeter to make sure we don't have any witnesses or surprises." He'd seen nothing coming in, but the last thing he wanted was to miss something that might result in an easy escape for Merton or jail time for him and the others.

Elsie pressed her lips together and tugged on her sleeve, but she nodded. "I'll look around in here."

Master Raven scoffed, but said nothing.

Outside, the air was growing progressively cooler, though it was still midsummer. A storm must have been blowing in. The clouds were shades of gray and blue, pierced through with gold on the western horizon. Nightfall was on its way. Distant trees swayed with a strong gust of wind. With the help of other physical aspectors, Bacchus could have hurried the storm along or even stopped it entirely, for a time, but a lone person couldn't direct Mother Nature. Not that he wanted to. The cover might come in handy, though he wasn't sure about rain.

He scanned the tree line, waiting for shadows to move, but there was nothing. This land had been abandoned a while ago, and no one had yet put in the work to restore it. He walked around the barn, stopping once to reinforce a sad-looking brace with a spell. As he came around the back of the barn, he heard movement and stopped, squinting across the darkening field, but it was only a hare bounding away, startled by him or some other carnivore lurking in the grass.

And then Bacchus felt the most euphoric sensation overcome him. His chest warmed, his nerves calmed, his muscles relaxed. There was something familiar about it . . . Distantly he questioned why he would feel so peaceful now, outside a dilapidated barn, awaiting his greatest enemy—

It came to him then. This feeling; it was something he got when he attended church in the city, when an attending spiritual aspector invoked inner peace, or the calling of the Holy Spirit. Raven—

He turned around, startling at the shadow beside him. A hand whipped up to his neck, cool fingers pressing into the skin. He jerked away, a shout ready on his lips.

"Be quiet," a familiar voice murmured.

And Bacchus was, as though a string tied to his lips had jerked up, holding his jaw shut. Panic pulsed through his chest, but as soon as he thought to flee, his body ceased to obey him.

The shadow shifted forward, dim light revealing the face of someone he had dined with on multiple occasions. The moment he saw her eyes, he knew what had happened, and his stomach fell. Dread leaked into his limbs like spilled oil, cold as a January breeze.

Bacchus pushed against the magic, trying to pry open his mouth. If he could just warn them—

"None of that." The hold on his lips doubled. Merton frowned at him, the expression drawing heavy lines down her face. "You're an easy one to track, Master Kelsey. You stand out in the crowd. I would kill you and take your magic for myself, but she would never forgive me. Instead, we're going to work together. Won't that be fun?"

Somehow, without speaking, Merton told him to turn around, and even in his desperation not to heed her, his body obeyed.

∽

It was going to work. It had to.

Elsie rubbed her hands together as she paced the length of the barn, eyeing a spider disappearing through a knot in a wooden floor plank. The lighting was uneven with the lamp and the darkening sky, which might affect their vision, should they need to dash outside. Would it be best to extinguish that light? But no, they needed Merton to know Master Raven was here.

She glanced at the spiritual spellmaker, who looked lost in thought, arms folded, mouth twisted. His long, gray-streaked hair fell over both shoulders, and his beard nearly touched it. He still wore his hat.

Then she heard the faint hum of a spell.

She straightened. "What are you doing?"

Master Raven didn't respond right away. His movements were slow, like he was stuck in honey. Then he scowled.

"I was projecting myself to the road. It lets me see what's going on." Dismissing her with a dip of his head, he cast the spell again. For a moment its song seemed to be a harmony, two sounds dancing together, but when Elsie focused, she found it was the same spell as before.

She went back to rubbing her hands together. Everything would be fine. Merton was powerful, yes, but they outnumbered her. Ogden could seize her mind, and Bacchus could seize her body so she couldn't escape, couldn't cast spells. Elsie and Irene were on hand in case she tried. Emmeline would come with the police if they needed backup, and they had Master Raven. Elsie couldn't imagine what a duel between two spiritually aligned spellmakers would look like, but hopefully it wouldn't come to that.

The most critical thing was protecting Master Raven. They knew Merton had at *least* one rational opus in her possession. A master mind-reading spell would be able to dig deep enough into Master Raven's brain to pull out the contagion spell Merton was after, with or without the man's cooperation. They could not allow that to happen.

The question was whether Merton would come alone. It would be an easy matter for her to acquire another Master Phillips to fight at her side, but even if she did, their numbers would still be greater . . .

The alley door opened and Bacchus strode in, the sight of him relaxing muscles Elsie hadn't known were tight. "Anything?"

Bacchus shook his head. "It's all clear."

Master Raven snorted, but said nothing more.

Elsie crossed the floor and stood next to Bacchus, finding comfort in his warmth. She got only a flicker of it before he moved to the window in one of the paddock doors.

"They're coming." Master Raven blinked and straightened, adjusting the lapels of his coat. "This had better work."

"If you can spy ahead, so can Merton," Elsie said.

"She'll know it's a trap."

"Of course it's a trap." Elsie's anxiety was making her words hard and quick. "We're luring her with ravens. But if she's willing to kill for your spell, then she'll risk a trap for it as well." Unless Elsie was entirely wrong in guessing the woman's motives. But between receiving regular missives from Lily Merton for ten years and their recent tête-à-tête, she was sure she was right.

Taking a deep breath, she stepped beside Bacchus. The last tendrils of golden sunlight were seeping behind the cloud-tipped horizon. The farm was so overgrown she could almost pretend they were in a meadow, though the distant fence ruined the effect somewhat.

"There's enough light for them to get here without problem. They'll park the carriage around back." She could hear the horses approaching the barn now, struggling through the weeds.

Bacchus nodded. "All will be well. I was just admiring the dogwood."

"Oh." She peered out the window, but didn't see any of the tall branches or white buds that hugged the stonemasonry shop. She leaned forward, searching, but saw only meadow, distant trees, and far-off hills slowly being swallowed by night's shadow.

"Where is—"

Ice flashed through her limbs.

Dogwood.

Her mind flashed back to their moment outside the stonemasonry shop, standing in the bushes' shade. *It will be a password, of sorts.*

She'd heard *two* songs when Master Raven cast his spell. Bacchus had been outside, alone.

Merton was already here. And she hadn't brought a lackey—she'd made one on the fly.

Bacchus.

Her heart blenched as one of the alley doors flew open, Irene hurrying inside, breathless, Ogden right behind her. He nearly shut her skirt in the door.

"That's that," he said. "Now we—"

Elsie whirled around. "Take Raven and run!"

Confusion flashed across Irene's features, but Ogden stiffened, tense.

Elsie rushed for them. "Get him out—"

The old floorboards of the barn bucked and shook, sending Elsie to a knee. They threw Master Raven and Irene to the ground; Ogden grabbed the door latch and stayed upright, his eyes darting to Bacchus, whose hand was outstretched.

"What are you doing?" Ogden barked, just as the floor grew up over their feet.

Elsie's heartbeat threatened to break skin. "She's controlling him!" She slid her hands over the misshaped mounds binding her down and broke the spell. Irene had already done the same and ran to Ogden to free him, only to have the floor swallow her steps and knock her down, nearly twisting her ankle.

Bacchus turned and marched toward Raven, throwing a spell at Elsie that thickened the air around her. She might as well have been walking through a ball of yarn. She saw the glimmering rune ahead of her, but reaching it was like trying to breathe honey.

Bacchus grabbed Master Raven by the lapels and shoved him onto the floor. Master Raven's clothing stiffened around him, making him look more like a nutcracker than a man. Pinning one of his hands down, Bacchus made the wood mold up around it and harden into a shackle.

Elsie, lungs struggling to breathe, reached the rune and untied it. The return of normal gravity had her collapsing to the floor, gasping for air.

"Now that I have your attention," said a sweet voice. Elsie whirled around to see Merton near the center paddock door, dressed in simple violet, her gray hair pulled back into a thin twist. The smile on her face faltered. "We have a spellbreaker on the loose, Master Kelsey."

She pointed not at Elsie, but at Irene, who had again freed herself and was crawling toward Ogden. Standing, Bacchus motioned his right forward, and a burst of wind swept across the barn, picking Irene up off her feet and slamming her into the alley doors.

"Stop!" Elsie cried, running for her friend, but a rune sparked to life near her knees, thickening the air once more. This time, however, it was only the air around her legs.

"Ogden!" Elsie screamed.

Ogden shook his head. His face was red and perspiring from his struggle against Bacchus's spell. "I can't get to her! She has the same thing Phillips had . . ." The air tingled as a rational spell swam to Merton. "No, not the same. Different—"

"You're so noisy on your own, Cuthbert," Merton said, dismissing him with a wave of her hand. Her gaze moved to Master Raven. "After all these years, this is how we meet? I was hoping it would be on friendlier terms."

Master Raven spat in Merton's direction.

She was unfazed, her eyes shifting to Elsie. "I still want to have a real chat, my dear. Just you and I."

Incredulous, Elsie didn't know what to say. She bent over and untied the spell holding her in place.

"I'll let him go if you come with me."

She froze. Merton didn't mean Master Raven.

Elsie's gaze moved to Bacchus, who stood guard over the American, waiting for his next command. He was straight and unmoving, yet in his eyes Elsie saw despair. Resistance.

Blinking to clear her vision, Elsie whispered, "Where is it? The spell?"

"Really?" Merton complained, but she was looking past Elsie. "You can't stay down?"

Elsie turned to see Irene freeing Ogden from his binds.

"It really is pointless to keep you alive." She waved a hand, and Bacchus raised his.

"Bacchus, no!" Elsie ran toward him. The air crackled as lightning shot from his fingertips.

Elsie intercepted it, feeling a jolt up her arm as she dis-spelled the blast just as she had with Nash at Seven Oaks.

"Impressive!" Merton cheered. "You're such a wonderful asset, Elsie. Surely we can work things out. I'll move on without you if I must, but—"

Elsie didn't hear what else the psychotic woman had to say, because Bacchus sent out another blast, this one sailing past Elsie and slamming into the alley door. Which, Elsie noted, also had floor growth up and over it, preventing escape. Ogden dodged the blow and sprinted toward Merton.

Bacchus ran to intercept him. The men collided. Bacchus was larger, but Ogden was dense and strong in his own right. Bacchus's left hand came up to Ogden's windpipe and squeezed.

"Stop!" Elsie darted forward and grabbed Bacchus's arm, trying to wrench it back. She succeeded, but Bacchus's hand leapt at her like a viper, a rune of speed glittering into existence before Elsie's eyes. His fingers grabbed her bodice and threw her with alarming force. Her dress tore, and she hit the floorboards hard on her shoulder, hissing through her teeth as pain radiated across her collarbone. Bruised, but not broken.

Bacchus shoved Ogden back, and a rune twisted around his feet, fusing him to the floor. Whipping around, Bacchus sent another wind spell over Elsie's head to where Irene was trying to reach Raven. Raven still had one free hand, and the barn sang with his spells.

Merton laughed. "Your curses won't work on me, old man."

"Merton, stop this!" Elsie pushed herself onto her knees. "You want to talk, let's talk!"

Merton smiled. "Later, dear. When we're not so distracted."

Raven shifted his attention to Bacchus, and a spell hummed over Elsie's head, striking him. He faltered, suddenly clumsy. Elsie took the opportunity to rush to Ogden and free him.

A sensation like a cool breath washed over Elsie's skin as Ogden joined the assault, sending a rational spell into Bacchus's mind. Bacchus grabbed his head and roared. Lightning started streaking from him in every direction, a bolt nearly hitting Raven. The walls of the barn began to groan and shift as though caught in a storm—but Bacchus couldn't cast two spells at once. That had to be Merton employing a physical spell. If she'd brought a large enough arsenal of opus spells, they were going to lose.

Elsie scrambled to Raven and freed one of his feet before lightning hit the back of her thigh. She screamed and jerked away, putting out the small flames erupting on her skirt. It burned terribly. Irene flew to her side, limping, helping with Raven. One of Bacchus's fists found a home in Ogden's face, breaking the rational spellmaker's hold on him.

Raven, free, ran to the alley doors behind them. Bacchus's attention shot to him, and the entire barn began to shake with another earthquake.

All the while Merton watched them, tapping a folded opus page against her shoulder, as though she had all the time in the world to see Bacchus destroy them. Why didn't she just use the spell and end it? She'd have Ogden's and Bacchus's opuses to add to her collection. She'd lock Elsie up, kill Irene, torture Raven for more information—

It was so strange, the way she nonchalantly stood there as violence erupted around her. Merton *never* partook in the violence. She'd run from the dinner at Seven Oaks when Nash attacked. She'd hired and controlled lackeys to kill, kidnap, and steal on her behalf—and always kept far away in the aftermath. The two times she'd risked revealing herself to Elsie, in jail and in Phillips's cellar, she'd done so as an astral projection.

Squinting, Elsie studied Merton.

I can't get to her! She has the same thing Phillips had, Ogden had said. *No, not the same. Different . . .*

How could two guard spells against rational invasion be *different?*

Why had Merton cast only one opus spell, and on the barn walls, no less?

A spell that could be cast from *outside?*

Elsie gasped. Merton didn't have a protection spell against Ogden. And Master Raven's curses *would* work against her.

That was, if Merton were really here.

This was an astral projection. It had to be. But it was so crisp, so pristine . . . Merton had to be very close to make it this realistic.

Elsie pulled the spiritual aspector up and shoved him in Irene's direction. "Get Raven out!"

Irene grabbed Master Raven's arm and bolted for the back alley door.

Bacchus whirled on them, still clumsy from his spiritual curse. Lightning flashed from his hands—

Elsie didn't stop to see where it landed. She rushed for the nearest paddock door and dived through its window, her skirts getting caught twice. Something bit into her knee as she struggled to free the material. She landed, swallowing a cry as she hurt her bruised shoulder. Dust flew into her mouth, and wild grass stabbed her eye. She found her footing and stood, a chill running down her torso as night air seeped through the tear in her dress, showing off a handful of chemise underneath.

It was dark, save for moonlight filtered through clouds. But it wasn't much brighter in the barn. Her eyes took only a moment to adjust.

Balling up her skirts immodestly, wincing as they brushed the burn on her leg, Elsie walked around the barn, searching for another presence. Nothing. Her pulse raced, her body hurt, her hands and the dip of her spine perspired, but Elsie closed her eyes, imagining she was in Master Phillips's cellar again.

Irene screamed.

Elsie ground her teeth and focused. Spells lit up like waking fire-flies—physical, spiritual, and rational enchantments radiating from the barn. The building quivered with a physical spell threatening to destroy its walls. The floors shuddered with a quake.

But there was another spell, to the north. Away from the rest, in a copse of trees. Elsie moved around it until she could see the faintest silhouette of a woman. Until she could hear the slightest whisper of a song.

Her mind spun. Holding her breath, she approached. Her thoughts were a jumble of half-remembered missives on silver paper. Of clipped discussions at dinner tables, in prison cells, in cellars. They pieced themselves together a little more with every step.

She didn't get too close before Merton snapped to attention and turned toward her.

"You were right." Elsie rushed to speak first. She dropped her skirts and held up both hands in surrender. "I want to talk. Don't hurt them. Just talk to me."

It was too dark to see the expression on Merton's face. "You always were a bright one, Elsie. That's why I like you. No farther, mind you."

"You know about my parents. My family." A lump started to form in Elsie's throat; she swallowed it down. "You lost yours, too."

Merton didn't respond.

"They left me," Elsie whispered.

"They didn't know what you were." The silhouette turned, an opus spell ready in one hand, an array of spiritual spells ready in the other. Merton seemed a little distracted—she had to actively control Bacchus, after all, and present herself in a way that made her projection in the barn seem like the real her. All of which should work to Elsie's advantage.

"I wish I'd known it was you from the beginning," Elsie pressed, inching a little closer, moving so slowly—that burn *hurt*—she hoped it was imperceptible. "We've disagreed, yes, but you're right. About everything. I fell in love with a rich man and didn't want to see it anymore. The pain, the suffering, the unfairness. You only want to make the world better—"

"The world *will* be better." Merton's tone was firm. "I will make it better. I will pull that spell from Raven and make it better." Her voice grew steely. "He's a coward. I could have done it differently if he'd listened. He forced my hand."

"But you don't want to be alone," Elsie guessed. "And you don't have to be. I can help you bear that burden. I can *help* you."

Merton paused.

Elsie got in another step. She was four paces from the woman now. "I wish I'd known it was you," she repeated, softer, "because then I might have had a mother."

No response. Elsie gained another inch.

"I don't like the deaths. You know that." Elsie needed to be careful with her words. She needed to sound genuine. "But you're the only one who's ever really been there for me. I realized it when I thought you'd died. Not my family, not Ogden, truly. Even my husband is only my husband because of some twisted sense of chivalry." Another step. She pressed her hands to her heart. "You rescued me, Lily." A few more inches. Elsie's thumb dipped down into her corset. "You saved me from a life as a pauper in a workhouse. I wish you hadn't hidden from me all these years—"

"I didn't want to," Merton said. Her posture was still stiff, but her expression had softened. "I couldn't have loose ends. I had to know you were trustworthy. Not many will do what it takes to bring true unity to the world. True peace and equality. I had to test you. Train you. My dear, you exceed expectations. But you spent too long in that mason's household. I never should have sent you to Seven Oaks. No farther."

Elsie halted. "What can I do to you, Lily? I'm only a spellbreaker. If I wanted you out of that barn, I would have disenchanted the projection."

She swallowed against the lump in her throat and let herself stew in the dark feelings she'd been suppressing. Her love for Bacchus, and the anxiety it instilled in her. Her fear that he, Ogden, Irene, and even Raven might be killed tonight. She reached even deeper: the shock of knowing her eldest brother had died without her ever knowing him. The grief of having a lost sister. Of knowing her parents had abandoned her. The guilt of having played a part, however unintentional, in the killing of so many aspectors.

Her throat squeezed, and the tears came. More importantly, they leaked into her voice. They sounded like conviction.

"Lily, please. I-I don't want them to die. Of course I don't." Because no version of herself would wish that upon people she loved. "But . . . maybe we can start over. Maybe you can tell me your story. All of it."

Another step.

"I want to understand you. Please."

Merton's shoulders slackened. "Only you know what it feels like. To be truly alone."

Elsie nodded. "As you do."

And she dared to close the gap between them. To embrace her enemy.

Merton didn't stop her. Nor did she notice the whisper of paper as Elsie pulled it from her corset.

Elsie embraced Master Lily Merton. Let the woman feel the tears on her cheek. Pressed both her hands into her back.

And whispered, *"Excitant."*

The opus spell vanished from her fingers. For a moment, Merton went limp in her arms.

The chaos in the barn quieted.

"Oh." The older woman pulled back from the embrace. A sliver of moonlight fell upon them, and in Merton's face Elsie saw surprise. Confusion. "Oh, my dear . . . Who are you?" She stepped back and took in the old farm. "Goodness, where am I? I . . . was just in my office at the atheneum . . ." She patted her cheeks, perhaps making sure she was all there. "Oh my. My dear, what is your name?"

"Elsie Amanda Kelsey," Elsie said, every part of her wound like a spring.

"Elsie. A lovely name."

Elsie swallowed. The master spell must have taken at least ten years off Merton's memory if the aspector didn't remember her. But it needed to be more if she were to forget the one person who mattered most.

"What year is it?" Elsie asked.

Merton blinked. "Why, it's 1880, of course. Tomorrow is Christmas . . ." She spun around, taking in the cool summer night. A hand pressed to her mouth. "I . . . I don't understand. Is this a temporal spell of some sort?"

Then she pulled her hand back and examined it, as though unused to the wrinkles there.

Heavy footsteps sounded behind Elsie. She turned, seeing a dark figure approach. But without someone upholding the other end of the control spell, it was as good as moot.

Elsie held up her hands. "It's fine. She's harmless."

Bacchus stopped in his tracks. "Harmless? What do you mean?"

"Master Kelsey," Elsie said carefully, "this is Master Lily Merton. The atheneum has been looking for her. You were right to check out here, but I'm afraid she doesn't remember a thing."

Bacchus's eyes narrowed. Behind him, Ogden was coming out of the barn, holding the lamp high over his head. When he neared, Elsie grasped Merton's hand to show she was harmless. "I didn't throw all the spells in the Thames," she admitted.

Bacchus's brows drew only closer together, but Ogden understood, even without reading her mind. His eyes shifted between Elsie and Merton several times before he said, "Which did you keep?"

"Forgetfulness. She thinks it's December of 1880."

Merton tensed. "What . . . Who are you?" She looked between the new faces. "What am I doing here?" She touched her forehead with her free hand.

Elsie let out a shaky breath. "It's fine now. Everyone is safe."

"Not enough."

Elsie turned, barely making out Raven's shadow at the edge of Ogden's light. "Fifteen years gone," she said. "She doesn't remember any of it. She doesn't remember *you*."

"Who?" Merton's voice carried a note of anxiety. Elsie squeezed her hand.

But Raven shook his head. "She's the same person with the same motivations. Having her *forget* isn't enough. Your little spell doesn't undo her crimes. It won't bring my friends back."

Merton was crying now. "What crimes?"

Elsie set her jaw. "Ogden, distract her, please."

She felt a slight distortion in the air between Ogden, who stood still as an ancient tree, and Merton, whose breathing suddenly calmed. Her eyes slipped away from them, seeing something that wasn't there, and her lips turned up. The image Ogden had pushed into her mind must have been beautiful.

Elsie turned her focus back to Raven. "She doesn't remember."

"It doesn't matter," he pressed.

"But in her mind she's innocent—"

"Elsie." Ogden's voice was soft, his concentration on his spell. His eyes remained on Merton, but he said, "She isn't innocent. I will—" His voice strained, and he swallowed. "I will never get those years back. *I* will never be able to forget."

A sore ache bloomed over her heart. She blinked away a new tear. "Of course you won't." No one could ever forget their deepest hurts, only learn to better shoulder them.

Bacchus murmured, "We could take her to the authorities. But she won't be able to confess."

"She will if they know which questions to ask." Raven stepped into the light, dry weeds crunching under his boots. Approaching Merton from behind, he put a hand on her shoulder, and a clear, sweet note rang out from the spell he cast. A strong note, a rich pitch—a master spell.

"What did you do?" Elsie whispered.

"I cursed her," he said, and Elsie's stomach tightened. "She can only speak the truth now."

That gave Elsie pause. The song was similar to the truthseeking spell he'd used on her in Juniper Down.

"You want to take her to the police," Bacchus guessed, "with a note containing incriminating questions. Anonymous, I presume."

Raven merely nodded, his face stern.

Elsie took in a deep breath and let it all out at once. "I suppose it's only fair. Perhaps you should write it, Raven. I think your handwriting will be the least easy to identify."

"She'll write it," Ogden said, straightening. "I'll guide her hand."

Elsie looked at him, then lifted her gaze to Bacchus's. His brow was resolute, but his eyes were sad. Elsie was sad, too, though this *was* the right thing to do. Still, not everything she'd said to Merton was a lie. They *were* similar, in so many ways. In another world, perhaps they could have been family.

"All right." She rubbed her arm uneasily. "But make sure she confesses to everything. Including the control and framing of Master Phillips. We need to make this right." She looked between them, a chill embracing her. "Oh God, Irene. Where is Irene?"

Ogden released his spell suddenly, and Merton startled. "Where am I?"

"Help me get Miss Prescott to the carriage." Ogden gestured to Bacchus. "She needs a doctor."

As the two men hurried back to the barn, Merton pulled her hand from Elsie's—Elsie had forgotten she was holding it. "My dear," she said, "I'm quite confused. Will you help me?"

Elsie gave her the best reassuring smile she could muster. "Of course." She glanced to Raven. "We'll get you to where you need to be."

CHAPTER 24

Elsie hadn't stayed to see Merton interrogated. None of them had. They'd swiftly taken Irene to a hospital, retrieved Emmeline and Reggie, and escorted Merton to the local constable's home early the following morning. She carried with her a letter sealed with plain wax.

The story hit the newspapers two days later.

Forgetful Aspector Raised from Death Confesses to Murders, the headline read. It was the top story that day. Three days later, Master Enoch Phillips Acquitted replaced it as the leading headline. They all collectively let out a breath of relief. It was hard for Elsie to believe it was over, but it was. Merton was taken to Her Majesty's Prison Oxford. Her state of mind would likely spare her the penalty of death. She could speak no lie; when she said she didn't remember, it was true.

Though Merton would not remember setting her control spell on Bacchus, its song remained, and Elsie had promptly removed it the moment he returned from aiding Irene.

And like that, it was over, as though it had never begun. The remainder of the stolen opuses had not yet surfaced, as Master Merton did not remember where she had hidden them, but from Ogden's sleuthing they knew the authorities were on the hunt, combing through Merton's estate and local haunts as thoroughly as possible. The missing spells gave Elsie an uneasy feeling, like she was reading a novel with the last page missing. Like it wasn't a true ending.

Master Quinn Raven disappeared before Merton's story spread like wildfire through England, offering no goodbyes—but little more could be expected of a recluse who'd had no social ties for years. But weeks later, Ogden found an interesting article on the second page of Brookley's local paper. The headline read, **American Artist Honors British Compatriots with Gratitude**. The article was brief and poorly written, switching back and forth between American and British English. There wasn't even a picture of the "art" the article mentioned, but the author named himself *Blackbird*. Whether or not he would return to the public eye was yet to be determined.

Ogden fell behind on his commissions for a time, enough so that when he got his wits about him again, Elsie put in three days' work per week for four weeks to help him catch up. Ogden didn't talk about it, but Elsie suspected there was still need for healing, despite his abuser being behind bars. If anyone knew minds, it was Cuthbert Ogden. The last time Elsie visited, he was smiling again, and had finally hired her replacement—a rather charming young man from Aylesbury who seemed utterly enthralled by Ogden's nonmagical talents and was an adept sketch artist himself.

Irene Prescott spent six weeks at home with a broken leg—such a thing can happen when one is sprinting in one direction and a sudden magical rise of a floorboard makes the bone surge in the opposite direction. Elsie had heard her scream, and knowing what caused it pained her. Not nearly as much as it pained Bacchus, whose guilt kept him from visiting the spellbreaker the first two weeks of her recovery. It had taken both Elsie's and Irene's reassurance to finally drag him to her townhome in London, where friendships were mended, "training" continued, and a recommendation for a maid was given.

As for guilt, or perhaps for the resolving of it, Bacchus did attend the Duke of Kent's funeral with Elsie at his side. He stood beside the duchess and her daughters, and even said a few words at the duke's graveside, not one of them limned with bitterness. The duke had been forgiven.

Bacchus struggled to accept his own forgiveness, however readily it was bestowed. He'd witnessed it all, of course. Merton's spell affected the spirit, not the mind. He was aware of every attack on his wife and his friends, and for a week he wouldn't touch Elsie, not when he could see the burn so prominently displayed on her leg. It wasn't until Elsie's patience snapped and they had their second-greatest argument yet— Elsie believed the struggle at their first meeting still took the cake—that he accepted her love and forgiveness, stopped being a stubborn lummox, and finally started bedding her again.

As for Master Enoch Phillips, he had been released from prison and exonerated of all charges, but his reputation would likely never recover. It had come as no surprise to anyone when he'd resigned from the London Physical Atheneum. Based on the rumor mill via Irene, he and his family sold his country estate and relocated to Paris. Much to Elsie's and Bacchus's delight, Master Ruth Hill replaced him as the head of the assembly, and even offered Bacchus the ambulation spell he'd originally come from Barbados to receive.

He, of course, accepted.

 ❧

It was high time Elsie had a proper honeymoon. And what better place to spend the autumn months than under the sunny Barbadian sky?

Elsie crammed her last petticoat in her trunk, shoving it down despite knowing she'd wrinkle her entire wardrobe. She'd insisted she could fit everything in one trunk for easier travel, and this petticoat would not make her a liar. The lid refused to shut, so she turned around and sat on the blasted thing, bouncing to pack in every fold of fabric. She'd never traveled anywhere outside of England—how was she to know which dresses would be most comfortable on a tropical island? Obviously it was better that she pack all of them, to be on the safe side. She had just managed to get the latches secure when Bacchus strode in, come up from the carriage awaiting them outside.

He cocked an eyebrow at her, amused. "If I pick that up, will it explode?" His Bajan accent was at its fullest expression.

Elsie smirked. "If you can pick this up by yourself, I will be doubly impressed." Reggie was due any moment now, come to help them get their luggage downstairs.

"Oh?" He strode across the room and bent toward her, placing one hand on either side of her hips. His nose brushed hers. "How impressed?"

She laughed and kissed him, his beard tickling her lips.

"It is a long way to Barbados," he murmured against her mouth. "This may be the last opportunity we have to—"

Steps sounded up the stairs. Groaning, Bacchus pulled away and straightened himself just as Reggie popped his head into the bedroom, removing his hat and fanning himself with it. His eyes dropped to the trunk. "That thing is massive! Yer gonna kill me, Els."

Elsie grinned. "I only have two books in there, if that garners any confidence. Thank you again for helping us."

Reggie shrugged and stuffed his head into his cap. "What's family for?"

Elsie pulled herself from the trunk. She was going to miss her brother. They'd visited frequently over the last two months, building up the relationship that had been so cruelly torn from them. "You're still coming for Christmas?" Elsie asked. She and Bacchus intended to be back in London for the holidays.

"Of course." He glanced to Bacchus. "I saw the carriage—I was going to wait until after we were done, but might as well do it before the heavy lifting."

"Do what?" Bacchus asked.

Reggie dug into his jacket, pulling a newspaper clipping from an interior pocket. Elsie's stomach clenched—she'd become wary of unexpected newspaper articles. What did this mean? Surely they'd put the whole Merton episode behind them.

He handed it to her, his grin throwing her off. "Look."

Elsie turned the article about, holding it so Bacchus could read over her shoulder. It had been hastily torn, bearing the corners of other articles. The story at the center read, New Recruits for Newcastle upon Tyne Temporal Atheneum. A short list of names followed.

"And?" Elsie scanned down the list.

"Second to bottom," Reggie said.

She skipped ahead. Her breath hitched.

There, the print clear, was the name *Alice Camden*.

Reggie had claimed their baby sister's name was Alice.

"Don't get your hopes up." Her brother gingerly took the article from her fingers. "It's not an uncommon name. But maybe."

Elsie shook her head, trying to ignore the sensation of ants in her middle. "I . . . Alice was just a baby. She couldn't have known her name."

Bacchus rested a comforting hand on her shoulder. "She might not have been given up as an infant," he offered, his tone awed and hushed.

Reggie nodded. "Maybe she was left with someone who knew it. Maybe she was never left."

Never left. If that was the case, Alice would know where their parents were. Elsie wasn't sure she was ready to meet them. Or her. If this even was her!

She was getting ahead of herself. Taking a couple of deep breaths, she sat on the trunk once more.

"See, that's why I was gonna wait."

"We . . ." Elsie met Bacchus's gaze, trying to sort through the tumult of her thoughts.

"We can postpone," Bacchus assured her. "Find another ship."

"Will we get a refund?" she asked.

Bacchus batted the concern away with a wave of his hand. "It doesn't matter. This is important to you. We should inquire now."

"Don't fret over it." Reggie folded up the article and tucked it into his pocket. "I've checked up on leads for her before, only for it to amount to nothing. Don't hold up your plans. If this is something, I'll send word right away. Even spirit line it. I promise. Besides"—he smiled—"I have a date, and I'll be batty-fanged if I miss it."

Elsie's brows drew together. "What do you mean you have a date?"

Reggie grinned and hooked a thumb under his suspenders. "You know. Met a girl in Brookley. Asked if she'd see me and she said yes."

Elsie laughed despite herself. "You scamp!" Emmeline had been hinting about liking a lad, but she'd been rather close-lipped about the whole thing. Elsie had hoped, but she hadn't wanted to assume.

Reggie shrugged noncommittally, but Elsie knew she was right. She stood, her mirth mingling into something uncertain. She leaned on Bacchus. "But Alice."

"I'm going with one of my friends to look into it this weekend. Really, Els. Don't fret over it. Go have yer honeymoon. I'd feel awful if I spoiled it."

Bacchus ran his hand up and down her back.

Elsie straightened, nodded, and dug into her reticule for a few coins. "The spirit line, if you would." She put the money in Reggie's palm.

Reggie whistled. "Yes, ma'am. I'd feel bad taking this if you weren't so fancy 'n' all."

Bacchus snorted.

Below them, the front door opened, and Elsie heard Mariah's voice call out in greeting. She was the new maid, who would be looking after the house while they were away.

Slipping her reticule away, Elsie embraced her brother. "Thank you for your help. Let me know immediately."

"You won't even be in Barbados yet—"

"Immediately," she reaffirmed, releasing him. She stared into his blue eyes, so much like her own. "Promise."

He gave her a lopsided smile. "Promise."

Elsie stepped back. Even if it wasn't *her* Alice Camden, it would drive her mad thinking about it. She itched for something to do. Some kind of distraction. Perhaps Bacchus could offer her one in the confines of their carriage. The thought tempted her mouth into a mischievous smile.

"I suppose we shouldn't miss our boat. If you two would be so kind." She gestured to the devilish trunk.

Reggie bowed. "Yes'm." As he and Bacchus took up the handles, he added, "Can't you enchant this to be lighter or something?"

"No magic on my clothes," Elsie quipped, which earned her chuckles from both men as they hauled the thing through the doorway and down the stairs.

Despite the hiccup of information from her brother, Elsie was glad for the journey, though she was not yet sure how strong her seafaring legs were. She'd finally get some blissful time alone with her husband and see his other side—the side that craved oranges and loved the ocean. She was looking forward to promised walks on the beach and picnics beneath palm leaves. She was looking forward to being with *him*, without any doubts, fears, worries, or secret murderers riding their trail. Then they'd come home for Christmas, where they'd host Ogden and Emmeline and Reggie, and perhaps hear rumor of engagements, and they'd spend the New Year at Seven Oaks with the duchess, and everything would be how it was meant to be.

They had already set up a tutor for her in Barbados, who would record all the remarkable progress she was to start having, which would push her ahead of schedule once she returned to England. Then it would be only another year for her to be official. To put away the hiding and be what she'd always wanted to be.

A spellbreaker.

ACKNOWLEDGMENTS

Thus ends my first duology. I am so grateful to those who have stuck with me through thick and thin, supporting me in this amazing career, helping me refine and polish one story after another. I am forever and always indebted to each of you.

Many thanks to Jordan, who is my rock. I had quite a stumble in 2019 when drafting this book, and he was there to hold my hand through all of it, always making sure I had what I needed to get back on my feet. I could not accomplish half of what I do without him.

Thank you to Tricia, Rebecca, and Leah for reading through my rough draft and helping me get that first round of edits done. Your input was golden, and I'm very grateful for the time you spend on my projects!

Many thanks to my editor Adrienne, who adopted me and took this series under her wing. And to Angela, who has edited with great finesse and farseeing almost every single book I've published. Thank you to Marlene, my agent, for digging up opportunities and defending me on the battlefield. It took fourteen books, but I finally got you on that dedication page!

And again, thank you to my Father in Heaven, who guides me in fiction as well as in real life. I recognize I am very blessed to be able to do what I do and have others read what I write, and that blessing comes straight from Him.

ABOUT THE AUTHOR

Charlie N. Holmberg is the author of the *Wall Street Journal* best-selling Paper Magician series, which has been optioned by the Walt Disney Company. She is also the author of the Numina series, the Spellbreaker series, and five stand-alone novels, including *Magic Bitter, Magic Sweet*; *Followed by Frost*, a 2016 RITA Award finalist for Young Adult Romance; and *The Fifth Doll*, winner of the 2017 Whitney Award for Speculative Fiction. Born in Salt Lake City, Charlie was raised a Trekkie alongside three sisters who also have boy names. She is a proud BYU alumna, plays the ukulele, and owns too many pairs of glasses. She currently lives with her family in Utah. Visit her at www.charlienholmberg.com.